NEON GODS

KATEE ROBERT

sourcebooks
casablanca

Copyright © 2021 by Katee Robert
Cover and internal design © 2021 by Sourcebooks
Cover design by Dawn Adams/Sourcebooks
Cover image © Alexxxey/Shutterstock
Internal images © Julia Dreams/Creative Market, etse1112/Getty Images,
GreenTana/Getty Images, LokFung/Getty Images, Roberto Scandola/Getty
Images, Vectors Market/Noun Project, Vectorstall, PK/Noun Project

Published by Sourcebooks Casablanca, an imprint of Sourcebooks
P.O. Box 4410, Naperville, Illinois 60567-4410
(630) 961-3900
sourcebooks.com

Library of Congress Cataloging-in-Publication Data is on file with the publisher.

Printed and bound in the United States of America.
PAH 10

To Erin and Melody—your podcast has brought me so much joy over the last few years, and I hope Hades's boastful floors give you a little joy in return.

PERSEPHONE

"I REALLY HATE THESE PARTIES."

"Don't let Mother hear you say that."

I glance over my shoulder at Psyche. "You hate them, too." I've lost count of the number of events our mother has dragged us to over the years. She's always got her eye on the next prize, on the newest piece to move in this chess game only she knows the rules to. It might be easier to stomach if most days I didn't feel like one of her pawns.

Psyche comes to stand next to me and bumps me with her shoulder. "I knew I'd find you here."

"It's the only room in this place I can stand." Even though the statue room is the very essence of hubris. It's a relatively plain space—if shining marble floors and tasteful gray walls can be called plain—filled with thirteen full-body statues arranged in a loose circle around the room. One for each member of the Thirteen, the group that rules Olympus. I name them off silently as my gaze skips over each one—Zeus, Poseidon, Hera, Demeter,

Athena, Ares, Dionysus, Hermes, Artemis, Apollo, Hephaestus, Aphrodite—before turning back to face the final statue. This one is covered in a black cloth that pours over it, spilling down to pool on the floor at its feet. Even still, it's impossible to miss the wide-set shoulders, the spiky crown that adorns his head. My fingers itch to grab the fabric and rip it away so I can finally see his features once and for all.

Hades.

In a few short months, I'll have won my freedom from this city, will have escaped, never to return. I won't have another chance to look on the face of Olympus's boogeyman. "Isn't it weird that they never replaced him?"

Psyche snorts. "How many times have we had this conversation?"

"Come on. You know it's weird. They're the Thirteen, but really they're only twelve. There's no Hades. There hasn't been for a very long time." Hades, the ruler of the lower city. Or at least he used to be. It's a legacy title, and the entire family has long since died out. Now, the lower city is technically under Zeus's reign like the rest of us, but from what I hear, he doesn't ever set foot on that side of the river. Crossing the River Styx is difficult for the same reason leaving Olympus is difficult; from what I hear, each step through the barrier creates a sensation like your head will explode. No one voluntarily experiences something like that. Not even Zeus.

Especially when I doubt the people in the lower city will kiss his ass the same way everyone in the upper city does. All that discomfort and no payoff? It's no surprise Zeus avoids the crossing just like the rest of us. "Hades is the only one who never spent time in the upper city. It makes me think he was different from the rest of them."

"He wasn't," Psyche says flatly. "It's easy to pretend when he's dead and the title no longer exists. But every one of the Thirteen is the same, even our mother."

She's right—I know she's right—but I can't help the fantasy. I reach up but stop before my fingers make contact with the statue's face. It's just morbid curiosity that draws me to this dead legacy, and *that's* not worth the trouble I'd be in if I gave in to the temptation to snatch the dark veil away. I let my hand drop. "What's Mother up to tonight?"

"I don't know." She sighs. "I wish Callisto were here. *She*, at least, gives Mother pause."

My three sisters and I all found different ways to adapt when our mother became Demeter and we were thrust into the shining world that exists only for the Thirteen. It's so sparkling and extravagant that it's almost enough to distract from the poison at its core. It was adapt or drown.

I force myself to act the part of the bright and sparkly daughter who is always obedient, which allows Psyche to play it cool and quiet as she flies under the radar. Eurydice clings to every bit of life and excitement she can find with a borderline desperation. Callisto? Callisto fights Mother with a ferocity that belongs in the arena. She will break before she bends, and as a result, Mother exempts her from these mandatory events. "It's better that she's not. If Zeus makes a pass at Callisto, she might try to gut him. Then we'd truly have an incident on our hands."

The only person in Olympus who murders without consequence—allegedly—is Zeus himself. The rest of us are expected to uphold the laws.

Psyche shudders. "Has he tried anything with you?"

"No." I shake my head, still looking at Hades's statue. No, Zeus hasn't touched me, but at the last couple of events we've attended, I could feel his gaze following me around the room. It's the reason I attempted to beg off tonight, though my mother all but dragged me out the door behind her. Nothing good comes from gaining Zeus's attention. It always ends the same—the women broken and Zeus walking away without so much as a bad headline to tarnish his reputation. There was exactly one set of charges officially leveled against him a few years ago, and it was such a circus that the woman disappeared before the case ever went to trial. The most optimistic outcome is that she somehow found a way out of Olympus; the more realistic is that Zeus added her to his alleged body count.

No, better to avoid him at every turn.

Something that would be significantly easier to do if my mother weren't one of the Thirteen.

The sound of heels clicking smartly against the marble floors has my heartbeat picking up in recognition. Mother always strides like she's marching into battle. For a moment, I honestly consider hiding behind the covered statue of Hades, but I discard the idea before Mother appears in the doorway to the statue gallery. Hiding would only delay the inevitable.

"There you are." Tonight she's wearing a deep-green gown that skims her body and feeds into the whole earth-mother role she's decided best fits her branding as the woman who ensures the city doesn't go hungry. She likes the people to see the kind smile and helping hand and ignore the way she will happily mow down anyone who tries to stand in the way of her ambition.

She pauses in front of the statue of her namesake, Demeter. The statue is generously curved and wearing a flowing dress that melds with the flowers springing up at her feet. They match the floral wreath circling her head, and she smiles serenely as if she knows all the secrets of the universe. I've caught my mother practicing that exact expression.

Mother's lips curve, but the smile doesn't reach her eyes as she turns to us. "You're supposed to be mingling."

"I have a headache." The same excuse I used to try to get out of attending tonight. "Psyche was just checking on me."

"Mm-hmm." Mother shakes her head. "You two are becoming as hopeless as your sisters."

If I realized that being hopeless was the surest way to avoid Mother's meddling, I would have gone with that role instead of the one I chose. It's too late to change my path now, but the headache I faked is becoming a real possibility at the thought of going back to the party. "I'm going to cut out early. I think this might evolve into a migraine."

"You most definitely are not." She says it pleasantly enough, but there is steel in her tone. "Zeus wants to speak to you. There's absolutely no reason to make him wait."

I can think of half a dozen off the top of my head, but I know Mother won't listen to a single one. Still, I can't help but try. "You know, he's rumored to have killed all three of his wives."

"It's certainly less messy than a divorce."

I blink. I honestly can't tell if she's joking or not. "Mother…"

"Oh, relax. You're so tense. Trust me, girls. I know best."

My mother is likely the smartest person I know, but her goals are not my goals. There's no easy way out of this, though, so I obediently fall into step next to Psyche and follow her out of the room. For a moment, I imagine I can feel the intensity of Hades's statue staring at my back, but it's pure fantasy. Hades is a dead title. Even if he wasn't, my sister is probably right; he'd be just as bad as the rest of them.

We leave the statue room and walk down the long hallway leading back to the party. It's like everything else in Dodona Tower—large and excessive and expensive. The hallway is easily twice as wide as it needs to be, and each door we pass is at least a foot taller than normal. Deep-red curtains hang from the ceiling to the floor and are pulled back on either side of the doors—an extra touch of extravagance that the space most certainly didn't need. It gives the impression of walking through a palace rather than the skyscraper that towers over the upper city. As if anyone is in danger of forgetting that Zeus has styled himself as a modern-day king. I'm honestly surprised he doesn't walk around with a crown that matches his statue's.

The banquet room is more of the same. It's a massive, sprawling space with one wall completely taken up with windows and a few glass doors leading out to the balcony that overlooks the city. We're on the top floor of the tower, and the view is truly outstanding. From this point, a person can see a good portion of the upper city and the winding swath of blackness that is the River Styx. And on the other side? The lower city. It doesn't look all that different from the upper city up here, but it might as well be on the moon for all that most of us can reach it.

Tonight, the balcony doors are closed tight to avoid anyone being inconvenienced by the icy winter wind. Instead of the view of the city, the darkness behind the glass has become a distorted mirror of the room. Everyone is dressed to the nines, a rainbow of designer gowns and tuxes, flashes of horribly expensive jewels and finery. They create a sickening kaleidoscope as people move through the crowd, mingling and networking and dripping beautiful poison from painted-red lips. It reminds me of a fun-house mirror. Nothing in the reflection is quite what it seems, for all its supposed beauty.

Around the remaining three walls are giant portraits of the twelve active members of the Thirteen. They're oil paintings, a tradition that goes back to the beginning of Olympus. As if the Thirteen really do think they're like the monarchs of old. The artist certainly took some liberties with a few of them. The younger version of Ares, in particular, looks nothing like the man himself. Age changes a person, but his jaw was never that square, nor his shoulders that broad. That artist also depicted him with a giant broadsword in his hand, when I know for a fact this Ares won his position by submission in the arena—not in war. But then, I suppose that doesn't make for as majestic an image.

It takes a certain kind of person to gossip and mingle and backstab while their likeness stares down at them, but the Thirteen is filled with monsters like that.

Mother cuts through the crowd, perfectly at ease with all the other sharks. With nearly ten years serving as Demeter, she's one of the newest members of the Thirteen, but she's taken to moving in these circles like she was born to it instead of elected by the people the same way Demeters always are.

The crowd parts for her, and I can feel eyes on us as we follow her into the brightly colored mix. These people might resemble peacocks with the way they go the extra mile for these events, but to a person, their eyes are cold and merciless. I have no friends in this room—only people who seek to use me as a stepping stool to claw their way to more power. A lesson I learned early and harshly.

Two people move out of my mother's way, and I catch a glimpse of the corner of the room I do my best to avoid when I'm here. It houses an honest-to-gods throne, a gaudy thing made of gold and silver and copper. The sturdy legs curve up to armrests and the back of the throne flares out to give the impression of a thundercloud. As dangerous and electric as its owner, and he wants to be sure no one ever forgets it.

Zeus.

If Olympus is ruled by the Thirteen, the Thirteen are ruled by Zeus. It's a legacy role, one passed from parent to child, the bloodline stretching back to the first founding of the city. Our current Zeus has held his position for decades, ever since he took over at thirty.

He's somewhere north of sixty now. I suppose he's attractive enough if one likes big barrel-chested white men with great boisterous laughs and beards gone winter gray. He makes my skin crawl. Every time he looks at me with those faded blue eyes, I feel like I'm an animal at auction. Less than an animal, really. A pretty vase, or perhaps a statue. Something to be *owned*.

If a pretty vase is broken, it's easy enough to purchase a replacement. At least it is if you're Zeus.

Mother slows down, forcing Psyche back a few steps, and takes my hand. She squeezes hard enough to convey her silent warning to behave, but she's all smiles for *him*. "Look who I found!"

Zeus holds out his hand, and there's nothing to do but place mine in his and allow him to kiss my knuckles. His lips brush my skin for the barest moment, and the small hairs on the back of my neck stand on end. I have to fight not to wipe the back of my hand on my dress when he finally releases me. Every instinct I have is screaming that I'm in danger.

I have to plant my feet to prevent myself from turning and running. I wouldn't make it far anyway. Not with my mother standing in the way. Not with the glittering crowd of people watching this little scene play out like vultures scenting blood on the wind. There's nothing this lot loves more than drama, and making a scene with Demeter and Zeus will result in consequences I don't want to deal with. At *best*, it will anger my mother. At worse, I run the risk of being a headline in the gossip mags, and that will land me in even more hot water. Better to just ride this out until I can escape.

Zeus's smile is a touch too warm. "Persephone. You look lovely tonight."

My heart beats like a bird trying to escape its cage. "Thank you," I murmur. I have to calm down, to smooth my emotions out. Zeus has a reputation as the kind of man who enjoys the distress of anyone weaker than he is. I won't give him the satisfaction of knowing he scares me. It's the only power I have in this situation, and I refuse to relinquish it.

He moves closer, edging into my personal space, and lowers his voice. "It's good to finally have a chance to speak with you. I've been trying to corner you for the last few months." He smiles, though it doesn't reach his eyes. "It's enough to make me think you're avoiding me."

"Of course not." I can't edge back without bumping into my mother…but I put several seconds of serious consideration into that option before discarding it. Mother will never forgive me if I make a scene before the all-powerful Zeus. *Ride it out. You can do this.* I dredge up a bright smile even as I begin chanting the mantra that's gotten me through the last year.

Three months. Just ninety days between me and freedom. Ninety days until I can access my trust fund and use it to get out of Olympus. *I can survive this. I will survive this.*

Zeus practically beams at me, all warm sincerity. "I know this isn't the most conventional approach, but it's time to make the announcement."

I blink. "Announcement?"

"Yes, Persephone." My mother edges in close, shooting daggers from her eyes. "The announcement." She's trying to beam some knowledge directly into my brain, but I have no idea what's going on.

Zeus reclaims my hand and my mother practically shoves me after him as he starts for the front of the room. I shoot a wild look at my sister, but Psyche is just as wide-eyed as I feel right now. What's going on?

People fall silent as we pass, their gazes a thousand needles against the back of my neck. I have no friends in this room. Mother would say it's my own fault for not networking the way she's instructed me to time and time again. I tried. Really, I did. It took all of a month to realize that the cruelest insults come with sweet smiles and honeyed words. After the first lunch invitation resulted in my misquoted words being splashed across the gossip headlines, I gave up. I will never play the game as well as the vipers in this room. I hate the false fronts and slippery insults and knives hidden in words and smiles. I want a normal life, but that's the one thing that's impossible with a mother in the Thirteen.

At least, it's impossible in Olympus.

Zeus stops at the front of the room and snags a champagne glass. It looks absurd in his large hand, like he'll shatter it with one rough touch. He raises the glass and the last few murmurs in the room fade away. Zeus grins at them. It's easy to see how he holds such devotion despite the rumors that circulate about him. The man practically has charisma oozing from his pores. "Friends, I haven't been completely honest with you."

"That's a first," someone says from the back of the room, sending a wave of faint laughter through the space.

Zeus laughs along with them. "While we are technically here to vote on the new trade agreements with Sabine Valley, I also have a little announcement to make. It's long past time for me to find a new Hera and make our number complete again. I've finally chosen." He looks at me, and it's the only warning I get before he speaks the words that light my dreams of freedom on fire so completely I can only watch them burn to ash. "Persephone Dimitriou, will you marry me?"

I can't breathe. His presence has sucked up all the air in the room, and the lights flare too bright. I teeter on my heels, only keeping my feet through sheer force of will. Will the others fall on me like a pack of wolves if I collapse now? I don't know, and because I don't know, I have to stay standing. I open my mouth, but nothing comes out.

My mother presses into me from the other side, all bright smiles and joyful tones. "Of course she will! She'll be honored to." Her elbow digs into my side. "Isn't that right?"

Saying no isn't an option. This is *Zeus*, king in everything but name. He gets what he wants when he wants it, and if I humiliate him right now in front of the most powerful people in Olympus, he'll make my entire family pay. I swallow hard. "Yes."

A cheer goes up, the sound making me dizzy. I catch sight of someone recording this with their phone and know without a shadow of a doubt that it will be all over the internet within an hour, on all the news stations by morning.

People come forward to congratulate us—really, to congratulate *Zeus*—and through it all he keeps his tight grip on my hand. I stare at the faces that move in a blur, a tidal wave of hate rising in me. These people don't care about me. I know that, of course. I've known that since my first interaction with them, since the moment we ascended to this vaulted social circle by virtue of my mother's new position. But this is a whole different level.

We all know the rumors about Zeus. *All* of us. He's gone through three Heras—three wives—in his time leading the Thirteen.

Three *dead* wives, now.

If I let this man put his ring on my finger, I might as well let him put a collar and leash on me, too. I will never be my own person, will never be anything but an extension of him until he grows tired of me, too, and replaces that collar with a coffin.

I will never be free of Olympus. Not until he dies and the title passes to his oldest child. That could be years. It could be *decades*. And that's making the outrageous assumption that I'll outlive him instead of ending six feet under like the rest of the Heras.

Frankly, I don't like my odds.

PERSEPHONE

2

THE PARTY CONTINUES AROUND ME, BUT I CAN'T FOCUS ON anything. Faces blur, colors meld together, the sound of gushing compliments are static in my ears. A scream is building in my chest, a sound of loss too big for my body, but I can't let it escape. If I start shrieking, I'm certain I'll never stop.

I sip champagne through numb lips, my free hand shaking so badly that the liquid sloshes around in the glass. Psyche appears in front of me as if by magic, and though she's got her blank expression firmly in place, her eyes are practically shooting lasers at both our mother and Zeus. "Persephone, I have to go to the bathroom. Come with me?"

"Of course." I barely sound like myself. I almost have to pry my fingers from Zeus's, and all I can think about are those meaty hands on my body. Oh gods, I'm going to be sick.

Psyche hustles me out of the ballroom, using her voluptuous body to shield me, dodging well-wishers as if she's my own personal security. The hallway doesn't feel any better, though. The walls are closing in. I can see Zeus's imprint on every inch of this place. If I marry him, he'll put his imprint on *me*, too. "I can't breathe," I gasp.

"Keep walking." She rushes me past the bathroom, around a corner, and to the elevator. The claustrophobic feeling is even worse when the doors close, trapping us in the mirrored space. I stare at my reflection. My eyes are too large in my face, and my pale skin is leached of color.

I can't stop shaking. "I'm going to be sick."

"Almost there, almost there." She practically carries me out of the elevator the second the doors open, taking us down another wide, marbled hall to a side door. We slip into one of the handful of courtyards that surround the building, a little bit of carefully curated garden in the midst of so much city. It's dormant now, dusted with the light snow that started to fall while we were inside. The cold cuts through me like a knife, and I welcome the sting. Anything is better than being up in that room for another moment longer.

Dodona Tower is in the very center of downtown Olympus, one of the few pieces of property that is owned by the Thirteen as a whole rather than any one of the individuals, though everyone knows it's Zeus's in every way that counts. It's a grand skyscraper that I used to find almost magical when I was too young to know better.

Psyche guides me to a stone bench. "Do you need to put your head between your knees?"

"It won't help." The world won't stop spinning. I have to... I don't know. I don't know what I'm supposed to do. I've always seen my path before me, stretching out through the years to my ultimate goal. It's always been *so clear*. Finishing my master's degree here in Olympus, a compromise with my mother. Wait until I turn twenty-five and gain my trust fund and then use the money to break free of Olympus. It's hard to fight your way through the barrier that keeps us separate from the rest of the world, but it's not impossible. Not with the right people helping, and my money ensures that will be the case. And then I'll be free. I can move to California to do my PhD at Berkeley. A new city, a new life, a fresh start.

Now I can't see anything at all.

"I can't believe she did this." Psyche starts pacing, her movements short and angry, her dark hair so like our mother's swinging with each step. "Callisto is going to kill her. She *knew* you didn't want any part of this, and she forced you into it anyway."

"Psyche..." My throat feels hot and tight, my chest tighter yet. As if I've been impaled and am only now noticing. "He killed his last wife. His last *three* wives."

"You don't know that." She answers automatically, but she won't quite meet my gaze.

"Even if I don't... Mother knew what everyone believes he's capable of and didn't care." I wrap my arms around myself. It does nothing to quell my shakes. "She sold me to cement her power. She's already one of the Thirteen. Why isn't that good enough for her?"

Psyche perches on the bench next to me. "We'll figure out a way through this. We just need time."

"He's not going to give me time," I say dully. "He's going to push the wedding through just like he pushed the proposal." How long do I have? A week? A month?

"We should call Callisto."

"*No.*" I nearly shout the word and make an effort to lower my voice. "If you tell her now, she'll come straight here and make a scene." When it comes to Callisto, that might mean yelling at our mother...or it might mean taking off one of the spike heels she favors and trying to stab Zeus in the throat. There would be consequences either way, and I can't let my older sister bear the burden of protecting me.

I have to figure my own way through this.

Somehow.

"Maybe making a scene is a good thing at this point."

Bless Psyche, but she still doesn't understand. As daughters of Demeter, we have two choices—play within the rules of Olympus or leave the city behind entirely. That's it. There is no bucking the system without paying the cost, and the consequences are too severe. One of us stepping out of line will create a ripple effect impacting everyone connected to us. Even Mother being one of the Thirteen won't save us if it comes to that.

I should marry him. It would ensure my sisters remain protected, or as near to it as is possible in this pit of vipers. It's the right thing to do, even if the very thought makes me ill. As if in response, my stomach surges and I barely get to the nearest bushes in time to be sick. I'm vaguely aware of Psyche holding my hair away from my face and rubbing my back in soothing circles.

I should do this...but I can't.

"I can't do this." Saying it aloud makes it feel more real. I wipe my mouth and force myself to stand.

"We're missing something. There's no way that Mother would send you into a marriage with a man who might harm you. She's ambitious, but she loves us. She wouldn't put us in danger."

There was a time when I agreed. After tonight, I don't know what to believe. "I can't do this," I repeat. "I *won't* do this."

Psyche digs through her tiny purse and comes up with a stick of gum. When I make a face at her, she shrugs. "No use getting distracted by puke breath while you're making life-changing statements of intent."

I take the gum and the peppermint flavor *does* help ground me a bit. "I can't do this," I repeat again.

"Yes, you've mentioned that." She doesn't tell me how impossible this situation is going to be to get out of. She also doesn't list all the reasons fighting it will never go my way. I'm just a single woman against all the power Olympus can bring to the fore. Stepping out of line isn't an option. They'll force me to my knees before they let me go. Getting out of this city was already going to take every resource I had. Getting out now that Zeus has claimed me? I don't know if it's even possible.

Psyche takes my hands. "What are you going to do?"

Panic bleats through my head. I have the budding suspicion that if I walk back into that building, I'll never walk back out again. It feels paranoid, but I'd felt weird about how furtive Mother was acting for days now and look how that turned out. No, I can't afford to ignore my instincts. Not any longer. Or maybe my fear is clouding my thoughts. I don't know and I don't care. I just know I absolutely *cannot* go back.

"Can you go get my purse?" I left both it and my phone upstairs. "And tell Mother that I don't feel so well and that I'm going home?"

Psyche is already nodding. "Of course. Anything you need."

It takes ten seconds after she's gone to register that going home won't solve any of these problems. Mother will just come collect me and deliver me back to my new fiancé, trussed up if necessary. I scrub my hands over my face.

I can't go home, I can't stay here, I can't *think*.

I shove to my feet and turn for the entrance to the court-yard. I should wait for Psyche to get back, should let her talk me down into something resembling calm. She's just as cunning as Mother; she'll come up with a solution if given enough time. But letting her get involved means running the risk that Zeus will punish her alongside me the second he realizes I desperately don't want his ring on my finger. If there's a chance to spare my sisters from the consequences of my actions, I'm going to do it. Mother and Zeus will have no reason to punish them if they had no part in helping me defy this marriage.

I have to get out and I have to do it alone. Now.

I take one step and then another. I almost stop when I come even with the thick stone archway leading out onto the street, almost let my rising reckless fear fail me and turn back to submit to the collar Zeus and my mother are so keen to put around my neck.

No.

The single word feels like a battle cry. I surge forward, past the entrance and out onto the sidewalk. I pick up my pace, moving at a brisk walk and turning south on instinct. Away from my mother's home. Away from Dodona Tower and all the predators contained within. If I can just get some distance, I can *think*. That's what I need. If I can get my thoughts in order, I can come up with a plan and find a way out of this mess.

The wind picks up as I walk, cutting through my thin dress as if it doesn't exist. I move faster, my heels clicking along the pavement in a way that reminds me of my mother, which only serves to remind me of what she's done.

I don't care if Psyche is likely right, that Mother undoubtedly has some scheme up her sleeve that doesn't put my head on a literal chopping block. Her plans make no difference. She didn't talk to me, didn't give me the benefit of the doubt; she simply sacrificed this pawn to get access to the king. It makes me sick.

The tall buildings of downtown Olympus do a bit to cut off the wind, but every time I cross a street, it barrels down from the north and whips my dress around my legs. It feels extra icy coming off the water of the bay, so cold my sinuses hurt. I have to get out of the elements, but the thought of turning around and walking back to Dodona Tower is too awful to bear. I'd rather freeze.

I laugh hoarsely at the absurd thought. Yes, that'll show them. Losing a few toes and fingers to frostbite will definitely hurt my mother and Zeus more than it hurts me. I can't tell if it's panic or the cold making me loopy.

Downtown Olympus is just as carefully polished as Zeus's tower. All the storefronts create a unified style that's elegant and minimalist. Metal and glass and stone. It's pretty but ultimately soulless. The only indicator of what kind of businesses are contained behind the various glass doors are tasteful vertical signs with the business names. The further from the city center, the more individual style and flavor seep into the neighborhoods, but this close to Dodona Tower, Zeus controls everything.

If we marry, will he order clothes for me so that I fit seamlessly in with his aesthetic? Supervise my hair stylist visits to mold me in the image he wants? Monitor what I do, what I say, what I *think*? The thought makes me shudder.

It takes me three blocks before I realize my footsteps aren't the only ones I hear. I glance over my shoulder to find two men half a block back. I pick up my pace, and they match it easily. Not quite trying to close the distance, but I can't shake the sensation of being hunted.

This late, all the shops and businesses in the downtown area are closed. There's music a few blocks away that must be a bar still open. Maybe I can lose them in there—and get warm in the process.

I take the next left turn, aiming in the direction of the sound. Another look over my shoulder shows only a single man behind me. Where did the other one go?

I get my answer a few seconds later when he appears in the next intersection from my left. He's not blocking the street, but every instinct I have tells me to stay as far away from him as possible. I veer right, once again heading south.

The farther I get from the center of downtown, the more the buildings begin to break away from the cookie-cutter image. I begin to see trash on the street. Several of the businesses have bars on their windows. There is even a foreclosure sign or two taped to dirty doors. Zeus only cares about what he can see, and apparently his gaze doesn't stretch to this block.

Maybe it's the cold muddling my thoughts, but it takes me far too long to realize that they're driving me to the River Styx. True fears clamps its teeth into me. If they corner me against the banks, I will be trapped. There are only three bridges between the upper city and the lower city, but no one uses them—not since the final Hades died. Crossing the river is forbidden. If legend is to be believed, it's not actually possible without paying some kind of terrible price.

And that's if I even managed to reach a bridge.

Terror gives me wings. I stop worrying about how much my feet hurt in these ridiculously uncomfortable heels. The cold barely registers. There has to be a way to get around my pursuers, to find people who can help.

I don't even have my fucking phone.

Damn it, I shouldn't have let emotions get the best of me. If I'd just waited for Psyche to bring me my purse, none of this would be happening... Would it?

Time ceases to have meaning. The seconds are measured in each harsh exhale tearing itself from my chest. I can't think, can't stop, am nearly sprinting. Gods, my feet hurt.

At first, I barely register the rushing sound of the river. It's almost impossible to hear over my own ragged breathing. But then it's there in front of me, a wet, black ribbon too wide, too fast to swim safely, even if it were summer. In the winter, it's a death sentence.

I spin around to find the men closer. I can't quite make out their faces in the shadows, which is right around the time I realize how quiet the night's gotten. The sound of that bar is barely a murmur in the distance.

No one is coming to save me.

No one even knows I'm here.

The man on the right, the taller of the two, laughs in a way that has my body fighting off shudders that have nothing to do with the cold. "Zeus would like a word."

Zeus.

Had I imagined this situation couldn't get worse? Foolish of me. These aren't random predators. They were sent after me like dogs retrieving a runaway hare. I hadn't really thought he'd stand idly by and let me escape, had I? Apparently so, because shock steals what little thought I have left. If I stop running, they will collect me and return me to my fiancé. He will cage me. There is absolutely no doubt in my mind that I won't get another opportunity to escape.

I don't think. I don't plan.

I kick off my heels and run for my life.

Behind me, they curse, and then their footsteps pound. Too close. The river curves here, and I follow the bank. I don't even know where I'm headed. Away. I have to get away. I don't care what it looks like. I'd throw myself into the icy river itself to escape Zeus. Anything is better than the monster who rules the upper city.

Cypress Bridge rises up in front of me, an ancient stone bridge with columns that are larger around than I am and twice as tall. They create an arch that gives the impression of leaving this world behind.

"Stop!"

I ignore the yell and plunge through the arch. It hurts. Fuck, *everything* hurts. My skin stings as if being scraped raw by some invisible barrier, and my feet feel like I'm sprinting on glass. I don't care. I can't stop now, not with them so close. I barely notice the fog rising around me, coming off the river in waves.

I'm halfway across the bridge when I catch sight of the man standing on the other bank. He's wrapped in a black coat with his hands in his pockets, fog curling around his legs like a dog with its master. A fanciful thought, which is only further confirmation that I am not okay. I'm not even in the same realm as okay.

"Help!" I don't know who this stranger is, but he's got to be better than what pursues me. "Please help!"

He doesn't move.

My steps falter, my body finally beginning to shut down from the cold and fear and strange slicing pain of crossing this bridge. I stumble, nearly going to my knees, and meet the stranger's eyes. *Pleading.*

He looks down at me, still as a statue draped in black, for what feels like an eternity. Then he seems to make a choice: lifting a hand, palm extended toward me, he beckons me across what remains of the River Styx. I'm finally close enough to see his dark hair and beard, to imagine the intensity of his dark gaze as the strange buzzing tension in the air seems to relax around me, allowing me to push through those final steps to the other side without pain. "Come," he says simply.

Somewhere in the depths of my panic, my mind is screaming that this is a terrible mistake. I don't care. I dredge up the last bit of my strength and sprint for him.

I don't know who this stranger is, but anyone is preferable to Zeus.

No matter the price.

HADES

THE WOMAN DOESN'T BELONG ON MY SIDE OF THE RIVER Styx. That alone should be enough to make me turn away, but I can't help but notice her limping sprint. The fact that she's barefoot without a fucking coat in the middle of January. The plea in her eyes.

Not to mention the two men chasing her down, trying to get to her before she reaches this side. They don't want her to cross the bridge, which tells me all I need to know—they owe allegiance to one of the Thirteen. Normal citizens of Olympus avoid crossing the river, preferring to stick to their respective sides of the River Styx without fully understanding what makes them turn back when they reach one of the three bridges, but these two are acting like they realize she'll be out of their reach once she touches this bank.

I motion with my hand. "Faster."

She glances behind her, and panic sounds from her body as loudly as if she'd screamed. She's more afraid of *them* than she is of me, which might be a revelation if I stopped to think about it too hard. She's almost to me, a few short yards away.

That's when I realize I recognize her. I've seen those big hazel eyes and that pretty face plastered on all the gossip sites that love following the Thirteen and their circles of friends and family. This woman is Demeter's second daughter, Persephone.

What is *she* doing here?

"Please," she gasps again.

There's nowhere for her to run. They're on one side of the bridge. I'm on the other. She must be truly desperate to make the crossing, to push past those invisible barriers and throw her safety in with a man like me. "Run," I say. The treaty keeps me from being able to go to her, but once she reaches me—

Behind her, the men pick up their pace, fully sprinting in an effort to get to her before she gets to me. She's slowed down, her steps closer to hobbling, indicating that she's injured in some way. Or maybe it's purely exhaustion. Still, she stumbles on, determined.

I count the distance as she covers it. *Twenty feet. Fifteen. Ten. Five.*

The men are close. So fucking close. But rules are rules, and not even I can break them. She has to make it to the bank of her own power. I look past her at them, an ugly recognition rolling through me. I know these men; I have files on them that stretch back years. They are two enforcers who work behind the scenes for Zeus, taking care of tasks he'd rather his worshipping public not know he engages in.

The fact that they're here, chasing *her*, means something big is happening. Zeus likes to play with his prey, but surely he wouldn't try that game with one of Demeter's daughters? It doesn't matter. She's almost out of his territory…and into mine.

And then, miraculously, she makes it.

I catch Persephone around the waist the second she hits this side of the bridge, spin her and pin her back to my chest. She feels even smaller in my arms, even more breakable, and a slow anger rises in me at the way she shivers. These fuckers have chased her for some time, terrorizing her at *his* command. No doubt it's a punishment of sorts; Zeus always did like driving people to the River Styx, letting their fear build with each block they passed until they were trapped on the banks of the river. Persephone is one of the few to actually attempt one of the bridges. It speaks to an inner strength to attempt the crossing without an invitation, let alone to succeed. I respect that.

But we all have our roles to play tonight, and even if I don't plan to harm this woman, the reality is that she's a trump card that's fallen right into my hands. It's an opportunity I won't pass up. "Hold still," I murmur.

She freezes except for her gasping inhales and exhales. "Who—"

"Not now." I do my best to ignore her shivering for the moment and bracket her throat with a hand, waiting for these two to catch up. I'm not hurting her, but I exert the slightest bit of pressure to keep her in place—to make it look convincing. She stills against me. I'm not sure if it's instinctive trust or fear or exhaustion, but it doesn't matter.

The men stumble to a stop, unwilling and unable to cross the remaining distance between us. I'm on the bank of the lower city.

I haven't broken any laws and they know it. The one on the right glares. "That's Zeus's woman you have there."

Persephone goes rigid in my arms, but I ignore it. I draw on my rage, injecting it into my voice in icy tones. "Then he shouldn't have let his little pet wander so far from safety."

"You're making a mistake. A big mistake."

Wrong. This isn't a mistake. It's an opportunity I've been waiting thirty fucking years to find. A chance to strike right to the heart of Zeus in his shining empire. To take someone important to him the same way he took the two most important people to *me* when I was a child. "She's in my territory now. You're welcome to try to steal her back, but the consequences for breaking the treaty will be on your head."

They're smart enough to know what that means. No matter how much Zeus wants this woman returned to him, even he can't break this treaty without bringing the rest of the Thirteen down on his head. They exchange a look. "He's going to kill you."

"He's welcome to try." I stare them down. "She's mine now. Be sure to tell Zeus how much I intend to enjoy his unexpected gift." I move then, throwing Persephone over my shoulder and striding down the street, deeper into my territory. Whatever held her paralyzed up to this point shatters and she struggles, beating my back with her fists.

"Put me down."

"No."

"Let me go."

I ignore her and stalk around the corner, moving quickly. Once we're out of sight of the bridge, I set her on her feet. The woman tries to take a swing at me, which might amuse me under other circumstances. She's got more fight in her than I expected from one of Demeter's socialite daughters. I had planned on letting her walk on her own, but lingering out in the night after that confrontation is a mistake. She's not dressed for it, and there's always the chance that Zeus has spies in my territory who will report this interaction back to him.

After all, I have spies in *his* territory.

I shrug out of my coat and shove her into it, zipping it up before she has a chance to fight me, trapping her arms at her sides. She curses, but I'm already moving again, lifting her back over my shoulder. "Be quiet."

"The fuck I will."

My patience, already whisper thin, nearly snaps. "You're half-frozen and limping. Shut up and be still until we get inside."

She doesn't stop muttering under her breath, but she *does* stop struggling. It's enough. Getting away from the river is the first priority right now. I doubt Zeus's men will be foolish enough to attempt to finish the crossing, but tonight's already brought the unexpected. I know better than to take anything for granted.

The buildings this close to the river are intentionally run-down and empty. All the better to preserve the narrative the upper city likes to tell itself about my side of the river. If those glittering assholes think there's nothing of value down here, they leave me and my people alone. The treaty only lasts as long as the Thirteen are in agreement. If they ever decide to band together to take the lower city, it means the worst kind of trouble. Better to avoid it altogether.

A great plan up until tonight. I've kicked the hornet's nest and there's no unkicking it. The woman over my shoulder will either be the tool I use to finally bring Zeus down, or she'll be my ruin.

Cheery thoughts.

I barely reach the end of the block before two shadows peel off from the buildings on either side of the street and fall into step a few feet behind me. Minthe and Charon. I've long since gotten used to the fact that my nightly wanderings are never truly solo. Even when I was a kid, no one ever tried to stop me. They just made sure I didn't get into any trouble I couldn't get out of again. When I finally took over the lower city and my guardian stepped down, he handed over control on everything except this.

A softer person would assume my people do it out of care. Maybe that's part of it. But at the end of the day, if I die now without an heir, the carefully curated balance of Olympus teeters and crumbles. The fools in the upper city don't even realize how vital a cog I am to their machine. Unspoken, unacknowledged... but I prefer it that way.

Nothing good comes when the other Thirteen turn their golden eyes this way.

I cut through an alley and then another. There are parts of the lower city that look like the rest of Olympus, but this isn't one of them. The alleys stink to high heaven and glass crunches under my shoes with each step. Someone who only saw the surface would miss the carefully concealed cameras arranged to take in the space from all angles.

No one approaches my home without my people knowing about it. Not even me, though I've long since learned a few tricks for when I need *actual* alone time. I turn left and stride to a nonde-script door tucked into an equally nondescript brick wall. A quick glance at the tiny camera angled at the top of the door and the lock clicks open beneath my hand. I shut the door softly behind me. Minthe and Charon will sweep the area and double back to ensure the two almost intruders don't get any foolish ideas.

"We're inside now. Put me down." Persephone's voice is as frigid as any princess at court.

I start down the narrow staircase. "No." It's dark, the only light coming from faint runners on the floor. The air goes breath-takingly cold as I reach the end of the stairs. We're fully under-ground now, and we don't bother with climate control in the tunnels. They're here for easy traveling or a last-minute escape route. They're not here for comfort. She shivers over my shoulder, and I'm glad I took the time to throw the coat on her. I won't be able to see her injuries until we're back in my home, and the quicker that happens, the better for everyone.

"Put. Me. Down."

"No," I repeat. I'm not about to waste my breath explaining that she's running on sheer adrenaline right now, which means she's not feeling any pain. And she *will* be feeling pain once those endorphins wear off. Her feet are fucked up. I don't think she has hypothermia, but I have no idea how long she was exposed to the winter night in that sad excuse of a dress.

"Do you often kidnap people?"

I pick up my pace. Gone is the spiky fury, replaced by a calm that has concern rising. She might be going into shock, which will be damned inconvenient. I have a doctor on call, but the fewer people who know Persephone Dimitriou is in my possession right now, the better. At least until I figure out a plan to use this unexpected gift.

"Did you hear me?" She shifts a little. "I asked if you often kidnap people."

"Be quiet. We're almost there."

"That's not really an answer." I get a few seconds of blessed silence before she keeps talking. "Then again, I've never been kidnapped before, so I suppose expecting an answer about your kidnapper's prior experience is just silly."

She sounds downright *chipper*. She's definitely in shock. Continuing this line of conversation is a mistake, but I find myself saying, "You ran to me. That's hardly kidnapping."

"Did I? I was just running to get away from the two men pursuing me. Your being there or not is immaterial."

She can say that all she likes, but I saw the way she zeroed in on me. She wanted my help. Needed it. And I had been unable to deny her. "You practically threw yourself into my arms."

"I was being chased. You seemed the lesser of two evils." The tiniest of pauses. "I'm beginning to wonder if I've made a terrible mistake."

I wind my way through the maze of tunnels to another set of stairs. This one is nearly identical to the ones I just descended, right down to the pale runners on each stair. I take them two at a time, ignoring her faint *oof* in response to my shoulder jarring her stomach. Once again, the door clicks open the second I touch it, unlocked by whoever is on shift in the security room. I slow down enough to ensure the door is properly closed behind me.

Persephone twists a little on my shoulder. "A wine cellar. I don't think I saw this coming."

"Is there a part of tonight that you *did* see coming?" I curse myself for asking the question, but she's acting so strangely unflappable that I'm genuinely curious. More than that, if she's actually verging into hypothermia, keeping her talking right now is the wise course of action.

At that, her strangely cheerful tone fades down to almost a whisper. "No. I didn't see any of it coming."

Guilt pricks me, but I ignore it with the ease of long practice. One last set of stairs out of the wine cellar and I stop in the back hallway of my home. After a quick internal debate, I head for the kitchen. There are first aid supplies tucked in a number of rooms around the building, but the two largest kits are in the kitchen and in my bedroom. The kitchen is closer.

I push open the door and stop short. "What are you two doing here?"

Hermes freezes, two bottles of my best wine in her small hands. She gives me a winning grin that isn't the least bit sober. "There was a snore-fest of a party in Dodona Tower. We cut out early."

Dionysus has his head in my fridge, which is enough to tell me that he's already drunk or high—or some combination of both. "You have the best snacks," he says without pausing in his raiding of my food.

"Now's not a good time."

Hermes blinks behind her oversize yellow-framed glasses. "Uh, Hades."

The woman over my shoulder jolts as if struck by a live wire. "*Hades?*"

Hermes blinks again and shoves back her cloud of black curls with one forearm. "Am I really, really drunk, or is that Persephone Dimitriou thrown over your shoulder like you're about to role-play some sexy pillaging?"

"That's impossible." Dionysus finally appears with the pie my housekeeper left in the fridge earlier today. He's eating it directly from the container. At least he's using a fork this time. He also has some crumbles in his beard and only one side of his mustache is curled; the other is only a little crimped, as if he's scrubbed a hand over his face recently. He frowns at me. "Okay, maybe not impossible. Either that or the weed I smoked with Helen in the courtyard before leaving was laced with something."

Even if they hadn't told me they'd come directly from a party, their clothing says it all. Hermes is wearing a short dress that would double as a disco ball, reflecting little sparkles against her dark-brown skin. Dionysus probably started the night with a suit, but he's down to a white V-neck and there is a ball of wadded-up cloth on my kitchen island that's no doubt his jacket and shirt.

Over my shoulder, Persephone has gone stock-still. I'm not even sure she's breathing. The temptation arises to turn around and walk away, but I know from past experience that these two will just follow along and pepper me with questions until I give in to frustration and snap at them.

Better to rip off the Band-Aid now.

I set Persephone on the counter and keep a hand on her

shoulder to prevent her from taking a nosedive. She blinks big hazel eyes up at me, little shivers racking her body. "She called you Hades."

"It's my name." I pause. "Persephone."

Hermes laughs and sets the wine bottles on the counter with a clink. She points at herself. "Hermes." She points at him. "Dionysus." Another laugh. "Though you already knew that." She leans against my shoulder and whisper-yells, "She's going to marry Zeus."

I turn slowly to look at Hermes. "What?" I knew she had to be important to Zeus in order for him to send his men after her, but *marriage*? That means I have my hands on the shoulders of the next Hera.

"Yep." Hermes works the cork out of one of the bottles and takes a long drink directly from it. "They announced it tonight. You just stole the fiancée of the most powerful man in Olympus. It's a good thing they aren't married yet, or you would have kidnapped one of the Thirteen." She giggles. "That is positively *devious*, Hades. I didn't think you had it in you."

"I knew he did." Dionysus tries to eat another bite of pie but has a bit of trouble finding his mouth, getting the fork tangled in his beard instead. He blinks down at the utensil as if it's the one to blame. "He's the boogeyman, after all. You don't get that kind of reputation without being a tiny bit devious."

"That's about enough of that." I dig my phone out of my pocket. I need to see to Persephone, but I can't do that while fielding dozens of questions from these two.

"Hades!" Hermes whines. "Don't kick us out. We just got here."

"I didn't invite you." Not that that's stopped them from crossing the river whenever they feel like it. Part of that is Hermes—she can go where she pleases, when she pleases by virtue of her position. Dionysus technically has a standing invitation, but it was only meant to be for business purposes.

"You *never* invite us." She pouts red lips that she's somehow managed not to smudge. "It's enough to make a person think you don't like us."

I give her the look that statement deserves and dial Charon. He should be back by now. Sure enough, he answers quickly. "Yeah?"

"Hermes and Dionysus are here. Send someone to take them to their rooms." I could toss them in a car and send them home, but with these two, there's no guarantee that they won't get a wild hair and come right back—or make even more questionable decisions. Last time I sent them home like this, they ended up ditching my driver and trying to take a drunken swim in the River Styx. At least if they're under my roof, I can keep an eye on them until they sober up.

I am aware of Persephone staring at me like I've sprouted horns, but getting this pair of idiots taken care of is the first priority. Two of my people arrive and usher them out, but only after a strained negotiation that has them taking the pie and wine with them.

I sigh the moment the door closes behind them. "Those are thousand-dollar bottles of wine. She's drunk enough that she's not even going to taste it."

Persephone makes a strange hiccupping sound, which is my only warning before she shoves my coat off—having unzipped it while I was distracted—and makes a run for it. I'm surprised enough that I stand there and watch her try to hobble for the door. And she *is* hobbling.

A glimpse of red streaking the floor in her wake is enough to snap me out of it. "What the fuck do you think you're doing?"

"You can't keep me here!"

I snag her around the waist and carry her back to the kitchen island to drop her on it. "You're acting like a fool."

Big hazel eyes glare at me. "You *kidnapped* me. Trying to escape you is the smart thing to do."

I grab her ankle and lift her foot to get a good look at it. It's only when Persephone scrambles to hold her dress in place that I realize I probably could have gone about this in a different way. Oh well. I carefully touch her sole and show her my finger. "You're bleeding." There are several large gashes, but I can't tell if they're deep enough to need stitches.

"Then let me go to the hospital and I'll get it taken care of."

She's nothing if not persistent. I tighten my grip on her ankle. She's still shivering. Damn it, I don't have time for this argument. "Let's say I do that."

"Then *do* it."

"Do you think you'll get ten feet inside a hospital without the staff calling your mother?" I hold her gaze. "Without them calling your...fiancé?"

She flinches. "I'll figure it out."

"Like I said—you're being foolish." I shake my head. "Now hold still while I check for glass."

PERSEPHONE

HE'S REAL.

I know I should be screaming or fighting or trying to make it to the nearest phone, but I'm still grappling with the fact that *Hades is real*. My sisters are never going to hear the end of this. I *knew* I was right.

Besides, now that my panic is fading, I can't exactly fault him for anything. He might have threatened me a smidge in front of Zeus's men, but the alternative was to be dragged back to Dodona Tower. And yes, my stomach might have the permanent imprint of his shoulder there, but as he keeps growling at me, my feet are injured.

Not to mention the careful way he cleans my wounds doesn't exactly support the rumor that Hades is a monster. A monster would have left me to my fate.

He's...something else.

He's built lean and strong, and there are scars across his knuckles. A full beard and shoulder-length dark hair just lean in to the imposing presence he creates. His dark eyes are cold but not entirely unkind. He just looks as exasperated with me as he was with Hermes and Dionysus.

Hades pulls out a tiny shard of glass and drops it into the bowl he brought over. He glares at the glass like it insulted his mother and kicked his dog. "Hold still."

"I *am* holding still." Or at least I'm trying. It hurts and I can't stop shivering, even with his coat back around my shoulders. The longer I sit here, the more it hurts, as if my body is just catching up with my brain to realize the trouble we've gotten ourselves into. I can't believe I left, can't believe I walked for far too long through the dark and cold until I landed here.

Thinking about that now is out of the question. For the first time in my life, I don't have a plan or a clear bullet-pointed list to get me from point A to point B. I'm free-falling. My mother might kill me when she tracks me down. Zeus... I shudder. My mother will threaten to toss me out the nearest window or drink herself to death, but Zeus might actually hurt me. Who would stop him? Who is *powerful* enough to stop him? No one. If there was someone who could stop that monster, the last Hera would still be alive.

Hades pauses, a pair of tweezers in his battered hands and a question in his eyes. "You're shivering."

"No, I'm not."

"For fuck's sake, Persephone. You're shaking like a leaf. You can't just say you're not and expect me to believe it when I can see the truth with my own eyes." His glare is really impressive, but I'm too numb to feel anything right now. I simply sit there and watch him stalk to the door tucked back in the corner of the room and return with two thick blankets. He sets one on the counter next to me. "I'm going to lift you now."

"No." I don't even know why I'm arguing. I'm cold. Blankets will help. But I can't seem to stop myself.

He gives me a long look. "I don't think you're hypothermic, but if you don't warm up soon, you might end up there. It'd be a shame if I had to use body heat to get you back to a safe temperature."

It takes several long seconds for his meaning to penetrate. Surely he can't mean that he'd strip us down and bundle us up together until I warm up. I stare. "You wouldn't."

"I sure as fuck would." He glares. "You're no use to me if you die now."

I ignore the outrageous impulse to call him on his bluff and instead hold up a hand. "I can move on my own." I'm painfully aware of his close attention as I shift myself up and over until I'm sitting on the blanket instead of the cold granite countertop. Hades wastes no time wrapping the second blanket around me, covering up every inch of exposed skin above my ankles. Only then does he go back to his work of extracting glass from my soles.

Damn him, but the blanket really does feel good. Warmth starts seeping into my body almost immediately, fighting the chill that's taken up residence in my bones. My shivering gets more violent, but I'm aware enough to realize that's a good sign.

Desperate to grab on to any distraction, I focus on the man at my feet. "The last Hades died. You're supposed to be a myth, but Hermes and Dionysus know you." They were at the party I fled—my…engagement party—but I don't really know them any better than the rest of the Thirteen. Which is to say I don't know them at all.

"Is there a question in there?" He pulls out another sliver of glass and drops it into the bowl with a clink.

"*Why* are you supposed to be a myth? It doesn't make any sense. You're one of the Thirteen. You should be…"

"I'm a myth. You're dreaming," he says drily as he prods my foot. "Any sharp pain?"

I blink. "No. It just aches."

He nods, as if that's exactly what he expected. I watch numbly as he lays out a series of bandages and proceeds to wash and bandage my feet. I don't… Maybe he's right and I really am dreaming, because this doesn't make the slightest bit of sense. "You're friends with Hermes and Dionysus."

"I'm not friends with anyone. They just show up periodically like stray cats I can't get rid of." No matter his words, there's a thread of fondness in his tone.

"You're friends with two of the Thirteen." Because he *was* one of the Thirteen. Just like my mother. Just like *Zeus*. *Oh gods, Psyche is right and Hades is just as bad as the rest of them.*

The events of the night crash over me. Flashes of scene after scene. The sculpture room. My mother's caginess. Zeus's hand trapping mine as he announced our engagement. The terror-stricken run alongside the river. "They ambushed me," I whisper.

At that, Hades looks up, a frown pulling his strong brows together. "Hermes and Dionysus?"

"My mother and Zeus." I don't know why I'm telling him this, but I can't seem to stop. I clutch the blanket more firmly around my shoulders and shiver. "I didn't know the party tonight was announcing our engagement. I didn't *agree* to our engagement."

I'm exhausted enough I can almost pretend I get a flash of sympathy before irritation writes itself across his features. "Look at you. Of course Zeus wants to add you to his long list of Heras."

He *would* think that. The Thirteen see something they want, and they take it. "It's *my* fault that they made that decision without even talking to me *because of what I look like?*" Is it possible for the top of a person's head to literally explode? I have a feeling I might find out if we continue this conversation.

"It's Olympus. You play power games, you pay the consequences." He finishes wrapping my second foot and pushes slowly to his feet. "Sometimes you pay the consequences even if it's your parents playing the games. You can cry and sob about how unfair the world is, or you can do something about it."

"I *did* do something about it."

He snorts. "You ran like a frightened deer and thought he wouldn't chase you down? Sweetheart, that's practically foreplay for Zeus. He'll find you and drag you back to that palace of his. You'll marry him just like the obedient daughter you are, and within a year, you'll be popping out his asshole children."

I slap him.

I don't mean to. I don't think I've ever raised my hand to a person in my entire life. Not even my irritating younger sisters when we were children. I stare in horror at the red mark blooming on his cheekbone. I should apologize. Should...something. But when I open my mouth, that's not what comes out. "I'll die first."

Hades looks at me a long time. I'm usually pretty good at reading people, but I have no idea what's going on behind those deep, dark eyes of his. Finally, he grinds out, "You'll stay here tonight. We'll talk in the morning."

"But—"

He picks me up again, scooping me into his arms like I'm the princess he named me, and gives me such a cold look, I swallow my protest. I have nowhere to go tonight, no purse, no money, no phone. I can't afford to look this gift horse in the mouth, even if he's growly and goes by the name parents have threatened their children with for generations. Well, maybe not *this* Hades. He looks like he's somewhere in his early to midthirties. But the role of Hades. Always in the shadows. Always catering to dark deeds best done out of the sight of our normal, safe world.

Is it really that safe? My mother just effectively sold me in marriage to Zeus. A man who *empirical* facts paint not as the golden king, beloved by all, but as a bully who's left a string of dead wives in his wake. And those are just his wives. Who knows how many women he's victimized over the years? Thinking about it is enough to make me sick to my stomach. No matter which way you spin it, Zeus is dangerous and that's a fact.

By contrast, everything surrounding Hades is pure myth. No one I know even believes he exists. They all agree that at one point, a Hades *did* exist but that the family line that held the title has long since died out. That means I have next to no information to pull from about *this* Hades. I'm not sure he's the better bet, but at this point, I'd take a man in a bloody trench coat with a hook for a hand over Zeus.

Hades takes me up a winding staircase that looks straight out of a gothic movie. Honestly, the bits of this house I've seen are the same. Bold, dark hardwood floors, crown molding that should be overwhelming but somehow just creates the illusion of leaving both time and reality behind. The hallway of the second floor is covered in a thick deep-red carpet.

The better to hide the blood.

I give a hysterical giggle and clamp my hands to my mouth. This is not funny. I should not be laughing. I'm obviously thirty seconds away from losing it completely.

Hades, of course, ignores me.

The second door on the left is our destination, and it's not until he's walking through it that my missing self-preservation kicks in. I'm alone with a dangerous stranger in a bedroom. "Put me down."

"Don't be dramatic." He doesn't drop me on the bed like I expect. He sets me down carefully and takes an equally careful step back. "If you bleed all over my floors trying to escape, I'll be forced to track you down and haul you back here to clean them."

I blink. It's so close to what I was thinking that it's almost eerie. "You are the strangest man I've ever met."

Now it's his turn to give me a wary look. "What?"

"Exactly. *What?* What kind of threat is that? You're worried about your *floors?*"

"They're nice floors."

Is he joking? I might believe it of anyone else, but Hades looks just as serious as he has since I saw him standing there on the street like some kind of grim reaper. I frown up at him. "I don't understand you."

"You don't have to understand me. Just stay here until morning and try to resist the urge to do anything to injure yourself further." He nods at the door tucked back in the corner. "Bathroom is through there. Stay off those feet as much as possible." And then he's gone, sweeping out the door and shutting it softly behind him.

I count to ten slowly and then do it three more times. When no one rushes in to check on me, I inch up the bed to the phone sitting innocently on the nightstand. Too innocently? Surely there's no way to make a call without being overheard. With those secret tunnels, Hades doesn't seem the type to leave anything resembling a security breach just sitting here. It's probably a trap, something designed to have me spilling secrets or something.

It doesn't matter.

I'm afraid of Zeus. Angry with my mother. But I can't leave my sisters frantic for my whereabouts any longer. Psyche will have called Callisto by now, and if there's anyone in my family who will rampage through Olympus, stepping on toes and making threats until I'm found, it's my eldest sister. My disappearance will already have set fire to the hornet's nest. I can't let my sisters do anything to aggravate a situation that's already an unmitigated mess.

Taking a deep breath that does nothing to brace me, I pick up the phone and dial Eurydice's number. She's the only one of my sisters who will answer an unfamiliar number on the first try. Sure enough, three rings later, her breathless voice comes across the line. "Hello?"

"It's me."

"Oh, thank the gods." Her voice gets a little distant. "It's Persephone. Yes, yes, I'll put it on speaker." A second later, the line gets a little fuzzy as she does exactly that. "I have Callisto and Psyche here, too. Where are you?"

I look around the room. "You wouldn't believe me if I told you."

"Try." This from Callisto, a flat statement that says she's half a second from trying to figure out how to crawl through the telephone line to throttle me.

"If I realized you were going to take off the second I went to get your purse, I wouldn't have left you alone." Psyche's voice wobbles as if she's on the verge of tears. "Mother is tearing apart the upper city looking for you, and Zeus..."

Callisto cuts her off. "Fuck Zeus. And fuck Mother, too."

Eurydice gasps. "You can't say things like that."

"I just did."

Against all reason, their squabbling calms me. "I'm okay." I glance at my bandaged feet. "I'm mostly okay."

"Where are you?"

I don't have a plan, but I know I can't go home. Walking back into my mother's household is as good as admitting defeat and agreeing to marry Zeus. I can't do it. I *won't*. "That doesn't matter. I'm not coming home."

"Persephone," Psyche says slowly. "I know you're not happy about this, but we have to find a better way forward than running into the night. You're the woman with a plan, and right now, you have no plan."

No, I don't have a plan. I'm free-falling in a way that feels dangerous and has terror licking up my spine. "Plans were meant to be adapted."

All three of them are silent, a rare enough occurrence that I wish I could appreciate it. Finally, Eurydice says, "Why are you calling now?"

That's the question, isn't it? I don't know. "I just wanted you to know I'm okay."

"We'll believe you're okay when we know where you are." Callisto still sounds ready to mow down anyone who gets between her and me, and I manage a smile.

"Persephone, you just disappeared. Everyone is frantically looking for you."

I digest that statement, picking it apart. Everyone is frantically looking for me? They mentioned Mother before, but I didn't really connect the dots until now. It doesn't make any sense that she doesn't already know my location because... "Zeus knows where I am."

"*What?*"

"His men followed me all the way to Cypress Bridge." Thinking about it makes me shudder. I have no doubt they had instructions to haul me back, but they could have easily taken me a few blocks from Dodona Tower. They chose to pursue me, to drive my desperation and fear higher. No underling of Zeus would dare do something like that to his intended bride...unless they were ordered to by Zeus himself. "He's acting like he doesn't know where I am?"

"Yes." The anger hasn't quite bled out of Callisto's voice, but it's dampened. "He's talking about organizing search parties, and Mother is fluttering at his elbow as if she hasn't already ordered the same thing done with her people. He's mobilized his private security force, too."

"But why would he do that if he already knows where I am?"

Psyche clears her throat. "Did you cross the Cypress Bridge?"

Damn. I hadn't meant to let that slip. I close my eyes. "I'm in the lower city."

Callisto snorts. "That shouldn't make a difference to Zeus." She's never paid much attention to the rumors that crossing the river is nearly as impossible as leaving Olympus. I honestly didn't quite believe it, either, not until I felt that horrible pressure when I did it myself.

"Unless..." Eurydice has gotten ahold of her emotions and I can practically see her mind whirling. She plays the ditzy damsel when it suits her, but she's probably the smartest of the four of us. "The city used to be divided into three. Zeus, Poseidon, Hades."

"That was a long time ago," Psyche murmurs. "Zeus and Poseidon work together now. And Hades is myth. Persephone and I were just talking about this tonight."

"If he weren't a myth, Hades would be enough to give Zeus pause."

Callisto snorts. "Except even if he existed, there's no way he wouldn't be just as bad as Zeus."

"He's not." The words slip free despite my best efforts to keep them internal. Damn it, I meant to keep them out of it, but obviously that isn't going to work. I should have known that the moment I dialed Eurydice. *In for a penny, in for a pound.* I clear my throat. "No matter what he is, he's not as bad as Zeus."

My sisters' voices comingle as they voice their shock.

"*What?*"

"Did you hit your head while you were running from those assholes?"

"Persephone, your obsession is getting out of control."

I sigh. "I'm not hallucinating, and I didn't hit my head." Best not to tell them about my feet or the fact that I'm still shivering a bit, even after being bundled up. "He's real, and he's been here this whole time."

My sisters are silent once again as they digest *that*. Callisto curses. "People would have known."

They should have. The fact that we've all believed him a myth this whole time speaks to a larger influence that wanted to wipe Hades's memory from the face of Olympus. It speaks of *Zeus's* meddling, because who else has the power to pull something like that off? Maybe Poseidon, but if it doesn't concern the sea and the docks, he doesn't seem to care about it. None of the rest of the Thirteen operate with the same amount of power as the legacy roles. None of them would dare take out the title of Hades, not on their own.

But then, no one really talks about how little crossover there is between the upper and lower city. It's just taken as the way things are. Even I never questioned it, and I question so much else when it comes to Olympus and the Thirteen.

Finally, Psyche says, "What do you need from us?"

I think hard. I only have to last to my birthday and then I'm free. The trust fund our grandmother set up releases to me then, and I don't have to rely on my mother or anyone in Olympus for anything ever again. But not until then, my twenty-fifth birthday. I have some funds of my own now, but they aren't *really* my own. They're my mother's. I could ask my sisters to bring me my purse, but Mother will have already frozen my accounts.

She likes to do that to punish us, and she'll want to ensure I come crawling back after humiliating her like this. More, I don't want my sisters in the lower city, even if they could make their way across the River Styx. Not when danger seems to be around every corner.

Really, there's only one answer. "I'm going to figure something out, but I'm not coming back. Not right now."

"Persephone, that's not a plan." Callisto huffs out a breath. "You have no money, no phone that isn't likely to be tapped, and you're shacking up with Olympus's boogeyman, who also happens to be one of the Thirteen. He is the very definition of dangerous. This is the opposite of a plan."

I can't argue that. "I'll figure it out."

"Yeah, no. Try again."

Psyche clears her throat. "If Eurydice can distract Mother, Callisto and I can bring you a burner phone and what money we have on hand. It should at least buy you time to figure things out."

The last thing I want to do is drag my sisters into this, but it's too late now. I lean back against the headboard. "Let me think about it. I'll call tomorrow with more details."

"That's not—"

"I love you all. Goodbye." I hang up before they can find another angle to argue from. It's the right call to make, but that doesn't stop me from feeling like I've cut off my last connection to my past. I've been working out a way to leave Olympus for a very long time, so this break was bound to happen, but I thought I'd have more notice. I thought I'd still be able to connect with my sisters without putting them in danger. I thought, given enough time, Mother would even come around and forgive me for not playing a pawn in one of her schemes.

It seems that I was wrong about a lot of things.

To give myself something else to think about, I look around the room. It's just as opulent as the parts of the house I've seen so far, the bed large and with a dark-blue canopy that would do any princess proud. The hardwood floors that Hades is so fond of are covered with a thick carpet and there's yet more crown molding everywhere. It's as atmospheric as the rest of the house, but it doesn't really give me many clues about the man who owns this place. It's obviously a spare bedroom, and as a result, it's doubtful it'll tell me anything about Hades.

My body chooses that moment to remind me that I walked for hours in the cold in those godforsaken heels and then ran over gravel and glass barefoot. My legs ache. My back hurts. My feet... Best not to think too hard about them. I am so incredibly exhausted, enough that I might actually sleep tonight.

I look around the room again. Hades might not be as bad as Zeus, but I can't take any chances. I climb gingerly to my feet and limp to the door. There's no lock, which has me cursing softly. I limp to the bathroom and nearly whimper with relief when I find that this door *does* have a lock.

My muscles seem to turn from flesh to stone with each second that passes, weighing me down as I drag the massive comforter off the bed and into the bathroom. The tub is more than large enough to sleep in, uncomfortable or no. After a quick internal debate, I go back to the bedroom door and drag the side table in front of it. At least I'll hear someone coming this way. Satisfied I've done all I can, I lock the bathroom door and practically collapse into the tub.

In the morning, I'll have a plan. I'll figure out a way forward and this won't seem like the end of the world.

I just need a plan...

HADES

AFTER A FEW HOURS OF RESTLESS SLEEP, I HEAD DOWN TO the kitchen in search of coffee only to find Hermes perched on my kitchen island, eating ice cream out of the carton. I stop short, faintly alarmed by the fact that she's dressed in a pair of cutoff shorts and an oversize T-shirt that she was most definitely *not* wearing last night. "You keep clothes at my house."

"Duh. No one wants to wear the aftermath of their drunken adventures home." She motions behind her without looking. "I put on coffee."

Thank the gods for small favors. "Coffee and ice cream is one way to deal with a hangover."

"Shhh." She makes a face. "My head hurts."

"Imagine that," I murmur and walk around to grab us both mugs. I pour her two-thirds of the way full and pass it over. She promptly drops a giant dollop of ice cream into the coffee, and I shake my head. "You know, I seem to remember locking up last night. And yet here you are."

NEON GODS 55

"Here I am." She gives me a slightly rumpled version of her usual wicked grin. "Come now, Hades. You know that there isn't a lock in this city that can keep me out."

"I've become aware of it over the years." The first time she showed up was a mere month after she earned the title of Hermes, some five or six years ago now. She startled me in my office and almost ended up with a bullet in her head as a result. Somehow, that interaction translated into her deciding that we're great friends. It took me a year to figure out that it didn't matter what *I* thought of the so-called friendship. Then Dionysus started appearing with her about six months after that, and I gave up fighting their presence.

If they're spies for Zeus, they're completely ineffectual and aren't gaining any information I don't want him to have. If they aren't...

Well, it's not my problem.

She takes a long drink of her ice-cream-dosed coffee and makes a disturbingly sex-like sound. "Are you sure you don't want some?"

"I'm sure." I lean against the counter and try to decide how to play this. I can't really trust Hermes. No matter that she seems to consider us friends, she is one of the Thirteen and I'd be a fool ten times over to forget that. More, she makes her home in the shadow of Dodona Tower and answers directly to Zeus—at least when it suits her. Showing my hand before I have a concrete plan is a recipe for disaster.

But the cat's out of the bag in every way that matters. Zeus's men will have reported Persephone's location to him already. Hermes confirming it changes nothing.

Dionysus stumbles through the door. His mustache is a mess and his pale skin is nearly green. He waves vaguely in my direction and makes a beeline for the coffee. "Morning."

Hermes snorts. "You look like death."

"You're to blame. Who drinks wine after whiskey? Villains, that's who." He contemplates the coffeepot for a long moment and finally pours himself a mug. "Just shoot me in the head and put me out of my misery."

"Don't tempt me," I mutter.

"Yes, yes, you're very broody and terrifying." Hermes spins on the island to face me. Her dark eyes light up with mischief. "All these years I thought it was an act, but then you stalk in, carrying your kidnapping victim."

I start to clarify that I didn't actually *kidnap* anyone, but Dionysus barks out a laugh. "So I didn't hallucinate that. Persephone Dimitriou always seemed a bit of a sunny bore, but she just got interesting. She stepped out of that party less than thirty minutes after Zeus announced their engagement, and then she turns up on the other side of the River Styx, where good upper-city girls most definitely don't go? Very, very interesting."

I frown, unable to stop myself from focusing on the least important part of what he just said. "A sunny bore?" Admittedly, we hardly met under ideal circumstances, but the woman is anything but a bore.

Hermes shakes her head, sending her curls bouncing. "You've only seen her in her public persona when her mom drags her to events, Dionysus. She's not too bad when she's not locked down, especially when she's hanging out with her sisters."

Dionysus opens one eye. "Darling, spying is highly frowned upon."

"Who said I'm spying?"

He opens the other eye. "Oh, so you've been spending time with the Dimitriou sisters, have you? The four women who hate the Thirteen with a passion that's truly outstanding considering who their mother is."

"Maybe." She can't even keep a straight face. "Okay, no, but I was curious because their mother is so determined to match them up with as many powerful people as she can get her hands on. It pays to know these things."

I watch this play out with fascination. Hermes, being one of the Thirteen, should be someone I dislike on principle, but her role edges her into the shadows in a number of ways. Private messenger, the holder of secrets I can only begin to guess at, a thief when it suits her. She's nearly as much a patron of the darkness as I am. It should make her even less trustworthy than the rest of them, but she's so damned transparent that sometimes it makes my head ache.

Then the rest of their words penetrate. "So it's true. She's set to marry Zeus."

"They announced it last night. It would have been sad if I had any room in my heart for pity. She was trying so hard to keep her smile in place, but the poor thing was terrified." Dionysus closes his eyes again and leans back against the counter. "Hopefully she lasts longer than the last Hera. It's enough to wonder what game Demeter is playing. I thought she cared more about her daughters' safety than that."

I'm aware of Hermes watching me closely, but I refuse to show my interest. I have too many years of locking everything away until there's a thick wall between me and the rest of the world. Tolerating these people in my house does not translate to bringing them into my confidence. No one earns that. Not when I've seen how spectacularly it can backfire and get people killed in the process.

Hermes inches to the edge of the island and kicks her legs out, a study in casualness. "You're right, Dionysus. She didn't agree to it. A little birdie told me that she had no idea it was happening until they dragged her to the front of the room and put her in a position where she had to agree or piss Zeus off with the entire Thirteen present—well, the Thirteen minus Hades and Hera. We all know how well that goes over."

"You work for Zeus," I say mildly, forcing down the instinctive anger that rises every time that fucker's name comes up.

"Nope. I work for the Thirteen. Zeus just happens to take advantage of my services more often than the others—including you." She leans forward and gives me an awkward wink. "You should consider utilizing my skills to their fullest extent. I'm rather outstanding at my role, if I do say so myself."

She might as well dangle the bait right in front of my face and give it a good shake. I raise my brows. "I'd be a fool to trust you."

"He's right." Dionysus burps and looks even greener, if that is possible. "You're tricksy."

"I don't know what you're talking about. I'm the very paragon of innocence."

Hermes plays a deeper game than anyone else. She has to in

order to maintain her balance of a vaguely neutral party in the midst of all the politicking and manipulation and schemes of the other Thirteen. Trusting her is like putting my hand in a tiger's mouth and hoping it's not in the mood for a snack.

Still...

Curiosity sinks its fangs into me and refuses to let go. "Most people in Olympus would happily give their right hand to become one of the Thirteen, marriage to Zeus or no." The tabloids paint a picture of Persephone as a woman with more money than sense— the exact kind of person who'd jump at being married to a rich and powerful man like Zeus. That Persephone is nothing like the strong yet terrified person who fled across the bridge last night. Which one is real? Only time will tell.

Hermes's smile widens as if I've just given her a gift. "One would think, wouldn't they?"

"Put him out of his misery and share the gossip." Dionysus groans. "You're making my headache worse."

Hermes pulls her legs up, and I have to bite back the urge to tell her to get her goddamn feet off my counter. She cups her mug in both hands and holds it in front of her mouth. "Demeter's daughters aren't interested in power."

"Right." I snort. "Everyone's interested in power. If not power, then money." I can't count how many times the Dimitriou daughters have been photographed shopping for things they certainly don't need. At least once a week.

"That's what I thought, too. Which is why I feel I can be forgiven for snooping." She shoots a look at Dionysus, but he's too lost in his hangover misery to notice. "Not a single one of them cares about their mother's ambitions. The youngest has even let Calliope's favorite son tempt her into a relationship."

That gets my interest. "Apollo's little brother?"

"The very one." She laughs. "The ultimate fuckboy."

I let that pass, because it doesn't really matter what I think of Orpheus Makos. His family might not be a legacy one in Olympus, but they've had plenty of power and fortune through the generations, even before Orpheus's older brother became Apollo. From the rumors I've heard of the guy, he's a musician on a permanent quest to find himself. I've heard his music, and it's good, but it doesn't quite excuse the excess he indulges in to pursue his various muses. "You have a point."

"Do I?" She waggles her eyebrows. "I'm just saying that you might want to sit the woman down and ask what she wants." She shrugs and hops off the counter, only weaving a little on her feet. "Or you could just play to expectation and lock her up in a dungeon. I'm sure Zeus would *love* that."

"Hermes, you know very well that I don't have a dungeon."

"Not a dank and dark one." More eyebrow waggling. "We've all seen the playroom, though."

I refuse to acknowledge that. The parties I host from time to time are as much part of my role as Hades as anything else. A carefully crafted persona that is designed to inspire the darker emotions and, as a result, ensure the few people who know about my existence in the upper city don't fuck with me. If I happen to enjoy this particular part of said persona, who can blame me? Persephone would take one look at that room and run screaming for her life. "Time for you to go home." I nod to the hall. "I can have Charon take you."

"Don't bother. We'll catch our own ride." She pops up onto her tiptoes and presses a quick kiss to my cheek. "Have fun with your captive."

"She's not my captive."

"Keep telling yourself that." Then she's gone, dancing out of the room in her bare feet as if it's the most natural thing in the world. The woman exhausts me.

Dionysus seems to have no intention of leaving my mug behind, but he stops in the doorway. "You and the sunshine girl might be able to help each other." He grimaces at my look. "What? It's a perfectly legitimate thought to have. She's probably one of the few people in Olympus who hates Zeus as much as you do." He snaps his fingers. "Oh, and I'll have that shipment for you by the end of the week. I didn't forget."

"You never do." As soon as he walks out the door, I snag Hermes's abandoned coffee cup and put it in the sink. The woman leaves mess wherever she goes, but I'm used to it at this point. Last night was relatively tame on the Hermes-Dionysus scale. Last time they broke in, they brought a chicken they'd found gods alone knew where. I was finding feathers for *days* afterward.

I stare at the coffeepot, pushing away thoughts of those two troublemakers. They aren't the ones I need to be worried about right now. Zeus is. I'm honestly surprised he hasn't contacted me already. He's not one to sit back and wait when someone takes away one of his toys.

It's so fucking tempting to reach out first, to rub his nose in the fact that this little socialite was willing to run to *me* rather than marry him. Doing so is too impulsive and petty. If I intend to use Persephone to actually get some measure of revenge...

I'll be just as bad as he is.

I try to push the thought aside. My people have suffered from Zeus's machinations. *I* have suffered, have lost just as much as anyone. I should be jumping at this chance to get a measure of revenge. And I *do* want revenge. But do I want it at the expense of this woman who has already played a pawn to both her mother and Zeus? Am I cold enough to push forward despite her protests?

I suppose I could ask *her* what she wants. What a novel thought.

I grimace and pour a second cup of coffee. After a moment's consideration, I find the cream and sugar and dose it. Persephone doesn't seem the type to drink her coffee black. Then again, what do I know? The only information I have on her is what's written in the gossip columns that follow the Thirteen and the people in their sphere. Those "journalists" adore the Dimitriou women and follow them around like a pack of dogs. I'm actually kind of impressed Persephone made it out of that party without acquiring an entourage.

How much is real and how much is creatively put together fiction? Impossible to say. I know better than most that reputation often has little to do with reality.

I'm stalling.

The second I realize it, I curse and stalk out of the kitchen and up the stairs. It's not late, but I'd half expected her to be up and terrorizing someone in the household by now. Both Hermes and Dionysus managed to stir from the drunken coma they call sleep and leave before Persephone woke.

I hate that tendril of concern that worms its way through me. This woman's mental health is not my business. It just fucking isn't. Zeus and I already dance on the edge of a sword every time we're forced to interact. One wrong move and I'll be sliced in two. More importantly, one wrong move and my people suffer the consequences.

I'm putting myself and my people in danger for this woman who's probably just as power hungry as her mother and will likely wake up realizing that her best way to that power is with Zeus's ring on her finger. It doesn't matter what she said on the phone last night to her sisters. It can't matter.

I knock on the door and wait, but no sound emerges. I knock again. "Persephone?"

Silence.

After a quick internal debate, I open the door. There's the slightest bit of resistance, and I push harder, making something crash on the other side. With a long sigh, I step into the room. It takes one look around the room—to see the tipped-over side table and the missing comforter—for me to come to the conclusion that she hid in the bathroom all night.

Of course she did.

She's in big, bad Hades's house so she just assumes that she'll be harmed in some way while she's defenseless in sleep. She *barricaded* herself in. It makes me want to throw something, but I haven't allowed myself that kind of loss of control since I was barely out of my teens.

I set down the coffee mug and pick up the side table, taking a moment to put it back exactly where it belongs. Satisfied with the placement, I stride to the bathroom door and knock.

A shuffling on the other side. Then her voice, so close she has to be pressed against the door. "Do you often break into people's rooms without permission?"

"Do I need permission to enter a room in my own house?" I don't know why I'm engaging in this. I should just open the door, drag her out, and send her on her way.

"Perhaps you should have people sign a waiver before crossing the threshold if that's how you think home ownership works."

She's just so *strange*. So...unexpected. I frown at the whitewashed wood. "I'll consider it."

"See that you do. You woke me rather abruptly."

She sounds so damn prim that I want to rip this door off the hinges just to get a good look at the expression she's wearing right now. "You were sleeping in a tub. Hardly the recipe for a good night's rest."

"That's a very narrow worldview you have."

I glare, though there's no way she can see it. "Open the door, Persephone. I'm tired of this conversation."

"You seem to do that a lot. If you find me so tiresome, you shouldn't be breaking down my door at ungodly hours of the morning."

"Persephone. The door. Now."

"Oh, if you insist."

I step back at the click of the lock and then she's there, standing in the doorway and looking deliciously rumpled. Her blond hair is a mess, there's a crease pressed into her cheek from her pillow, and she's got the comforter wrapped around her like a suit of armor. A very fluffy, very ineffective suit of armor that requires her to shuffle into the room with tiny steps to avoid falling on her face.

The ridiculous urge to laugh rises, but I smother it. Any reaction will only encourage her, and this woman already has me set back on my heels. *Get her sorted out. Either use her or get her out.* That's all that matters. I wave at the mug. "Coffee."

Persephone's hazel eyes widen the tiniest bit. "You brought me coffee."

"Most people drink coffee in the morning. It's really not a big deal." I make a face. "Though Hermes is the only one I know who doses it with ice cream."

If anything, her eyes get wider. "I can't believe Hermes and Dionysus have known about you this entire time. How many other people know that you're not a myth?"

"A few." A nice, safe, noncommittal answer.

She's still staring at my face as if searching for evidence of someone she knows, as if I'm somehow familiar to her. It's disconcerting in the extreme. I have the irrational suspicion that she's fisting that comforter so tightly to avoid reaching out and touching me.

Persephone tilts her head to the side. "Did you know there's a statue of Hades in Dodona Tower?"

"How would I know?" I've only been to the tower once, and Zeus hardly gave me the full tour. I never want to repeat the experience, unless it's to end that bastard once and for all. That particular vengeful fantasy has gotten me through more rough days than I want to number.

She continues on as if I didn't respond, still studying my features too closely. "There's these statues of each of the Thirteen, but yours has a black shroud over it. I guess to signify that your line has ended. You're not supposed to exist."

"Yes, you keep saying that." I consider her. "It certainly seems like you've spent a lot of time studying this Hades statue. Hardly the kind of man Demeter would want you chasing down."

Just like that, something shutters in her eyes and her smile brightens to blinding levels. "What can I say? I'm an eternal disappointment as a daughter." She takes a step and winces.

She's injured. Fuck, I forgot. I move before I have a chance to consider the wisdom of it. I scoop her up, ignoring her squawk, and set her on the bed. "Your feet are hurting you."

"If they're hurting me, I will happily sit down under my own power."

I look down at her, meeting her eyes, and realize exactly how close we are. An unwelcome frisson of awareness pulses through me. I sound too harsh when I manage to speak. "Then do it."

"I will! Now *get back*. I can't think with you so close."

I take a slow step back and then another. Setting her on the bed was a mistake, because now she's looking deliciously rumpled *on the bed*, and I'm far too aware of other bed-related activities that would accomplish the same look. Fuck, but she's beautiful. It's the warm kind of beauty that feels like summer sunlight on my face, like if I get too close, I'll smudge it. I stare at this beautiful, baffling woman, and I'm not sure I can go through with using her, even to punish Zeus for all the harm he's caused me and mine.

I slip my hands into my pockets and strive for a neutral tone. "It's time we spoke about what comes next."

"Actually, I was thinking the same thing." Persephone carefully dismantles her blanket armor and gives me a long look. It's all the warning I get before she smashes through the wall of my good intentions. "I believe we can help each other."

PERSEPHONE

6

A NIGHT SLEEPING IN A STRANGER'S BATHTUB HAS A WAY of bringing perspective to a situation. I have nowhere to go. No resources. No friends who won't bow to my mother's will. A winter didn't seem like that long when I was still moving through my normal life. Now? Three months might as well be an eternity for all I can breach it.

My sisters would help me—Callisto would drain *her* trust fund to ensure I get out of Olympus unscathed—but I can't let them get that involved. I might be leaving this city, but they aren't and it would be cowardly in the extreme to accept their help and then whirl away, leaving them to deal with the consequences.

No, there really isn't another option.

I have to throw myself on Hades's mercy and convince him that we can help each other.

It doesn't help that the soft morning light does nothing to make him look less forbidding. I'm getting a feeling like this man walks around with a little bit of midnight in his pocket. He's certainly dressed the part in a black-on-black suit. Expensive and tasteful and very, very atmospheric when combined with the perfectly groomed beard and long hair. And those eyes. Gods, the man looks like some kind of crossroads demon designed specifically to tempt me. Considering the deal I'm about to offer, maybe that's not a bad thing.

"Persephone." A single eyebrow arches. "You think we can help each other." A reminder that I'd let my voice trail off immediately after throwing that into the air between us.

I smooth back my hair, trying not to let his presence fluster me. I've spent the last few years rubbing elbows with powerful people, but this feels different. *He* feels different. "You hate Zeus."

"I would think that's glaringly clear."

I ignore that. "And for some reason, Zeus is hesitant to move against you."

Hades crosses his arms over his chest. "Zeus can pretend the rules don't exist for him, but even he can't stand against the entirety of the Thirteen. We have a very carefully constructed treaty. A small selection of people can cross back and forth from the upper to the lower city without consequence, but he can't. And neither can I."

I blink. This is all news to me. "What happens if you do?"

"War." He shrugs as if it's of no concern. Maybe it isn't for him. "You crossed of your own free will, and he can't take you back without risking a conflict that will embroil all of Olympus." His lips quirk. "Your fiancé never does anything that might endanger his power and position, so he'll let me do whatever I want to you to avoid that fight."

He's trying to scare me. Little does he realize that he's actually reassuring me that this haphazard plan has a chance of working. "Why does everyone believe you're a myth?"

"I stay in the lower city. It's not my problem the upper city likes to tell tales that have nothing to do with reality."

That's not even close to a complete answer, but I suppose I don't need that information right now. I can see the framework well enough without all the details. Treaty or no, Zeus has a vested interest in keeping Hades a myth. Without the third legacy role in place, the power balance lands firmly in Zeus's favor. It was always strange to me that he effectively ignored half of Olympus, but now that I know Hades is real, it makes more sense.

I straighten my spine, holding his gaze. "Regardless, that doesn't explain the way you spoke to his men last night. You *hate* him."

Hades doesn't blink. "He killed my parents when I was very young. Hate is too gentle a word."

Shock nearly steals my breath. I'm not surprised to hear Zeus accused of another set of murders, exactly, but Hades speaks of his parents' death so neutrally, as if it happened to someone else. I swallow hard. "I'm sorry."

"Yeah. People always say that."

I'm losing him. I can see it in the way his gaze tracks around the room as if debating how quickly he can bundle me up and send me on my way. I take a deep breath and press forward. No matter what he told those men last night, it couldn't be clearer that he has no intention of keeping me around. I can't allow that. "Use me."

Hades refocuses on me. "What?"

"It's not the same thing, not even on the same level, but he claimed me and now *you* have me."

Surprise colors his features. "I didn't realize you'd resigned yourself so fully to playing the pawn in a chess match between men."

Humiliation heats my cheeks, but I ignore it. He's trying to provoke a reaction, and I won't give it to him. "A pawn between you or a pawn to be used by my mother—it all amounts to the same." I smile brightly, enjoying the way he flinches as if I've struck him. "I can't go back, you see."

"I'm not keeping you."

No reason for that to sting. I don't know this man, and I have no intention of being *kept*. It still irks that he's so ready to dismiss me out of hand. I keep my smile firmly in place and my tone bright. "Not forever, of course. I have somewhere to be in three months' time, but until I turn twenty-five, I can't access my trust fund to get there."

"You're twenty-four." If anything, he looks grumpier, as if my age is a personal affront.

"Yes, that is how math works." *Tone it down, Persephone. You need his help. Stop needling him.* I can't seem to help myself. Normally, I'm better at putting people at ease, which makes them more inclined to do what I want. Hades makes me want to dig in my heels and stick it to him until he squirms.

He turns to look out the window, which is when I notice that he's replaced the side table exactly how it was before I moved it. How wonderfully anal of him. It doesn't line up in the least with the boogeyman of Olympus. That man would have kicked down the door and dragged me out by my hair. He'd be only too happy to take me up on my offer instead of looking at the open bathroom door like I've left my wits behind me in the tub.

By the time he turns back to me, I have my placid, happy expression firmly in place. Hades glowers. "You want to stay here for *three* months."

"In fact, I do. My birthday is April sixteenth. I'll be out of your hair the day after. I'll be out of everyone's hair."

"What does that mean?"

"Once my trust fund is in my hands, I'm bribing someone to get me out of Olympus. The details aren't important; the fact that I'm leaving is."

He narrows his eyes. "Leaving the city isn't that easy."

"Neither is crossing the River Styx, but I managed that last night."

He finally stops glaring and studies me. "What a pale revenge you sketch out. Why should I care what you do? As you said, you won't go back to Zeus and your mother, and I'm the one who took you from him. Whether or not I keep you here, whether you leave now or in three months, it makes no difference to me."

He's right, and I hate that he's right. Zeus already knows I'm here, which means Hades effectively has me over a barrel. I stand carefully, muscling down my flinch at the aching pain putting weight on my feet causes. From his narrowed eyes, he sees it regardless, and he doesn't like it. No matter how cold this man pretends to be, if he was *really* that cold, he wouldn't have sat me in his kitchen and bandaged my feet, wouldn't have wrapped blankets around me to ensure I warmed up. He wouldn't be fighting himself in order not to shove me back onto the bed to keep me from hurting myself.

I clasp my hands in front of me to prevent myself from fidgeting. "What if you twisted the knife, so to speak?"

He's watching me so closely, I have the hysterical thought that this must be how a fox feels before the hounds are loosed. If I run, would he chase me? I can't be certain, and because I can't be certain, my heart picks up its rhythm in my chest.

Finally, Hades says, "I'm listening."

"Keep me for the rest of the winter. And all that that entails."

"Don't be vague now, Persephone. Spell out what you're offering, in detail."

My face must be crimson, but I don't let my smile falter. "If he thinks I chose you over him, it will drive him mad." When Hades continues to wait, I swallow hard. "You live in the lower city, but surely you know how it works across the river. My perceived value is directly tied to my image. Among the other things, there's a reason you haven't seen me publicly dating anyone since my mother became Demeter." In hindsight, I intensely regret submitting to my mother's meddling in that regard. I thought it easier to not make waves as she cultivated a certain reputation for me and my sisters; I had no idea she'd use that same reputation to sell me to Zeus.

"Zeus is notorious for not wanting what he considers tarnished goods." I take a deep breath. "So...tarnish me."

Hades finally smiles and, good gods, it's like being hit by a laser beam. Heat strong enough to make my fingertips tingle and curl my toes. I stare up at him, caught in the intensity of those dark eyes. And then he's shaking his head, smothering the rush of strangeness through my body. "No."

"What do you mean, *no?*"

"I'm aware that you've likely not heard the word often in your privileged life, so I'll spell it out for you. No. Nein. Nyet. Non. Absolutely not."

Irritation rises. It's a very good plan, especially when I had such short notice to come up with it. "Why not?"

For a moment, I think he won't answer me. Finally, Hades shakes his head. "Zeus isn't stupid."

"I suppose that's a fair assumption." One doesn't gain and keep power in Olympus without some level of intelligence, even if they *are* in a legacy role. "What's your point?"

"Even if one takes Hermes out of the equation, he has spies in my territory the same way I have spies in his. No surface-level charade will fool him. It will take one report to prove it all to be a sham, which will entirely defeat the purpose of said sham."

If he's correct, my plan won't work. How frustrating. Now it's my turn to cross my arms over my chest, though I refuse to glare out of principle. "Then we do it for real."

Hades's slow blink is a special kind of reward. "You're out of your mind."

"Hardly. I'm a woman with a plan. Learn and adapt, Hades." My breezy voice doesn't belie the way my heart is racing so hard that it's leaving me a bit dizzy. I can't believe I'm offering this, can't believe I'd be this impulsive, but the words just keep pouring out of my mouth. "You're attractive enough in a broody sort of way. Even if I'm not your type, I'm sure you can close your eyes and think of England or whatever it is the boogeyman does when he engages in carnal activities."

"Carnal activities." I don't think he's taken a breath in the last sixty seconds. "Are you a virgin, Persephone?"

I scrunch up my nose. "That's not really your business. Why do you ask?"

"Because only a virgin would call sex 'carnal activities.'"

Ah, that's what's holding him up. I shouldn't enjoy poking this man so much, but despite what I told him earlier, I honestly don't think he'll hurt me. My skin doesn't try to crawl off my body every time I'm in a room with him, which is a marked improvement from Zeus and some of the other people who frequent that social circle. More, Hades might growl and snap and attempt to slap me down verbally, but he keeps sneaking glances at my feet as if it physically pains *him* that I'm standing on them. He's irritating, but he's not going to hurt me if he's that concerned with my current level of comfort.

I give him a faintly pitying look. "Hades, regardless of the ridiculous importance the upper city puts on virginity, there are plenty of activities that can be termed 'carnal' that don't involve penis-in-vagina sex. Really, I would think you'd know that already."

His lips twitch, but he manages to get control of himself before actually smiling. Then he's back to glowering at me. "You're so eager to sell your virginity for your safety."

I roll my eyes. "Please. Whatever fiction my mother sold to Zeus, I'm not a virgin, so if *that's* what's having your head in danger of exploding, you can let it go. It's fine."

If anything, he glares harder. "That doesn't make your offered bargain more attractive."

Oh, this is just ridiculous. I sigh, letting my exasperation through. "Silly me for thinking that you're among the percentage of the human population that doesn't worship at the altar of the hymen."

He curses, looking like he wants to drag his hands over his face. "That is not what I meant."

"It's what you said."

"You're twisting my words."

"Am I?" I'm already well past my frustration limit with this conversation. I'm usually better at selling people on my ideas than this. "What is the problem, Hades? We have similar interests at this point. You want to punish Zeus for the harm he's caused you. I want to ensure his plans to marry me die a quick and efficient death. Ensuring that he believes we're fucking on every available surface until you're imprinted on my skin accomplishes both of these goals. He won't touch me with a ten-foot pole, and he'll never be able to get over the fact that it was *you* who 'ruined' me."

Still he doesn't say anything. I sigh again. "Is it because you think you'd be coercing me? You're not. If I didn't want to have sex with you, I wouldn't offer."

His shock is so delicious, I can almost taste it. Like the rest of Olympus, this man has seen the various media coverage of me and my family and made assumptions. I can't say all of them are wrong, but I get a special delight in this interaction. I know the role my mother crafted for me among my four sisters—the sweet, sunny Persephone who always smiles as she does what she's told.

Little do they know.

I'm not exactly lying. Yes, I don't have much in the way of options right now, but the idea of sleeping with Hades to ruin any chances of Zeus's ring on my finger... It appeals to a very dark, very secret part of me. I want to twist the knife, to punish Zeus for acting like I'm a piece of art up for auction instead of a person with thoughts and feelings and plans. I want him to writhe in pain around a blade of *my* crafting, to undermine his authority by slipping through his fingers to take up with his enemy. A small thing, perhaps, but nothing is truly small when it comes to reputation. My mother has taught me that lesson well.

Power is as much about perception as it is about the resources one has at their disposal.

"I don't know how you pick sexual partners, but I don't usually bargain for the privilege." His hand twitches at his side. "Sit your ass down before you bleed all over my carpet."

"First hardwood floors, now carpet. Hades, you are positively rabid for your floors." After a quick internal debate, I perch on the edge of the mattress. He won't be able to focus on a single thing I'm saying if I remain standing. I fold my hands primly on my lap. "Better?"

Hades has the same look on his face that my mother gets before she starts threatening to throw people out windows. I don't think she's ever actually thrown *anything* in a fit of anger, but the threat was good when we were children. He shakes his head slowly. "Hardly. You're still here."

"Ouch." I hold his gaze. "I still don't understand the problem. Last night you were all throat-grabbing and snarling *Mine*, and today you're acting like you can't wait to kick me to the curb. Am I just not your type?" It's possible, though it seems a strange thing to trip him up if he really wants vengeance. I have access to a mirror. I know what I look like. Traditional beauty and all that, and that was before my mother insisted we sink a truly absurd amount of money into hair and skin care and wardrobe, though I drew the line at a nose job.

"Unless you're more into the helpless damsel in distress? I suppose I could play the role for you if that'll get the job done." I look up at Hades, and I don't bother to paint my expression with any artifice or seduction. It won't work on him, I'm sure of it. Instead I give him a mocking smile, the tiniest bit of edge to my normally sunny self. "Do you want me, Hades? Even a little bit?"

"No."

I blink. Maybe I imagined the heat in his gaze? If that's the case, I've just been an unbelievable asshole. "Well then. I suppose this plan won't work after all. Apologies." I wrap up my disappointment in a small box and shove it deep.

It was a good plan, and I'm self-aware enough to know that I would very much like to have a fling with this broody, handsome man in addition to accomplishing my other goals. *Oh well.* There's another path forward. I just need to figure out the steps to get there. As much as I don't want to involve my sisters further, between the four of us, we should be able to figure out how to hide me for the next few months.

I push to my feet, mind already a thousand miles away. I might have to take a loan from Callisto, but I'll be sure to pay her back with interest. I don't know if the passage I've been promised will be available early, but I suppose if I throw enough money at the problem, I can find a way. I'll just have to make sure I don't think too hard about how much of my trust fund I'll be eating up in the process once I repay Callisto.

"Persephone."

I stop short before I run into Hades's chest and look up at him. He isn't a particularly large man, but he feels bigger up close, like his shadow looms larger than the man himself. We're close enough that a careless move would press my chest to his. It's a terrible idea. He just told me he doesn't want me, and I may be stubborn to a fault, but I know how to accept a rejection.

I start to take a step back, but he catches my elbows, holding me in place. Holding me almost close enough to be an embrace. His dark eyes give me absolutely nothing, which shouldn't be thrilling. It truly shouldn't. Watching this man's control crack in real time is a desire I can't afford to have.

That doesn't stop me from taking a particularly deep inhale, and it certainly doesn't quell the surge of victory when his attention drops to the way my breasts press against the thin fabric of my dress. His jaw flexes beneath his perfectly groomed beard. "I'm not in the habit of bargaining for sex."

"Yes, you said that." My voice is too breathy to pass as unaffected, but I can't help it. He's so overwhelming, the kind of presence an unwary partner could get lost in. They might not even mind it. But I am not unwary. I know exactly what I'm getting myself into. I hope.

"I suppose there's a first time for everything," he murmurs. Convincing himself or convincing me? I could tell him the latter is completely unnecessary, but I keep my mouth shut. Hades finally focuses on me. "If I agree to this, you're mine for the next three months."

Yes. I barely manage to damper my enthusiasm. "That sounds like agreeing to more than sex."

"It is. I'll protect you. We'll play out the narrative you want. You'll belong to me. You'll obey." His fingers tighten ever so briefly on my elbows, like he's fighting not to haul me against him. "We act out every depraved thing I want to do to you. In public." At my confused look, he clarifies. "Zeus knows that I engage in public sex on occasion. That's what you're agreeing to."

Temper your reaction, Persephone. Let him play the big, bad wolf he's so determined to cast himself as. I lick my lips and give him wide eyes. I've never had sex in public, not really, but I can't say I'm opposed to the idea. It's startlingly hot. "I'll just have to grin and bear it, then."

"You shouldn't."

Oh, he is too delicious. I can't help leaning a little forward, pulled by the sheer gravitational force he exudes. "I agree to your terms, Hades. Protected by you, belonging to you, and having depraved public sex with you, oh my." I should let it stop there, but I've never been that good at denying myself what I want. "I suppose we should seal our bargain with a kiss. That's the traditional way of things."

"Is it." His inflection makes the words less question and more mocking absolute. He's so cold, he might freeze me down to my very core. It should scare me. Every partner I've had to date has been the very opposite of Hades—people willing to take what I give and ask no questions, require no further commitments from me. My mother's reputation ensured that their desire for me didn't outweigh their fear of her, so they all went out of their way to keep our relationship a secret. At first sneaking around was fun. Later, it became exhausting. But it was safe, as safe as someone can be as Demeter's daughter while living in Olympus.

Hades is not safe. He's so far from safe, I should be rethinking this bargain before it's even begun. I can tell myself I have no choice, but it's not the truth. I want this with every shadowy part of my soul that I work so hard to keep locked down. There's no room in the public narrative of the sweet, sunny, biddable woman for the things I find myself craving in the dark of night. Things I'm suddenly sure Hades is capable of giving me.

And then his mouth is on mine and I'm not sure of anything at all.

7

HADES

SHE TASTES LIKE SUMMER. I DON'T KNOW HOW IT'S POSSIBLE, not when she was just sleeping in a bathtub, not when it's the dead of winter outside, but it's the truth. I dig my hands into her mass of hair and tilt her head back, angling for better access. Sealing a bargain is the flimsiest of excuses to kiss her; I have no excuse to keep the contact, to deepen it. No excuse beyond wanting her. Persephone moves to close the fraction of distance between us and then she's fully in my arms, warm and soft and, fuck, she nips my bottom lip as if she actually wants this.

As if I'm not taking advantage.

The thought slams me out of my haze, and I force myself to take a step back and then another. There have always been lines I refused to cross, boundaries sketched out that are just as flimsy as the ones keeping Zeus from the lower city. That doesn't change the fact that I've never crossed them before.

Persephone blinks up at me, and for the first time since I met her last night, she looks completely real. Not the personification of a sunbeam. Not the scarily calm woman in over her head. Not even the perfect daughter of Demeter she plays for the public. Just a woman who enjoyed that kiss as much as I did.

Or I'm projecting and this is just another one of her many masks. I can't be sure, and because I can't be sure, I take a third step back. No matter what the rest of Olympus thinks of me—of the *boogeyman*—I can't allow myself to prove them right. "We begin today."

She blinks again, her impossibly long eyelashes fanning against her cheek in a motion I can almost hear. "I need to contact my sisters."

"You did that last night."

It's fascinating to watch her gather her armor around herself. First comes the straightening of her spine, just the tiniest bit. Then the smile, cheerful and deceptively genuine. Finally the guileless look in those hazel eyes. Persephone clasps her hands in front of her. "You have the phones tapped. I suspected as much."

"I'm a paranoid man." It's the truth, but not the full truth. My father wasn't able to protect his people, protect his family, because he took things at face value. Or that's what I've always been told. Even without Andreas coloring the events with his own perception, the facts remain. My father trusted Zeus, and he and my mother died as a result. I would have died, too, if not for sheer dumb luck.

Persephone shrugs that off as if it's nothing more than she expected. "Then you'll know that my sisters are more than capable of showing up on your doorstep if properly motivated, crossing the River Styx or no. They're difficult like that."

The last thing I need is *more* women like Persephone in my household. "Call them. I'll have someone find clothing for you and bring it up." I turn for the door.

"Wait!" A tiny fracture in her perfect calm. "That's it?"

I glance back, expecting fear or maybe anger. But no, if I'm reading her expression right, there's *disappointment* lurking in her eyes. I can't trust it. I want her more than I have a right to, and she's only here because she has nowhere else to go.

If I were a better man, I'd smuggle her out of the city myself and give her enough money to survive until her birthday. She's right; if she has the strength to cross the river, she likely has the strength to leave the city with the proper help. But I'm not a better man. No matter how conflicted this deal makes me, I want this woman. Now that she's offered herself to me in a devil's bargain, I mean to have her.

Just not yet.

Not until it serves our mutual purpose.

"We'll talk more tonight." I enjoy her huff of irritation as I walk out the door and head down to my study.

There are consequences for my actions last night, consequences for the bargain I just made with Persephone. I have to prepare my people for them.

I'm not the least bit surprised to find Andreas waiting in my study. He's nursing a mug that might be coffee or might be whiskey—or both—and wearing his customary slacks and wool sweater like the strangest cross between a fisherman and a CEO anyone's ever met. The tattoos peppering his weathered hands and climbing his neck only add to the disconnect. What's left of his hair has long since gone white, leaving him looking every minute of his seventy years.

He glances up as I walk in and close the door. "I hear you stole Zeus's woman."

"She crossed the border on her own."

He shakes his head. "Thirty years and change of avoiding trouble and then you throw it all away for a pretty thing in a short skirt."

I give him the look that statement deserves. "I bend too much when it comes to that asshole. It was necessary before, but I'm not a child any longer. It's time to put him in his place." It's what I've wanted since I was old enough to understand the sheer scope of what he took from me. It's why I've spent years compiling information on him. An opportunity that I can't pass up.

Andreas exhales, long and slow, some remembered fear lingering in his watery blue eyes. "He'll crush you."

"Maybe ten years ago he was capable of it. He isn't now." I've been too careful, have built my power base too intentionally. Zeus killed my father when he was still new to the title, too inexperienced to know friend from foe. I've had my entire life to train to take that monster on. Though I was little more than a figurehead Hades before I turned seventeen, I've had sixteen years actually at the helm. If ever there was a time to do this, to draw my line in the sand and dare Zeus to cross it, it's now. There's no telling if I'll get another opportunity like Persephone, a chance to humiliate Zeus and step into the light once and for all. The thought of all the eyes in Olympus on me is enough to open up a pit in my stomach, but it's been far too long that Zeus overlooks the lower city and pretends *he's* the ruler here. "It's time, Andreas. It's long since time."

Another of his headshakes, like I've disappointed him. I hate how much that matters to me, but Andreas has been the strong guiding light in my life for so long. His retirement a few years ago doesn't lessen that. He's the uncle I never had, though he never tried to play the father. He knows better than that. Finally, he leans forward. "What's your plan?"

"Three months of giving him the middle finger. If he comes across the river and tries to take her back, not even the other Thirteen will stand by him. They put that treaty in place for a reason."

"The Thirteen didn't save your father. What makes you think they'll save you?"

We've had this argument a thousand times over the years. I smother my irritation and give him my full attention. "Because the treaty didn't exist when Zeus killed my father." It's shitty beyond belief that my parents had to die for the treaty to be put into place, but if things become a free-for-all among the Thirteen, it hurts their bottom line, which is the only thing they care about. It was one of the few times in Olympus history that the Thirteen worked together long enough to challenge Zeus's power and strong-arm an agreement that no one is willing to break.

Zeus cannot come here and I can't go there. *No one* can harm another member of the Thirteen or their families without being erased from existence. It's a damn shame that rule doesn't seem to apply to Hera. That role used to be one of the most powerful, but the last few Zeuses have whittled it down until it's little more than a figurehead position for their spouse. It's allowed Zeus to act however he damn well pleases without consequence because Hera is seen as an extension of his position rather than one that stands on its own.

If Persephone marries him, the treaty won't keep *her* safe.

"Hardly a foolproof plan."

I allow myself a grin, though it feels haggard on my face. "Will it make you feel better if we double the guards at the bridges in case he attempts to march Ares's small army over the river?" It won't happen and we both know it, but I've already planned on increasing security in the unlikely event Zeus tries to attack. I won't be caught flat-footed like my parents were.

"No," he grumbles. "But I suppose that's a start." Andreas sets his mug down. "You can't keep the girl. Thumb your nose at him if you must, but you can't keep her. He won't allow it. Maybe he can't move against you directly, but he'll bait a trap to put you in violation of the treaty, and then the full might of those pretty fools will come down on you. Not even you can survive that. Certainly not your people."

There it is. The constant reminder that I am not a mere man, that the weight of so many lives rest on my shoulders. In the upper city, the responsibility for the lives of its citizens falls on twelve sets of shoulders. In the lower city, there is only me. "It won't be an issue."

"You say that now, but if it were true, you never would have brought her back here."

"I'm not keeping her." The very idea is ludicrous. I can't blame Persephone for not wanting to wear Zeus's ring, but she's still a pretty princess who's been given everything her entire life. She might like her walk on the wild side for the duration of the winter, but the thought of something permanent would send her screaming into the night. It's fine. I have no long-term use for a woman like that.

Andreas finally nods. "I suppose it's too late to worry about it now. You'll see it through."

"I will." One way or another.

What would it take to incite Zeus to break the treaty? Very little, I expect. His rage is legendary. He won't take kindly to me "defiling" his pretty bride for everyone to see. It's easy enough to orchestrate a little show to the proper people who are guaranteed to get the rumor mill spinning, and the story will spread through Olympus like wildfire. Enough people talking and Zeus might feel he has to do something rash. Something that will have actual consequences.

More, the people of Olympus will finally come face-to-face with the truth. Hades is not a myth, but I'm more than happy to play the boogeyman in real life if it accomplishes my goals.

Andreas has a contemplative look on his face. "Keep me in the loop?"

"Sure." I sit on the edge of my desk. "This would be when I remind you that you're retired."

"Bah!" He waves that away. "You sound like that little shit, Charon."

Considering Charon is his biological grandson and well on his way to becoming my right-hand man, "little shit" hardly fits as a descriptor. He's twenty-seven and more capable than most of the people under my command. "He means well."

"He's meddlesome."

A knock on the door and the man himself pokes his head in. He's a spitting image of his grandfather, though his shoulders are broad and his dark hair covers his full head. But the bright-blue eyes, square chin, and confidence are all there. He catches sight of Andreas and grins. "Hey, Pop. You look like you need a nap."

Andreas glares daggers. "Don't think I can't paddle your ass the same way I did when you were five."

"Wouldn't dream of it." His tone says otherwise, but he always likes to play with fire when it comes to Andreas. Charon steps into the room and closes the door behind him. "You wanted to see me?"

"We need to go over the changes to the sentry schedule."

"Trouble?" His eyes light up at the idea of it. "This have anything to do with the woman?"

"She's going to stay on for a bit." I might have been frank about my plans with Andreas, but he's earned that after everything he's sacrificed to keep me alive and keep this territory together. I'm not ready to talk about it with anyone else, though my window for keeping shit to myself is rapidly closing. "Have Minthe raid her closet for a few things Persephone can borrow until I have a chance to order more."

Charon raises his eyebrows. "Minthe's going to love that."

"She'll get over it. I'll reimburse her for whatever she comes up with." It won't completely soften the request, not when Minthe is so damn territorial about anything she views as *hers*, but it's the best I can come up with right now. I need all of today to get the defenses in place to protect my people from what I'm about to do.

And tomorrow?

Tomorrow we have to make our announcement with enough splash that even those golden assholes up in Dodona Tower hear it.

My phone rings, and I know who it is before I round my desk to answer it. I glance at the two men in my office, and Charon drops into the chair next to his grandfather. They'll be quiet. I don't allow myself a deep breath to brace. I simply answer. "Yeah?"

"You have some brass balls, you little shit."

Satisfaction seeps through me. Zeus and I have had cause to deal with each other several times over the years, and he's always been condescending and blustery, as if gifting me with his presence. He doesn't sound anything but furious now. "Zeus. Nice to hear from you."

"Give her back immediately, and no one has to know about this little transgression. You wouldn't want to do anything to endanger the fragile peace we have going."

Even after all these years, it amazes me that he thinks I'm that short-sighted. There was a time when his bluff would have sent panic searing through my chest, but I've come a long way since then. I'm not a child for him to bully. I keep my voice mild, knowing it will infuriate him further. "I didn't break the treaty."

"You took my wife."

"She's not your wife." That comes out too sharp, and I take half a second to remove any emotion from my tone. "She crossed the bridge on her own power." I should leave it at that, but cold fury takes me. He thinks he can fuck with people's lives simply because he's Zeus. That might be true in the upper city, but the lower city is *my* kingdom, no matter what the rest of Olympus believes. "In fact, she was so desperate to get away from you, she bloodied her feet and nearly gave herself hypothermia. I'm not sure what passes for romance in the upper city, but that's not a normal reaction to a proposal down here."

"Return her to me or you'll suffer the consequences. Just like your father did."

Only years of learning to mask my emotions keep me from flinching. That fucking *bastard*. "She crossed the River Styx. She's mine now, by might and by terms of the treaty." I lower my voice. "You're more than welcome to her when I'm through with her, but we both know what games I like to play. She'll hardly be the unsullied princess you're panting after." The words taste foul in my mouth, but it doesn't matter. Persephone agreed the goal is to twist the knife. Playing this verbal game of chicken with Zeus is only part of it.

"If you lay one filthy finger on her, I'll skin you alive."

"I'm going to lay more than one finger on her." I force a thread of amusement into my voice. "It's funny, don't you think? That she'd rather welcome every depraved thing I want to do to that tight little body than let you touch her." I chuckle. "Well, *I* think it's funny."

"Hades, this is the last time I'll make this offer. You'd do well to consider it." The anger disappears from Zeus's voice, leaving only icy calm in its wake. "Return her to me within the next twenty-four hours, and I'll pretend this never happened. Keep her, and I'll destroy everything you love."

"Too late, Zeus. That ship sailed thirty years ago." When he caused the fire that killed my parents and left me covered in scars. I let the pause stretch out several beats before I say, "Now it's my turn."

PERSEPHONE

A SMALL SELECTION OF DRESSES IS DELIVERED TO ME BY A tall brunette with a surly attitude who looks like she could crush my head with one hand. I don't catch her name before she's gone, leaving me alone once again.

The call with my sisters went about as well as can be expected. They're furious I'm cutting them out for their own good. They think my plan is terrible. I'm certain they'll continue to try to find another option, but I can't stop them.

It's almost enough to distract me from the sun tracking across the sky and down to the horizon. From the knowledge of what comes next. Or, rather, the *lack* of knowledge. Hades is a fan of dire statements with little information to support them. He instructs me to be ready but gives me no information about what I'm supposed to be ready for. And there's that kiss. I've spent most of the day trying and failing to avoid thinking about how good it felt to have his mouth on mine. If he hadn't stepped away, I don't know what I would have done, and that should scare me.

Everything about this situation should scare me, but I'm not about to let Hades intimidate me into backing out. Whatever he has planned for tonight, it can't be worse than Zeus. *That*, I'm sure of.

I take my time getting ready. This room offers a surprising selection of hair products, which leads me to wonder if Hades has a habit of keeping women here. None of my business. I could walk out of this room and this house at any time, and that's all I need to know.

The dresses are all beautiful but several sizes too big for me. I shrug and pull on the simplest one, a beaded sheath that's a similar style to the dress I had on last night. The beads add some weight to the fabric, and it swings in a really satisfying way. I'm eyeing the shoes the woman left and considering my options when a knock sounds on my door.

Showtime.

I take a deep breath and pad to open the door. Hades stands there and, good gods, I've never seen a man pull off a black-on-black suit the way Hades can. He's like a living shadow, a sexy, sexy living shadow. He looks down and glares at my feet. I shuffle back, suddenly self-conscious. "I'm just putting on shoes."

"Don't be absurd."

I grasp on to my irritation with both hands. Better to step onto a verbal battleground than to let fear and uncertainty override everything. "I'm not being absurd."

"You're right. Wearing high heels after your feet were maimed less than twenty-four hours ago isn't absurd. It's stupid." He's full-on glowering now. "Just like running through Olympus in nothing more than a silk dress in the middle of the night."

"I don't know why we're bringing that up again."

"We're bringing *that* up because I'm beginning to see a trend of you not prioritizing your health and safety."

I blink. "Hades, they're just shoes."

"The fact remains." He steps into the room, his intent clear.

I dance back. "Don't you dare pick me up." I swat at the air between us. "I've had about enough of that."

"Cute." He sounds like it's anything but. Hades moves so quickly that even anticipating him, I barely let out an undignified squawk before he lifts me into his arms.

I freeze. "Put me down." Kissing Hades earlier was one thing. Agreeing to sleep with him was something else. This is totally different. Having him hold me close as he walks through the hallways of his house so I don't hurt myself further... It feels very, *very* different. Knowing that he doesn't want me to injure myself was a useful tool in negotiating this morning. Now it just feels like a hurdle I'm not sure how to get past. "You don't need to take care of me."

"Yes, you're doing a stand-up job of it yourself." He sounds so put out by the whole situation that it immediately cheers me up.

My peevish desire to irk him rises again, and I don't bother to resist it. Instead, I lay my head on his shoulder and tug his beard. "Maybe I just want to be carried about by a big, strong man who's determined to save me."

Hades arches a single eyebrow, managing to convey skepticism and mocking at the same time. "Is that so?"

"Oh, yes." I flutter my eyelashes at him. "I'm very helpless, you see. What would I do without Prince Charming in dented black armor showing up to save me from myself?"

"I'm no Prince Charming."

"On that, we can agree." I give his beard another gentle tug. I like the way his grip tightens on me when I do it. He's being careful to keep his hands on my dress and off my skin, but the thought of his fingers digging in as he does...other things...is enough to make me squirm.

"Hold still."

"There's a very simple solution to this. Put me down and let me walk. Problem solved."

Hades takes the stairs down to the main floor...and then keeps going. Apparently he's going to ignore me, which is one way to win an argument. I used to employ the same tactic against Psyche when we were children and she constantly stole my toys to take them off on fantastic adventures. Fighting didn't work to make her stop. Going to our mother was out of the question. Telling Callisto would just result in her "fixing" the problem by destroying the toys in question. No, the only thing that worked was ignoring Psyche entirely. Eventually, she always broke and returned the toys. Sometimes she even apologized.

I will not break.

Since our conversation is apparently over, I settle into Hades's arms like this is exactly where I want to be. Because we're touching so much, I can feel him getting tenser and tenser. I hide my smile against his shirt. *Take that.*

He finally stops in front of a door. A *black* door. It's perfectly flat, with no panels to mar its surface, and it shines eerily in the low light. I stare at our faintly distorted reflection in it. It's almost like looking into a pool of water under the new moon. I have the strangest suspicion that if I touch it, my hand will sink right through its surface. "Are we diving right in?"

Only now does Hades hesitate. "This is your last chance to change your mind. Once we walk through there, you're committed."

"Committed to depraved acts of public sex." It's really cute how he keeps insisting on giving me an out. I lean back enough to see his face, to let him see mine. I feel none of the conflict I see in his dark eyes. "I already said yes. I'm not changing my mind."

He waits a beat. Two. "In that case, you need to pick a safe word."

My eyes widen before I can temper the reaction. I read widely and know a very specific set of entertainments comes with the use of a safe word. I wonder which flavor Hades prefers. Whips or bondage or dealing out humiliation? Maybe all of the above. How deviously delicious.

He takes my surprise as confusion. "Consider it a safety brake. If things get too intense or you become overwhelmed, you say your safe word and everything stops. No questions asked, no explanations required."

"Just like that."

"Just like that," he confirms. Hades glances at the door and then back at me. "When I said I didn't bargain for sex, that wasn't strictly true. Each encounter has an element of bargaining and negotiation in it. What I actually meant is that I value consent. Consent because you have no other options isn't consent."

"Hades, do you plan on putting me down before walking through that door?" Wherever it leads.

"No."

"So this consent only applies to sex?"

He tenses as if he's about to turn around and march me back to my room. "You're right. This was a mistake."

"Wait, wait, wait." He is so stubborn, I could kiss him. I frown up at him instead. "We've had this conversation before, no matter how you want to paint it now. I have other options. I want this one. I was just teasing you about carrying me."

For the first time since we met, it feels like he's *really* looking at me. No holds barred. No growly masks in place. Hades looks down at me like he wants to consume me one decadent bite at a time. Like he's already thought of a dozen ways he wants to have me, and he has them planned down to the barest detail. Like he already owns me and he fully intends to stake his claim for anyone to see.

I lick my lips. "If I tell you that I like you carrying me, are you going to do it nonstop for the next three months? Or will you decide to punish me by making me walk of my own power?" A few minutes ago, I'd say I was playing with reverse psychology, but in this moment, even I don't know what I want his answer to be.

He finally registers that I'm mostly joking and shocks me by rolling his eyes. "It never ceases to surprise me how difficult you are determined to be. Pick a safe word, Persephone."

A shiver of apprehension goes through me. All joking aside, this is real. We're truly doing this, and once we go through that door, he might honor my safe word, but at the end of the day, I have no way of knowing. Two days ago, Hades was little more than a faded myth that might have been a man a few generations ago. Now, he's all too real.

In the end, I have to trust my instincts, which means trusting Hades.

"Pomegranate."

"Good enough." He pushes through the door and into another world.

Or at least that's what it feels like. The light moves strangely here, and it takes me a few moments to realize it's a clever trick of lamps and water that sends ribbons of light dancing across the ceiling. It's like the polar opposite of Zeus's banquet room. There aren't any windows, but thick, red wall hangings give the room a decadently sinful feel rather than making it claustrophobic. There's even an honest-to-gods throne, though like the rest of the room, it's black and actually looks comfortable.

Realization rolls through me and I laugh. "Oh wow, you're really petty."

"I have no idea what you're talking about."

"Yes, you do. All it's missing is a giant portrait of you." He must have seen the banquet room at some point, because he's built something that is its antithesis. It's a smaller room and has more furniture, but it's impossible not to see the connection. More, it's not like the rest of the house. Hades obviously likes expensive things, but the bits of the house I've seen so far feel cozy and lived in. This is as cold as Zeus's tower.

"I have no need for a giant portrait," he says drily. "Everyone who walks through these doors knows exactly who rules here."

"So petty," I repeat. I laugh. "I like it."

"Noted." I can't be sure, but I think he's fighting back a smile. To keep from staring up into his handsome face like a lovestruck fool, I peer at the comfortable couches and chairs—all leather—gathered strategically around the space as well as a number of pieces of furniture that I recognize by description if not by sight. A spanking bench. Saint Andrew's cross. A frame that might be used to suspend a person from if one got creative with rope.

The room is also completely empty.

I twist in Hades's arms to look at him. "What is this?"

He sets me down on the nearest couch, and I skim my fingers over the smooth leather. Like every other piece of furniture I can see, it's flawless and pristine. And cold. So incredibly cold. It's exactly what I would have expected from Hades, based on the myth surrounding him, and nothing like the man himself. I look up to find him watching me closer. "Why isn't anyone here?"

Hades slowly shakes his head. "You thought I'd throw you to the wolves on the first night? Give me a little credit, Persephone."

"I don't have to give you anything." That comes out too sharply, but I had built up my courage for this, and the letdown is leaving me dizzy. This *place* is leaving me dizzy. It's nothing like I expected. *He* is nothing like I expected. "You have to stake your claim, and you have to do it now."

"And *you* have to stop telling me what I *have* to do." He looks around the room, expression contemplative. "You say you're no virgin, but have you done any kink before?"

That takes the wind right out of my sails. No point in lying, at least not at this juncture. "No."

"That's what I thought." He shrugs out of his jacket and slowly rolls up his sleeves. He's not even looking at me, isn't paying attention to the way I devour each inch of revealed skin with my eyes. He's got nice forearms, muscled and tattooed, though I can't make out the design. It looks like swirls, and it takes me several long moments to realize the tattoos are moving around scars.

What *happened* to this man?

He sits next to me, keeping a full cushion between us. "There are some preliminary questions I need answered."

That surprises a laugh out of me. "I didn't realize this was an entrance interview."

"Hardly." He shrugs, looking like a king with the way he unapologetically takes up more than his fair share of space. It's not even his body—he's not particularly huge. It's his presence. It fills this large room until I can barely breathe past it. Hades is watching me too closely, and I have the uncomfortable feeling that he's clocking every single one of my micro expressions.

He finally motions around the room. "This arrangement might have a purpose beyond pleasure, but I'm not interested in traumatizing you. If you're going to fuck me, you might as well have a good time, too."

I blink. "That's so very considerate of you, Hades."

My sarcasm rolls right off him like water off a duck's back. Though I am *certain* his lips twitch. "Answers are yes, no, maybe."

"I—"

"Bondage."

My body goes hot at the thought. "Yes."

"Fucking in front of people."

No. But that answer isn't the truth. The truth is the very idea sets me aflame. I look at his face, but he's not offering me a single thing. No encouragement. No judgment. Maybe that's why I'm able to answer honestly. "We already talked about this. Yes."

"It pays to be sure." He goes on like that. Him naming thing after thing and me trying to answer as honestly as I can. Most of these things, I've never thought about too hard outside of fiction. I know what makes me hot and squirmy in the books I read, but the possibility of acting it out in reality is almost too much to contemplate.

The conversation, if one can call it that, is hardly comfortable, but it reassures me all the same. He really is doing the proper homework instead of throwing me into the deep end. I can't remember the last time I was the recipient of focus this intense; the realization has heat working its way through me in slow surges, and my breath picks up at the thought of acting out all the things Hades names.

He finally sits back, expression contemplative. "That's enough."

I wait, but his gaze is a thousand miles away. I might as well not be in the room. I open my mouth but decide against interrupting wherever his thoughts have gone. Instead, I stand and turn for the nearest kinky furniture. It looks a bit like a less soulless version of the table you sit on at the doctor's, and I want to see exactly how it works.

"Persephone."

The snap in his tone has roots growing from my soles and freezing me in place. I glance over my shoulder. "Yes?"

"'Yes, Sir' is the proper response when we're in this room." He points at the spot I just vacated. "Sit down."

"What happens if I don't obey like that?" I snap my fingers.

He's back to watching me closely, his body poised and tense as if he'll spring at me given half the chance. Maybe that should scare me, but it's not fear beating a pounding drum in my blood. It's excitement. Hades leans forward very slowly, very pointedly. "Then you'll be punished."

"I see," I say slowly. A choice, then. There's no one watching right now, no one to playact for. I don't have to be perfect or sunny or bright or any of the labels I've acquired over the years. The realization leaves me feeling giddy and almost drunk.

I look around the room again. "What is this place for you? Freedom from labels?"

"This place *is* the label." When I frown, he sighs. "There are only so many methods of holding power. Fear, love, loyalty. The latter two are fickle at best, the first difficult to acquire unless you're willing to get your hands dirty."

"Like Zeus," I murmur.

"Like Zeus," he confirms. "Though that bastard has enough charm that he doesn't have to get his hands dirty when he doesn't want to."

"Do *you* get your hands dirty?" I glance around the room again, beginning to understand. "But then, you wouldn't have to if everyone is scared of you, would you?"

"Reputation is everything."

"That's not an answer."

Hades studies me. "Do you need one?"

Do I? It's not required for our bargain; I've already agreed and I have no intention of backing out now. But I can't help the curiosity that sinks its fangs into me and refuses to let go. My fascination with Hades goes back years, but meeting the real man behind the myth is a thousand times more compelling. I've already divined the purpose of this room, this carefully curated stage. I want to know more about *him*. I hold his gaze. "I'd like an answer, if you're willing to give it."

For a moment, I think he won't respond, but he finally nods. "People are already primed to fear Hades. As you keep pointing out, the title is the boogeyman of Olympus. I use that, amplify that." He motions around the room. "I have exclusive parties for carefully selected members of the upper city here. My tastes already ran kinky; I simply use that predilection to serve my purposes."

I study the room, focusing on the throne. All the better to create the larger-than-life image of Hades, a dark king to Zeus's golden one. Neither of the images they present to their audience are the truth, but I much prefer Hades's version. "So you sit there and preside over this den of iniquity and indulge your desires in a way that gives everyone watching a shiver of fear and a story to whisper."

"Yes." Something strange in his voice makes me turn to look at him. Hades is staring at me like I'm a puzzle he's dying to put together. He leans forward. "They really don't know what an asset you are in the upper city, do they?"

I paint my usual sunshine smile across my features. "I'm sure I have no idea what you're talking about."

"You're wasted on those fools."

"If you say so."

"I do." Hades rises slowly. All he needs is a cape to flow

around him to complete the menacing-sexy picture he creates. "Shall I give you a demonstration of how our first night here will go?"

Suddenly, this is all too real. A shiver works its way through me that's part nerves, part anticipation. "Yes, Sir."

He glances at my feet. "Are they bothering you?"

Truth be told, they already ache just from standing here for a few minutes. "Nothing I can't handle."

"Nothing you can't handle," he repeats slowly and shakes his head. "You'll run your body right into the ground, given half a chance. I wondered if that first night was the exception, but it's not, is it? It's the rule."

I flinch, guilt flickering through me even as I tell myself I have no reason to feel guilty. It's *my* body. I can do with it what I need to in order to survive. If sometimes my flesh bears the cost? That's the price of life. To distract myself from the uncomfortable feeling unfurling within me, I take another step back. "I said it's fine, and I mean it."

"I will take your word on it. This time." He continues before I can say anything. "But I *will* be checking your bandages at the end of the night, and if you've damaged yourself further out of stubbornness, there will be consequences."

"You are outstandingly arrogant. It's my body."

"Wrong. For the duration of this scene, it's *my* body." He motions to the low stage set up in the center of the room. "Up."

I'm still processing *that* statement as I set my hand in his and allow him to assist me the mere twelve inches up onto the dais. It's not high, but it gives the impression of looking down at the rest of the room. Of being on display. It doesn't matter that there's no one else here but us. Imagining all the chairs and couches filled has my heartbeat kicking into high gear.

Hades releases my hand. "Stay there a moment."

I watch him weave through the furniture to a nondescript door tucked behind a carefully draped curtain. A few seconds later, a set of lights flick on over the dais. They aren't particularly bright, but in the relative darkness, they immediately cut off my view of the room. I swallow hard. "You weren't kidding about making a scene, were you?"

"No." His voice comes from an unexpected direction—to my right and slightly behind me.

I turn to face him, but I can't see much in the glare. "What is this?"

"Tell me your safe word."

Not an answer, but did I really expect one? I can't tell if he's trying to scare me or if this truly *is* a preview of what he intends to do in front of an audience. I lick my lips. "Pomegranate."

"Take off your dress." This time, he speaks from somewhere in front of me.

My hands fall to the hem of the dress and I hesitate. I don't think I'm shy, but every remotely sexual encounter I've had to date has been behind closed doors and mostly in the dark. The exact opposite of this experience. I close my eyes, trying to still the shaking in my body. *This is what I want, what I asked for.* I grip the hem and begin to lift.

Cool air teases my thighs, the lower curve of my ass, my hips.

"Persephone." His voice is deceptively mild.

I can't quite catch my breath. We haven't even *done* anything, and I feel like my body is on fire. "Yes...Sir?"

"You're not wearing anything under your dress." He states it like he's commenting on the weather.

I have to fight the urge to squirm, to drop the dress to cover my nakedness. "My borrowed wardrobe is missing a few items."

"Is that the truth?" He steps out of the darkness and joins me on the dais, and it's almost as if the light shies away from him. Hades circles me slowly, stopping at my back. He doesn't touch me, but I can *feel* him there. "Or did you think you could tempt me into doing what you want?"

The thought had crossed my mind. "Would it work if I tried?"

He lifts my hair off the back of my neck. An innocent touch as such things go, but I feel like he's doused me in gasoline and lit a match. Hades's other hand drifts to brush the bared skin at my hip. "The dress, Persephone."

I take a slow breath and continue easing it up my body. He's perfectly still behind me, but I swear I can feel his gaze devouring each newly bared inch of skin as the fabric rises. It feels horribly intimate and also sexy beyond belief. I finally pull the dress over my head and, after the briefest hesitation, drop it on the floor.

There's nothing hiding my body from him now.

I jump at the press of his fingertips to my upper arms. Hades chuckles darkly. "How do you feel?"

"Exposed." Having to answer the question only makes the sensation more acute.

"You *are* exposed." He trails his fingers up to my shoulders. "The next time we do this, every eye in the room will be on you.

They'll look at you and want you for their own." And then he's there, his body against mine, one hand lightly bracketing my throat. Not applying any pressure. It's a simple touch of ownership that has me fighting not to curl my toes. "But you're not theirs, are you?"

I swallow hard, the move pressing my throat more firmly against his palm. "No. I'm not theirs."

"They can look their fill, but I'm the only one who gets to touch you." His breath ghosts the shell of my ear. "I'm going to touch you now."

I can't stop shivering, and it has nothing to do with the temperature in the room. "You're touching me right now." Is that my voice, all breathy and low and filled with invitation? I feel like I'm floating above my body and yet devastatingly grounded in my flesh.

His hand drifts down to my sternum, tracing a line between my breasts. Still not where I suddenly desperately need him to be. He's barely done anything and I can't stop shaking. I bite my bottom lip hard and try to hold still as his fingers feather over my ribs and down my stomach. "Persephone."

Gods, the way this man says my name. Like it's a secret just between us. "Touch me."

"As you said, I *am* touching you." There it is, that sliver of delicious amusement. He goes still, his hand resting on my lower stomach. The weight feels like it's the only thing keeping me tethered to this world. He traces one of my hip bones. "This is how it's going to go. Listen closely."

I'm trying, but every bit of my concentration is wrapped up in not spreading my legs and trying to contort myself to get his hand where I desperately need it. I settle for a shaky nod. "Yes, Sir." Funny, but calling him that hardly feels strange at all.

"I will give you every fantasy you've dreamed up in that ambitious brain of yours. In return, you follow my every command."

I frown, trying to think past the feel of his body against my back, his hard length pressed against me. I desperately want to get up close and personal with this man, to strip him down and touch him as intimately as he's touching me now. "I have a lot of fantasies."

"Of that, I have no doubt." His lips brush my temple. "Are you shaking out of nerves or desire?"

"Both." So tempting to leave it at that, but I need him to understand. "I don't hate it."

"And the thought of people actually filling this room and watching me touch you like this?"

"I don't hate it," I repeat.

"I'm going to make you come, little Persephone. And then I'm taking you upstairs and changing the bandages on your feet. If you're very good and manage to restrain from complaining, I'll let you orgasm a second time." He gives my stomach another slow stroke. "Tomorrow, we'll get you clothed appropriately."

It's so very hard to focus with his fingers drifting closer and closer to my pussy, but I try. "I thought we were negotiating orgasms."

"This is about more than orgasms."

I only understand this game in broad strokes, but I recognize that he's asking for permission in his way, as if I haven't given him the green light half a dozen times today alone. He's not exactly throwing me into the deep end to wait and see if I sink or swim. He's drawing me carefully, inexorably toward a single destination. I don't believe in fate, but this moment feels like we've both spent years barreling down our respective paths to this point. I can't turn away now. I don't want to.

"Yes. I say yes."

HADES

I'M WRONG ABOUT PERSEPHONE. EVERY TIME I PUSH HER, test her, see if this will be the thing to send her scurrying home to the upper city, she steps to the line. But it's more than that. I think going around with each other excites her as much as it does me. Every time her lips curve and she embodies a human-shaped sunbeam, I know things are about to get interesting.

And now?

I have no words to describe what I'm feeling now, not with her naked in my home, her tanned skin flush with desire for *my* touch. I skate my hand over her stomach, hating her mother and the rest of the upper city for creating circumstances where this woman is so focused on surviving and getting out that she ignores her body's needs. She's too thin. Not breakable, exactly, but she as much as admitted that she doesn't take care of herself the way she should.

"Hades." Persephone presses back against me, leaning her head against my shoulder, giving herself to me entirely. "Please."

As if I could stop now, even if I wanted to. We're on this road to the Underworld together, well past the point of no return. I don't waste any more time. I cup her pussy, and I can't help my growl when I find her wet and wanting. "You enjoy these games. Enjoy being on display."

She nods. "I already said I did."

I concentrate on moving slowly, because the alternative is to fall on her like a starving creature and undo all the fragile trust I've built. She's soft and wet and hot as fuck. I work two fingers into her and she lets loose the most delicious whimpering sound and clamps around me. I explore her slowly, looking for that spot that will make her go molten, but it's not enough. I need to see her. See all of her.

Soon.

I reach down with my free hand and hook her thigh, lifting it and spreading her wide to give me better access. Putting her on display for an audience of none. I've always liked to play publicly, and I can't deny how intensely I anticipate claiming her like this in front of a crowded room. Her response tonight indicates that she'll get off on it just as hard as I will.

I stroke her clit with my thumb, experimenting until I find the right motion that has her whole body going tight. I lean down until my lips brush her ear. "Tomorrow night, this room will be filled with people. Everyone showing up to get a look at your pretty pussy, to hear how sweetly I can make you come."

"Oh, gods."

"Will you put on a good show for them, Persephone?" I can't help dragging my mouth along her neck. It's like the realization that I can touch her however I want, that she's dancing on the edge of orgasm, that she wants more... It's finally hitting me. This woman is *mine*, even if it's only for a few months. It's heady knowledge.

"Hades, *please*."

I go still, and she tries to roll her hips to keep fucking my fingers. That earns her a nip on her shoulder. "Please what? Be explicit."

"Make me come." Her inhale is ragged. "Kiss me. Fuck me. Just don't stop."

"I won't stop." My words come out as a growl, but I don't give a damn. I kiss Persephone and resume driving her toward orgasm. She still tastes like summertime. I want to wrap her up and keep her safe. I want to fuck her until all her masks shatter and she cries as she comes around my cock.

I *want*.

As much as I intended to draw this moment out, we're both dancing on the edge of control. I press the heel of my hand against her clit, giving her that extra bit of friction. She moans, breathy and low, and I'd give anything to hear her make that sound again. To know that I'm the one causing it. "Let go. I've got you." I move back to her neck, kissing her as she writhes against me. Her breath comes in harsh pants and then she tips over the edge, her pussy clamping around my fingers as she orgasms.

I gentle my touch, towing her back to earth even as I lift my head. Persephone shivers in my arms, leaning against me and letting me carry her weight in a way that indicates a trust I don't deserve. I ease her leg back down, but I can't quite help kissing her neck one last time. We haven't even had sex and I'm already craving the feeling of her in my arms, her taste on my tongue, with a desire bordering on frenzy.

I have to close my eyes for several long moments to fight down the impulse to lay her down on this dais and fuck her now. The reasons why I shouldn't feel flimsy as spiderwebs, easy enough to tear through without a second thought.

Not yet.

It takes effort to lock myself down, to retreat behind the cold mask that usually feels more natural than my actual self. I shift back from Persephone, keeping a hand on her hip in case she wobbles. She doesn't. Naturally.

I ignore her questioning look as she turns to face me. I can barely look at her for fear that the need coursing through me will take control, so I scoop up the discarded dress and drag it over her head. She gives a muffled curse but manages to get her arms in the proper place and pull it the rest of the way down her body. It was a tantalizing tease even before I knew everything that lay beneath it. Now I have to concentrate to keep myself on task. It would be so easy to fall into this woman and spend the rest of the night learning what I can do to draw those delicious whimpers from her lips. To memorize the taste and feel of her until I'm imprinted on her skin.

Impossible. If I give an inch, Persephone will run a mile with it. I may not know her well, but I know that beyond a shadow of a doubt. This woman is no blushing princess in a tower. She's a goddamn shark, and she'll attempt to top from the bottom if given half a chance.

My reputation, my power, my ability to protect the people in the lower city, they all depend on me being the biggest, baddest motherfucker this side of the River Styx. That reputation is the reason I don't have to bloody my hands; everyone is too scared to test me.

If a pretty upper-city socialite starts leading me around by the cock, that will jeopardize everything I've spent my entire life fighting for.

I can't allow it.

I scoop her into my arms. For such a big personality, she feels so small when I hold her like this. That sends protective instincts I thought nonexistent rising to the surface. With each step toward the door, it's easier to ignore my body's demand for her. I have a plan, and I'm sticking to it. End of story.

Persephone leans her head against my shoulder and looks up at me. "Hades?"

I sense the trap, but I couldn't ignore this woman if I wanted to. "Yeah?"

"I know you have this plan for tonight and tomorrow."

"Mm-hmm." I open the door and pause to ensure it's closed firmly behind us. Then I start down the hallway in the direction of the stairs. Five minutes and we'll be back in her room so I can get a little distance between us.

She runs her hand up my chest to lightly hook my neck. "I meant it when I said I wanted to have sex with you."

I almost miss a step. Almost. It takes everything I have not to look at her. If I do, we'll be fucking in the middle of this hallway. "That so?"

"Yes." She strokes the sensitive skin at the nape of my neck.

"The orgasm was nice, really nice, but don't you think we should have a trial run before you fuck me in front of a room full of people?"

The little vixen. She knows exactly what she's doing. I reach the stairs and concentrate on moving swiftly but not so swiftly it could be termed running.

Persephone keeps up that light stroking that has me feeling like I'm about to come out of my skin. "I suppose there's your plan to consider. You seem like a man who likes a plan, and I can respect that." She cuddles closer and rubs her cheek against my chest. "How about a compromise? Why don't you reassure yourself that I am, in fact, just as fine as I told you I was, and then I'll suck your cock?"

I don't answer until I reach her room and we're inside. Then I sit her on the bed and tangle my fingers in her silky hair. The way her lips part when I wrap it around my fist has me fighting not to growl again. "Persephone." I give her hair another tug. "It strikes me that you're used to getting your way."

She's watching me like she expects me to pull my cock out and fuck her mouth until we're both undone. She arches her back a little. "Only in some arenas."

"Mmmm." One last tug and I force myself to stop touching her. I *cannot* lose control now, or I'll never gain it back. If I was just another man, I wouldn't hesitate to accept everything she's offering. But I'm not just another man. I'm Hades. "I have a word you'd do well to get used to."

Her brows pull together. "What word?"

"No." It takes more effort than I'll ever admit to turn away from a rumpled Persephone sitting on her bed and walk into the bathroom. The distance does nothing to help. This woman is in my blood. I dig through the cabinet under the sink for the first aid kit. We keep them in every bathroom in the house. I'm not technically at war with anyone, but my line of business means that sometimes my people are dealing with unexpected injuries. Like gunshot wounds.

I half expect to find Persephone ready to mount her next seduction when I return to the room, but she's sitting primly where I left her. She's even managed to smooth her hair a bit, though the flush in her skin betrays her. Desire or anger, or some combination of both.

I go to one knee beside the bed and shoot her a look. "Behave."

"Yes, Sir." The words are sugary sweet and poisonous enough to knock me on my ass if I wasn't expecting it.

I've never kept a submissive. I prefer to confine things to the playroom and to individual scenes, even if there are repeat partners. The only rule is that it stops the second the scene ends. This is something else, and I'm not prepared for the conflicting feelings that twist through my chest as I unwrap Persephone's feet and examine them. They're healing well, but they're still a mess. That sprint through the upper city truly did come close to maiming her. Not to mention that she was dangerously close to hypothermia by the time she made it to me. Much longer out in the night and she might have done irreparable damage to herself.

She might have fucking *died*.

I'd hope Zeus's men would have stepped in at that point, but I have no faith when it comes to Zeus. He's just as likely to let her run herself to death to punish her for the act of fleeing him as he is to sweep in and haul her back to his side.

"Why didn't you call a cab when you left the event?" I don't intend to voice the question, but it lands in the space between us all the same.

"I wanted to think, and I do that better on the move." She shifts a little as I spread Neosporin on the worst of the wounds. "I had a lot to think about last night."

"Stupid."

She tenses. "It's not stupid. By the time I realized that I was being pursued, I was being herded to the river, and then it just…" Persephone lifts a hand and lets it fall. "I couldn't go back. I *won't* go back."

I should let it stand at that, but I can't seem to keep my mouth shut around this woman. "Hurting yourself when they cross you doesn't do a damn thing to them. If anything, it's what they want. You treat your body like it's the enemy; it makes you too weak to fight them."

Persephone huffs out a breath. "You act like I'm committing self-harm or something. Yes, sometimes I put my body's needs on the back burner because of stress or dealing with all the various bullshit being one of Demeter's daughters entails, but I'm not doing it to hurt myself."

Once I'm satisfied that I've got the ointment on every cut, I begin the process of wrapping her feet in bandages again. "You only get one body, and you're a shitty custodian of yours."

"You're taking a tiny injury really personally."

Maybe I am, but the way she insists on downplaying the

danger she was in aggravates me in the extreme. It means she's done it before, often enough for it to be barely worth mentioning. It means she'll do it again if given half a chance. "If you can't be trusted to take care of your body, then I'm going to do it for you."

The silence stretches on so long that I finally look up to find her staring at me with her mouth in a perfect O. She finally gives herself a shake. "It's a nice thought, I suppose, but hardly necessary. I might have agreed to sex—and happily—but I did not agree to you signing on as the world's crankiest babysitter. Are you planning on feeding me by spoon, too?" She laughs brightly. "Don't be absurd."

Her dismissal rankles more than it has a right to. Not because she's attempting to deny me. No, there's something brittle beneath her feigned amusement. Has anyone ever truly taken care of Persephone? It's not my business. I should get up and leave the room and leave *her* until the required public scenes.

To do anything else invites the kind of ruin a man like me might not recover from.

PERSEPHONE

WHEN HADES SAID HE INTENDS TO TAKE CARE OF ME, I didn't believe him. Why would I? I'm a grown woman and more than capable of taking care of myself, no matter what he seems to think. If he wasn't so incredibly pushy, I might even be able to admit how dangerous the night we met was for my health. I hadn't *meant* to ignore the cold and the pain, but by the time I realized it was an issue, I didn't have any other choice but pushing forward. I might even reassure him that though I sometimes forget to eat or other small things like that, I don't make a habit of putting myself in the way of actual harm.

But Hades *is* being pushy, and as much as part of me enjoys it in a kind of baffled sort of way, the rest of me can't help but push back.

He rises slowly to his feet, towering over me, and my body tenses in anticipation. Even with the irritating conversation, my earlier orgasm was...beyond words. He claimed my pleasure as his due, and it took him approximately thirty seconds to figure out how to wind me up and set me off. If he can do that with his fingers alone, what can he accomplish with the rest of his body?

More selfishly, I want to touch and taste him. I want to get beneath the fancy black suit and see everything this man has to offer. I haven't craved someone so intensely since... I can't remember when. Maybe Maria, the woman I met in a little hole-in-the-wall bar just outside the upper warehouse district a few years ago. She turned my world upside down in the best way possible and we still text sometimes, though our time together was never meant to be more than a fling.

Am I destined to have connections with people I'm only meant to be with for a short time?

The thought depresses me, so I put it away and reach for Hades. He catches my hands before I can touch him and shakes his head slowly. "You seem to be under the mistaken impression that you can simply reach out and take whatever you desire."

"No reason not to take it when it's what we both want."

He drops my hands and takes a step back. "Get some sleep. We have a lot of work to do tomorrow."

It's only when he reaches the door that I realize this isn't a bluff. "Hades, wait."

He doesn't turn, but he does pause. "Yes?"

If humiliation could kill, I'd be a puddle of goo on the floor. Pride demands that I let him walk out of this room and curse his name until I finally fall asleep. I can't hold a grudge nearly as well as Psyche or Callisto, but I'm no slouch. I instinctively know exactly what he wants from me, and I hate it. Yes, I definitely hate it.

I lick my lips and try for an unaffected tone. "You promised me a second orgasm if I behaved."

"Do you really think you've *behaved*, Persephone?"

Every time he says my name, it feels like he's running rough hands all over my bare skin. I shouldn't love it as much as I do. I certainly shouldn't want him to do it again and again and again. He still hasn't looked at me. I lift my chin. "Do you know, I'm just hedonistic enough to be orgasm-motivated. I suppose I can promise to be on my best behavior tomorrow if you make it worth my while tonight."

He laughs. The sound is a little ragged, almost rusty, but as Hades laughs, he turns to lean against the door. At least he's not leaving yet. He slides his hands into his pockets, a move that should be completely mundane but has me fighting not to clench my thighs together. Finally, he says, "You're making promises you have no intention of following through on."

I give him innocent eyes. "I'm sure I have no idea what you're talking about."

"You, little Persephone, are a brat." He gives another rusty chuckle. "Do those assholes in the upper city know that?"

I want to slap back with a quip, but for some reason, the question gives me pause. "No." I shock myself by answering honestly. "They see what they want to see."

"They see what *you* want them to see."

I shrug. "I suppose that's a fair assessment." I don't know what it is about this man that tempts me to put down the sunny persona—or weaponize it—but Hades is under my skin. I might be impressed under different circumstances. He is so determined to *see* me, when I am equally determined not to be seen. Not in that way. Vulnerability is an invitation to be cut down and taken apart piece by piece. I learned that the hard way the first year my mother took over as Demeter. The only people I can truly trust are my sisters. Everyone else either wants something from me or wants to use me to further their own agenda. It's exhausting and so much easier to give them nothing at all.

Apparently that isn't an option with Hades.

He's watching me closely, as if he can draw the thoughts directly from my head like warm taffy. "I don't expect perfection."

That makes me give a scratchy laugh of my own. "Could have fooled me. You want perfect obedience."

"Not really." Now it's his turn to shrug. "The game can be played many ways. In a single scene, most things are negotiated beforehand. This situation is infinitely more complicated. So I'll ask you again—what do you want? Perfection obviously chafes. Do you want me to force obedience? Allow you your freedom and punish you when you step out of line?" His dark eyes are an inferno just waiting to burn me up. "What will get you off the hardest, Persephone?"

My breath stalls in my chest. "I want to misbehave." I don't mean to say it. I truly don't. But Hades offering me whatever I need? It's more intoxicating than any alcohol I've tasted. He's offering a strange sort of partnership, one I didn't realize I desired. He might dominate. I might submit. But the power balance is startlingly equal.

I didn't know it could be like this.

"There you are." He says it like I've revealed something profound with those four little words. Hades stalks back to the bed, and if he was casually dominant before, now he feels overwhelming. I inch back onto the mattress, unable to take my eyes off him. He snaps his fingers. "The dress. Take it off."

My hands move to the hem before my brain catches up. "What if I don't want to?"

"Then I'll leave." He raises that blasted eyebrow again. "It's your choice, of course, but we both know what you really want. Take off the dress. Then lie back and spread your legs."

He has me cornered and I can't even pretend he doesn't. I glare, but it feels half-hearted at best with anticipation licking at my skin. I don't waste time teasing him; I just yank the dress off and toss it to the side.

Hades follows the movement of the fabric, disapproval radiating from him. "Next time, you fold it, or I'm going to make you crawl across the floor in penance."

Shock. Anger. Pure lust.

I lean back on my elbows and glare. "You can try."

"Little Persephone." He shakes his head slowly as I spread my legs. "You don't even know what you crave, do you? It's okay. I'll show you."

I should let it go. I really should. But for some reason, I can't manage to keep myself locked down in Hades's presence. "Please. I know what I like."

"Prove it."

I blink. "Excuse me?"

He waves a casual hand as if he's not devouring my pussy with his gaze. "Show me. You want an orgasm so desperately? Give yourself one."

Now my glare is hardly playing. "That's not what I want."

"Yes, it is." He climbs onto the bed to kneel between my spread thighs. Hades doesn't touch me, but it feels like he's tattooed his possession on every part of my body. His obvious desire for me stokes my need higher.

I'm going to do this. I'm going to reach between my thighs and stroke my clit until I come apart in front of him. With how turned on I am right now, it won't take much time at all. And I...I do want to do it, damn him. I can't just give in, though. It's not in my genetic makeup. I lick my lips. "I propose a bargain."

There goes his eyebrow again, but he only says, "I'm listening."

"I would very much like to..." I don't know how to say this without dying of embarrassment, so I simply charge forward. "I want you to come when I come." When he keeps watching me, waiting, I force myself to continue. "If I'm making myself orgasm...I would very, *very* much like for you to make yourself orgasm, too."

He stares at me a long moment as if waiting for me to change my mind. I could tell him that there's absolutely no danger of *that*, something he seems to realize a few seconds later.

Hades's hands move as if he can't help himself, resting on my thighs and giving me a light stroke. "You might have your way tonight, but don't get in the habit of expecting it."

I give him a sunny smile that makes a muscle in his cheek twitch. "If I had my way, you'd already be inside me."

"Mmmm." He shakes his head. "You're incorrigible."

"Fancy words." I can't resist any longer. I snake a hand down my stomach and part my pussy. I'm drawing this out because I enjoy the way his hands clench on my thighs, as if he's fighting himself not to touch me more. This man has control wrapped around him like chains. I wonder what it would take for those restraints to snap. What will happen when they finally do?

I use my middle finger to draw my wetness up and around my clit, and Hades snorts. "Cheeky."

"I don't know what you're talking about." Even with me going intentionally slowly, intentionally lightly, pleasure coils through me. I have the borderline hysterical thought that I might be able to come simply from the force of his gaze on my body. I circle my clit again. "Hades, *please*."

"I like the way you say my name." He releases me, peeling his fingers away from my thighs so slowly that it's obvious he doesn't want to stop touching me. I don't want him to stop, either, but the end result is worth the temporary detour. He reaches for the front of his slacks. I hold my breath as he draws out his cock. He's... Wow. He's perfect. Big and thick and my body clenches with the need to have him inside me. Hades gives himself a rough stroke. "Don't stop."

I realize I had slowed my movements to a standstill and pick up my pace again. I can't take my eyes from his cock as he strokes himself. "You're beautiful."

He gives one of those ragged laughs I'm already learning to crave. "You're drunk on lust."

"Maybe. Doesn't make it less true." I bite my bottom lip. "Touch me? Please?" When he doesn't immediately respond, I press on. "Please, Hades. Please, *Sir*."

Hades curses and knocks my hand away from my clit. "You are shit for my self-control."

"I'm sorry," I murmur, trying to look apologetic.

"No, you're not. Do *not* move, or this ends."

"I won't. I promise."

I stare down my body as Hades wraps a fist around his cock and angles it down to drag the blunt head over my clit. It feels dirty and a little bit wrong, and I never want it to stop. Gods, how is this hotter than some of the sex I've had? Is it purely because it's *him*? I don't have an answer. Not now. Maybe not ever.

He waits a beat and then strokes me again, circling my clit just like I did with my fingers earlier. I hold my breath, willing him to do more. It's as if Hades draws the thought right out of my head, because he drags his cock down, wetting himself with my desire. Wicked. This is so beyond wicked.

It's on the tip of my tongue to beg him to fuck me now, but I bite the words back. No matter how delirious pleasure makes me, I'm still aware enough to know that I've pushed him to his limit tonight. If I try for more, there's every chance he'll push back. That he'll stop the decadent motion of his cock through my folds. Down, and then up to circle my clit, and then back down.

He tenses as he presses to my entrance, but I don't have a chance to throw caution to the wind before he speaks. "Hands above your head."

I don't hesitate. He's not going to leave me hanging tonight. Despite what he seems to think, I *am* capable of obedience when properly motivated. The look he gives me says he's noted how quickly I stop arguing now that I'm getting what I want. He shifts forward to press my body hard against the mattress, his solid weight pinning me in place. And then he shifts his hips and the whole length of his cock is suddenly rubbing against my clit with each slow thrust.

So careful. He's so fucking careful with me, even now. Holding me down but ensuring his weight doesn't drive the breath from my lungs. I could have told him it's a lost cause—pleasure has already accomplished that. I'm gasping out each exhale, fighting to hold still, to obey, to not do anything that might cause him to stop.

His slow movements have his clothing sliding against my bare skin. In this moment, I'd give my right lung to have him as naked as I am.

I expect him to kiss me, but he kisses along my jaw to nip my earlobe. "See how good it feels to obey, little Persephone?" Another long drag of his length against my clit. "Do as I ask tomorrow, and I'll let you have my cock."

My thoughts scatter, shooting in a thousand different directions. "Promise?"

"I promise." He picks up his pace the tiniest bit. My toes curl, and I can't help arching into him. Hades hooks one arm under my thigh and spreads me up and further out. The smallest shift and he'll be inside me. I want it so desperately, I'm in danger of begging.

My body doesn't give me a chance to. I orgasm hard, every muscle clenching and my toes curling. Hades keeps moving, drawing it out, and then he jerks back and comes across my stomach. I stare dazedly down at the liquid marking my skin and have the absurd desire to run my fingers through it.

While I'm still recovering, Hades fixes his clothing and sits back on his heels. The way he watches me... We haven't even had sex yet, and this man looks at me like he wants to keep me. It should be enough to send me running, but I can't quite work up the energy to be concerned. We have our deal. I don't know why I'm so sure, but I *know* Hades won't break his word. At the end of this, he'll ensure I get out of Olympus unscathed.

"Don't move." He climbs off the bed and walks to the bathroom. A few seconds later, he returns with a damp cloth. I reach to take it, but he shakes his head. "Hold still."

I watch him clean me up. This should bother me…shouldn't it? I'm not sure, not when I'm still riding high from my orgasm. Hades sets the cloth aside and arranges himself against my headboard. "Come here."

Again, part of me protests that I should dig in my heels, but I'm already moving to him and allowing him to arrange me on his lap. Still, I can't quite keep silent. "I'm not a big cuddler."

"This isn't about cuddling." He smooths a hand down my back and guides my head to his shoulder.

I wait, but he doesn't seem overly motivated to keep talking. A little laugh escapes. "By all means, don't feel like you have to elaborate. I'll just sit here in pleasant confusion for the duration."

"For someone with your reputation, you've got quite the mouth on you." He doesn't sound annoyed by this fact. No, if I don't miss my guess, he's positively amused.

I sigh and relax against him. He's obviously not going to let me go until he's finished with whatever this not-cuddling thing is, and holding myself tense through the whole thing is too exhausting. Plus…it's kind of nice to lie like this. Just for a little while. "I don't know why you're so surprised. You've already admitted you use your reputation as a weapon. Is it so strange to think I might do the same?"

"Why did you land on sunshine? None of your other sisters made the same choice."

At that, I lean back a little so I can raise my brows at him. "Hades...you seem to know a lot about us. You must follow the gossip sites."

He doesn't look remotely sorry. "You'd be surprised at the information someone can glean from them if they read between the lines and have a little insider perspective."

I can't argue that. I feel the same way. With a small laugh, I relax against him again. "Eurydice isn't playing a part, not entirely. She really is the innocent dreamer, which is how she ended up with that asshole of a boyfriend."

Hades's chuckle rumbles through his chest. "You don't approve of Orpheus."

"Would you if he were in a relationship with someone you care about? He embraces the starving artist trope to an absurd degree, especially considering he's a trust-fund baby like the rest of us. He might think Eurydice is his muse right now, but what happens when he gets bored with her and starts looking outside their relationship for *inspiration*?" I know exactly what will happen. Eurydice will be crushed. It might actually break her. We've kept our youngest sister as sheltered as a person can be when they're one spot removed from the Thirteen. The thought of Eurydice losing her innocence... It hurts. I don't want that for her.

"And your other sisters?"

I shrug as much as I'm able to. "Psyche prefers to fly under the radar. She never lets them know what she's thinking, and sometimes it seems like all of Olympus loves her for it. She's something of a trendsetter, but she makes it look effortless, like she can't be bothered to try." Though sometimes I catch an empty look in her eyes when she thinks no one is looking. She never used to have that look before Mother became Demeter.

I clear my throat. "Callisto isn't playing a role. She really is as fierce as she seems. She hates the Thirteen, hates Olympus, hates everyone except us." I've wondered time and time again why she hasn't left. She's the only one of us who has access to her trust fund, and instead of using it to craft an escape hatch, she's only seemed to settle deeper into her hate.

Hades slowly winds a strand of my hair around his finger. "And you?"

"Someone has to keep the peace." It was my role in our little family unit even before we moved up the social and political ladder in Olympus, so it felt natural to extend it. I smooth things out, make plans, and get everyone on board. It wasn't meant to be forever. Only until I could craft my ship out of here.

I never could have anticipated that wearing the mask of the sweet, biddable daughter might be the very thing that traps me here forever.

HADES

IT TAKES MORE DETERMINATION THAN I ANTICIPATE TO leave Persephone's bed after she falls asleep. It feels good to have her in my arms. Too good. It's like waking up to find that the happy dream was real all along, and that fantasy is the one thing I can't allow. That's ultimately what pushes me to press a kiss to her temple and leave.

Exhaustion weighs me down, but I won't be able to rest before I do my nightly rounds. It's a compulsion I've given in to too many times, and tonight is no exception. I'm better than I used to be, though. At one point, I couldn't close my eyes before I checked every single door and window in this house. Now, it's only the doors and ground-floor windows, finishing with a stop in our security hub. My people never comment on me checking their work, which I appreciate. It's less about their capabilities and more about the fear that licks at my heels when I let my guard down.

I didn't expect Persephone's presence in the house to make the feeling worse. I've promised her my protection, have given my word that she'll be safe here. The threat of the Thirteen might be enough to deter Zeus, but if he decides it's worth the risk to attempt an attack that might not be tracked to him...

Would he really set fire to this place knowing Persephone is inside?

I know the answer before the thought has even registered in my mind. Of course he would. Not yet, no, not when he still thinks he has a chance of retrieving her. But the recklessness of his men pursuing her over such a distance proves that if he ever decides she's beyond his reach, he will not hesitate to strike. Better she be dead than belong to anyone else, *especially* me.

It's something I need to bring up to her, but the last thing I want is to renew the fear I saw in her eyes the first night. She feels safe here, and I want to make damn sure I don't betray the trust she's put in me. My hesitation to give her the full rundown speaks more to me than it does to her, and I need to correct that tomorrow, no matter how little I like the idea of it.

The moment I walk into my bedroom, I know I'm not alone. I move to the gun I keep stashed in the magnetic safe tucked beneath the side table, but I only get a single step when a feminine voice emerges from the darkness. "Surprise a friend and almost get shot in the bargain. *Tsk, tsk.*"

Some of the tension slides out of me, exhaustion rising in its wake. I frown into the darkness. "What are you doing here, Hermes?"

She waltzes out of my closet, one of my more expensive ties wrapped around her hand, and gives me a bright grin. "I wanted to see you."

It's an effort not to roll my eyes. "More like you came back for the rest of my wine cellar."

"Well, sure, and that, too." She moves aside as I walk into my closet and shrug out of my jacket. Hermes leans against the doorframe. "You know, keeping all your windows and doors locked sends a special kind of message to your friends. It's almost as if you don't want company."

"I don't have friends."

"Yes, yes, you're a lone mountain of solitude." She waves that away.

I hang my jacket in its proper place and kick off my shoes. "It's not as if it keeps you out."

"That's true enough." She laughs, the sound deceptively loud considering how small she is. That laugh is part of the reason I haven't tried to up my security. As aggravating as I find her and Dionysus's antics, the house feels less large and looming when they're around.

She frowns at me and motions to my shirt and pants. "You're not continuing the strip show?"

I might tolerate her presence here, but we have nowhere near the trust level required for me to fully undress in front of her. I trust no one that much, but instead of saying so, I keep my tone cautiously light. "Is it a strip show if you weren't invited?"

She grins. "Dunno, but I'd enjoy it nonetheless."

I shake my head. "Why are you here?"

"Oh. That. Duty calls." She rolls her eyes. "I have an official message from Demeter."

Persephone's mother. There's one element of this shitshow Persephone hasn't really addressed, and it's how her mother decided to push her into a marriage with a dangerous man solely for the sake of ambition *without talking to her about it.* I have plenty of thoughts about that, none of them kind.

I slide my hands into my pockets. "Well, let's hear what she has to say."

Hermes straightens and lifts her chin. Despite a whole host of differences, I have the sudden impression of Demeter. When Hermes speaks, it's *Demeter's* voice that emerges. Hermes's mimicry is part of how she ended up as Hermes, and it's perfect, as always. "I don't know what grudge you're nursing against Zeus and the rest of the Thirteen, and frankly, I don't care. Free my daughter. If you harm her or refuse to return her, I'll cut off every resource under my control to the lower city."

I sigh. "It's nothing more than I expected." The cruelty is almost beyond comprehension, though. She wants her daughter to play along, so she has every intention of dragging Persephone back to the upper city—and to the altar. And she'll step on my people to ensure it happens.

Hermes relaxes her posture and shrugs. "You know how the Thirteen are."

"*You* are a member of the Thirteen."

"So are you. And besides, I'm quirky." She scrunches up her nose. "Also cute and lovable and lacking a certain level of power madness."

I can't exactly argue that. Hermes never seems to play the games the others do. Even Dionysus is focused on expanding his little corner of Olympus's map of power. Hermes just...flits about. "Then why take the position?"

She laughs and smacks me on the shoulder. "Maybe it's just because I like poking fun at powerful people who take themselves too seriously. Know anyone who fits the bill?"

"Charming."

"Yes, I am." She sobers. "I hope you know what you're doing. You're pissing off a lot of people right now, and I have a feeling that you intend to piss off a lot more before this is finished."

She's not wrong, but I still have to fight back a growl. "Everyone is so quick to forget that Persephone ran from them because she didn't want the marriage Zeus and Demeter plotted."

"Oh, I know. And, no lie, it makes me like her a tiny bit." She holds her pointer finger and thumb a fraction of an inch apart. "But it won't make a difference. Zeus waves his giant dick around and everyone scrambles to give him whatever he wants."

I ignore that. "For someone so invested in the kind earth-mother persona, Demeter is quick to put her daughters on the chopping block."

"She *does* love her girls." Hermes shrugs. "You don't know how it is out there. On this side of the river, you're king and you've carved out a really good thing for your people. They don't waste effort and resources re-creating the glitz and glam of the upper city, and they aren't stabbing each other in the back with diamond-encrusted daggers." At my look, she nods rapidly. "It happened. You must remember that fight between Kratos and Ares. That motherfucker just walked up to him in the middle of the party, whipped a dagger out, and…" She makes stabbing motions. "If Apollo hadn't intervened, it would have been straight-up murder instead of just assault with a deadly weapon."

"I'm sure I must have glossed over the part of the report where Ares was arrested on said charges."

She shrugs. "You know how it is. Kratos isn't one of the Thirteen, and he *had* been skimming off Ares's bottom line. The fight was delightful drama; a trial wouldn't have been."

If ever there was a good example of how the Thirteen abuse their power, there it is. "It changes nothing. Persephone crossed the bridge. She's here." *And she's mine.* I don't say the latter, but Hermes's perceptive gaze narrows on my face. I clear my throat. "She's free to walk away at any time. She's choosing not to." I should leave it at that, but the thought of Demeter and Zeus dragging Persephone back to the upper city against her will has anger surging through me. "If they try to take her, they'll have to go through me to do it."

"'They'll have to go through me to do it.'"

I blink. Hermes's impression of me was spot-on. "That was not a message."

"Wasn't it?" She examines her nails. "Sounded like a message to me."

"*Hermes.*"

"I take no sides, not as long as everyone is following the rules. Threats don't violate them." She grins suddenly. "They just add a little spice to everyone's life. Ta!"

"Hermes!"

But she's gone, darting out my door. Chasing her down won't change a damn thing. Once she's set her mind on something, she'll do it no matter what anyone around her says. For the *spice*. I drag my hands over my face. This is a fucking mess.

I don't know if Demeter is capable of following through on her threat. She's been in the role for years now, but her reputation is too carefully curated to get a good read on what she'll do in a situation like this. Is she really willing to hurt thousands of people whose only crime is to live on the wrong side of the River Styx?

Fuck. I don't know. I really don't know.

If I wasn't a goddamn myth to most of the upper city, I'd be able to fight this more effectively. She would never try this bluff with one of the other Thirteen because of the potential blow to her reputation. I'm in the shadows, so she thinks she's safe, that I have no recourse. She'll find out how wrong she is if she goes through with this.

At this point, I'm inclined to call Demeter's bluff. The other Thirteen don't overly give a fuck about the lower city, but even they have to see how dangerous it is to let Demeter run amok. Beyond that, I've had a lifetime of not trusting the Thirteen, so my people are prepared to weather any storm they try to throw at us.

If Demeter thinks she can fuck with me without seeing consequences, she has another think coming.

After a mostly sleepless night, I get ready and head down to the kitchen in search of coffee. The sound of laughter echoes through the empty halls as I reach the ground floor. I recognize Persephone's voice, even if she's never laughed that freely around *me*. It's silly to feel jealous of that fact after only knowing her a few days, but apparently reason has gone out the window where this woman is concerned.

I take my time walking to the kitchen, enjoying how much more alive the house feels this morning. I hadn't really noticed the lack until now, and the realization doesn't sit well with me. It doesn't matter what *life* Persephone brings to my home, because she's leaving in a few weeks. Getting used to the idea of waking up to her laughing in my kitchen is a mistake.

I push through the door to find her standing at the stove with Georgie. Georgie is technically my housekeeper, but she's got a small army of staff to take care of cleaning this place, so she mostly presides over the kitchen and cooking. There's a reason most of my people find their way through these doors for at least one meal a day; she's a happy, middle-aged white woman who could be fifty or could be eighty. All I know is that she hasn't appeared to age in the twenty years since she took over the position. Her hair has always been a sleek silver, and there have always been laugh lines around her eyes and mouth. Today, she's wearing one of her customary aprons with frills around the edges.

She points to my normal chair without looking. "I just put a new pot of coffee on. Breakfast sandwiches incoming."

I eye the pair of women as I sit. Persephone is on the other side of the island, and she's got a little flour on her dress. Obviously, she's been an active participant in breakfast. The realization makes me feel strange. "Since when do you let us help?"

"There is no 'us.' Persephone offered to handle a few small tasks while I set things up. Simple."

Simple. As if she hasn't chased off any offer of assistance I've made for the last two decades. I accept my coffee and try not to glare at it. The closest Georgie has let me get to "help" is watching a pot of water for fifteen seconds while she dug through the pantry for a few ingredients. Certainly nothing involved enough to put flour on my clothing.

"Maybe that expression is why Georgie doesn't want you playing the role of a human storm cloud in her kitchen."

I shoot a look at Persephone and find her fighting back a smile, her hazel eyes dancing with mirth. I raise my eyebrows. "Someone's in a good mood this morning."

"I had good dreams." She winks at me and turns back to the stove.

I already had no plans to hand her back to Demeter and Zeus, but even if I were entertaining the idea, this morning would have nuked it. She's been in my house less than forty-eight hours and something has already unwound in her. If I were any more arrogant, I'd chalk it up to the orgasms last night, but I know better. She feels safe, so she's let down a layer or two of her guard. I might be a bastard, but I can't repay that fledgling trust by throwing her to the wolves.

I'll keep my word.

For better or worse.

PERSEPHONE

I EXPECT HADES TO CALL IN PEOPLE TO DRESS ME RATHER than let me leave the house. All in the name of safety, of course. So I'm surprised when he leads me to the front door. A pair of sheepskin boots sit there. He points at the bench tucked back in an alcove of the foyer. "Sit."

"You bought me boots." They're hideous, but that's not what has me raising my brows. "This is your idea of a compromise?"

"Yes, I do believe I've heard the word before." He waits for me to pull them on, watching closely as if he's about to jump in and do it for me. When I raise my eyebrows, he slips his hands into his pockets, nearly successful at pretending he's not an overprotective mother bear. "I'm well aware that you won't submit to being carried down the street."

"Very astute of you."

"Like you said: compromise." Next comes a large trench-coat type of jacket that covers my borrowed dress. I look absolutely ridiculous, but that doesn't stop my heart from going warm.

Hades, king of the lower city, boogeyman of Olympus, someone more myth than reality, is taking care of me.

I find myself holding my breath as Hades opens the front door and we step out onto the street. It looks nothing like the alley that led to the underground passage he used to bring me into his house. No trash. No close quarters and filth.

The upper city is all skyscrapers, the buildings nearly blocking out the sky; they might gain more character the farther one gets from the city center, but they don't lose any height. The buildings on *this* street all stop at three or four stories, and as I look around, I pick out a laundromat, two restaurants, a few places with businesses I can't determine, and a little corner grocery store. All the buildings have a feeling of age, as if they've stood here a hundred years and they'll still be here a hundred years from now. The street is clean and there's plenty of foot traffic on the sidewalks. The people are varied, dressed in everything from business casual to jeans to one guy in pajama pants and bedhead who ducks into the corner store. It's all so *normal*. These people obviously aren't worried that paparazzi are going to pop out around a corner or that one wrong move will cause catastrophic social consequences. There's an ease here that I don't know how to explain.

I turn around and look at Hades's home. It appears exactly how I would expect from the parts of the interior I've seen. Almost Victorian with its steep roofs and all the stylistic extras. It's the kind of house that speaks of a long and complicated history, the sort of place kids dare each other to run up to and touch the gates after dark. I bet there are just as many legends about this house as there are about the man who lives in it.

It shouldn't fit with the rest of the neighborhood, but the eclectic clash of styles isn't a clash at all. It feels strangely seamless, but with character that the city center in the upper city lacks.

I love it.

I glance back, only to find Hades watching me. "What?"

"You're ogling."

I suppose I am. I give the street another scan, lingering on the pillars that bracket the laundromat. I can't be sure at this distance, but it almost looks like there are scenes carved into them. "I've never been across the river." It never struck me as odd before—the way that Olympus is carved in two by the River Styx. The sheer lack of crossover between the two sides. Surely other cities aren't like that? But then, Olympus isn't like any other city.

"Why would you?" He takes my hand and slips it into the crook of his elbow like an old-world gentleman. "Only the more stubborn—or desperate—get across the river without an invitation."

I fall into step beside him. "Would you…" I take a deep breath. "Would you show me around?"

Hades stops short. "Why would you want that?"

The harshness of the question shocks me, but only for a moment. Of course he'd be protective of this place, these people. I carefully touch his arm. "I just want to understand, Hades. Not gape at them like a tourist."

He glances at my hand and then at my face, his expression unreadable. Except it's not entirely unreadable, is it? He only goes icy when he wants distance or doesn't know how to react. "We can go for a short walk after we get you some weather-appropriate clothing."

Part of me wants to argue about the *short* part of the walk, but the truth is that my feet do ache, and after the events of the last few days, it's smart to keep from overextending. "Thank you."

He nods and we begin walking again. After a block, I can't keep my questions bottled up any longer. "You say the people aren't allowed here without an invitation, but Hermes and Dionysus were here not two days ago. Did you invite them?"

"No." He makes a face. "There's no boundary that can hold those two. It's annoying as fuck." His words say one thing, but there's a certain level of fondness in his tone that has me fighting down a smile.

"How did you meet them?"

"It was less a meeting than an ambush," he rumbles. He's watching the street as if he expects an attack, but his posture is loose and relaxed. "Not long after Hermes took over the position, I found her in my kitchen, eating my food. I'm still not sure how she got past security. How she *keeps* getting past security." Hades shakes his head. "Dionysus and I are familiar because distribution is something we both handle different parts of, but it wasn't until Hermes that he started showing up outside business meetings, too. The man can drink like a fish, and he's always in my goddamn fridge, eating my desserts."

I've met both of them previously, of course, but unlike many of the other Thirteen, they don't seem to care about politicking. At the last party, they were sitting in a corner and engaged in a rather loud running commentary critiquing everyone's clothing choices as if they were on a red carpet. Aphrodite, in particular, had not been amused when they called her dress "a puffy vagina."

Hermes is an ambiguous role. She's a technical genius who handles all the security features in the upper city. It always struck me as strange that the Thirteen let her be so close when they guard their secrets like jealous lovers, but I'm one position removed. Maybe they understand something I don't. Or maybe they fall victim to this glaring weakness in their defenses because it's the way things have always been done. Difficult to say.

Dionysus? He's a jack of all trades beneath the umbrella of entertainment. Parties and events and social positioning are his forte. And so are drugs and alcohol and other illicit entertainments. Or at least that's the rumor. My mother has always gone out of her way to ensure we're never around him, which is slightly ironic considering how she's trying to effectively sell me to *Zeus*.

I shudder.

"Cold?"

"No, just thinking too hard." I give myself a shake. "We live in a strange world."

"That's an understatement." He guides me around the corner, and we walk in easy silence for a few blocks. Once again, it strikes me how *comfortable* people seem to be here. They don't stare at Hades and me as we walk past, something I didn't realize I missed. In the upper city, the only thing people love more than politicking and ambition is gossiping, and as a result, the gossip sites pay a pretty penny for pictures and news about the Thirteen and those in their respective circles. My sisters and I are constantly being photographed like midtier celebrities.

Here, I could be anyone. It's incredibly refreshing.

I'm so busy contemplating the differences between upper and

lower city that it takes me a good ten minutes to realize Hades is moving far slower than he would naturally. I keep catching him checking his stride. "I'm fine."

"I didn't say anything."

"No, but I'm pretty sure that old lady just lapped us around the block." I point to the gray-haired Latina woman in question. "Honestly, Hades. My feet are doing much better. They barely ache today." It's even the truth, not that I think he'll believe me.

As expected, he ignores my attempt to be reasonable. "We're almost there."

I fight down the urge to roll my eyes and let him lead me one more block into what appears to be a warehouse district. We have several areas like this in the upper city, large building after large building, all varying shades of gray and white. My mother is in charge of the one connected to the food supply.

Hades moves to a narrow unmarked door and holds it open for me. "In here."

I take one step inside and stop short. "Wow." The warehouse is one massive room that has to take up most of the city block, a divine space filled with fabric and clothing in every color and texture imaginable. "Wow," I say again. My sisters would *die* to get a chance to peruse this space.

Hades speaks softly, the words designed not to carry. "Juliette used to be the premier designer for Hera—the one two Heras ago—but when she died, Juliette was a little too vocal about her suspicions of Zeus so he set out to destroy her business. She crossed the river seeking sanctuary."

I drift closer to the nearest dress form, clothed in a magnificent red gown. "I saw Zeus's oldest daughter, Helen, wearing something similar to this two weeks ago."

"Yeah." Hades snorts. "Just because Juliette is effectively exiled doesn't mean she lost her clientele. That's how the Thirteen work. They do one thing publicly and something else behind closed doors."

"Once again, just reminding you that *you're* one of the Thirteen."

"Technicality."

A woman's voice comes from somewhere farther in the warehouse. "Is that Hades I hear?"

He lets loose an almost silent sigh. "Hello, Juliette."

The Black woman who appears from between racks of clothing has the kind of timeless beauty that starts on runways and only gets better with age. Her short black hair leaves her face on full display and I actually sigh a little at how gorgeous she is. Like a painting or a piece of art. Flawless. She walks toward us, each movement graceful, and I am doubly sure that she used to spend time on runaways. Juliette takes me in with a single look. "You brought me a gift. How thoughtful."

He gives me a little nudge in her direction. "We need the works."

"Hmmm." She circles me like a shark, all elegant predatory movement. "I know this girl. She's Demeter's middle daughter."

"Yes."

She stops in front of me and tilts her head to the side. "You're a long way from home."

I'm not sure what I'm supposed to say to that. I can't get a good read on this woman. Normally, I would lump her in with the other beautiful, powerful people I've come across, but Hades trusts her enough to bring me here and that means something. Finally, I shrug. "The upper city can be exceedingly cruel."

"Isn't that the truth?" She glances at Hades. "Are you staying or going?"

"I'll stick around."

"Suit yourself." She waves me forward. "This way. Let's get you measured and see where we stand."

The next few hours pass in a blur. Juliette takes my measurements and then brings forth rack after rack of clothing for me to try on. I expect the gowns. I don't expect the loungewear or the casual clothes. By the time she brings out the lingerie, I'm weaving on my aching feet.

She notices, of course. "Almost done."

"I'm not here for that long. I don't know that all this is necessary." Not to mention that the prospective bill makes me cringe. I highly doubt Juliette functions on IOUs.

She shakes her head. "You know better. The peacocking might not be as blatant in the lower city, but if Hades is using you to make a statement, then you must *make a statement*."

"Who says Hades is using me to make a statement?" I don't know why I'm arguing. That's exactly why Hades and I made our bargain.

She gives me a long look. "I'm going to pretend you didn't just insult my intelligence. I've known Hades years now. The man does nothing without reason, and he certainly wouldn't steal Zeus's fiancée out from under his nose if he didn't want to stir the pot."

I don't ask how she knows that I'm promised to Zeus. The lower city has access to the same gossip sites that the upper city does; just because I haven't looked at the headlines doesn't mean they don't exist. They'll have reported on both my engagement and my disappearance. Maybe if Zeus and my mother weren't so sure of me, it wouldn't have come to this. Now we're both painted into a corner and I'm determined not to be the one who blinks first.

I take a deep breath and turn to the last rack. "Lingerie it is."

It's another hour before I wind my way through the racks to find Hades camped out in the corner of the warehouse that seems to be solely for this purpose. It's got several chairs, a television that's currently set to mute, and a stack of books on a coffee table. I get a glimpse of the one in Hades's hands as he closes it and drops it on top of the stack. "I didn't take you for a true crime fan."

"I'm not." He pushes to his feet. "You look comfortable."

"I'm going to take that as a factual statement and not an insult." I glance down at my fleece-lined leggings and sweater. Juliette also gave me an incredibly warm coat to combat the temperature outside. "You promised to show me around."

"I did." He takes the coat from my hands, examining it as if to determine its ability to keep me warm. I *should* be bristling at his overprotectiveness, but all I feel is a strange sort of warmth in my chest. The feeling flares hotter as he settles the coat around my shoulders and looks down at me. He strokes the lapels, and it almost feels like he's touching *me* instead of the cloth. "You look good, Persephone."

I lick my lips. "Thank you."

He glances over my shoulder as Juliette approaches, but he doesn't step back, doesn't drop his hands. "Charon will be by to pick up the order later today."

"Of course. Enjoy yourselves, you two." And then she's gone, bustling several of the racks deeper into the warehouse.

I watch her go, unable to stop myself from frowning. "I didn't pay."

"Persephone." He waits for me to look at him. "You have no money."

Shame heats my skin. "But—"

"I've taken care of it."

"I can't let you do that."

"You haven't *let* me do anything." Hades takes my hand and tugs me toward the front door. It almost slips past me how casual he is touching me now. It feels so natural, as if we've been doing this far longer than a few days.

Hades doesn't release my hand when we reach the street. He simply turns and heads back the way we came. Boots or no, my feet hurt and exhaustion settles over my skin in a wave. I ignore both feelings. When will I get another chance to see the lower city, let alone with Hades leading the way? It's too great an opportunity to pass up just because my body isn't at one hundred percent yet.

And maybe I just want to spend some more time with Hades, too.

Halfway back to the house, he takes a right turn and leads me to a doorway with a mass of cheerily painted flowers on it. Like some of the other businesses I've seen on our walk, it has white columns on either side of the entrance. I haven't been able to get close looks at the others, but these depict a group of women by a waterfall, surrounded by flowers. "Why do some of the businesses have columns and not others?"

"It's a sign that this place has been here since the founding of the city."

The sense of history staggers me. We don't have that in the upper city. Or if we do, I've never seen it. History is less important to the people in power than presenting a polished image, no matter how false. "They're so detailed."

"One artist did all of them. Or at least that's how the story goes. I have a team whose sole job is to maintain and repair these as needed."

Of course he did. Of course he would see this sign of history as an assent instead of something to be smudged out and erased in favor of the new and shiny. "They're beautiful. I want to see them all."

He's got a strange look on his face. "I don't know if we could make it to all of them before spring. But we can try."

The strange warm feeling in my chest blossoms. "Thank you, Hades."

"Let's go in and get out of the cold." He leans past me to open the door.

I don't know what I expect to find inside, but it's a small flower shop, with groupings arranged in cute tin buckets around the counters. A white man with a shaved head and truly impressive black mustache sees us and jerks away from the wall he was just leaning on. "Hades!"

"Matthew." Hades nods. "Is the greenhouse open?"

"For you? Always." He reaches under the counter and tosses over a set of keys. If I wasn't looking closely, I might mistake his eagerness for fear, but it *is* eagerness. He's delighted that Hades is here, and he's barely concealing it.

Hades nods again. "Thanks." Without another word, he tugs me through the room to a small door tucked in the back corner. It leads to a narrow hallway and up a set of steep stairs to another door. I make the climb in silence, fighting not to wince when each step sends a dull pain echoing up my legs.

The sight that greets us behind this final door makes the discomfort more than worth it. I press my hand to my mouth and stare. "Oh, Hades. It's beautiful." A greenhouse covers what I expect is the entirety of the roof of the building, housing row after row of flowers of every kind and color. There are hanging pots with vines and pink and white flowers cascading down. Roses and lilies and flowers I have no name for lined up carefully beneath cleverly concealed water lines. The air is warm and faintly humid and it heats me straight through.

He stands back and watches as I move down the aisle. I stop before a cluster of giant, purple ball-like flowers. Gods, they're pretty. I find myself speaking without meaning to. "When I was a little girl, back before my mother was Demeter, we lived out in the country that surrounds Olympus. There was this field of wildflowers that my sisters and I would play in." I move to the mass of white roses and lean over to inhale, enjoying their scent.

"We pretended we were fairies until we grew out of those types of games. This place reminds me of that." For all that it's cultivated instead of flowers left to grow wild, there's an aura of magic about this place. Maybe it's the little bit of springtime in the midst of a city cloaked in winter. The glass is faintly steamed, concealing the outside and giving the impression of us standing in the middle of another world.

Hades seems determined to take me through portal after portal. First the room behind the black door. Now this little slice of floral heaven. What other treasures does the lower city hold? I want to experience them all.

I feel Hades at my back, though he keeps a careful distance between us. "It's easy to forget you're in Olympus when you're up here."

An asset when someone carries the burdens Hades does. Even if he's not a publicly active member of the Thirteen, it's becoming clear that he holds plenty of responsibility behind the scenes. With the entire lower city resting on his shoulders, it's no wonder he craves escape from time to time.

I turn and look at him. He's so out of place here in his black suit and broody good looks, like a hellhound that wandered into a garden party. "Why here?"

"I like the flowers." His lips curve a little. "And the view is outstanding."

For a breathless second, I think he's talking about *me*. It's there in the way he looks at me as if the room ceases to exist around us. I can't help holding my breath, waiting for what he'll do next, but Hades just takes my hand again and tugs me down the aisle and through a set of glass doors I hadn't noticed before. They lead into a second, smaller room that's been set up almost like a sitting room. There are still flowers around the walls but the center of the room holds a number of chairs and a couch, all perched atop a thick rug. There's a low coffee table with a stack of books, and the entire scene just invites a person to curl up and lose themselves for a few hours.

Hades bypasses the furniture and stops in front of the glass wall that edges up to the perimeter of the roof. "Look."

"Oh," I breathe.

He's right. The view is outstanding. The greenhouse overlooks the River Styx's curving journey, carving a swath between upper and lower city. This section of the river curves into a deep reversed C shape, creating a little peninsula on the upper-city side, bringing the water closer to us. The divide between the two parts of the city is barely noticeable from this position. We're nowhere near the city center; the buildings on the upper-city side are older and more varied than I'm used to seeing. I wonder if they have the same type of columns that I've seen in the lower city, if the artist who created them crossed the river to leave their imprint.

"The shop is owned by an old family friend. At one point, I got into some trouble as a kid, and my punishment was tending the greenhouse for a few weeks."

I manage to tear my gaze away from the view to shoot him a look. "What kind of trouble?"

He grimaces. "It doesn't matter."

Oh, now I have to know. I edge closer to him and grin. "Come on, Hades. Tell me. What kind of trouble could you possibly have gotten up to?"

He hesitates, and disappointment threatens to sour the mood, but finally he grudgingly grinds out, "I took the owner's car for a joyride. I was fourteen. It seemed like a good idea at the time."

"How scandalous of you."

He looks out over the river. "I wanted to get the hell out of Olympus and never look back. Some days, it's just all too much, you know?"

"I know," I whisper. The desire to touch him rises, but I'm not sure he'll accept comfort from me. "You got caught?"

"No." He glares at the glass. "I got to the city limits and I couldn't do it. I didn't even try to cross the boundary out of the city. I just sat there in that idling car for a couple hours, cursing myself, my parents, Andreas." At my questioning look, he clarifies. "He was my father's right-hand man. After my parents died, he took care of me." He drags a hand through his hair. "I drove back, returned the car, and told Andreas what I'd tried to do. I'm still not sure if the greenhouse was a punishment or his way of giving me a break for a little bit."

My heart aches for the fourteen-year-old version of this man, who must have hurt so much. "It sounds like working here helped."

"Yeah." He shrugs as if it doesn't mean anything, when it couldn't be more obvious that it means everything. "I still come around and help sometimes, though since Matthew took over for his father, he's as jumpy as a cat in a room full of rocking chairs every time I show up."

I laugh a little. "He's got some serious hero worship going on."

"That's not it. He's afraid of me."

I blink. "Hades, if he had a tail, it would have been wagging the second you walked through the door. That's not what fear looks like. Trust me, I know." He doesn't look convinced. But then, it's becoming startling clear that Hades holds himself apart from everyone else. It's no wonder he doesn't recognize the truth of how people look at him when he's only searching for fear in their eyes.

I reach out and touch his arm. "Thank you for showing me this."

"If you want to come back here at any point and I'm not available, I'll send someone with you." He shifts, almost like he's uncomfortable. "I know the house can get stifling, and while it's safe enough here, I don't trust Zeus not to try something if his people find you walking alone."

"I'm actually looking forward to exploring the house." I look around the room. "But I will undoubtedly take you up on that invitation. This place is really soothing." A yawn surprises me, and I press my hand to my mouth. "Sorry."

"Let's go back."

"Okay." I don't know if it's stress, my late night, or if Hades is right and I'm too good at ignoring my body's signals. Surely not the latter. I take a step and then another, propelling myself forward from sheer stubbornness. But on the third step, the room goes sickeningly wavy and my knees turn to jelly. I'm falling, and I already know I won't get my hands up in time to save myself.

"You stubborn little fool." Hades curses and sweeps me into his arms before I have a chance to hit the floor. "Why didn't you say you were feeling light-headed?"

It takes me a moment to reconcile the fact that I'm once again in Hades's arms, that the harsh contact with the floor never came. "I'm fine."

"You're not fucking fine. You nearly took a dive." He stalks through the greenhouse and takes the stairs down two at a time, his expression thunderous. "You and everyone else in your life might be willing to play fast and loose with your health, but I am not."

I get a glimpse of a startled Matthew as Hades tosses back the keys, and then we're out on the street. I shift in his arms. "I can walk."

"You most assuredly can*not*." He covers the blocks between the flower shop and his home at a startling pace. He really *was* checking his stride when we strolled casually around earlier. Part of me wants to keep arguing, but the truth is that I'm still feeling a little dizzy.

He practically kicks down the front door. Instead of putting me down like I expect, he marches up the stairs, bypassing the second landing. As much as I resent being treated like a child— even if *maybe* I should have said something on the way to the greenhouse about not feeling well—he's sparked my curiosity. Georgie caught me this morning before I had a chance to do any real exploring, so the only bits I've seen are the sex dungeon, my room, and the kitchen. The third floor is all new to me.

That perks me up a little. "Where are we going?"

"You obviously can't be trusted to take care of yourself, so I have to keep a better eye on you."

I give up and rest my cheek against his shoulder. I really shouldn't enjoy being carried about by this man as much as I do.

"I probably just have low blood sugar," I murmur. "It's no big deal. I just need to eat something."

"No big deal," he repeats, as if he doesn't understand the words. "You ate breakfast only a few hours ago."

My skin heats and I can't quite meet his gaze. "I had a snack."

"Persephone." He makes a sound impressively like a growl. "When is the last time you had a full meal?"

I don't want to be honest, but I know better than to lie to him when he's like this. I examine my fingernails. "Maybe breakfast the day of the party."

"That was three days ago."

"I've eaten since then, of course. Just not what I suspect you mean." He doesn't immediately respond and I finally look at him. Hades has gone so cold, it's a wonder my breath doesn't show in the air between us. I frown. "I don't eat when I'm stressed."

"That changes now."

"You can't just decree that something will change and make it so."

"Watch me," he snarls.

Hades opens a door to what appears to be a study, though I can see a bed through the doorway on the other side of the room. He walks to the couch and sets me down. "Do not move."

"Hades."

"Persephone, I swear to the gods, if you don't obey me this once, I will tie you down and feed you by hand." Hades points a blunt finger at me. "Do not fucking move from that couch." Then he's gone, sweeping out of the room.

I stick my tongue out at the closed door. "Drama queen."

The temptation to snoop is nearly overwhelming, but I don't think he's bluffing with his threat to tie me down, so I manage to stifle my curiosity and sit still. Hades doesn't make me wait long. Less than ten minutes later, the door opens and he stalks through, followed by half a dozen people.

I can feel my eyes going wider and wider as one of them sets up a little table in front of me and the other five place takeout food from five different restaurants on it. "What is this, Hades? Did you steal someone's food to have it here this fast?" Then the sheer amount registers. "I can't possibly eat *all* of this."

He waits for his people to file out and then shuts the door. "You will eat *some* of it."

"That's so wasteful."

"Please. My people love leftovers to a truly unholy degree. The remainder of the food won't last the day once you're finished." He rearranges the cartons on the table and pushes the whole thing closer to me. "Eat."

A not-insignificant part of me wants to resist just for the sake of resisting. But that's shortsighted. If I'm light-headed, it means I need calories, and there's a feast of them right in front of me. That's simple logic. I still glare at him. "Stop staring at me while I try to eat."

"Gods forbid." He strides to the desk on the other side of the room. It's smaller than I expected, though the dark wood and figures carved into its legs give it a dramatic flair. The first chance I get, I'm going to be on the floor trying to figure out what those carvings depict. To see if they match the style of the columns on the buildings.

This isn't where he conducts actual work. There's no way. Hades seems anal enough to prefer his work space clean and organized, but this is too pristine to be used day in and day out. More than that, his room is right through the door in the corner. No one conducts meetings that close to where they sleep. It would be foolish in the extreme.

Which doesn't quite explain why he brought me *here* instead of to one of the many other rooms in the house.

I set the thought away, and as I examine my options for food, my mind goes back to the greenhouse. Annoyance at how overbearing Hades is or no, I can't ignore the fact that he gave me the barest glimpse behind the curtain. That place is special to him and he allowed me access to it, plans to *continue* to allow me access to it. For someone as obviously closed in as Hades, it's a gift of the highest order.

I'm not sure it means anything, but it feels like it does. If he can trust me that much, I suppose I can attempt to stop being such a pain in his ass, at least when it comes to taking care of myself. Even if I kind of like the way Hades gets overprotective and growly.

I'm sure I can find another way to poke at him.

In fact, I have several ideas already.

HADES

PERSEPHONE HAS PUT ME IN AN UNENVIABLE POSITION.
She's right—we need to get the word out that we're together sooner
rather than later—but she's also proving time and time again that
she will put her health and safety last in her long list of priorities.
Those fuckers in the upper city might applaud her for that, but
down here, it means I can't trust her to be honest with me. Which
means I could harm her if I'm not careful.

I don't want to be careful. Fuck, but I've never been so
close to losing control with another person before. Every smart
comment out of those pretty pink lips and sign of arch amusement in those hazel eyes makes me want to drag her down into
the dark with me. To divine all her darkest, filthiest fantasies that
she's barely been able to admit to herself she wants...and then
give them to her.

That doesn't explain why I took her to the greenhouse, though.
That place has nothing to do with reputation or sex. It's one of
my few refuges. I only took her there because it seems like she

could use a little refuge right now, too. That's it. Simple, really. No reason to look further into it.

I flip a page in the book in my hands and watch her eat out of the corner of my eye. Her motions are short and irritated, but she's stopped staring at me like she wants to stab me with her fork.

It takes longer than I expect before she sits back with a sigh. "I can't eat another bite."

I ignore her and turn another page. It's going to be a pain in the ass to go back and figure out where I actually was in this book, because I'm sure as hell not reading it right now. Persephone huffs out a low curse that almost, *almost* makes me smile and slouches back against the couch.

Within five minutes, she's snoring softly.

I shake my head and stand. How in the gods' name did she manage to make it this far while ignoring her most basic needs? Her mother has been Demeter for years. A person can only charge blindly ahead for so long before everything collapses around them. Apparently no one taught Persephone that lesson.

I send a text to Charon, and a few minutes later, he and two others appear to silently take the food away. I pull a throw blanket out from the small chest tucked against the wall and drape it over Persephone. She looks smaller in sleep. That has instincts I thought nonexistent rising to the fore. Then again, everything about this woman fucks with my instincts.

I watch her sleep for a few moments, measuring her breathing. She's fine. I know she's fine. I don't know why I'm so sure the moment I turn around, she's going to be rappelling down the side of my house or creating chaos.

My original plans for tonight need an update, which means I need to make a few calls.

By the time Persephone wakes a few hours later, I have things in motion to my satisfaction. She sits up like someone fired a gun next to her head and blinks at me. "I fell asleep."

"Yes."

"Why did you let me fall asleep?"

She sounds so accusing that I almost smile. Again. "You needed it. You have an hour to get ready. Juliette already sent over a few things for tonight. They're on my bed." When she just stares at me, I make a shooing motion. "You're so determined to convince me that you're fine. Unless you really aren't feeling up to this..."

"I'm fine." She nearly gets tangled up in the blanket as she stands but manages to right herself before she takes a tumble. Persephone gives me a sharp look. "I have my own room, you know."

The longer she's here, the harder it is to remember that she's not *really* mine to protect. I've promised her safety, yes, but the mundane day-to-day things don't fall under that umbrella. Unless I want them to. I have no business telling her that she's staying in my room going forward, no matter how appealing I find the idea. "Get ready."

She frowns but finally moves into my bedroom. Persephone pauses just inside the door. "If I take too long, are you going to kick down the door because you're sure I've collapsed?"

It's a good thing I don't feel guilt, or I might be blushing. "You have a history of ignoring your body's needs. And that's in the last forty-eight hours alone."

"That's what I thought." She gives me a positively angelic smile; if I had hackles, they'd be raised seeing that. Persephone bites her bottom lip. "Why don't we save the dramatic entrance? You can play guard dog and supervise at the same time." She presses her fingers to her temple. "I'm not in danger of passing out, but one can never be too sure, right?"

Heat courses through me, and I have to lock myself down to resist taking a step toward her. "You wouldn't be trying to tempt me into losing control, would you?"

"Of course not." She turns and there's definitely a little more swing in her step than there was earlier. As I watch, Persephone pulls her sweater over her head and drops it on the floor. She's not wearing anything underneath it.

Even as I tell myself to hold firm, I follow her into my bedroom. She pauses in the doorway to the bathroom and works her leggings off, bending at the waist. *Fuck.* I am treated to the sight of her round ass and then she disappears into the bathroom.

Following her in there is a mistake. She's attempting to top from the bottom again, and if I let her direct this...

I'm having a hard time remembering why I need to keep control. She might light the spark that turns us into an inferno, but I'm too dominant to let her drive things for long. I'm also self-aware enough to realize when I'm making excuses. That knowledge isn't enough to keep me from following her into the bathroom.

Persephone meanders into the walk-in shower as if she isn't temptation personified. I like that she's not the least bit self-conscious about being naked in front of me. That she's fearless enough to grab the tiger by the tail. Fuck, I kind of like *her*.

"Persephone."

She stops and glances over her shoulder at me. "Yes, Sir?"

She knows exactly what she's doing to me, and the little brat is enjoying every moment. Truth be told, I am, too. I take a position on the bench near the entrance of the shower, well out of the water's spray. "Come here."

Her smile is nothing less than radiant. She waltzes back to me and stops right before her knees touch mine. She's a golden goddess with long, blond hair, her body a temptation I have no intention of ignoring. "Yes, Sir?"

"Your mouth is being obedient, but your actions aren't."

She does that adorable lip-biting thing again, her eyes dancing. "I suppose that means you want to reward my mouth."

That surprises a laugh out of me. It feels as rusty as it sounds, but I like the way her lips curve in response. It's not her beaming sunshine smile. No, this expression is genuine amusement. I snort. "I'm not remotely surprised you jumped to that conclusion."

She leans forward a little, putting her rosy nipples right at eye level. "Do I get to name my reward?"

I shake my head slowly. "You're wasting time. Shower, Persephone."

She hesitates a beat, as if I've surprised her, and then moves to obey. Within a few seconds, hot steam is curling around me. She steps beneath the spray and runs her hands over her body slowly. Teasing me. Teasing herself. I don't know which is her main goal, but it doesn't matter. My cock is so hard, I can barely think straight enough to remember why I can't touch her. Not yet.

If I start, I won't be able to stop. Last night was my limit. If she wasn't practically begging for my cock, I might have a better chance of resisting, but Persephone wants this even more than I do, which is something I didn't think possible twenty-four hours ago. Now? I don't trust us together. If I drag this woman to my bed, we won't surface for days, weeks even. It might result in a whole hell of a lot of pleasure, but it won't do a damn thing to strike at the heart of Zeus. What the rest of Olympus doesn't know won't hurt him.

Which is the problem.

Persephone plucks her nipples and skates her hands down her stomach. I'm already shaking my head. "No."

"No?"

"You heard what I said."

She props her hands on her hips. "You want me."

"Yes."

"Then *take* me."

Yeah, it's official. I like her. I bite back a grin. "I will. When I'm ready." I push slowly to my feet. "You seem to have things well in hand. Don't take too long. Whether you're ready or not, we leave in..." I check my watch. "Forty minutes. So you'd better hurry."

Her curses follow me into the bedroom. It's only then that I allow myself to grin. I didn't expect to tango with her, let alone to enjoy it so much. I head back into the study and sit down to wait.

Thirty-eight minutes later, Persephone sweeps into the room. "Tell me the truth, Hades. You have a Princess Leia fetish, don't you?"

I stare at her. Speechless. I'm fucking *speechless*. She's twisted her hair up into a style that looks almost like a crown, and she's wearing the clothing I set out for her. It's a bra and panty set that would be mundane if not for the silk straps that crisscross around her breasts and waist and hips. I can admit that skirt is strikingly similar to Leia's bikini costume, with a long, sheer panel in the back and a narrow one in the front.

She looks like a present I can't wait to unwrap.

I make a spinning motion with my finger. Persephone huffs but obeys, turning slowly. Both the bra and panties are technically full coverage but they're lace and give a tantalizing peek-a-boo to both nipples and pussy. I want her on my mouth, and I want it now.

By the time she faces me again, I have myself under control. Mostly. I stand and hold out my hand. "I have something special planned tonight."

"I should hope so. It took me a full twenty minutes to get into this thing." She tugs on one of the straps and winces. Each step she takes toward me puts her legs on display. She's magnificent. I cast a look at her feet, and she quickly cuts in before I can say anything. "I have small bandages on. I didn't need the large ones."

It's tempting to check, but the fiery look in her eyes says she's just waiting for me to try so she can tear me a new one. I'm not willing to say I've been overly careful with her, not when apparently I have to be careful for both of us, but I plan to keep a close eye on her tonight. The thought makes me smile. "Let's go."

We walk out of the room together to find Charon waiting. He flicks a glance over Persephone but keeps his attention on me. "We're ready."

I don't entertain as often as I used to. There are other locations around the lower city that cater to the rich and kinky who are looking to get their rocks off playing on the dark side. *My* home isn't open to just anyone; it's strictly invite only. There was a time in my early twenties where I didn't give a fuck who showed up, my recklessness giving my parties nearly legendary status, which only added to the myth of Hades. That was a long time ago. Now, I pick and choose who walks through those doors.

Tonight, I've loosened the reins a bit, have picked a select few names off the long waiting list. Charon and my other people will ensure the new invitees stay in the appropriate places and don't get any funny ideas about snooping. "Two people at the door?"

"Yes, Hades."

"More at the other entrances."

He doesn't roll his eyes, but he looks like he wants to. "We went over the entire plan earlier. I've followed it to your specifications. We're all good. No one will end up where you don't want them."

It doesn't feel like enough, but it will have to do. "Good."

We make our way down to the door I showed Persephone yesterday. It's so glossy, it's almost a mirror as we approach, and the reflection of me in my suit and her in that outfit... Persephone is a pretty present—a pretty captive—and I'm the scary fucker who will cut down anyone who tries to take her from me.

I give myself a mental shake. No use thinking like that. She might be mine for the duration, but she's not really *mine*. She's not for keeping. I can't afford to forget that, not even for a second.

Charon takes up position next to the door. I adjust Persephone's hand against the bend in my arm. "We're about to have an audience. It'll be real this time."

She takes a deep breath. "I'm ready."

She's not, but that's part of what tonight is about. Easing her into it. Staking my claim, yes, but doing so in a way that doesn't throw her into the deep end to drown. "I'm your anchor. Remember that."

Her lips quirk like she wants to make a smart-ass response, but she finally nods. "I can be obedient."

I laugh. Fuck, that's four times in a twenty-four-hour period. I ignore the surprised look Charon sends me and nod at the door. "Let's go."

Walking into the room is always a bit like walking into another world, but tonight the effect is more pronounced. The lights are all lowered, making the room appear larger than it really is. Persephone nailed it on the head yesterday; it really is the antithesis to Zeus's banquet hall. The silvery light cast onto the ceiling by the water gives the impression that we're somewhere below the surface of the world. A true Underworld fantasy.

The lights aren't fully lighting up the dais yet. That will be the signal that the show is about to begin. Right now, people are mingling on the couches and chairs. Some chatting, some already getting their own little parties started. The rules of the upper city don't apply here, and the people invited to cross the river tend to throw themselves into pleasure with a reckless abandon.

I slow down, giving Persephone time to acclimate to the lower lighting. Giving our guests time to see us, to realize that things are finally getting started. Eyes turn our way, and a low murmur surges through the room when they realize who's on my arm.

I guide Persephone to the dark throne situated against the wall in the center of the room. It's dramatic as fuck and absolutely ridiculous, but it serves its purpose. A king is only king if everyone around him acknowledges it. I might never set foot in the upper city again, but it advances my interests to remind every single person in this room who rules *here*.

I have a reputation to uphold, after all.

I sink into the chair and pull Persephone down to sit on my lap. She's so rigid, I might as well have a statue perched on my thighs. I raise a brow. "You're going to be sore if you don't relax."

"Everyone is staring," she says out of the corner of her mouth.

"That's the point."

She looks at her clasped hands, her jaw tight. "I know that's the point, but knowing it and experiencing it are two very different things."

This right here is why I changed my initial plans for the night. She's too fucking fearless—she rushes forward even when her mind and body are screaming at her to slow down. I sink back farther into the chair, taking her with me. At first, she resists, but when I give her a significant look, she allows me to arrange her so that she's leaning against my chest. "The show's starting soon." And then she'll be too distracted to worry about everyone else in the room.

"*What* show?"

I allow myself a smile and loosely wrap an arm around her waist. Throughout the room, the lights dim the tiniest amount, and the ones aimed at the center dais brighten a little. "Do you remember being on display?"

"Of course. It happened yesterday."

I settle her more firmly on my lap. Another night, it would serve my interests to keep her off-center, but I want her at ease. "You won't be up there tonight."

I don't miss the way her muscles subtly loosen. I know the idea of being watched turns her on, but she's also new to this. Being thrust into the center would be too much, too soon, and I can't deny that I very much want her to enjoy this time with me. "I won't?"

"No. Now relax and enjoy the show," I murmur in her ear. "It's just for you."

PERSEPHONE

HOW AM I SUPPOSED TO FOCUS ON THE "SHOW" WHEN Hades is touching me *everywhere*? His thighs are hard beneath mine, his chest solid at my back, his arm an iron band across my hips that I don't mind in the least. I shift a little just to feel the tension of him holding me down without holding me down.

"Be still."

I shift again just to be contrary and then live to regret my decision when I feel his hard cock against my ass. A temptation I am not allowed to indulge in, at least not yet. I thought I could entice him into changing his mind in the shower, but I should have known better. Hades hasn't wavered. If I couldn't convince him to take me while naked and wet, I certainly don't have a shot now, intricate lingerie or no.

I'm temporarily distracted by two people stepping onto the dais. A white man and plus-sized white woman I don't recognize. He's wearing a pair of low-slung leather pants and she's got on nothing at all. There have to be nearly fifty people in the room, but he's only got eyes for her. I can't hear what they say to each other from here, but she sinks gracefully to her knees as if the motion is pure muscle memory.

An answering pulse goes through me, a deep recognition. I relax back against Hades and turn my head slightly. "Who are they?"

"Does it matter? Eyes forward. Pay attention."

I huff out a breath and turn back to the dais. The man presses his finger beneath the woman's chin and tilts her head up. Whatever he says has a beatific smile pulling at her lips. He hasn't *done* anything yet, but I'm enraptured despite myself. He moves a few steps away, and that's when I notice there's a bag at the edge of the dais. The man grabs a corded length of rope and begins to bind his partner.

It's *almost* enough to miss the fact that heads are still turning in our direction. I can't see most of the audience clearly because of the shadows, but there's no mistaking a low murmur that started when we arrived and hasn't abated. I catch my name spoken and have to fight not to tense.

There's no going back now.

There never was.

I close my eyes for a long moment, fighting against the fluttering feeling in my chest. I chose this. I will continue to choose this. And a small, forbidden part of me enjoys the attention, enjoys the shock I know some of these people are experiencing. I want to keep shocking them.

I take a slow breath and refocus on the couple on the dais. He's halfway through binding his partner already. Every twist, every line he visually cuts across her curvy body, has tension winding tighter and tighter through me. It's like watching an artist create a masterpiece except the masterpiece is another person and the obvious desire between the two of them pulses with each minute that ticks past. My breath gets choppy, and I have to fight my body's urge to shift against Hades.

His lips touch the curve of my ear. "Is it the bondage or the exhibition making you all hot and jealous?"

"Everyone is watching," I whisper back. "We can see *all* of her." At least we can now that he's bound her legs wide and is working on a series of knots between her thighs. The flush spreading across her skin says that she's enjoying experiencing it even more than I'm enjoying watching.

Hades shifts, moving to lightly drag his fingertips across my stomach. It takes me several seconds to realize he's tracing the straps crisscrossing my body and another few seconds to make the connection between what I'm clothed in and the scene playing out before us. His breath ghosts against my neck. "I'm going to touch you now."

"You *are* touching me." I don't know why I'm arguing, acting as if I'm not holding my breath to keep from begging him to touch me more.

"Persephone." A tiny bit of censure mixed with amusement. "Tell me you won't get off harder than you did last night if I finger you right here in front of everyone... Tell me and I'll stop."

I can't say it without lying. I suddenly want him to take me onto that stage, to bend me over a chair or just throw me to the floor and fuck me right there with so many eyes on us. There are *already* eyes on us, even if they can't see us any clearer than I can see them. Will they notice Hades slipping his hand into my panties? Do I want them to?

Yes.

I carefully shift back and move my arms down to press against his hips. The new position leaves my body completely open to him. I swallow and strive for a nice, contrite tone instead of a demand. "Please touch me, Hades."

"You are singularly motivated with your pleasure on the line." He chuckles against my shoulder. Despite my damn near begging, he doesn't pick up his pace. He drags his middle finger along the strap spanning my waist. "Half the eyes in this place are on you, Persephone."

I shiver, pressing my hands harder to his hips in an effort to keep still. "Well, we're sending a message, aren't we?"

"Yes. Look around." If he were a literal demon on my shoulder, he couldn't be more tempting. Hades drops his hand another inch until his pinkie finger brushes the top of my panties through the front of the skirt.

Sure enough, he's right. Despite the low light, I can clearly see that half the people in the room are watching *us* and not the couple on the dais. It almost feels like *they* are here to boost *my* pleasure. Didn't I imagine eyes on me when Hades had me strip yesterday? When we stood on that same dais and he made me come so hard my legs shook? It turns out the real thing is exponentially hotter.

Hades's beard tickles my bare shoulder. "Sheer skirt. Lace panties. They're going to be able to see everything I do to your pretty pussy. Are you prepared for that?"

Am I prepared for it?

I'm pretty sure I might expire on the spot if he doesn't follow through on the lustful spell he's weaving about me. I lick my lips and fight not to lift my hips to guide his hand lower. "Yes, Sir."

He presses a kiss to my shoulder. "Say the word and this all stops. No harm, no foul."

For someone so determined to be labeled a monster, he's incredibly invested in my pleasure and consent. A thrill of power licks through me. I'm not in charge. Not by any stretch of the imagination. But the knowledge that no matter what Hades does to me, *I* am choosing it? It's beyond sexy. "I know. I trust you."

The barest hesitation, as if I've surprised him. "Good." Still, he moves slowly, gliding his hand down to cup my pussy through the skirt. The fabric is so thin as to not exist at all, and I can't help a small jump at the heat of his palm. He gives a low curse. "I can feel how wet you are."

"Do something about it."

He tightens his grip, holding me in that intimate place like he owns me. "One day, you'll learn to stop trying to top from the bottom." He moves his free hand to my right breast and yanks the lace down, baring me to the room. I jerk back, but his chest gives me nowhere to go and his hand between my legs follows me, pressing my body more firmly against his. Then Hades repeats the treatment to my left breast. I'm still covered in the silk straps, but my nipples are bare and on display. He makes a low tsking sound. "Just for that defiance, I'm going to make you come, loud and messy, right here in front of them."

It doesn't even occur to me to cover my breasts. Instead, I spread my legs a little wider. "Do your worst."

"My worst, Persephone?" His voice gets lower, almost a growl. "You dip one toe into the water and think you're ready to swim the length of the River Styx. You can't begin to handle what my *worst* has to offer." He finally moves his hand up, only to shove it into my panties and spear me with two fingers. The contact bows my back, but his other hand is there, bracketing my throat and holding me in place. "Can you feel their eyes on you?"

I want to keep defying him, but my brain has gone all fuzzy with pleasure. He's not even fucking me with his fingers. He's holding me down, possessing me in a way I've never experienced before. Like he's staking his claim in front of an entire room of witnesses in the most primitive way possible. *No, the most primitive way possible would be to bend me over this chair and fuck me until I scream.* I shiver. "Yes," I gasp. "I can feel them watching."

"Do you know what they see?" He doesn't move, just pins me to him. "They see a monster about to devour a pretty princess. They see me taking one of their own and dragging her down into the dark with me. I'm ruining you before their very eyes."

"Good," I whisper fiercely. "Ruin me, Hades. I want you to."

"You're clenching around me." His voice has gone deeper yet. "You like this."

"Of course I do." Hades shifts his hand, his palm rubbing against my clit, and suddenly words are pouring from my lips. "I like you staking your claim on me."

"Is that what I'm doing?" He finally begins to move his hand, his searching fingers finding my G-spot and stroking it lightly.

"Isn't it?" I have to fight not to lift my hips, fight not to moan. "Staking your claim. Tarnishing me. Warning off everyone else."

"Persephone." He says my name like it's a song he's recently memorized. "Who said anything about warning off everyone else?" He nips my earlobe lightly. "What if I want to share? What if I pull your panties to the side and let whoever is interested come over here and fuck you against my chest?"

My entire body clenches, but I'm too dazed to decide if it's in protest or desire. "You'd do that?"

He goes still for one endless moment. Then Hades curses and pulls me up so I'm sitting crosswise on his lap. He grips my hair with one hand and knocks my legs wide with his other elbow. Then he stops messing around. Each stroke of his fingers drives me closer to the edge. "No, little Persephone. Sharing isn't my kink. I'll be the only one touching you. Your pussy is mine until it's not, and I'm not wasting a single moment by gifting it to someone else."

Crude words.

Sexy words.

I reach up with a shaking hand to cup his neck. "Hades?"

"Yeah?" He slows his strokes, adds his thumb into the mix, tracing devastating circles around my clit. "You want something."

I forget to be coy. I forget the rules. I forget everything but the edge of pleasure bearing down on me, a wave I'm suddenly certain will drown me if I'm not careful. There's nothing left but perfect honesty. "I want you."

"You love your words so much. Use them."

"Fuck me," I breathe. "Fuck me in front of them. Show every

single one of them who I belong to." I need to stop, to keep the words in, but I can't with him touching me like this. "Yours, Hades. Not Zeus's. Never his."

Something like conflict dances across his face, there and gone as quickly as moonlight flickering across choppy water. "I haven't decided if you've earned it."

I might laugh if I had the air. I drag my hand down his chest to press against his cock. "Punish me later if you want to. Just give us what we both need now." I'm distantly aware of the sound of sex coming from the dais, the slapping of flesh against flesh, but I only have eyes for Hades. "Please." I kiss him. He tastes of whiskey and sin, a temptation I want to embrace fully. My reasons for agreeing to this bargain start to feel distant in this moment, with lust pounding through my body. I need him. I need him more than food, more than water, more than *air*. I lightly drag my teeth over his bottom lip. "*Please*, Hades."

"You're going to be the death of me," he mutters.

Before I can come up with a response for that, he withdraws his fingers. There's a rip and the front of my skirt is gone. Another vicious yank and my panties follow. I blink up at him and he gives a wicked grin. "Second-guessing yourself?"

"Not in the least." I don't need his urging to move to straddle him. I'm in danger of grinding away at his cock through his slacks like a sex-drugged monster. I barely, *barely* manage to hold myself off him. "Condoms?"

"Mmmm." He reaches down the side of the chair and comes up with a foil package. I expect... I'm not sure. I should know better than to try to anticipate Hades at this point. He presses the condom into my hand and nudges me back enough for him to undo his slacks.

I rip open the condom as he draws his cock out. I lick my lips. "Promise me that soon I get to have you naked."

"No."

I glare, but it feels half-hearted at best. I'm too eager for him. It takes less than no time to roll the condom over his hard length. He grabs my hip with one hand, holding me in place until I look at him. "What?"

"No going back if you do this. If you ride my cock with them watching, they'll really believe you're mine."

The words feel serious, full of layers I can't delve into with my body practically weeping with need for him. Tomorrow. I'll figure it all out tomorrow. "Yes, you've said that." I'm suddenly afraid that he's going to change his mind. I suspect there will be an orgasm for me either way, but I want his cock inside me too much to play fair. I lean down until my lips brush the shell of his ear. "Take what's yours, Hades. I want you to."

"You aren't a princess. You're a fucking siren." He yanks me forward and then he's inside me. I can barely breathe as he drags me down his cock, filling me almost uncomfortably full.

"Oh, gods."

"They have nothing to do with it." He looks furious and turned on and yet he's still nowhere near as rough as I suddenly need him to be. "This is what you wanted, little siren. My cock inside you." Just like that, he releases me and drapes his arms over the chair, looking every inch the indulgent king. "Ride me, Persephone. Use me to make yourself come."

Shock stills me. Having sex in front of a roomful of people is one thing when he's right there with me, but he's forcibly putting distance between us even if he hasn't moved an inch. Suddenly, *I'm* the one on display, rather than *us* being on display.

I...like it.

Not a single person can watch this scene and think that I'm anything but an enthusiastic participant. Hades has to know that, has to know how much that will matter. Fucking him here, like this, is as good as screaming to all of Olympus that I truly am his.

I slide my hands up his chest, wishing I was feeling skin instead of his shirt. Another time. And there *will* be other times. I grip his shoulders and begin to move. No matter how frantic my pulse beats through me, I want this to last.

Because it's a show, yes, but more importantly, because it's our first time. I don't want this to end too soon.

I ride him slowly, working myself up and down his cock, winding my pleasure higher and higher. It's not enough and yet is too much at the same time. More. I need more. Endlessly more.

As much as I want to close the distance and kiss Hades again, the way he's watching me is too intoxicating. His gaze travels over my body in a sweep I can almost feel against my skin. Drinking in the sight of me fucking him even as his hands clench the arms of the chair. He might have the cold mask in place, but he's fighting not to touch me.

I hold his gaze and lean back, bracing my hands on his thighs and arching my back, putting my breasts on display. A distant part of me is aware that I'm putting on a show for more than him, but right now, he's the only one I care about. "See something you like?"

"A mouthy brat."

My orgasm dances closer. I feel like Hades and I are playing a game of chicken, barreling toward each other to see who will bend first. I've always, always bent in the past. With my family, with the Thirteen, with *everything*. Bend so they don't break me, keeping my eyes on the horizon.

I won't do it now. I refuse.

I bite my bottom lip and slow down further, circling my hips in tiny, agonizingly good rotations. "Hades."

"Mmmm?"

My breathing hitches and he watches my breasts rise and fall with the move. It takes me two tries to find the words. "You have a threat to follow through on."

"Do I?" He arches that damn eyebrow. "Feel free to remind me."

"You said you'd make me come, loud and messy, right in front of everyone." I can't quite dredge up my normal sunshine smile. "That you'd take me in a way that shows everyone here that I'm yours."

His body tenses beneath me. "I did, didn't I?" He has me up and off his cock before I register his movement. I don't get a chance to protest before Hades turns me around and guides me down onto him again. With my legs on either side of his thighs, I'm facing the room and spread wide open. His hand is at my throat again, thumb stroking the sensitive skin as his voice growls in my ear. "Would hate for them to miss the rest of the show."

On the dais, the man has the woman facedown on the ground, tied and helpless, as he fucks her from behind. The blissful expression on her pretty face is matched only by the look of utter concentration on his. It's sexy as hell.

But most of the people I can make out are turned *our* way. They're watching me fucking Hades, watching him touch me as he drives my pleasure higher.

Hades skates his hand down my stomach and lightly circles my clit. "Don't stop. Take what you need."

My exhale comes out almost like a sob. It's a little harder to ride him like this, but I make do. Every move has his fingers sliding against my clit, but he's forcing me to do all the work. In this position, there's no ignoring how many people are watching us. The attention only makes me hotter, more desperate. "Hades, please."

"Don't beg me for it. Take it."

I'm having an out-of-body experience and yet I'm suddenly sure I can feel every single nerve ending individually. His strength at my back, his arms anchoring me in place as I fuck him, the attention of so many people… It's all creating an experience unlike any I've had before. I brace my hands on the chair and roll my body, riding his cock, rubbing my clit against his fingers. Pleasure coils tighter and tighter through me, so intense I have to close my eyes. A held breath, a feeling of being tipped over the edge, and then I'm coming harder than I ever have before. Words pour out of my mouth, but I'm too overwhelmed to understand what I'm saying. All I know is that I never want this to stop.

Nothing lasts forever.

The cresting waves slowly recede, Hades's gentle touch bringing me back to earth. He slides out of me and shifts me enough to tuck his cock away, but I'm incapable of doing more than allowing him to move me to his will. When he finally gathers me into his lap, I rest my head against his chest and exhale slowly. "Um."

His laugh rumbles my cheek. "Yes?"

I'm not sure what I'm supposed to say. Thank him? Ask him if he dosed me with some magical aphrodisiac because I've never orgasmed like *that* before? Accuse him of playing dirty? I cuddle closer. "You didn't come."

"No, I didn't."

Something like insecurity winds through me, dampening the deliciously weightless feeling in my bones. "Why not?"

He strokes a hand down my spine. "Because I'm nowhere near done with you yet."

HADES

THERE'S NOTHING I WANT MORE THAN TO CARRY Persephone up to my room and finish what we've started. Even though I should know better by now, she surprised me again. I want to keep learning her, to find every single fantasy she has so I can make her come over and over again.

Unfortunately, the night is far from over. We've had our fun. Now it's time for politics.

I can't help pressing a kiss to her temple. "The show's almost over."

"At least one of them already is." She nuzzles my chest like a cat seeking pets. It makes my heart give an uncomfortable thud. She's closed her eyes and cuddled into me like I'm her favorite blanket. It's...cute.

"Persephone." I put just enough bite into my tone to get her to look at me. "We have to play court, at least for a little while. That's what tonight is all about." Except it was all too easy to forget that once I got inside her. The room faded away until all I could see was her.

Her brows draw together and she sighs. "I knew it was too much to ask to just keep fucking until dawn."

I have to fight down a smile. "I think we can spare the time this will take."

"Uh-huh." She fiddles with one of the buttons of my shirt and gives me a sly look. "I don't suppose you'll make it up to me later?"

"You're impossible."

"You're the only one who seems to bring out that side of me."

I like that, in a perverse sort of way. Persephone might get under my skin like no one I've ever met but I enjoy our bantering more than I have a right to. I enjoy a lot of things about Persephone. I'm saved from having to come up with a response by the lights coming up a bit and a white man approaching. He's breathtakingly beautiful, his features so perfect it almost hurts to look at him. Square jaw, sensual lips, a wild riot of curly blond hair on his head. He looks too pretty to take seriously, but he's Aphrodite's son. I know for a fact that he handles unsavory tasks for her so she can keep her hands pristine. He's dangerous in the extreme.

I tap a finger against Persephone's hip and lean back. "Eros."

He grins, teeth white and straight. "Thank you for the show." His gaze slides to Persephone. "You've pissed off a lot of people in the upper city."

She shifts in my lap. I wait for her to blush, to stammer, to do something to signal her regret for letting things go so far in front of others. She's never done anything like we just did; having sex in front of an audience is a big fucking deal to a sheltered princess like Persephone. I start to verbally step in to save her.

She surprises me yet again. Her voice goes sickly sweet and coated in poison. "Funny, but a lot of people in the upper city have pissed *me* off."

His grin doesn't falter, though his blue eyes are cold. "Zeus is furious, and it's in everyone's best interest to keep him happy."

"I have no interest in keeping Zeus happy." She gives her sunshine smile. "Do be a dear and give Aphrodite my regards. She's been managing Zeus this long. I'm sure she's more than capable of managing him a bit longer."

That kills Eros's smile. He looks down at her like he's never seen her before. I can understand the sentiment. He whistles softly. "Looks like someone underestimated Demeter's perfect daughter."

Persephone's voice gains a hard edge. "Be sure and tell them that, too, when you deliver your report for tonight."

Eros holds up his hands, his easy grin returning. It's a mask, but nowhere near as good as Persephone's. "Tonight, I'm just here to enjoy myself."

Tonight. It's the barest of reassurances. I hold his gaze. "Then enjoy yourself...tonight. But remember whose hospitality you're currently benefiting from."

He tips an imaginary hat to me and moves away. A couple on a couch on the other side of the dais wave at him, and he joins them. Within a few seconds, they're stripping him to participate in the fun. I look down to find Persephone watching with a frown. She nibbles her bottom lip. "You know he's here as a spy."

"Better than him being here to act out Aphrodite's vengeance." Something he's rumored to do on the regular.

She looks around the room, and I can practically see her mind whirling as she's finally able to make out the faces of the crowd. "There are a lot more people from the upper city here than I expected. People who attend the same parties I used to."

"Yes." I wind a strand of her blond hair around my fingers, waiting for her to work through whatever she's chewing on.

"They *knew* you were here. Why are you only a rumor if all these people know you exist?"

I stroke my thumb over her hair. "That's an easy question and a complicated answer. The simplified version is that Zeus has a vested interest in keeping me a myth."

She looks at me. "Because it gives him more power. Poseidon mostly keeps to his territory around the docks and doesn't have the patience for politicking. You're the only other legacy title. Without you in the mix, there's no one to stand in the way of Zeus playing king of all Olympus."

Smart little siren.

"Yes." All the other Thirteen answer to Zeus in their way. Not a single one of them can bring forth the power that one of the legacy titles can. Not even Demeter, with her control of the city's food supply, or Ares with his small army of private contract soldiers.

When Persephone keeps frowning, I give her hair a gentle tug. "What else?"

"It's just so...hypocritical. In the upper city, it's all purity culture and pretending that they're above such base human needs, putting value on denying themselves. Then they come down here and take advantage of your hospitality to play the kind of sex games that would get them exiled from their social circles and publicly shamed." She looks around the room. "Though it's not only sex games, is it? They come to the lower city for a number of things they don't want others to know about."

It doesn't really surprise me that Persephone connects the dots so quickly, not when she's already proven to have a sly mind behind that persona of pretty fluff. "If their sins happen in the dark, do they even count?"

Her expression is downright ferocious. "They use you and then they tuck you back into the shadows and pretend you're a boogeyman. It's not right."

That strange pulse in my chest strengthens. I think I'm speechless. It's the only explanation for me staring at her like I've never seen her before. That's not only it, though. I've seen her fierce as fuck, but she's never directed that in defense of *me*. It's strange and novel and I don't know what to do with it.

Thankfully, I'm saved from having to come up with a response by Hermes and Dionysus strolling up. Since the shows—official and unofficial—are finished, everyone around us are in various states of undress and beginning scenes. Not these two. They always show up, but Hermes is the only one who ever participates, if rarely. For Dionysus's part, his vices don't include sex of any flavor.

Dionysus points at a chair occupied by two women. "Move."

They move, taking themselves a few feet away, and he drags the chair over to ours. "Nice party."

"Glad you like it," I say drily. He drops into the chair and Hermes perches on the arm of it. She runs her fingers through Dionysus's hair absently, but her dark eyes are shrewd. I sigh. "Yes, Hermes?"

"You know I don't like to tell you how to live your life."

"When has that ever stopped you?" I feel Persephone tense like a coiled snake, and I smooth my hands down her body, tucking her more firmly against me—and banding an arm around her waist. I don't *think* my little siren will physically attack someone, let alone one of the Thirteen, but I didn't expect her to cut Eros down so efficiently, either. She's full of surprises, which shouldn't delight me nearly as much as it does.

Dionysus wraps an arm around Hermes's waist and tilts his head so she has better access to keep up her absent stroking. No matter how relaxed he appears, he's just as sober and shrewd as she is right now. "You're poking the bear, my friend. Are you prepared for what happens next?"

It shouldn't be possible that both Hermes and Dionysus are *more* dramatic when they're sober than when they're drunk. And yet here we are. "Not all of us make decisions on the fly."

"You know, when we said you should loosen up, we didn't exactly mean you should bang Zeus's fiancée in front of fifty people who are frothing at the mouth to run back to the upper city and tell him what they've seen in explicit detail." Hermes adjusts her glasses. "Not us, of course. We don't indulge in spreading tales like that."

I snort. "If there's anyone in this room who believes that line, I have a nice oceanfront property in Ohio to sell them."

"Hades." She stops stroking Dionysus and sits up straight. "Was that a *joke?*" She points at Persephone. "What have you done to him? Three days and he's cracking jokes. It's weird and unnatural, and you both need to stop this immediately."

Persephone huffs out a breath. "Maybe you'd know he has a dry sense of humor if you stopped talking long enough to let him get a word in edgewise."

Hermes blinks slowly. "Um."

"And for another thing, if you're such good friends, maybe consider not running directly back to Zeus and tattling about everything you've seen here every time you visit. That kind of thing makes you a *terrible* friend, not a good one, no matter how many nights you end up drunkenly crashing at Hades's house."

Hermes does another slow blink. "Hades, I'm in love."

"Down, girl."

"That's *another* joke." She whoops and does a full body wiggle that forces Dionysus to move fast to keep her from toppling off the arm of the chair. "Oh my gods, I *love* her." She straightens and grins at Persephone. "You are seriously a delight."

Persephone turns to me. "I just yelled at her, and now she's talking about how much she loves me. What's wrong with her?"

"She's just Hermes." I shrug. "Carrying tales back and forth across the River Styx is part of her job. It's why all these people are here."

Persephone's cheeks gain two bright spots of color. "Right. I forgot for a second."

She forgot because she was so quick to rush to my defense. I don't get it. She has nothing to gain from defending me. She came to *me* for protection, not the other way around. Once again, Dionysus saves me from having to come up with a suitable response.

He laughs. "You should see how pissed Zeus is. He's playing

it cool in public, but rumor has it that he destroyed an entire room when he found out where you'd gone. When he realizes that you're riding Hades's cock for everyone to see?" He shakes his head. "Nuclear doesn't begin to cover it."

Persephone goes tense, and I don't have to see her face to know she's thinking about her sisters. She might have conflicted feelings about her mother, but from everything she's said and everything I've seen, the same cannot be said of the other Dimitriou sisters. If there's one pressure point Zeus has available to him, it's them. *Fuck*. I should have thought of that sooner. I can't send my people to keep them safe without violating the treaty, and there's no way Zeus will stand by if I allow them into my home. It's a problem I don't have a ready solution to, but I'll figure it out.

I press a kiss to her temple. "Tired?"

"Is that a euphemism for do I want to get out of here and go up to your room?" She twists just enough for her lips to brush mine. "If so, then *yes*. If not, then be prepared for me to convince you otherwise."

"I. Love. Her." Hermes claps. "Hades, you have to keep her. She's turning you human and you're turning her interesting, and it's been less than a week. Imagine how entertaining you'll both be in a year or five."

"Hermes." I sink enough warning into my tone to shock anyone to their senses.

Naturally, she ignores me. "Though I suppose if you tempt Zeus into striking, then we're looking at war, and that will put a damper on things."

Persephone turns back to her. "Wait, war? If he breaks the treaty, the Thirteen will come after him. That's how it works."

"Correction, that's how it's *supposed* to work." Hermes shrugs a shoulder. "The truth is that at least a third of them are Zeus's little minions and are heavily invested in keeping the status quo. They'll join with him to stomp Hades into oblivion if they think he's going to rock the boat."

"And the other two thirds?"

Another shrug. "Could go either way."

The information isn't exactly a surprise, though it's one hell of a disappointment. If *I'm* the one to step out of line, all of them will unite to bring me down without hesitation. Hermes and Dionysus might feel bad about it, but they'll fall in with the others when push comes to shove. Of course the same doesn't apply when it comes to that piece of shit Zeus.

I gather Persephone in my arms and stand, ignoring her protests that she can walk. Carrying her right now isn't about what she can and can't do. It's about what I want, about the small bit of comfort I'll allow myself. I have to think, and I can't do that here. Though I don't know what I hope to accomplish. We've already laid out our plan and jumped into a free fall. There's no going back now. No matter what the consequences are, we have to see this through to the end.

I just have to figure out how to ensure that I don't get everyone I am responsible for killed in the process.

PERSEPHONE

16

I'M STILL CHEWING OVER THE NEW INFORMATION AS Hades carries me out of the room. I protest being hauled around like this, but a small, secret part of me really likes it. I like a lot of things about Hades, truth be told. He's prickly and overbearing, but even after only a few days, I can see the truth of him.

"Hades." I lay my head against his shoulder and let the steady beat of his heart soothe me. "I know your secret."

He heads up the stairs. "What's that?"

"You snarl and snap and growl, but you've got an ooey-gooey center beneath the crusty exterior." I circle his top button with my forefinger. "You *care*. I think you actually care more than any of the other Thirteen, which is ironic considering the role you've been shoehorned into in Olympus."

"What makes you say that?" He's still not looking at me, but that's okay. It's actually easer to talk to him this way, without feeling like he can read my mind with a single intense look.

"You want Zeus to pay, but not at the expense of your people.

And they are *your* people. I've watched how you are with Georgie, and again with Juliette and Matthew. It's like that with everyone, isn't it? They would all walk through fire for you, and you protect them with your big, broody presence."

"I don't brood."

"You are the very definition of brooding."

He snorts. "Surely I don't care more than your mother. She's the one who ensures the entire city is fed and supplied with necessities."

"Yes, she is." Impossible to keep the bitterness out of my tone. "She's very good at her job, but she isn't doing it out of the charity of her soul. She's chasing power and prestige. The feeling of *enough* is always over the next horizon. She was going to sell me to Zeus. She won't see it that way, but it's what that engagement was—a transaction. She loves me, but it's secondary to everything else."

Hades doesn't immediately respond, and I look up to find him with a strange expression on his face. He looks almost...conflicted. I tense. "What do you know that I don't?"

"A number of things."

I refuse to be distracted by that half-assed joke. "Hades, please. We're in this together, one way or another, for the rest of the winter. Tell me."

The longer he hesitates, the more anxiety starts to creep in around the edges. He waits until we reach his bedroom and the door is closed between us and the rest of the house to finally answer. "Your mother passed along an ultimatum of sorts."

I don't know why I'm surprised. Of course she did. She's no more happy with me fleeing than Zeus is. All her careful plans wasted because of a disobedient daughter. She wouldn't be able to let that stand, not if she knows where I am. I wiggle until Hades carefully sets me on my feet. It doesn't leave me any steadier. "Tell me," I repeat.

"If I don't return you, she'll cut off supplies to the lower city."

I blink, waiting for the words to rearrange themselves into an order that makes sense. "But that's... There are thousands and thousands of people in the lower city. People who have nothing to do with you or me or the Thirteen."

"Yes," he says simply.

"She's threatening to starve them."

"Yes." He doesn't look away, doesn't do anything but give me the honesty I demand.

I wait, but he doesn't continue. Surely this is the end of it. Surely we can't move forward with this plan when so many people will be harmed. The barrier keeping Olympus separate from the rest of the world is too strong for people to leave for supplies, not to mention that part of Demeter's role is to negotiate favorable prices to ensure everyone has access to resources for well-balanced nutrition, regardless of their income. Without those supplies coming in, people will go hungry.

I can't believe she'd do this, but my mother doesn't bluff.

I take a slow breath. "I have to go back."

"Do you *want* to go back?"

I give a helpless little laugh. "The irony, if it can be called that, is that the one thing my mother and I have in common is the eye-on-the-horizon thing. All I want is to be free of this place and figure out who I am if I'm not Demeter's middle daughter. If I don't have to play a particular role to survive, what kind of person might I turn into?"

"Persephone—"

But I'm not listening. "I guess that makes me as selfish as her, doesn't it? We both want what we want, and we don't care who else has to bear the cost." I shake my head. "No. I won't do it. I won't let your people be hurt for my freedom."

"Persephone." Hades reclaims the space between us and gently but firmly takes my shoulders. "Do you want to go back?"

I can't lie to him. "No, but I don't see how that—"

He nods as if I've answered more than that single question. "Then you won't."

"What? You just said—"

"Do you think I'm naive enough to trust the Thirteen with my people's health and well-being? We were always one step away from pissing one of them off and causing a disruption like this." His lips quirk, though his eyes remain cold. "My people won't starve. We have plenty of resources in the lower city. Things might get uncomfortable for a little while, but no one will be irreparably harmed."

What?

"Where are you getting supplies from?"

"Triton and I have an under-the-table arrangement." He's not surprised or angry or any of the emotions coursing through me right now. He's not even worried.

The shocks just keep coming. "You...you negotiated with Poseidon's right-hand man to get around the Thirteen. How long has this been going on?"

"Since I took over at seventeen." He holds my gaze. "I know better than most that you can't afford to trust the goodwill of the Thirteen. It was only a matter of time before one of them tried to use my people to hurt me."

I look at him with new eyes. This man... Gods, he's even more complex than I suspected. A true leader. "You knew this might happen when you agreed to help me."

"I knew it was a distinct possibility." He shifts his hands up to cup my face and drags his thumbs along my cheekbones. "A long time ago, I promised myself that I wouldn't let those assholes in the upper city harm anything of mine ever again. There's little they can do, short of war, that will overly affect things here."

What would it be like if Hades ruled Olympus instead of Zeus? I can barely wrap my mind around the very concept. Hades truly *cares*.

I kiss him before I realize I'm going to do it. There's no plan, no ploy, nothing beyond the need to show him... I'm not even sure. Something. Something I can't put into words. He goes still for half a breath, and then he shifts his hands to my hips and pulls me against him. He kisses me back with the same level of ferocity bubbling up in my chest. A feeling bordering on desperation, on something more intricate still.

I pull away enough to say, "I need you."

He's already moving, backing me toward the bed. Hades looks down at my mostly bared body and growls. "I want you naked."

"I hope you're prepared to wait."

"I'm not." He reaches into his jacket and comes up with a small knife. "Don't move."

I hold still. I hold my very breath as he slips the blade between my skin and the first strap. It's surprisingly warm, likely from being so close to his body. The strap gives easily beneath the sharp edge. And then another, and another, and another, until I'm standing before him completely naked. He snaps the blade closed and takes a step back, sweeping his gaze over me from my head to my feet and back again. "Better."

He stalks to the light switch and flicks it, ignoring my wordless protest. I want to *see*. Hades moves past me to the windows and shoves the heavy curtains open. My eyes adjust quickly enough and I realize I can see, at least a little. The lights from the city bathe the room in a low neon glow.

Hades strips as he walks toward me. Jacket and shirt. Shoes and pants. He stops a few feet away and I can't help reaching for him. He might be giving me the view I crave, but I need something even more vital—his skin against mine.

Except he catches my hand before I make contact with his chest and guides it up to his neck. He finishes closing the distance between us, bringing us chest to chest. I get the faint impression of rough scars against my skin, but Hades kisses me again and I forget anything else but getting him inside me as quickly as possible.

He lifts me, and I wrap my legs around his waist. The new position has his cock nearly lined up perfectly where I need him, but he moves before I can lose my mind enough to take advantage. My need is an all-consuming thing that's been building since the moment I laid eyes on him. Having sex in front of the crowd was one thing, but it barely took the edge off. That was about reputation. This is about *us*.

Hades walks us to the bed and climbs onto it. He takes my hands and guides them up to the headboard. "Keep them here."

"Hades." I'm panting as if I've run a great distance. "Please. I want to touch you."

"Keep your hands here," he repeats and gives my wrists a squeeze.

He doesn't have to say it again. I'm already nodding. Anything to keep this going, to prevent this moment from ending. "Okay."

Hades shifts back to kneel between my spread thighs. His front is in shadow, but I have the feeling that he can see me in detail from the light through the windows. He cups my breasts, but he doesn't linger long before he slides down my body and presses an openmouthed kiss to the sensitive spot just below my belly button. And then he's at my pussy. His breath shudders out against my clit as if he's just as affected by this moment as I am. Maybe more so.

"I'm going to have you, little siren. In every position, in every way."

I don't know if he's talking to me or talking to himself, but I don't care. I grip the headboard hard and fight to stay still. "Then take me." An echo of what I said to him on the throne, but it means something different now. I can't pretend I want this solely for the benefit of our mutual reputations.

No, I just want *him*.

My desire to hear Hades's dry, rasping laugh is becoming a serious addiction. It's a thousand times better when he's making the sound against my pussy. He drags his tongue over me. His growl is the only warning I get before he grabs my thighs and presses them up and out, holding me completely open. There is no savoring, no teasing, no tempting me. He goes after my pussy like he'll never get this chance again. Like he needs my orgasm more than he needs his next breath.

Each exhale sobs out. I can't think, can't move, can't do anything but obey his order to hang on and take the pleasure he has rising with every movement of his tongue. I start shaking and can't stop. "Hades!"

He doesn't respond, just keeps up the same movements that have desire coiling tighter and tighter through me. It's too good. I want it to last and want the promised finale and just flat-out *want*. Hades sucks my clit hard into his mouth and pushes two fingers into me. I come so hard, it feels like every system is shutting down.

It's as if that orgasm took his edge off because he takes his time now, dragging his mouth over my stomach, kissing the curves of my breasts. I'm still spinning, but each touch, combined with the weight of his body on mine, slowly draws me back to earth. I lick my lips. "Hades."

He pauses. "Yeah?"

"Can I touch you now? Please?"

His breath shudders out against my neck. "You are touching me."

"That's not what I mean and you know it." I don't release the headboard, won't break his command without permission. This feels like an important moment, like we're poised on the brink of something *big*. It doesn't make any sort of sense. This is only sex, an act that can be simmered down to its basic components.

I desire him, so naturally I want to touch him. I don't want this to stop, so of course I won't disobey his order.

Except it doesn't feel that simple.

Hades is very intentionally hiding from me. By sight, by touch, by everything. I shouldn't resent that last bit of distance between us, not when he's so invested in my pleasure. But I do. I want everything, just like he's demanding from me. My chest goes tight. "Hades, please."

He hesitates so long, I think he's going to deny me again. Finally, he curses and reaches over my head to take one of my hands and bring it down to press against his chest, and then repeats the motion with my other hand. The skin is marred, too smooth in some places and raised in others. Scars. I'm feeling scars.

I don't say a single thing as I slowly stroke my hands down his chest and back up again. Hades holds himself perfectly still. I'm not sure he's even breathing. Something—someone—hurt him, and badly. Even without seeing the extent of the damage, I can tell he's lucky to be alive.

Maybe one day, he'll trust me enough to let me see him fully.

I arch up and kiss him. We don't need more words right now. He instantly relaxes against me, and I have the distant thought that he expected me to reject him. Silly man. Every piece of him I discover, every little nuance and mystery, just makes me want him more. Hades is a puzzle I could spend a lifetime exploring and never quite have the whole picture.

It's a shame I only have three months.

He breaks the kiss long enough to reach down into the

nightstand and come up with a condom. I grab it from him and nudge him back with a hand on his chest. "Let me."

"You're terrible at submission," he murmurs, but he's got that raspy laugh in his voice.

"Wrong." I tear the condom open. "I am really excellent at submission. I'm equally excellent at communicating what I want when I want it. It's called being adaptable."

"Is that so?" His breath hisses out as I stroke his cock, so I do it again.

"Hades?"

He gives a strained laugh. "Yes?"

"Promise me that I can give you a blow job soon. Really soon. I need you inside me too much right now, but I want that."

He reaches up and drags his thumb across my bottom lip. "Whenever you decide you need my cock in your mouth, kneel and ask nicely. If I'm feeling agreeable, I'll even give it to you."

I nip his thumb. "Okay, I deserved that."

"Put the condom on, Persephone. Now."

It turns out I'm not in the mood to tease him further, either. I roll the condom down his length. I barely get my hands out of the way when Hades pushes me back down onto the bed. Before being with him, I would have said I'm not into being manhandled, carefully or otherwise. Turns out I just needed the right man handling me. He pushes me onto my side and lifts one leg to wrap over his arm as he kneels between my thighs. It's a strange position, but I don't have time to comment because half a breath later, he's inside me. He sheaths himself to the hilt and we exhale in tandem.

Hades barely gives me a second to adjust before he starts

fucking me. Long, thorough strokes that have me completely pinned to the bed. "Touch yourself," he growls. "I want to feel you come around my cock. No witnesses. No audience. This time, it's just for me."

I do as he orders, sliding my hand down to stroke my clit. It feels so, so good. It seems like everything we do together feels good. Being with Hades is like being in a fever dream I don't ever want to wake up from. I never, ever want this to stop.

Hades adjusts his angle and picks up his pace, sending pleasure rising in a wave that I can't hold back. "Oh gods."

"Don't stop. Don't you dare stop." It's like he's pulling the words right from my chest and speaking them back to me.

I couldn't even if I wanted to. Words slip from my lips, forming into his name, over and over again. He leans down, bending my body to his will, and claims my mouth as I come. His strokes get rougher, less even, and then he's following me over the edge.

My bones turn liquid even as I fight not to break the kiss. It's gone from fierce to something gentle, almost loving. As if he's telling me without words how pleased he is with me. It's not something I would have thought I needed before now, but it settles a jagged piece in my chest.

Hades finally pulls away. "Don't move."

"Couldn't even if I wanted to."

His rough chuckle trails behind him as he walks into the bathroom. A few seconds later, he's back. I watch him stalk toward the bed, wishing for better light. He barely looks human like this. It's almost as if he's an incubus sent to fulfill my dark desires and he'll be gone with the morning light. "Stay."

Hades stops short. "What?"

"Stay." I sit up, something akin to panic fluttering in my throat. "Don't leave."

"Persephone." He reaches the bed and climbs up to pull me into his arms. "Little siren, I'm not leaving." It takes some maneuvering to get us both beneath the blankets, but Hades doesn't stop touching me the entire time. We end up on our sides, him spooning me from the back.

It's only when I'm fully wrapped up in him that I can breathe again. "Thank you."

"Where would I go? You're in my bed."

I want to laugh, but I can't. Instead, I stroke my hands down his arms. "But you're leaving eventually. Or I am, rather." Eventually, no matter how good this is, it *will* end.

"Yes."

I close my eyes, hating how disappointed his answer leaves me. What did I expect? We've known each other less than a week at this point. The entire reason I pushed this deal so hard was so that I could be well and truly free. Jumping from an engagement with Zeus into this bargain with Hades... That's not freedom. I know that, and yet there's still a strange burning in my eyes at the thought of this being over.

Not yet.

I have a little longer yet, and I plan to enjoy every moment to the fullest.

HADES

I'M UP WITH THE SUN. OPENING MY EYES TO FIND Persephone in my bed does something to me that I'm afraid to examine too closely. I like her here. It *soothes* me, which is bullshit. I can't afford to look into her eyes half begging me to stay through the night. She was coming down from the adrenaline rush of scening and sex. Even if we weren't in my bed, I wouldn't have left her hanging in that moment.

It doesn't change the fact that I like seeing her golden hair spread out over a pillow next to mine. And the evidence of her being a restless sleeper, the sheet tangled around her waist, leaving her breasts bare to meet the morning light streaming through the windows. It's almost enough to make me forget myself and wake her up with my mouth.

Almost.

I look down at my chest, at the mess of scars left from the fire that killed my parents. A memory I can never escape because it's written on my very skin. With a sigh, I climb out of bed, careful to tuck the blankets up around Persephone so she doesn't get chilled, and walk to close the curtains. A quick shower later and I'm dressed. I almost head down to my study on the main floor but hesitate. Will Persephone see it as a rejection, as me leaving her? I can't be sure. Fuck, I shouldn't care one way or another. No matter how great the sex, we aren't dating. Forgetting that truth, forgetting the expiration date, is a recipe for disaster.

I keep telling myself that even as I drop into the chair in my barely used desk in the study off the bedroom. A quick check of my phone reveals half a dozen text messages. I scroll through them, stopping at one from Hermes.

Hermes: Mandatory meeting @9. Don't miss this, Hades.
I'm being uncharacteristically serious.

I knew this was coming, though I expected it days ago. I take a deep breath and open the laptop. It takes a few minutes to get everything booted up, but I'm still ten minutes early to the meeting. Unsurprisingly, everyone else is here.

The screen splits into four. One image is myself mirrored back. One is Hermes and Dionysus, who appear to be sitting on a hotel bed and eating Cheetos, still wearing their clothing from last night. The third shows Poseidon, his big, burly shoulders consuming the frame. He's wearing a pissed-off expression under his red hair and beard, like he doesn't want to be here any more than I do. The remaining square contains the other eight people who represent the remainder of the Thirteen seated around a boardroom table. Since Zeus is unmarried after the last Hera died, we're one short.

The thought of Persephone sitting at that table makes me sick to my stomach.

Zeus sits in the center, and I don't miss the fact that his chair is slightly higher than the rest of them. Even though technically the power lies in the group itself, he's always fancied himself a modern-day king. To his right is Aphrodite, her skin flawless and her blond hair flowing around her shoulders in carefully curated waves. To his left, Demeter.

I study Persephone's mother. I've seen her before, of course. It's impossible to avoid her image in the gossip columns and news feeds. I see a bit of Persephone in the piercing hazel eyes and in the line of her jaw, though Demeter's has softened a little with age. She's as regal as a queen in her pantsuit, and she looks ready to call for my head. Lovely.

For a long moment, no one speaks. I sit back. I'm certainly not going to be the one to break the silence. I didn't call this meeting. Zeus wants me here, so he had damn well better get on with it.

As if he can sense my thoughts, Zeus leans forward. "Return my fiancée."

"The treaty was honored and you know it. She ran from you, ran until she bloodied her feet and damn near froze to death, because she couldn't get away from you fast enough. She crossed the River Styx of her own power. She's free to return whenever she wants." I make a show of looking at everyone gathered before responding. "She doesn't want to. You're wasting everyone's time with this."

"You're defiling my baby, you monster."

I raise my eyebrows at Demeter. "You were prepared to sell

your *baby* to a man with a reputation for killing his wives. Let's not throw stones."

Demeter gasps, but it's all theatrics. I don't know her well enough to be sure if I'm seeing guilt or just fury on her face. It doesn't matter to me. Persephone will do anything to get away from these people, and I'll throw myself on a literal sword before I hand her back against her will.

Zeus shakes his head slowly. "Don't test me. The last Hades..."

"You mean my father. The one you murdered. The reason this treaty was created in the first place." I lean forward. "If you're going to threaten me, pick a better weapon." I meet the gazes of the other members of the Thirteen in turn. "I honored the treaty. Persephone is free to come and go as she pleases. Are we done here?"

"Prove it," Demeter snarls.

I sense her behind me a moment before Persephone lightly touches my shoulder. In the monitor, I see her at my shoulder, wrapped in my sheet. Her hair is tangled and there's whisker burn on her neck and what little of her chest is in view. She leans down and glares at the screen. "I am where I want to be, Mother. I'm *very happy* with Hades." She reaches over my shoulder and shuts the laptop.

I twist slowly to look at her. "You just hung up on the Thirteen."

"Fuck them."

I don't know whether to laugh or bundle her up and take her somewhere that will protect her from Zeus's inevitable revenge. "Persephone."

"Hades." She matches my censoring tone. "They weren't going to believe you if they didn't see it for themselves, and half of them still won't believe. Letting Zeus rant just wastes everyone's time. You should be thanking me."

"I should be thanking you?"

"Yes." She climbs into my lap and straddles me. "You're welcome."

I let my hands rest on her hips. "They have no idea who you truly are, do they?"

"No." She runs her hands up my chest, her expression contemplative. "But then, I don't really know who I truly am, either. I was hoping getting out of Olympus would help me figure it out."

I cover her hands with my own. "You're still getting out of Olympus." It pains me to say it, but none of that leaks into my tone. I made a promise, and no matter how much I've enjoyed going round with her the last few days, I will hold to it. We have until April. It will be enough.

It has to be enough.

She gives me a sad little smile. "I'm going to have to call my sisters soon to check in again if you don't want them storming the place."

"I'll get you a phone today." I pause. "One that isn't tapped."

"Thank you." She gives me a beautiful smile. I stare up at her in something akin to shock. I've seen Persephone cunning and sunshiny and angry. I've never seen her like this. Is this happiness? I'm afraid to ask, only to find it's just another version of her usual mask.

Persephone presses a quick kiss to my lips and then slides off my lap and down to the floor to kneel between my thighs. She gives me an expectant look, and I put aside my tangled feelings to focus on the here and now. "Want something, little siren?"

She runs her hands over my thighs and bites her bottom lip. "You promised if I hit my knees and asked nicely, I could have your cock." She reaches for the front of my slacks. "I would very, very much like your cock, Hades. Please."

I catch her hands. "You know you don't have to do this."

"Yes, I'm aware." She gives me an imperious look, as if she's indulging me. "Telling me I don't have to do anything I don't want to do is ridiculous, because I *want* to do everything with you. Absolutely everything."

She's just talking about sex, but my heart still gives a dull thump in response as if waking from a long sleep. Rusty and unused but still alive. I release her and press my shaking hands to the arms of my chair. "Then don't let me stop you."

"I'm so glad you're seeing things my way." She opens my slacks and draws my cock out. Persephone licks her lips. "Oh, Hades. I kind of wish I had any artistic ability at all, because I would love to paint you."

I'm still processing that strange statement when she leans down and takes my cock into her mouth. I expect... I don't know what I'm expecting. I should realize by now that Persephone is never quite what I think she'll be. She sucks me down as if she wants to taste and luxuriate in every inch. A warm, wet slide that has every muscle in my body going tense. I fight to hold still, to let her have this moment as she finishes her exploration and looks up.

Her eyes have gone dark and the color is high in her cheeks. "Hades?"

"Yeah?"

She kneads my thighs with her fingertips. "Stop being so freaking nice to me and tell me what you want."

Shock has me answering honestly. "I want to fuck your mouth until you cry."

She gives me a beautiful smile. "There. Was that so hard?" Persephone inches back. "You play the big, bad wolf, but you've been so careful with me since we met. You don't have to be. I promise I can take everything you give me." She lets the sheet fall to the floor around her. The woman says she wants to paint me, but *she's* the artwork, the very picture of the siren I've named her.

I'm starting to think I would gladly drown for this woman.

I push slowly to my feet and smooth back her hair. Fuck, she's so beautiful, she steals my breath. I want her more than I've wanted anything else in my life, a fact I'm not prepared to look too closely at. I twist her hair around one fist and give it a tug. "If it's too much, slap my thigh."

"It won't be too much."

I tap her bottom lip with my thumb. "Open."

Persephone is all wicked pleasure as I ease my cock into her mouth. I start off slowly, letting her adjust to the angle, but the dark desire to do exactly as I described is too strong. I pick up my pace, thrusting deeper into her mouth. Into her throat. She closes her eyes.

"No. Don't do that. Look at me while I fuck your mouth. Witness what you're doing to me."

Instantly, she opens her eyes. Persephone goes loose and relaxed, submitting to me fully in this moment. I know it won't last, which makes it all the sweeter. Pleasure builds with each thrust, threatening to tear me to pieces. It only gets more intense when tears slide from the corners of her eyes. I cup her face and wipe them away with my thumbs, tender even in this moment of restrained brutality.

It's too much. It will never be enough. "I'm going to come," I grind out.

She runs her hands up my thighs and gives me a squeeze. An assent. It's all the permission I need to let go. I try to keep my eyes open, try to savor every moment of this gift she's giving me as I drive into her willing mouth and orgasm. Persephone drinks me down, holding my gaze. She looks at me like she *sees* me. Like she's loving this just as much as I am.

I've never felt so fucking owned in my life.

I don't know what to do with it, how to process it. I force myself to release her, and she gives my cock one last lazy suck before leaning back and licking her lips. Tear tracks mark her cheeks and she grins, looking particularly pleased with herself. It's a contrast I don't know what to do with so I yank her to her feet and kiss her, hard and thorough. "You're a gift."

She laughs against my mouth. "I know."

I back her toward the door to my bedroom. "I have things to do today."

"Do you?" Persephone laces her arms behind my neck and beams at me, totally unrepentant. "I guess you should do them."

"Mmm." I catch the backs of her thighs and lift her to topple back onto the bed. "In a little bit." I kneel at the side of the bed and push her legs apart. Her pussy is pretty and pink and oh so wet. I part her lips with my thumbs and exhale against her clit. "You liked it when I fucked your mouth."

"I really, really did." She lifts her head enough to look down her body at me. "I told you that I can handle anything you can give. I should clarify. I *crave* anything and everything you do to me."

Sweet fuck, the trust she places in me. I'm still not sure I deserve it.

I hold her gaze and circle her clit with the tip of my tongue. "I suppose business can wait a little longer." Her smile in response is reward enough, but I have her practically vibrating with the need to ride my face...

Actually, that's a fantastic fucking idea.

I slide her up the bed and crawl onto the mattress. "Come here."

Persephone is already obeying, following my lead to climb up to straddle my chest. I slide down and then there she is, right where I want her. "Don't hold back, little siren. You know you want to be wicked."

She gives an experimental roll, and I reward it with a long lick. It doesn't take long before Persephone is rocking against my mouth, chasing her own orgasm even as I lose myself in the taste of her. She comes with a cry that sounds a whole lot like my name, her body shuddering above me as she grinds down against my tongue.

It's not enough. How many fucking times will I think that before I acknowledge that it will *never* be enough? It doesn't matter. At least once more.

I topple her back onto the bed and keep eating her out, driven by the need to make this... I don't know. I want to ensure that no matter where she goes or how much time passes, she'll always remember this.

That she'll always remember *me*.

PERSEPHONE

HADES AND I DON'T MAKE IT OUT OF BED UNTIL NEARLY lunchtime, and only then because my growling stomach seems to offend him on a personal level. Which is how I end up sitting at the kitchen island with three plates' worth of food in front of me. I'm still picking through the fries when Hermes strolls into the room.

I raise my eyebrows. "Do you ever go home?"

"Home is such a fluid concept." She nods at the brand-new phone sitting on the counter by my elbow. "So you *do* have a phone. Your poor sisters have resorted to using me as messenger because they can't get ahold of you."

I stare at it and then at her. "My sisters sent you here?"

"Apparently you were supposed to contact them a few days ago, and when you didn't, they assumed the worst. Also, Psyche sent along a message." She clears her throat and then my sister's voice emerges from her lips. "I can only hold Callisto off for another day or two. Call as soon as you get this so we can calm her down. She and Mother have been fighting, and you know how *that* goes." Hermes grins and steals a fry off my plate. "End message."

"Um, thanks." I've heard she can do that, but it's still eerie as hell to witness it.

"It's my job." She snags another fry. "So, you and Hades are making the beast with two backs in real life, not just pretend. I'm not exactly surprised but also very, very surprised."

I'm not about to start sharing secrets with the woman who's primary job is to collect them. I raise my brows. "You and Dionysus seem awfully close for just friends. Is it true that he's not particularly interested in sex?"

"Point taken." She laughs. "Better call your sisters. I'd hate for Callisto to do something to piss off Zeus."

The thought leaves me cold. Psyche knows well enough to play the game. Eurydice is all flavors of distracted by her boyfriend. Callisto? If Callisto and our mother go head-to-head, I'm not sure the city will survive it. If she goes after Zeus... "I'll call them."

"Good girl." She pats me on the shoulder and walks out of the room, presumably off to torment some other unsuspecting soul. Despite that, I like her. Hermes might play at deeper games than I can begin to guess at, but she's at least interesting. And I think she and Dionysus actually care about Hades. I'm not sure it's enough to prevent them from siding with the other Thirteen if it comes to that, but that's a worry for another day.

I take one last bite, grab the phone Hades gave me earlier, and head out of the kitchen and down the hall to the room I found during a cursory exploration of the first floor. I suppose it's a living room, but it feels like a cozy little reading nook with two comfortable chairs, a giant fireplace, and several bookshelves filled with everything from nonfiction to fantasy.

I sink into the deep-purple chair and turn on the phone. It's already got my sisters' contact information in it and the video chat app installed. I take a deep breath and call Psyche.

She answers immediately. "Oh, thank the gods." She leans back. "She's here!"

Callisto and Eurydice appear behind her. Anyone looking at the four of us wouldn't assume we're siblings. Technically, we're all half siblings. My mother went through four marriages before she achieved her goal to become one of the Thirteen and ceased needing men to further her ambitions. We all have our mother's hazel eyes, but that's where the similarities stop.

Eurydice looks ready to cry, her light-brown skin already blotchy. "You're alive."

"Yes, I'm alive." Guilt threads through me. I was too worried about getting as close to Hades as possible to remember to contact my sisters. Selfish. So selfish of me. But then, what else do you call my plan to leave Olympus forever? I push the thought away.

Callisto leans forward and runs a critical eye over me. "You look...good."

"I am good." As tempting as it is to downplay the situation, being perfectly honest with them is the only way to go. "Hades and I made a deal. He's going to keep me safe until I'm able to get out of Olympus."

Callisto narrows her eyes. "At what cost?"

Here's the crux of it. I hold her gaze. "If Zeus considers me less desirable because I've been sleeping with Hades, he won't try to pursue me when I leave." When my sisters just stare at me, I sigh. "And yes, I'm furious at Mother and furious at Zeus and I wanted to prove a point."

Psyche frowns. "There's a rumor circulating this morning that you and Hades were, well, having sex in front of half the lower city. I thought it was just people gossiping nonsense, but…"

"It's true." I can feel my face getting red. "Our plan won't work if it's just pretend. It has to be real."

It's Eurydice, my sweet and innocent sister, who speaks next, her voice low and furious. "We're coming to get you right now. If he thinks he can force you—"

"No one is *forcing* me to do anything." I hold up a hand. I have to get ahead of this. I should have known that trying to be vague would only incite every single one of their protective instincts. "I'll tell you the full truth, but you have to stop reacting and listen."

Psyche puts her hand on Eurydice's shoulder. "Tell us and then we'll decide how to react."

That's about as good an offer as I'm going to get. I sigh and then tell them everything. How I pushed the bargain. Hades's constant mothering. How *good* the sex is.

I leave out Hades's history with Zeus, the scars wrapping his body that no doubt came from the fire that killed his parents. The fire *Zeus* caused. I trust my sisters implicitly, but something in me rebels at sharing that story. It's not exactly a secret, but it feels like one, like a piece of knowledge that Hades and I share, that bonds us together further.

And…

I hesitate, but in the end, who else can I talk to about this? "I feel like I can breathe here. I don't have to pretend with Hades, don't have to be perfect and bright all the time. I feel like... Like I'm finally starting to figure out who I am behind the mask."

Eurydice has hearts in her eyes. "Only you could manage to run away and fall into bed with a sexy man determined to do anything to protect you. You're truly gods-blessed, Persephone."

"It didn't feel like it when they announced the engagement."

Eurydice's happiness dims. "No, I suppose it didn't."

Psyche is looking at me like she's never seen me before. "Are you sure it's not all an elaborate trap? You've developed those defenses *for a reason*."

I bite down on my instinctive denial and force myself to think about it. "No, it's not an elaborate trap. He hates Zeus just as much as I do; he has no reason to think breaking me would hurt anyone but me. He's not like that anyway. He's not like the rest of the Thirteen at all." That, I know for truth. I've survived moving through Olympus's circle of power and influence this long by trusting my instincts and lying through my teeth. I don't have to lie with Hades. More, my instincts mark him as safe.

"Are you sure? Because we all know you've had this fascination with the title Hades for—"

"*Hades* is not the problem." I don't want to tell them what I know about Mother, but they need to know. "Mother threatened to cut off the entire supply line to the lower city until Hades returns me."

"We know." Callisto drags her hand through her long dark

hair. "She's been ranting about it ever since you left, working herself up into a frenzy."

"She's worried," Eurydice says.

Callisto snorts. "She's *angry*. You defied her and left her with pie on her face in front of the rest of the Thirteen. She's going out of her mind trying to save face."

"*And* she's worried." Eurydice shoots our eldest sister a look. "She's been cleaning."

I sigh. Easy to paint my mother as the villain right alongside Zeus, but she *does* love us. She just doesn't let that love get in the way of her ambitions. My mother can be stone-faced when issuing her orders like a general about to go into battle, but when she's worried, she cleans. It's her only tell.

Ultimately, it changes nothing. "She shouldn't have sprung that on me."

"No one is arguing that." Psyche holds up her hands. "No one is arguing *anything*. We're just worried. Thank you for checking in."

"Stay safe. I miss you."

"We miss you, too." Psyche smiles. "Don't worry about us. We have things under control here as much as possible." She hangs up before I really register the statement.

Don't worry about them.

I *wasn't* worried about them, not really. Until now.

I call them back. It rings a long time before Psyche picks up. This time, Callisto and Eurydice are nowhere in evidence, and Psyche doesn't look as chipper as she did a few minutes ago. I frown. "What's going on? What aren't you telling me?"

"We're fine."

"Yes, you keep saying that, but it sounds like you're trying to reassure me and *I am not reassured*. Speak plainly. What's going on?"

She looks over her shoulder, and the light in the room gets a little dimmer as if she shut the door or a window or something. "I think someone is following Eurydice. Actually, not just her. Callisto hasn't said anything, but she's even more on edge than the situation warrants. And I think I've seen the same lady the last three times I've left the penthouse."

A chill cascades down my spine. "They know where I am. Why would they try to track you to me?"

Psyche presses her lips together and finally says, "I think they're making sure none of us try to flee."

"Why would Mother—" I stop short. "Not Mother. Zeus."

"That's my thought." Psyche runs her fingers through her hair and twists, a nervous gesture she's had since we were children. She's scared.

I did this. Zeus wasn't following any of us before I ran. I close my eyes, trying to play through possible scenarios, possible reasons for him to do this beyond safeguarding their presence in the upper city. I don't like what I keep coming back to. "You don't think she'll sub one of you into the marriage instead of me, do you?" If that's the case, I *have* to go back. I can't be the reason one of my sisters ends up married to that monster, even if I have to take the hit to ensure it doesn't happen.

"No." She shakes her head and shakes it again harder. "Absolutely not. They painted themselves into a corner by announcing it publicly. They *can't* force one of us to take your place without looking like fools, and that's one thing Zeus and Mother will not do."

That's a relief, but not as much of a relief as I'd like it to be. "Then why?"

"I think he might try to trick you into coming back across the River Styx." Psyche holds my gaze, as serious as I've ever seen her. "You can't do it, Persephone. No matter what happens, you stay the course with Hades and get out of Olympus. We have things covered here."

The chill bleeds through my entire body. What lengths will Zeus go to in order to get me back? I was so focused on how he might try to take me that I didn't look at the other angles. Mother would never hurt her daughters, even if she moves us around like chess pieces. She might allow us to experience a certain level of danger, but she isn't a complete monster. I have a feeling that if I actually went forward with the marriage, she had some sort of secondary plan in place to ensure I didn't end up like the other Heras. It doesn't matter, because she didn't ask me.

But Zeus?

His reputation isn't fabricated. Even if being a wife-killer is only rumor, the way he deals with enemies isn't. He doesn't maintain his ironclad grip on Olympus by being kind and considerate and shying away from making brutal calls. People obey him because they fear him. Because he's given them reason to fear him.

Psyche must see the fear on my face, because she leans in and lowers her voice. "I mean it, Persephone. We are fine and have things covered over here. Don't you *dare* come back for us."

The guilt I've been very carefully not thinking about for days threatens to claw out my throat. I've been so focused on my plan, on my endgame, I didn't really stop to consider that my sisters might be paying the price. "I'm the worst sister."

"No." She shakes her head. "Not even a little bit. You want out, and you should get out. All three of us could leave if we wanted to."

That doesn't make me feel better. It might actually make me feel worse. "Being in that penthouse, being around those people... It makes me feel like I'm drowning."

"I know." Her dark eyes are sympathetic. "You don't have to justify yourself to me."

"But my selfishness—"

"Stop it." A harsh note creeps into my sister's voice. "If you want to blame someone, blame Mother. Blame Zeus. Gods, blame the entire Thirteen if you want. We didn't choose this life. We're just trying to survive it. That looks different on all four of us. Do *not* apologize to me, and certainly don't call yourself selfish."

My throat is burning, but I refuse to indulge in self-pity enough to cry. I fight for a smile. "You're pretty smart for a younger sister."

"I have two brilliant older sisters to learn from." She looks away. "I have to go. Call if you need anything, but don't you dare change your plans for us."

The fierceness in her voice ensures that I won't. I force a nod. "I won't. I promise."

"Good. Be safe. Love you."

"Love you, too."

Then she's gone, leaving me staring into the empty fireplace and wondering if I've made a horrible mistake.

HADES

DUSK IS STEALING ACROSS THE SKY BY THE TIME I FINISH
with the various things that needed to be accomplished today
and go to find Persephone. Our territory is as prepared as we can
possibly be for what's coming. I've had my people put out word
that there might be supply disruptions and to plan accordingly.
The spies in the upper city are on high alert and ready to slip back
across the river to safety. Everyone is watching and waiting to see
what Zeus and Demeter will do.

I'm tired. Really fucking tired. The kind of exhaustion that
sneaks up and drags a person down between one step and the next.

I don't quite realize how much I'm looking forward to seeing
Persephone until I step into the mini library and find her curled up
on the couch. She's wearing one of the dresses Juliette delivered, a
happy bright blue, and reading a book. There's a small fire crack-
ling in the fireplace, and the sheer normalcy of the scene nearly
knocks me on my ass. For a fraction of a moment, I allow myself
to imagine that *this* is a sight that would greet me at the end of

every day. Instead of dragging myself to my bedroom and collapsing on my mattress alone, I'd find this woman waiting for me.

I put the fantasy away. I can't afford to want things like that. Not in general, and not with her. Temporary. This whole thing is *temporary.*

I brace myself and step farther into the room, letting the door close softly behind me. Persephone looks up, and the haunted expression on her face has me immediately moving to her. "What's wrong?"

"Besides the obvious?"

I sit on the couch next to her, close enough to be an invitation if she wants it but far enough away to give her space if she needs it. I've barely settled when Persephone crawls into my lap and draws her legs up until she's balanced on my thighs. I wrap my arms around her and rest my chin on her head. "What happened?"

"Hermes delivered a message from my sisters."

I'd known about that, of course. Hermes might have an uncanny ability to slip past my guards, but even she isn't able to dodge the cameras completely. "You called them and the conversation with your sisters upset you."

"I guess you could say that." She relaxes by inches against me. "I've just been sitting here, stewing in my self-pity. I'm a selfish asshole who threw this whole mess into motion because I wanted to be free."

I've never heard her sound so bitter. I give her back a tentative stroke and she sighs, so I do it again. "Your mother wasn't forced to take the position of Demeter. She went after it."

"I'm aware." She traces my buttons with a single finger. "Like

I said, it's self-pity, which is nearly unforgivable, but I'm worried about my sisters and afraid that I made the situation worse by taking off instead of just going along with my mother's plans."

I'm not sure what I'm supposed to say to make her feel better. One of the side effects of being an only child and an orphan is that I don't have much in the way of social skills. I can intimidate and threaten and rule, but comfort is beyond my expertise. I pull her closer as if that's enough to gather all her scattered pieces together again. "If your sisters are half as capable as you, they'll be more than fine."

She gives a shuddering laugh. "I think they might be more capable than me. At least Callisto and Psyche. Eurydice is still so *young*. We've kept her sheltered over the years, and now I'm wondering if that was a mistake."

"Because of Orpheus."

"He's not a bad guy, I guess. But he loves himself and his music more than he loves my sister. I'll never be okay with that." As she speaks, she relaxes, the last of the tension bleeding away. A distraction was all it took. Maybe I'm not nearly as bad at this comforting thing as I thought. I file away the information for later, even as I tell myself that it's worthless. The clock is already running out on us, for all that we have the rest of the winter. After that, it won't matter that I know how to comfort Persephone when she's upset. She'll be gone.

It's tempting to use sex to distract her, but I don't know that it's what she needs right now. "Would you like to get out of here for a little bit?"

The way she perks up confirms this was the right call. Persephone turns those big hazel eyes on me. "Really?"

"Yeah, really." I stifle the urge to tell her to dress in warmer clothing. We won't be going far, and the last thing I want right now is to push her too hard on anything, not when she's already feeling so fragile. I ease her off my lap and hold her hand while she stands. "Let's go."

Persephone beams at me. "Is this another secret like the greenhouse?"

I still can't believe how intimate it feels to have shared that with her. Like she's seen a part of me that no one else gets to. Instead of turning away, she seems to understand what that place means to me. I shake my head slowly. "No, this is something else. A little peek behind the curtain of the lower city."

If anything, her eyes light up even more. "Let's go."

Fifteen minutes later, we're holding hands while walking down the street. Part of me wonders if I should take my hand back, but I don't fucking want to. I like the feeling of her palm against mine, our fingers linked together. I lead her east away from the house, setting a pace that won't tax her overmuch. No matter what else is true, Persephone hasn't fully recovered from the night that brought her to me. Or maybe I'm just looking for an excuse to take care of her.

We walk in easy silence, but I can tell her thoughts are still occupied with her sisters. I have nothing to say that will actually comfort her on that note, so I set myself on providing an experience that will get her out of her head a bit. "We're almost there."

She finally looks at me. "Are you going to tell me where *there* is?"

"No."

"Such a tease."

I squeeze her hand. "Maybe I just like the look on your face when you first experience something."

It's hard to tell in the shadows of the growing dark, but I think she blushes. "You know, if you wanted to distract me, sex is always a good option."

"I'll keep that in mind." I turn us down a narrow alley. Persephone follows me without hesitation to the large metal door at the end. I glance at her. "Nervous?"

"No," she answers immediately. "I'm with you, and we both know you won't let anything happen to me."

I blink. "You're that sure of me?"

She smiles, some of the worry in her eyes dissipating. "Of course I am. You're the fearsome Hades. No one fucks with you, which means no one will fuck with me while I'm with you." She leans in, her breasts pressing against my arm. "Right?"

"Right," I say faintly. I can't even enjoy her teasing because I'm too busy reeling at her casual statement. *I'm with you, and we both know you won't let anything happen to me.* As if it's that simple. As if it's a truth.

It is. I would commit unforgivable acts to keep Persephone safe. But somehow hearing her say it aloud makes it so much more real.

She trusts me.

I motion to the door simply for something to do. "There's still enough light to study the columns if you like."

"I like." She keeps a hold on my hand as she peers at the white columns on either side of the door. I watch her instead of them, already knowing what she's seeing. A revel in a magical forest with satyrs and nymphs eating and drinking and enjoying themselves. Persephone finally leans back and grins at me. "Another portal."

"Portal?"

"Show me what's behind the door, Hades."

I push open the door, and Persephone's gasp is almost lost in the commotion on the other side. She starts to push past me, but I keep my grip on her hand. "No need to rush."

"Speak for yourself." Her eyes are even wider than normal as she takes in the scene in front of us.

The indoor market is open most nights of the week during the winter. The ceiling is lost to the darkness above us, the warehouse an echoing space—or it would be if it were empty. This time of year, it's filled with bustling shoppers and vendors. Semipermanent stalls are set up in narrow rows. They're all a uniform size, but the owners have made each space their own with brightly colored canopies and signs advertising everything from produce to soap to desserts to trinkets. All of them have shops scattered around the lower city, but they keep a sampling of their products here.

Some of these people have had shops since I was a small child. Some of them stretch back generations. The entire warehouse is filled with the clamor of people buying and selling and a tangled mix of delicious food smells.

I use the noise as an excuse to slip my arm around Persephone's waist and pull her close to speak directly into her ear. "Hungry?"

"Yes." She still hasn't taken her eyes off the market. It's not as crowded tonight as it will be on the weekends, but there is still a large number of people crammed into the rows between the stalls. "Hades, what is this?"

"Winter market." I inhale her summery scent. "During the warmer months, this whole setup moves out into a city block that's specifically designated for this purpose. It's open every night of the week, though some of the vendors cycle through."

She turns to look at me. "This is like a secret world. Can we... Can we explore?" Her curiosity and joy are a balm to my soul that I never knew I craved.

"That's what we're here for." Once again, I tug her back when she'd bolt into the crowd. "Food first. That's my only stipulation."

Persephone grins. "Yes, Sir." She bounces onto her toes and kisses my cheek. "Take me to your favorite food place here."

There it is again, the feeling of sharing parts of me with this woman that no one else gets to see. Of her appreciating and enjoying the bits of me that aren't strictly Hades, ruler of the lower city, the shadow member of the Thirteen. In moments like this one, it's as if she really *sees* me, and that's intoxicating in the extreme.

We end up at a gyro stall, and I nod at Damien behind the counter. He grins at me. "Long time, no see."

"Hey." I nudge Persephone closer to the stall. "Damien, this is Persephone. Persephone, this is Damien. His family has been selling gyros in Olympus for, what is it? Three generations?"

"Five." He laughs. "Though if you ask my uncle, it's closer to ten, and on top of that, we can trace our lines back to Greece to some head cook who served Caesar himself."

"I believe it." I laugh just like he wants me to. We've had this exchange dozens of times, but he enjoys it so I'm more than happy to indulge him. "We'll have two of the regular."

"Coming right up." It takes him a few moments to put the

gyros together, and I allow myself to enjoy the way his smooth movements speak of years of practice. I still remember coming here as a teenager and watching Damien's dad walk him through the process of taking an order and making the gyro, supervising his son with patience and love that I envied. They have a good relationship, and it was something I wanted to soak up peripherally, especially during those angsty teen years.

Damien holds up the gyros. "No charge."

"You know better." I pull cash out of my pocket and set it on the counter, ignoring his half-hearted protests. This, too, we do nearly every time I visit. I accept the gyros and hand one to Persephone. "This way." I lead her around the edge of the warehouse to where a handful of tables and chairs have been set up and tucked back against the wall. There are several similar sitting areas scattered throughout the area so no matter where one buys food, they don't have to walk far to find a place to sit and eat.

I glance over to find Persephone looking at me with a strange expression on her face. I frown. "What?"

"How often do you come down here?"

My skin prickles and I have the uncomfortable suspicion that I'm blushing. "Usually at least once a week." When she just keeps staring, I have to fight not to shuffle my feet. "I find the chaos soothing."

"That's not the full reason."

Once again, she's entirely too perceptive. Strangely enough, I don't mind elaborating. "This is just a small portion of the population in the lower city, but I like seeing people here going about their business. It's normal."

She unwraps her gyro. "Because they're safe."

"Yes."

"Because *you* make them safe." She takes a bite before I can respond and gives a downright sexual moan. "Gods, Hades. This is amazing."

We eat in silence, and the sheer normality of this moment hits me right in the chest. For just a little while, Persephone and I could be two normal people moving through the world without the entirety of Olympus threatening to topple if we make a wrong move. This might be a first date or a third or one ten years down the road. I close my eyes and push that thought away. We aren't normal and this isn't a date, and at the end of our time together, Persephone will leave Olympus. In ten years, I might be in this very spot enjoying a gyro alone just like I have countless times in the past, but she'll be somewhere far away, living the life she was always meant to.

One spent in the sunlight.

Her empty wrapper crinkles as she wads it up. She leans forward, expression intent. "Show me everything."

"There's no way we can see the whole thing tonight." Before she can wilt, I press on. "But you can explore a little bit tonight and come back again every few days until you see everything you want to."

The smile she gives me is so pure, it feels like she cracked open my sternum and wrapped her fist around my heart. "Promise?"

As if I'd deny her this simple pleasure. As if I'd deny her *any* pleasure. "I promise."

We spend an hour wandering the stalls before I herd Persephone back to the entrance. During that time, she's managed to charm every single person she meets, and we end up with an armful of bags filled with candy, a dress that caught her eye, and a trio of glass figurines for her sisters. I almost feel guilty for cutting her time short, but the wisdom of it becomes readily apparent as we walk back home. By the time we reach our block, Persephone is leaning on me.

"I'm not tired."

I fight down a smile. "Sure."

"I'm not. I'm just conserving energy."

"Mm-hmm." I lock the door behind us and consider her. "Then I suppose I should resist carrying you upstairs and putting you to bed."

Persephone nibbles on her bottom lip. "I mean, if you *want* to carry me, I suppose I can keep my protests to a minimum."

That feeling of her squeezing my heart only gets stronger. "In that case…" I scoop her up, bags and all, enjoying her little shriek. Enjoying the way she lays her head against my chest so trustingly. Just flat-out enjoying her.

I hesitate on the landing of the second floor, but she leans up and presses a kiss to my neck. "Take me to bed, Hades." Not hers. Mine.

I give a short nod and continue up the stairs to my room. I set Persephone on the bed and step back. "Do you want me to have your stuff brought up here?"

She does that adorable lip nibbling thing again. "Is that presumptuous? I know last night was one thing, but I'm being pushy about this, aren't I?"

Maybe, but I like the way she carves out a space for herself in my home, in my life. "I wouldn't offer if I didn't want you here."

"Then yes, please." She reaches for me. "Come to bed."

I catch her hands before she can start unbuttoning my shirt. "Put your things away. I need to do my rounds before anything else happens."

"Your rounds." She stares up at me, seeing too much, just like she always seems to. I tense, waiting for her to question, to ask why I feel the need to check the locks when I have one of the best security systems money can buy and a staff of security people. Instead, she just nods. "Do what you need to do. I'll be waiting."

Even though I want to rush, I know I won't be able to sleep until I've checked all the entrances and exits on the ground floor properly. Especially now that Persephone is here, trusting me to keep her safe. By all rights, the knowledge should add weight to my shoulders, but it just feels strangely comfortable. As if things were meant to be this way. It doesn't make any sense to me, so I put it from my mind.

I pause in the security room to check in with my people, but as expected, there's nothing new to report. Whatever move Zeus makes is yet to be seen, but it's unlikely he'll do it tonight.

There will be a time for *me* to make another move, but I'm hesitant to do so. Not yet, not when things are going so well with Persephone. Better to let things simmer a bit and see what Zeus does before we do anything else.

The excuse feels flimsy as fuck, likely because it is. I don't care. I push the thoughts away and head back up to my room. I'm not sure what I expect, but it isn't to find Persephone in my bed, sound asleep.

I stand there and stare, letting the scene wash over me in waves. The way she's curled on her side, the blankets clutched to her chest with a loose fist. Her hair already a tangled mass over her pillow. How she has her back to what was my side of the bed last night, as if she's just waiting for me to join her and curl my body around her.

I rub my thumb against my sternum, as if that will ease the ache there. It's tempting to join her in bed right now, but I make myself go to my closet, strip, and head into the bathroom to go through my nightly ritual.

She's exactly where I left her when I return, and I shut off the lights and ease between the covers. Maybe I'm reading too much into this. She's fallen asleep, but she already said she's not a big cuddler. Just because she's here doesn't mean it's an invitation...

Persephone reaches back and grabs my hand. She scoots back toward me as she tugs me closer, only stopping when we're sealed together from torso to thigh. She pulls my arm up to curl around her chest with the blanket and gives a sleepy sigh. "Night, Hades."

I blink into the darkness, no longer able to deny the fact that this woman has irreversibly changed my life. "Good night, Persephone."

PERSEPHONE 20

A DAY PASSES, AND THEN ANOTHER, ONE WEEK BLEEDING into the next. I spend my days alternately obsessing over when Mother and Zeus will make their move and sinking into the distraction that living with Hades offers. Each room is a new exploration, containing a secret to hold close to my heart. There are shelves tucked into every nook and cranny, all filled with books with spines weathered from many rereads. I conquer one room a day, drawing this journey out, feeling like I'm getting closer and closer to knowing the man who owns this place.

Several times a week, we revisit the winter market and Hades lets me tug him along like a well-loved stuffed animal as I explore. He's also taken to showing me other hidden gems the lower city has to offer. I get to see dozens of the columns, each depicting a unique scene that relates to the business they bracket. I never get tired of the way his expression goes from guarded to a little awestruck when he realizes how much I value these experiences. I feel like it's allowing me to get to know this part of the city, yes, but also the man who rules it.

And the nights? My nights are filled with knowing him in an entirely different way.

I close the book I wasn't reading and look at him. He's sitting on the other side of the couch with a stack of paperwork and a laptop. If I squint a little, I can almost pretend that we're normal people. That he's brought his work home with him. That I'm perfectly content to be a housewife or whatever label fits my current status.

"You're thinking rather hard over there," he says without looking up.

I fiddle with the book. "It's a very good book. A real puzzler." I don't sound remotely convincing.

"Persephone." The seriousness in his tone demands a response. A *truthful* response.

The words bubble up before I can call them back. "You haven't taken me back to your sex dungeon."

"It's not a sex dungeon."

"Hades, it's the very definition of a sex dungeon."

At this, he finally sets his laptop aside and gives me his full attention. His brows draw together. "We've been having a good time."

"'Good time' hardly begins to cover it. I enjoy exploring your house and the lower city. I enjoy exploring *you*." My cheeks heat, but I power on. "But you said you wanted people to take us seriously, and how can they take us seriously if you're not treating me like they expect you to?"

"I haven't wanted to share you with the voyeurs from the upper city." He says it so simply, as if he's not dropping a bomb. Hades tugs off the throw blanket I've curled up under and tosses it onto the floor. "You're right, though. It's possible they haven't moved yet because we haven't forced them to."

I go a little melty at the feeling of his hand closing around my ankle. It's always like this with him. I keep waiting for the intensity to fade, for ready access to each other to wear off the shine of having sex with each other. It hasn't happened yet. If anything, the last couple of weeks have made me want him more. I'm Pavlov's dog. He touches me, and I'm instantly aching for him.

What were we talking about?

I give myself a mental shake and try to focus. "Are we trying to make them act?"

"We're trying to hurt them. Or him, at least." Hades slides his hand up my calf to hook the back of my knee and tug me down the couch to him. We came straight up to his room after having dinner at a charming little restaurant down the street, so I'm still wearing one of the flirty dresses Juliette put together for me. From the heated way Hades rakes his gaze over me, he likes it even better when it's bunched around my upper thighs. "Show me."

I reach down with shaking hands and pull my dress up, just a little, just enough to give him a look beneath it.

Hades raises his brows. "Look at you, wearing panties like a good girl."

"Yes, well, sometimes I like the tease." I let the skirt fall to my waist and tug my panties to the side. It doesn't matter that Hades has seen and had his mouth over every inch of me. It *feels* wicked to do this, and riding the edge of that feeling is an addiction I'm not sure I'm ever going to shake. I can't think about that now, can't contemplate *after*.

After the winter is over. After I've gained my freedom. After I walk out of Hades's life forever.

He tugs me another few inches closer and leans down to settle between my spread thighs. A single look and I release my panties and prop myself up on my elbows. Hades presses an openmouthed kiss to the silk. I whimper. "Gods, that feels good."

He seems to have no interest in moving my panties out of the way, working me through the fabric slowly, getting me all wet and slippery. It's only when I'm breathing hard and fighting not to lift my hips that he looks up. "We'll have a party tomorrow."

"A...party."

"Mm-hmm." He finally, *finally* nuzzles the panties to the side and gives my pussy a slow, thorough kiss. "Tell me what you want. Describe it in detail."

I have to bite back a moan. "What?"

"Now."

I stare down at him. He wants me to describe what I want right now, while he's tongue-fucking me? Apparently so. I bite my bottom lip and try to focus through the waves of pleasure he's sending through my body. I've had a lot of time to get to know my tastes and Hades's tastes, but this feels like a completely different level. "I, uh, I want..."

I don't want to tell him.

I dig my fingers into his hair and lift my hips to give him better access. The next lick never comes. Despite my grip on him, Hades lifts himself easily away from me. His brows draw together as he searches my face. "With all we've done in the last few weeks, what could you possibly want that has you hesitating now?"

"I like being with you. I love what we do together."

He frowns harder. "Persephone, if I wasn't ready to give you whatever you need, I wouldn't have asked."

I don't want to. I really, really don't want to. It's too wrong, too dirty, even for us. I know it's hypocritical in the extreme to call Hades out for holding back with me and then turn around and do the same to him, but it feels different. It *is* different.

He moves while I'm still fighting with myself, sitting up and hauling me into his lap. My back to his chest, my legs spread to the outside of his thighs. Just like I was that night where he made me come and then I rode his cock in front of everyone.

The same night that seeded the fantasy I'm afraid to put to voice.

Hades slides his hand into my panties to palm my pussy and push two fingers into me. Then he stills, holding me in place in the most intimate way possible. "You're tense, little siren. Is this bringing back memories?"

"Of course not. Why would you say that?" I speak too quickly, my voice too breathy to make my bravado the least bit convincing.

He kisses my neck and moves up to my ear. "Tell me."

"I don't want to."

"Do you think I'll judge you?"

It's not that. I whimper as he curls his fingers along my inner wall. Just like that, the truth spills from my lips. "I don't want to do anything you don't want to do."

He goes still for one long moment and then chuckles against my skin. "I hit a nerve that night, didn't I?" Another delicious curl of his fingertips. His voice rumbles in my ear. "Say it. Tell me what fantasy you've had playing in the back of your mind since that party."

My resistance crumbles. I close my eyes. "I want to be the one on the dais. Not in the shadowy corner with you. Right out there in the spotlight while you fuck me in front of everyone. Where you claim me and make me yours where everyone can see."

He keeps stroking my G-spot. "Was that so hard?"

"*Yes*." I grip his forearm, but even I can't say if I'm trying to push him away or keep him touching me. "I know you don't like being exposed like that."

"Mmmm." He nips my earlobe. He presses the heel of his palm against my clit. "Do you think there's anything I wouldn't give you while you're mine? Fucking *anything*, little siren."

I don't have words, but that's okay because he apparently has words enough for both of us. He keeps up those slow movements, a steady coiling of pleasure through me, tighter and tighter, as if we have all the time in the world.

Time is one thing we don't have.

His free hand comes up to yank the straps of my dress off my shoulders and let it fall to my waist. Somehow this being half-dressed while he fucks me with his fingers feels even sexier than if I was naked. Hades always knows what gets me off the hardest, and he never hesitates to put it into reality. "I'll bend you over a chair and flip up your skirt so everyone can see your needy little pussy. Spread you wide with my fingers."

"Yes," I gasp out.

"I'll give this to you, love. I'll give you everything." He chuckles darkly. "Would you like to know a truth?"

"Yes."

"I'll get off on playing out that fantasy, too." He pushes a third finger into me. "If I want to strip you down and fuck you until you're begging for mercy, that's exactly what I'll do. Because it pleases me. Because it will get you off. Because there is nothing you can ask me that I won't give you. Do you understand?"

"*Yes*." This is it, the thing that I couldn't quite conceptualize, the reason why that dark threat held such promise for me. I should have known he'd understand, shouldn't have doubted him.

Hades hauls me up and bends me over the arm of the couch. He flips up my skirt and pulls my panties down to my thighs. "Don't move." He's gone for a few seconds and there's the crinkle of a condom wrapper. And then he's pushing his way inside me, one inch by devastating inch.

The position creates a tighter fit and my panties prevent me from spreading my thighs. It's the lightest bondage imaginable, but it makes this a thousand times hotter. Hades hooks his fingers at my hips and then he's fucking me. I scramble to get a good hold on the cushion, but my fingers slide across the leather, unable to find purchase. Hades doesn't hesitate. He pulls me up and back against his chest, one hand bracketing my throat and the other delving down to press against my clit. Each stroke creates a delicious friction that has me soaring to new heights.

His voice is so low, I can almost feel it more than hear it. "Your pussy is mine to do with as I please. In public. In private. Wherever I want it. The way you, little siren, are *mine*."

"If I'm yours…" And I am. I undoubtedly am. I can't catch my breath, can barely get the next words out. "Then you're mine, too."

"Yes." His rough voice in my ear. "Fuck, yes, I'm yours."

I come hard, writhing against his hand and around his cock. Hades bends me back over the couch and finishes in a series of brutal thrusts. He pulls out, and I barely get a chance to miss the feel of him at my back before he returns and lifts me into his arms. After that first night visiting the winter market, I've stopped pseudo complaining about him carrying me around. We both know it'd be a lie if I kept it up, because I enjoy these moments just as much as he seems to.

He walks us into what's become our bedroom and sets me down. I catch his wrist before he can move to the light switch like he normally does. "Hades?"

"Yeah?"

The urge to drop my gaze, to let this go, is nearly overwhelming, but after he's demanded I be honest and vulnerable with him, I can demand nothing but the same in return. I meet his eyes. "Keep the lights on? Please."

He goes so still, I think he stops breathing. "You don't want that."

"I wouldn't ask for it if I didn't want it." I know I should stop pushing, but I can't seem to help myself. "Don't you trust me not to turn away?"

His breath shudders out. "It's not that."

That's what it feels like. But saying as much puts him in a terrible position. I want his trust the same way he seems to crave mine; forcing the issue isn't the way to get it. Reluctantly, I release his wrist. "Okay."

"Persephone..." He hesitates. "Are you sure?"

Something flutters in my chest, as light and fluid as hope but somehow stronger. "If you're comfortable with it, yes."

"Okay." His hands move to the buttons of his shirt and pause. "Okay," he repeats. Slowly, oh so slowly, he begins to remove his clothing.

Even as I tell myself not to stare, I can't help drinking in the sight of him. I've felt his scars, but they're borderline gruesome to see in the light. The sheer danger he must have been in, the pain he survived, leaves me breathless. The burns cover most of his torso and down his right hip. His legs have some smaller scars, but nothing on the same level as his chest and back.

Zeus did this to him.

That bastard would have killed a small child the same way he killed Hades's parents.

The desire to wrap this man up and protect him makes my tone fierce. "You're beautiful."

"Don't start lying to me now."

"I mean it." I lift my hands and press them carefully to his chest. I've touched him there dozens of times now, but this is the first time I've seen him fully. Part of me wonders what happened to him in the years since the fire that has caused him to hide so effectively, even during sex, and the protective desire swirling through me gets stronger. I can't heal this man's scars, not internal or external, but surely I can help in some small way? "You're beautiful to me. The scars are part of that, part of *you*. They're a mark of everything you've survived, of how strong you are. That fucker tried to kill you as a child and you survived him. You're going to beat him, Hades. You will."

He gives me a ghost of a smile. "I don't want to beat him. I want him dead."

21

HADES

I WAKE UP WITH PERSEPHONE IN MY ARMS. IT'S BECOME MY favorite part of the day, that first slide of awareness and the warmth of her. Despite what she said that first time, she's a cuddler, and it doesn't matter where we start out when we fall asleep, because she finds her way to me in the dark. Over and over again, every night we spend together in my bed.

If I was a hopeful kind of man, I'd see this as a sign of something more. I know better. She likes what we do together. She even likes *me* at least a tolerable amount. But the only reason we're together right now is because we're on parallel paths to make Zeus pay. The second that's accomplished, this ends.

Neither of us is fool enough to believe the last few weeks are anything but the quiet before the storm. Everyone thinks Zeus is loud and brash, but he's only that way to distract from what he's doing behind the scenes. For three weeks, he's been attending parties and acting as if nothing is wrong. Demeter hasn't publicly followed through on her threat, but the shipments into the lower city have decreased a marked amount. If we hadn't spent years preparing to be cut off, my people would be suffering right now.

All for pride.

I smooth Persephone's golden hair back from her face. If I was a better man... But I'm not. I've set myself on this path and I'll see it through to the end. I should be delighted that she wants to play out the fantasy I described to her that night. Maybe her fucking me isn't enough to force Zeus's hand, but every time she rides my cock in public, we get closer to that point. Every time the rumor mill swirls with what people have witnessed while visiting my playroom, her perceived value decreases in Zeus's eyes. A brilliant move, even if I'm not making it for brilliant reasons.

She wants it. I want to give it to her. That's enough of a reason for me.

Persephone stirs against me and opens those hazel eyes. She smiles. "Morning."

The dull thump in my chest that happens more and more around her gains teeth and claws. I can't help smiling in response, even as part of me wants to get the fuck out of this bed and start walking and not stop until I have myself under control. Just because I've never felt like this before doesn't mean I'm not aware of what's happening.

I'm falling for Persephone.

Maybe there'd be time to save myself if I backed out now, but I'm not so sure. Either way, it doesn't matter. I'm not stopping until I have to, no matter how much pain it causes at the end of this. I smooth her hair back again. "Morning."

She cuddles closer and lays her head on my scarred chest as

if the sight doesn't repulse her. Who knows? Maybe it doesn't. She'd be the only one, though. I had one relationship very early on where I was naked with my partner, and his response was strong enough to ensure I never did it again. Maybe others would have been more welcoming, but I never gave them the chance.

Not like I'm giving her the chance now.

"Are things going okay?" Her hand quivers like she wants to touch me, but then she seems to forcibly still it on my waist. Respecting how hard it still is for me to lie here in the morning light with my scars exposed. "You haven't said much this week about supply lines and the like."

I release a slow breath and try to relax. I don't know if I want her to touch me or not touch me. I don't know shit when it comes to this woman, apparently. It's almost a relief to focus on the greater problem outside this bedroom. "We're in a holding pattern. The supplies keep dwindling, but we were prepared for that. Zeus hasn't so much as prodded our borders."

She tenses. "I can't believe my mother would be so cruel. I'm so sorry. I honestly thought…" She gives a mirthless laugh. "I don't know what I thought that first night. That no one would miss me if I disappeared? It seems very shortsighted when I look back now."

"It wasn't shortsighted so much as you were terrified and reacting." But I know Persephone well enough now to know that acting without a plan amounts to an unforgivable sin. "It just means you're human. Humans get scared and run sometimes. It's not something you need to beat yourself up over."

She huffs out a breath, but she's still staring at things beyond this room. "I don't get to be human. Not when my whole future hangs in the balance. And even then, I should have been thinking of someone other than myself."

So we're back to this.

I gather her into my arms and hold her close. "Do you trust me, Persephone?"

"What?" She cranes her neck to see my face, her dark brows pulled together. "What kind of question is that?"

"A legitimate one." I try not to hold my breath while I wait for a response.

Thank the gods she doesn't make me wait long. Persephone nods, suddenly solemn. "Yes, Hades, I trust you."

The clawing feeling in my chest only gets stronger. It feels like my heart is trying to dig its way through calcified tissue to get to her. I'm rapidly reaching the point where I'd cut my chest open and dig my heart out just so I can present it to her. What the fuck is wrong with me? She's leaving. She was always leaving.

I never thought she'd take my beaten-up heart with her when she walked away.

"Hades?"

I blink and push the new revelation away. "If you trust me, then trust me when I say you're doing better than anyone else would have in your situation."

She's frowning at me again. "It's not that simple."

"It's exactly that simple."

"You can't just decree it to be so and wipe all the doubt from my mind."

I chuckle. "I wouldn't even if I could. I like you when you're difficult."

Persephone shifts, sliding a leg over my hips and moving up to straddle me. With her hair a mess and her body backlit by the faint morning sun sneaking through the curtains, she looks like some kind of spring goddess, all warm and earthy.

She holds my gaze. "Since we're on the subject of trust, I want to talk about protection." She holds perfectly still, as if she doesn't notice my cock hardening against her. "As in, I would like to stop using it."

My breath catches in my throat. "You don't have to do that."

"I know, Hades. I don't have to do anything with you that I don't want to do."

The easy way she says it makes me feel... She just flat-out makes me feel. A lot. I gently set my hands on her hips. "I'm tested regularly."

She nods as if she expects no less, taking me at my word. The sheer trust she's putting in me is a little staggering. Persephone covers my hands with her own. "I haven't been with anyone since my ex-girlfriend, and I was tested after that. I'm also on birth control—an IUD."

"You don't have to do this," I repeat. I want to be inside her without a barrier more than I want almost anything right now, but I also don't want her to agree to something she's not one hundred percent ready for. I really should know Persephone better by now.

"Hades." She doesn't move. "Do *you* not want to? Because it's okay if you don't. I know there's some trust involved with the entire birth-control subject, and if you're not comfortable with it, that's okay, too. I promise it is."

For a moment, I just stare at her in shock. When was the last time someone took *my* comfort level into account? I don't know. I really have no fucking idea. When I was with partners in the past, *I* was the dominant one, the responsible party who designed the scenes and ran them. I like that role, like having others submit to me, but I didn't realize how *tired* I am until Persephone offers me the tiniest of considerations.

She's frowning again. "Oh gods, I crossed a line, didn't I? I'm sorry. Forget I said anything."

I tighten my grip on her hips before she can move. "Hold on. Give me a second."

"Take as long as you need." She says it so meekly, I almost laugh.

I finally get ahold of myself. "I think we're on the same page." I speak slowly, feeling my way. "If you change your mind at any point, we'll go back to condoms."

"If you change your mind, too." She gives me a happy smile and grips my wrists, slowly bringing my hands up to palm her breasts. "Never a better time to start than now."

"Can't argue that."

She arches her brows. "Really? You're not going to argue even a *little* bit? How disappointing."

I snag the back of her neck and tow her down to meet my mouth. As much as I enjoy sniping back and forth with her, I'm not in the mood right now. The amount of trust she's placing in me staggers me on a level I'm not prepared to deal with. This isn't anything as deceptively simple as telling each other truths. She's taking my word that she's safe with me in this moment.

Persephone melts against my chest, eagerly meeting my kiss. I slide my hands around to grip her ass and shift her up enough that my cock notches at her entrance. I hold perfectly still, giving her plenty of time to change her mind. I really should know better by now. She's set herself on this path and is ready to eagerly race forward just like she seems to do with everything else.

She circles her hips slowly, working the head of my cock inside her. Persephone shifts to whisper in my ear. "This feels so wicked, doesn't it? You're so hard, it makes me crazy." She gives her hips another swivel. "Talk to me, Hades. Tell me how good I feel. I love it when you spill sexy filth into my ears while you're inside me."

I love it, too. I let my hands coast down her ass to stroke the point where the curve meets the back of her upper thighs. "You're so tight and wet, little siren. I think you like being wicked."

"Yes." She sinks another slow inch onto me.

"Don't play coy. You wanted my cock. Now take it."

She moans and slams all the way down, sheathing me to the hilt. I tangle my fingers in her hair and draw her close for another kiss. It's messy and fucking perfect. It gets even better when she starts moving, rolling her hips even as she fights not to break the kiss. I can already tell it won't be enough.

I release her and nudge her back to press my hand to the center of her chest, urging her to sit up. "Ride me."

She obeys, arching her back and riding me in slow, decadent strokes. I watch my cock disappear into her pussy and have to fight not to come from the sight alone. The feel of her without a barrier between us, the sheer amount of trust she's placing in me, it's all too heady. I can't think. I feel like I'm having an out-of-body experience because the only thing I can do is hang on to her as she fucks me slowly and thoroughly.

She's a golden goddess and I'm just a mortal who will never deserve her.

Persephone grabs my wrists again, moving one hand to the apex of her thighs. "Touch me. Please, Hades. Make me come." She moves the other to bracket her throat and leans into the contact. "Don't stop."

Sweet fuck.

I tense my arm, letting her press her throat harder against the palm of my hand, letting her control the pressure, and trace slow circles around her clit with my thumb. Her eyes slide shut with pleasure, and then she's coming, her pussy clenching around my cock. It's too much. Another time, I'll go slower, last longer, but right now all I want is to follow her over the edge. I drive up into her, pleasure overwhelming me.

Persephone catches my mouth, catches *me*, in a kiss that slows everything and settles me back into my body, cell by cell. I wrap my arms around her and hold her close. My heart feels bloody and raw and that should scare me, but it's somehow cathartic as fuck. I don't understand it, but I don't need to.

I press a kiss to her forehead. "Let's take a shower and get moving."

"Really?" She stretches against me, an intoxicating sensation of her skin against mine. "I thought maybe we could just play hooky and stay in bed."

"If we do that, we can't visit the greenhouse again today."

She lifts her head so suddenly, she almost clocks me in the chin. "The greenhouse?"

If I had any doubts about my plans for the day, the happiness written across her features would have banished them. "Yes."

She's up and off me before I have a chance to brace for it. "Well then, what are you waiting for? Let's get moving."

I watch her ass as she strides across the room and disappears through the door to the bathroom. A few seconds later, the water turns on and her voice floats out. "Coming? I think we'll save time if we share a shower." The wicked lilt to her tone gives lie to the words.

I find myself grinning as I climb out of bed and stalk toward the bathroom. "Save time and water. Sounds like a plan."

PERSEPHONE

HADES AND I SPEND A BLISSFUL HOUR IN THE GREENHOUSE, and then we make a few stops as we head back toward the house so he can see and be seen. He doesn't explicitly say that's why we're wandering the aisles of a hardware shop after we did the same in a little market store, but I see the way people watch him. The careful way he notes empty shelves, I have no doubt that he's creating a mental list of gaps in the supply chain and looking for ways to plug those holes so his people don't suffer.

He's brusque and straightforward to the point of rudeness, but it couldn't be clearer that his people worship the ground he walks on. I lose count of how many times shop owners thank him for taking care of them while things are tight.

More, people are working together to ensure everyone is taken care of. It's a mentality that I vaguely remember from a time before moving to Olympus, but years in the upper city have made it feel new and novel. It's not that everyone in the upper city is selfish or evil. Hardly. It's more that they take their cues from the rest of the Thirteen and are very, very aware that they are never truly safe.

Yet another difference in the legion that separate Hades from Zeus.

We leave the hardware shop and walk down the street. It feels the most natural thing in the world to slip my hand into Hades's just like I always seem to when we take these walks. He laces his fingers through mine and it feels *so right*, I can't breathe for a few steps. I open my mouth to say... I'm not even sure.

I see the sign before I get a chance to. I stop short. "What's that?"

Hades follows my gaze. "It's a pet store. Family-owned, have been for three or four generations, if I'm remembering right. Not counting the three who currently run it." He rattles the history off just like he did about the family who runs the gyro stall in the winter market, without having any awareness of how novel it is that he has this information readily available from memory.

"Can we go in?" I don't bother to keep the excitement from my voice. When he raises a single brow, I can't help trying to explain. "When I was very young, we had two dogs. They were working dogs, of course—nothing goes to waste on a farm, industrial or not—but I loved them. Having pets in the high-rise is strictly forbidden, of course." I have to fight down the urge to bounce on my toes like a child. "Please, Hades. I just want to look."

If anything, his brow rises higher. "Somehow, I don't believe you." But he gives one of his slow smiles. "Of course we can go in, Persephone. Lead the way."

A bell dings above our heads as we walk through the door. I

inhale the mixed scent of animals and wood shavings, and a feeling wells up inside me that's part nostalgia and part something I can't identify. I don't spend much time thinking about my life before my mother became Demeter and we moved to the city. There's no way she'd leave us behind, and pining for a life that was no longer mine seemed a study in madness. Better, easier, to focus on the future and my path to freedom.

I'm not even sure why a pet store brings it all back, but my heart is in my throat as I wander the first aisle, looking at guinea pigs and brightly colored birds. We reach the end near a counter and see two pretty Black women standing there, heads bent over a computer. They look up and catch sight of us. One of them, the woman wearing a faded pair of jeans and an orange knit sweater, grins in recognition. "Finally decided to take my advice?"

"Hello, Gayle." He moves past me and she pulls him into a hug. "We're just doing the rounds."

"Oh, that." She waves it away. "We're fine. You've more than made sure of that." She grips his shoulders and looks up at him. "We support you. No matter what."

There it is again, the sheer loyalty Hades commands. He does it without threats or making lavish promises. His people will follow him to the end of the earth simply because he respects them and does his best to see they're taken care of. It's a powerful thing to witness.

He nods. "Appreciate it."

She drops her hands and grins again. "Don't suppose today is finally the day I convince you to get a dog or two so you aren't haunting that giant house by yourself?"

I perk up. "Dogs?"

She finally looks at me, and her attitude cools a little. "We don't normally keep any dogs but Old Man Joe in the shop." She motions behind her at a dog bed that I thought contained a bunch of towels. A head lifts and I realize it's not towels at all. It's a Komondor dog. He shakes his hair out of his eyes and gives a big yawn.

"Oh my gods," I whisper. "Hades, look at that magnificent creature."

"I see," he says drily.

Gayle shrugs. "Like I was saying, we don't normally keep dogs here, but Jessie found a box of them by Cypress Bridge. I don't know if someone from the upper city decided to dump them there or if it was one of ours, but…" She sighs. "People can be real assholes sometimes."

I manage to drag my attention away from the dog at that. "They just dumped them there?" I have absolutely no business feeling a kinship for these puppies I've never seen, but I can't deny that it feels like a strange twist of fate. "Can we see them?"

"Yeah." She jerks her thumb over her shoulder. "We have them back here. They look like they were old enough to be weaned, so that's a silver lining."

I'm already moving, slipping past Hades and Gayle in the direction she indicated. Sure enough, there is a large box set up near the back of the shop. I lean over and look in and gasp. "Oh my *gods*."

There are three of them, all perfectly black. I'm not quite sure of the breed—I suspect they're mutts—but they're cute as they sleep in a puppy pile against one corner. I reach out, then stop to look at Gayle. "May I?"

"By all means." Most of the frostiness is gone from her when she looks at me, and I'm certain I see amusement lingering in her dark eyes. "I take it you're a dog person."

"I'm an equal-opportunity pet person." I go to my knees next to the box and reach down to run a gentle hand over the back of the puppy on top of the pile. "I like cats, too. Fish, I can take or leave."

"Noted." Now Gayle is definitely fighting back laughter, but that's okay. I don't mind her finding me amusing.

"Hades, *look*."

He sinks to his knees next to me. "I'm looking." There's something strange in his tone, and it's enough to get me to drag my attention from the puppies. *Oh my gods, they're so soft.*

I study his face. He looks almost pained. "What's wrong?"

"Nothing."

I wrinkle my nose. "Your words are saying 'nothing' but your expression is saying something else altogether."

He sighs, but not like he's irritated. More like he's giving in. "They're very cute." He reaches down and lifts one carefully into his arms. Now he *really* looks pained. "They shouldn't have been left like that."

I'm aware of Gayle moving back to the computer with the woman who must be her mother, giving us space and at least the illusion of privacy. "It happens a lot, especially if they aren't purebred. They're essentially worthless to breeders and just more mouths to feed. It's crappy."

"Crappy," Hades echoes. The puppy nuzzles his chest and settles into his arms with a sigh. He strokes its head with a single finger like he's afraid of hurting it. "It's a terrible thing not to be wanted."

My heart gives a painful twist. I speak before giving myself a chance to think. "You should adopt one. She's right about that big, empty house, and no one loves like a dog. He or she will win you over before you know it."

He contemplates the puppy, still petting it methodically. "It's not a good idea."

"Why?"

"It's easier not to care."

I might laugh if there was any air left in the room. Hades might pretend he doesn't care, but this man cares more than any other I've ever met. He tries too hard to hold people at a distance, but he obviously hasn't noticed how epically he's failed. I'm not sure I should be the one to tell him, that it's my place to pull back the curtain and show him the truth of his circumstances. I'm not a permanent fixture in his life. The thought leaves me feeling hollow.

Suddenly, I'm determined to convince him to buy this puppy. The thought of Hades wandering the halls of his house alone after I leave, a lord of emptiness and sorrow... I can't stand it. I can't let it happen. "Hades, you should adopt the puppy."

He finally looks at me. "This is important to you."

"Yes." When he just waits, I give him a sliver of the truth. "Everyone should have a pet at least once in their lives. It's such a blessing, and I think it would make you happy. I like the thought of you happy, Hades." The last comes out almost like a confession. Like a secret, just between us.

He stares at me a long time, and I'm at a loss to guess what's going on behind his dark eyes. Is he thinking about the deadline looming over us, too? Impossible to say. He finally nods slowly. "Maybe a dog wouldn't be a bad idea."

I can't help holding my breath. "Really?"

"Yeah." His attention tracks down to the remaining two pups. "He'll be awfully lonely without his littermates."

"Um." I'm pretty sure my eyes are in danger of popping out of my head. "What?"

Instead of answering directly, he raises his voice. "Gayle?" When she reappears, he nods at the puppies. "We'll take them all."

She presses her lips together. "I'm not one to tell you how to do your business."

He arches a brow. "When has that ever stopped you?"

"Three dogs is a lot, Hades. Three puppies? You're biting off more than you can chew." She points at the puppies. "And they will chew the shit out of your expensive shoes."

He's undeterred. He's put himself on this path and he won't be dissuaded. "I'll give the staff hazard pay. It will be fine."

For a moment, I think she'll keep arguing, but she finally shrugs. "Don't come crying to me in a week or two when teething really sets in."

"I won't."

One final look and she shakes her head. "Better call some of your people to come help fetch and carry. You're not set up for puppies, so we'll need to load you up."

"Consider it done. We'll get whatever you think is best."

She walks away, still shaking her head and muttering about stubborn men. I turn back to Hades and can't stop from grinning widely. "You're buying three dogs."

"*We're* buying three dogs." He pushes easily to his feet, the pup still cradled in his arms. "You should know by now that I can't say no to you, Persephone. You turn those big hazel eyes on me, and I'm putty in your hands."

I snort. I can't help it. "You're so full of shit."

"Language," he murmurs, mirth lighting up his eyes.

I burst out laughing. The giddiness soaring through me is pure, undiluted happiness. A feeling I have no right to, not with everything hanging over our heads, but somehow that makes it more precious. I want to cling to this moment, to shove reality away and let us have this time uninterrupted.

Because no matter what he says, these dogs aren't really mine. They're his, the way it should be. I'll get them for the rest of the winter, but that's it. Then I'll leave and they'll be Hades's little pack. Companionship that he'll hopefully allow even if he holds the humans around him at a distance.

My little bubble of happiness deflates instantly. He deserves so much more than the hand life has dealt him. He deserves to be happy. He deserves to be surrounded by friends and loved ones who will fill his giant house with laughter and experiences. He's such a *good* person, even if he's a villain as far as Olympus is concerned—at least the parts of Olympus that even believe in him.

It takes a solid thirty minutes to get everything we need and for Hades's man Charon to show up with two guys to help haul it all back home. It's not until I walk through the front door that I realize I was thinking of this place as *home* before just today. That it feels more like a home than the high-rise penthouse my mother owns ever did, my sisters' presence or no.

A sliver of panic spears through me. No matter how much I'm enjoying my time with Hades, this *can't* be home. I've sacrificed too much, asked my sisters to sacrifice too much, to not follow through now. I have to leave after I turn twenty-five, have to take my trust fund and power my way out of Olympus. If I don't... What was even the point?

I'll have traded one beautiful cage for another.

And that's one thing I can't allow.

HADES

"HADES, WE'RE GOING TO BE LATE."

I sit on the floor while the three black pups play in and out of my lap. It took them most of the day to warm up to the space, and we decided to clear out a room near the interior courtyard so we have easy access to the outside for potty breaks. So much to consider, it almost distracted me from what's coming.

Almost.

I look up and my breath catches in my throat. Persephone is beautiful in everything she wears, but she's *stunning* in black. The stark color sets off her golden skin and blond hair. It doesn't exactly cover up her brightness but gives the feel of a stray sunbeam that's somehow found its way to the Underworld. The dress clings to her skin like oil, pouring over her breasts and down her hips to fall to the floor around her feet.

She looks like a fucking queen.

"Hades?"

I give myself a mental shake, but I can't take my eyes off her. "You look beautiful."

She glances down at herself and smooths her hands over her hips. "Juliette outdid herself with this one. It's deceptively simple, but the cut and fabric are just masterful."

I carefully move the pups off my lap and rise to my feet. "It wouldn't look nearly as masterful on anyone else."

"Now you're just teasing me." But she's smiling as if my compliments make her happy. I have to rein in the impulse to promise to compliment her every day if it puts that expression on her face. Has she noticed how she's slowly relaxed and unfurled in the last few weeks? I have. She's stopped guarding her words so closely, has stopped considering each conversation like a battlefield she might not come out the other side of. Another clear indication of the trust she places in me.

In how safe she feels.

She nods at the puppies, her expression going indulgent. "Have you considered names?"

"Dog." I don't mean it. I only say it to see her roll her eyes at me.

She doesn't disappoint. "Hades, you have three dogs. You can't call them all 'dog.' They need names."

"Cerberus." I point to the largest of the three, the one who's the clear leader, even at this age. "This one is Cerberus."

"I like it." She smiles. "Now, the other two."

"I want you to name them."

Her brows draw together, and for the first time since she walked into the room, she looks unsure. "I don't think that's a good idea." Because she's leaving.

Instinct tells me to back off, to protect myself, but the deadline makes me reckless. "Persephone."

"Yes?" Is there hope in her tone? I'm afraid to assume.

There are a thousand things I could say right now, a thousand things I want to say. Spending the last few weeks with her has made me the happiest I can remember being. She challenges me and delights me in turn, and I have a feeling I could know this woman for decades and she'd still find ways to surprise me. I suddenly, desperately want this winter never to end, want spring never to come, want to stay with her here forever.

But there is no forever. Not for us.

I cross to her and cup her face in my hands. "If we were different people in different circumstances, I would get down on my knees and beg you to stay at the end of the winter. I would move heaven and earth and the Underworld itself to keep you with me."

She blinks those big hazel eyes at me and licks her lips. "If…" She sounds so hesitant, I simultaneously want to gather her into my arms and don't want to move in case she never finishes that sentence. She doesn't leave me hanging long. "If we were different people, you wouldn't have to beg. I'd plant my roots right here in this house, and it would take a catastrophic event to make me walk away."

If. A key word, a vital word, one that might as well be a hundred-foot wall between us and that future I'm too goddamn foolish not to want. "We're not different people."

Her eyes go a little shiny. "No. We're not different people."

My whole body goes heavy as the truth settles in my bones. I love this woman. I have to steel myself to keep from doing exactly what I said, from dropping to my knees and begging her to stay. It's not fair to her to pull a stunt like that. I don't want to be yet another jailer who she'll come to resent. Persephone wants freedom, and the only way she can obtain that is to leave Olympus. I can't be the reason she doesn't follow through on her plan. I refuse to be.

My voice is hoarse when I finally pull forth words. Not ones that will keep her with me. I might love her—fuck, the very idea makes me light-headed—but if I tell her, it will change things. It's a trap I won't spring. "Leave me a piece of you, little siren. Name the pups."

She presses her lips together and finally nods. "Okay." Persephone steps back, and I release her. I watch as she bends down to pet the pups now trying to climb up her legs. "This one will be Charybdis."

"*Charybdis?*"

She ignores me. "And this little one will be Scylla."

I blink. "Those names are...something."

"They are, aren't they?" She gives me a mischievous smile. "They'll grow into them, I'm sure."

Georgie bustles into the room, takes one look at us, and plants her hands on her hips. "What are you still doing here?"

"Naming puppies," Persephone says easily. "Meet Cerberus, Charybdis, and Scylla."

Georgie nods as if those names are completely normal and expected. "Good strong names for good strong dogs. Now get out of here and let me play with them." She'd taken one look at us coming through the door earlier and declared the puppies the grandchildren she'll never have. I have a feeling I'm going to have to arm-wrestle her to get time with them going forward, but we'll figure it out.

I offer my arm to Persephone and she lays her hand on my forearm, as graceful and regal as the queen I named her earlier. As we walk through the halls toward the basement room, I allow myself to picture what it might be like if this didn't have an expiration date. If she ruled at my side, a dark queen to my king of the lower city.

I wouldn't let her stay in the shadows indefinitely. I'd fight to give her every bit of sunlight and happiness I could find.

It's not in the cards for us.

I force my attention forward and stop us just short of the door. "You know how this goes. If you change your mind or want things to stop, tell me and it all stops."

She gives me a ghost of a smile. "I know." For a second, she looks nervous, but she shuts it down almost immediately. "I'm ready."

"It's okay if you're not."

Persephone opens her mouth, seems to reconsider. "I'm more nervous than I thought I'd be. We had sex in the shadows last time, and even if people were watching, it felt different. The fantasy feels so hot and present when I'm thinking about it, but knowing it will actually happen is a little...intimidating."

I study her expression. I can't tell if she's got the good kind of nervousness or if she's starting to regret asking for this. "You don't have to do this."

"I know." The surety seeps back into her tone. "I know that I don't have to do anything I don't want to when I'm with you." Persephone takes a deep breath and squares her shoulders. "Maybe we can play it by ear?"

"That sounds like a plan." I don't know what I'm feeling right now. I'm not opposed to public sex in the spotlight. With the right parties involved and a clear set of expectations, it can be hot as hell. When Persephone finally confessed that it's what she wants, I was just as turned on as she was.

I didn't feel quite so raw that night. I knew I cared about her, but love? I've gone thirty-three years without feeling it, so I'd half convinced myself that I'm not capable of the emotion. Trust this woman to make a liar out of me.

I get us moving again and then we're through the door and into the room. Despite my sending out invites this morning, the space is packed. They might be here to play, but they really showed up to watch another spectacle with me and the society darling I stole from beneath Zeus's nose. If only that were the truth. Then I could keep her.

I take her hand and begin to weave through the room. The only path to the throne takes us through several sets of chairs and couches. It was designed that way, letting them look at me like a tiger in a zoo. Close enough to touch, but they know better than to try. I see familiar faces as we move through the room. Eros is here again, a man under one arm and a woman under the other. He gives me an arrogant smile as we pass. For once, no one seems to have started the party without us.

They're all waiting for the show.

With each step, Persephone's stride becomes more stilted. I look back and find her hazel eyes glassy even though her sunshine smile is in place. Her *mask*. Fuck.

My throne is empty, as always. I sink into it and pull Persephone into my lap. She's so tense, she's shaking, and that only further confirms what I suspect. I tuck her legs up and over my thighs, encompassing her as much as possible with my body. "Take a slow breath, Persephone."

"I'm trying." She sounds like she's drowning. Not in desire. Not in anticipation. In fear.

I capture her chin and guide her face up until she meets my gaze. "I changed my mind."

"What?"

I have to play this carefully. She won't thank me for managing her, but I'm also not going to let her soldier on simply for the sake of doing it. There will be other nights, other opportunities. I'm not engaging in something that will harm her. I give her a long look. "I'm not in the mood to fuck your pretty pussy on the dais tonight."

Relief flares in her eyes and she gives a shy smile. "I'm that transparent?"

"I've learned to read you better than most." I lean in. "Though I'm telling the truth. I'm not ready to put you on display on that level yet. I like that we stay in the shadows, that what we have is just for us. Forgive me?"

"Always." She relaxes against me and presses a quick kiss to the corner of my mouth. "It sounds so hot in theory, but now that I'm here…"

"If you decide you're never ready to take it out of fantasy, that's okay."

She leans back. "But it's something you want. Eventually."

I take her hand and play my thumb over her knuckles. "It

appeals to me, yes. Part of that appeal, however, is *your* enjoyment. If you're not turned on by it, then it's a moot point."

"Mmmm." She watches our hands. "Maybe we can start tonight with something in the shadows, in this throne? Then build up from there next time?"

"If you like," I say carefully. I don't comment that we would need a whole lot longer than six weeks to work through all the dirty things she's got pinging around in that impressive brain of hers. It wouldn't be playing fair, and I don't want to hurt her, even in passing.

"But not tonight?"

"Not tonight," I confirm.

"Okay." She seems to relax further, then a sly smile pulls at the edges of her lips. "In that case, Hades, I would very much like to start the night off with you fucking my mouth while you sit on your throne."

I go still. She's had her lips wrapped around my cock dozens of times since the first, but I don't think I'll ever get used to those filthy words coming from her. I won't ever stop craving them, either. I don't tell her that the night is young. She's been vulnerable with me, and now she's offering us something we both want to get us back on firmer ground. I release her and sit back, draping my arms over the chair. "By all means, little siren. Get on your knees."

She wastes no time sliding off me and obeying. Even on her knees, she looks every inch a queen. She undoes the front of my pants and draws out my cock. The little tease licks her lips and looks up at me. "They're all watching, aren't they?"

I don't have to look to know the answer, but I do it anyway.

Now that they've realized the agenda has changed, there are a handful of shadowy figures who are already in the midst of scenes and fucking, but the majority of them are lounging on couches and chairs and facing our direction. "They can't see clearly, but their imaginations are doing the work for them."

"Mmmm." She shivers, and this time it's all desire. "They look at us and see you debasing Zeus's property."

"You're not his property." It comes out harsher than I mean it to.

She wraps a hand around the base of my cock. "I know." Persephone gives me a heartbreaking smile. "Ruin my makeup, Hades. Put on a good show, just for us."

Us.

This woman will kill me if she keeps talking like that, like it's us against the world. Like we're a team, a unit, a pair. I don't correct her, though. Instead, I allow myself to sink into the fantasy the same way she seems to be doing. The fantasy of *us.*

I wrap her hair around my fist and steel my expression to something cold and contained. "Suck my cock, little siren. Make it good."

"Yes, Sir." She doesn't hesitate, just swallows me down until she has to move her hand for her lips to meet my base. She gags a little, but that doesn't deter her in the least. I'm not doing anything but holding on as Persephone picks up a rhythm easily enough, practically choking on my cock with every downstroke. But it looks like I am. As tears smudge her mascara and she leaves lipstick around my base and smears around the edges of her lips, it *seems* like I'm forcing her.

Even without looking, I can feel the sexual tension in the room heightening. But I do look. I survey the room while Persephone fights to take my cock into her throat, seeing those who look on the scene with lust and those who appear almost worried.

I hate it.

Every other time I've done a scene like this, it's been to build another layer to the myth of Hades, to add to the reputation that I am a man not to be fucked with. They've looked at me with fear before, and it's never bothered me because their fear serves a purpose. Persephone isn't just some anonymous partner playing a role before she drifts back to her normal life. It doesn't matter that she needs this scene, needs the end result as much as I do. The thought that they think I'm tarnishing Zeus's fiancée purely for revenge sits like broken glass in my chest.

The fact that they believe that something as earthy and natural as *sex* can tarnish a person only drives those shards deeper.

Her fingers dig into my thighs and I jerk my gaze from the room to Persephone. She moves off my cock enough to say. "Stay with me, Hades. We're the only ones who matter tonight."

She's right. I know she's right. I close my eyes for a breath, two, and open them. The only one in this room who matters is kneeling between my legs, staring up at me with hazel eyes gone so hot, it's a wonder we both don't combust on the spot. She's a beautiful mess and knowing that she allowed it for *me*? That's some intoxicating shit.

"I'm here." I clear my suddenly tight throat. "I'm with you."

She smiles and takes my cock back into her mouth, resuming driving me out of my mind with pleasure. I don't try to hold out.

Not when Persephone is sucking me so sweetly, not when she's turned this into something just for us instead of a show for *them*. I swipe my thumbs over her cheeks, catching her tears. "I'm almost there." A warning and a promise. She immediately picks up her pace, sucking my cock like her redemption is on the other side of this orgasm.

I let go. The entire rooms shrinks down to her and me, and pleasure takes over. She swallows me down as I come, sucking me until I have to nudge her off my cock. Persephone licks her lips and gives me a happy smile. "I really, really love seeing you undone like that."

I really, really love you.

Somehow, I keep the words inside. I can't tell her that without chaining her to me, without ruining everything. But... I can show her. I can give her a gift in return for everything she's given me over the last few weeks, cumulating in this scene. This woman doesn't deserve to be on her knees. She deserves to be worshipped. She deserves to be on the throne as my equal.

I intend to put her there.

I tuck myself back into my pants. "Up."

She must expect to end up back in my lap, because her eyes go wide when I move and nudge her onto the chair I just occupied. Onto the throne. Her brows draw together, but I don't give her a chance to question me. I simply go to my knees before her.

Her eyes go wide. "Hades, what are you doing?"

For a moment, I can only stare up at her. Her dress spills over her legs and down to the floor, the dark throne behind her and careful lighting giving her blond hair a halo effect. Even with her makeup less than perfect, there's no denying the power vibrating from every cell of her being. I thought she looked like a queen before, but I was fucking wrong.

She's a goddamn goddess.

PERSEPHONE

I CAN'T DEAL WITH LOOKING AT THE REST OF THE ROOM, SO I focus entirely on the man kneeling at my feet. Doesn't he understand how unnatural this is? Yes, he's been on his knees before me before, but it was different then. Private, just between us. No matter our positions, there's no doubt in my mind that he's dominant down to his very soul. He's never actually *submitted* to me.

He's not doing it now, either.

But it looks like he is, which is all that matters to the people witnessing. They're watching Hades of the Thirteen kneel at the feet of a woman sitting in *his* throne. I thought we were marking me as his and his alone, but this doesn't fit that plan.

"What are you doing?" I whisper.

"Paying tribute."

The words don't make sense, but he doesn't give me time to comprehend. He catches the hem of my dress and strokes his hands up my legs, taking the fabric with him. Baring my calves and knees and thighs and finally bunching my dress around my hips.

It's so different from the last time we were in this room. I wasn't worried about modesty then, was so out of my mind with desire that I didn't care who saw what we did in the shadows, but Hades's position makes this act feel secret.

Like it's just for us.

He looks at me like he's never seen me before, like I'm the powerful one in this equation and he truly is paying tribute to someone above his station. It doesn't make sense, but my confusion does nothing to dampen my desire. Especially when he skates his thumbs up my inner thighs and urges me to spread for him.

His attention narrows on my pussy. "You love sucking my cock."

"Guilty. But you knew that already." We're both speaking softly, barely above a whisper. It lends an extra layer of intimacy to this moment despite the eyes on us. "Hades..." I don't know what to say. I don't know what I'm *supposed* to say. "What are we doing?"

He answers with his mouth, but not with words. Hades lowers his head and kisses my pussy. A long, lingering caress that drives all the questions from my mind. They'll hold. Right now, the only rule is pleasure and he's dealing it out in spades. He guides one of my legs up and over the arm of the chair, spreading me wide for him.

Each lick and kiss is like he's memorizing me. He's not intent on my orgasm, that much is clear even as desire sings through my blood. He might be going down on me, but Hades does it like it's purely for *his* pleasure. Somehow, that makes the entire experience that much hotter.

And then I look up.

It's no exaggeration to say that every eye in the room is on us. People have stopped doing whatever they were up to before Hades and I started our own little show. Their lust drips over me, driving my own higher. Power and need twine through me as I meet one set of eyes after another, as I see jealousy and want there.

Some of them want to be me.

Some of them want to be the one kneeling at my feet.

Denying them feels like nothing else I've ever experienced before. We were right to stick to the shadows, to not put ourselves on display in the light. This is so much better, spinning a fantasy of forbidden fruit that everyone in the room is able to see but not touch.

Everyone except for Hades.

He sucks my clit into his mouth, working it with his tongue. It's so shocking after his light touches and teasing licks that it bows my back and draws a cry from my lips. The tension in the room ratchets up several notches, but I'm not looking at our audience any longer. No, only Hades holds my attention. I run my fingers through his hair and dig in, holding him to me.

He growls against my skin, and it feels so wicked, I can barely stand it. "Make me come," I whisper.

For a second, I think he might pull back, remind me that no matter how equal we are, *he* is the one in charge right now. He doesn't. He...obeys.

Hades wedges a finger and then two inside me, twisting his wrist as he searches for the spot that will turn all my joints liquid even as he traces my clit in steady circles with the tip of his tongue. Where before he built my pleasure in steady waves, lapping at my control, now he spins a tsunami of desire that I have no hope of fighting.

I never intended to fight it.

I come with his name on my lips, the sound of it seeming to sing to every corner of the room. Even as he gentles his touches and coaxes me back into my body, I'm shaken by the feeling that nothing will ever be the same again. We've crossed a point of no return that neither of us recognized. There's no going back now. I'm not sure I want to, even if the road remained open.

Hades finally shifts my dress back into place and rises. At first glance, he seems perfectly composed...at least until I get to his eyes. They're wild with the same need surging beneath my skin. This wasn't enough. It barely took the edge off.

He holds out his hand.

I stare at it for the space of a heartbeat. It seems such a simple gesture, but even as shaken as I am, I know better. He's not demanding. He's requesting. Putting us on equal ground. The thing I don't understand is *why*.

In the end, it doesn't matter. I slip my hand into his and let him tug me to my feet. He turns to face the rest of the room, all of whom have stopped pretending to do anything but stare at us. It feels...strange, but not necessarily in a bad way. They're waiting on our whim, and they'll wait as long as we demand.

Is this what power feels like?

Hades seems to stare down each and every person present. "Be sure, when you go running back to your high-rises and glamorous lives in the upper city, that you're telling the full truth of what happened here tonight. She's mine." His hand tightens ever so briefly around mine. "And I'm hers."

This wasn't part of the plan. I'm not exactly sure there *was* a plan going into tonight, not after I got cold feet. But Hades isn't declaring me his the same way he has been since the beginning of this, the way designed to provoke Zeus.

He's declaring it mutual.

It's something we spoke of privately, but doing it like *this* is something else altogether. I don't know what it means. Because I don't know what it means, I can only fight to keep my expression under control as Hades turns us toward the exit and we leave the room. The door barely closes behind me when I murmur, "Not holding court tonight?"

"Fuck them." He barely sounds like himself. "They're only here for the gossip, and I'm not in the mood to play villain." He moves down the hall toward the stairs, nearly dragging me behind him. "They don't see me. No one fucking *sees* me but you."

My heart lodges itself in my throat. "What?"

But he doesn't speak again until we enter his bedroom suite and he slams the door behind him. I've never seen him like this. Angry, yes. Even a little panicked. But this? I don't know what this is. "Hades, what's wrong?"

"I swore I wouldn't do this." He drags his hands through his hair. "What we have isn't simple, but it's the most honest I've been with another person for as long as I can remember. That means something, Persephone. Even if it doesn't mean something to you, it does to me."

I still don't understand, but I at least have an answer to this. "It means something to me, too."

That calms him a little. He drops onto the couch and exhales roughly. "Give me a minute. This isn't your fault. It's shit in my head. I just... I need a minute."

But I don't want to give him a minute. I want to understand what's upset him. I want to fix it. He's given me so much over the last few weeks, more than I can begin to categorize. I can't stand by and let him hurt while I twiddle my thumbs. So I do the only thing I can think of.

I walk to him and sink to my knees in front of him. When he just watches me, I wedge myself between his thighs until he's forced to either push me back or make way. He spreads his legs with another of those heartbreaking sighs. "You already sucked my cock once tonight, little siren."

"That's not what this is." If I thought for a second it would help, I'd have him in my mouth and gladly. Sex won't fix this, though. Of that I'm sure.

Instead, I press myself to his torso and wrap my arms around him as best I can. He goes so still I might think he was holding his breath if I couldn't feel his chest rise and fall against my face. Slowly, oh so slowly, he wraps his arms around me, gently at first and then hugging me tightly to him.

"It's going to hurt when you leave."

He speaks so softly, I barely register the words. When they hit, it's with the force of a nuclear explosion.

I had suspected he cared, of course. Hades might be fearsome in so many ways, but he's too honest to be able to lie with his body. He touches me like I mean something to him. He's drawn back the curtain on bits of the lower city, showing me things he cares about, letting me in. Even if I haven't allowed myself to contemplate the implications of *that* too closely, I've noticed. Of course I've noticed.

I care too.

"Hades—"

"I meant what I said before. I won't ask you to stay. I know that's not possible." He releases a long breath.

I bite my tongue before I can say anything else. He's right—it's not possible for me to stay—but that doesn't change the fact that I meant what I said earlier tonight. If we were different people, this place would be home and this man would be mine.

"Three months felt like an eternity when I agreed to this."

A soft laugh slips free, muffled against his shirt. "It doesn't feel like an eternity now." Just under two months left and it feels like a blip in time. Look away too long and it will slip past, leaving the distance between us growing.

I'll never see Hades again.

Somehow, with everything going on, *that* never occurred to me. That I might miss this man. That it will feel like tearing out a part of myself to walk away. Silly, foolish thoughts. It's only been a few weeks. Maybe one of my other sisters would fall so hard for a partner in that time, but that's not me. I understood the boundaries of this when I fought so hard to get Hades to agree to the deal. It was only for show, only because we had no other choice.

He wouldn't have chosen me if I hadn't been Zeus's before I was his.

He wouldn't have even looked at me twice, a woman who's the epitome of everything about the upper city that he hates. A walking sunbeam, a fake persona that I project to get people to do what I want.

I lean back and try for another laugh. It comes out broken, closer to a sob. "I..." What am I supposed to say? Nothing will change the course we're on. A path shared for a short time while his need for revenge and my desire for freedom overlap.

It was never meant to last forever.

It should fill me with relief to know that Hades won't ask me to stay, that he won't muddy the waters around us with things neither of us should want. It doesn't. Instead, a strange desperation claws its way through my body, up and up and up, until it spills from my lips. "Kiss me."

He only hesitates for the briefest of moments, as if to memorize my features before he closes the minuscule distance between us and takes my mouth. Hades kisses me roughly, with none of the tender care he's displayed time and time again. *Good.* I don't want his tenderness. I want the memory of him woven into the fabric of my very soul.

He pushes to his feet and yanks me up with him, barely breaking the kiss. We use rough hands to drag off each other's clothes, ripping my dress when the fabric doesn't move fast enough, sending buttons flying from his shirt. I'm still kicking free when he walks me backward through the room to his bed.

"I can't wait."

I'm already nodding. I don't need the slow seduction right now. I just need him. "Hurry."

He lifts me and I wrap my legs around his waist. The smallest adjustment and his cock is pushing into me, Hades's hands on my ass controlling my descent onto his length. Fast, fast, too fast. I don't care. I writhe, trying to get closer. We haven't stopped kissing, can't get enough. Who needs to breathe when I have Hades? He's my very air.

The thought should scare me. Maybe it will when I've had some time to think about this. Right now, all I have is need.

He lifts me and lowers me, using his strength to fuck me where he stands. It's enough to make me light-headed. I pull my mouth from his long enough to say, "More. Harder."

I expect him to take me to the bed. Instead, he turns and moves to the dresser to set me on it. Hades brackets my throat, pushing me back to pin me against the wall. "Watch." He barely sounds like himself, his voice gone low and vicious. "Watch how much you need me in this moment. When you're free and chasing that dream of a life you want, you remember how good it felt to be filled by me, little siren." He slams into me and then withdraws, his cock glossy with my wetness. I can't look away. I don't want to.

Hades keeps seducing me with his words, entrapping me. "Someday, when you let some asshole seduce you and you're riding their cock, remember tonight and know that they will never compare to me. You think of me when they're inside you."

My gaze flies to his face, the possessive fury there just as hot as what he's doing to my body. I want to sink into it and never surface. I can't, though. I *can't*. "Don't be cruel," I gasp.

"I *am* cruel." He slams into me again, sealing us together as closely as two people can be, and kisses me roughly. He lifts his head enough to say, "You've *ruined* me, Persephone. Forgive the fuck out of me if I want to return the favor."

And then there's nothing else to say. We devolve to our base selves, chasing our mutual shared pleasure. When I come, it feels like my orgasm has been ripped from me, like it's something I can never take back. Hades follows me over the edge a few moments later, sealing us together and burying his face in my neck as he comes.

Stillness descends.

I cling to him and keep my eyes closed, unwilling to let reality intrude. It's there, though, hovering at the edge of our fading pleasure. The coolness of the room against our sweat-slicked skin. The ache of various parts of my body from what we've done to each other. Hades's rough breathing slowing out even as mine does the same.

He finally lifts his head, but he doesn't look at me. "I'm sorry."

I should let it end at that. We can circle all we want, but it changes nothing about our situation, about our deadline. Instead, I swallow hard. "I'm not."

HADES

I DON'T SLEEP. EVEN AFTER SHOWERING AND CRAWLING into bed with Persephone, holding her in my arms as her breathing evens out, sleep won't come for me. I can't shed the dread that's risen with every minute from the moment when I pulled out of her, my harsh words still ringing in my ears. I crossed a line, and her being right there with me doesn't change the fact that it's done.

I don't want to let her go.

An impossible scenario. I might as well try to lasso the moon as try to keep Persephone with me. Even if she was willing, the price is too high. Her mother will never acknowledge that her darling daughter might prefer the lower city—might prefer *me*—to the sparkling poison Zeus's court has to offer. She'll continue to punish my people to try to force my hand. We can last a few years on our own, as long as we don't pull too hard on the supply lines I've set up with Triton, but the second Poseidon or Demeter realizes what's happening, that avenue will be closed to us. People who depend on me for safety will suffer.

And Zeus?

He'll never rest as long as Persephone's by my side. I'd thought he'd make his play by now, but that old bastard is craftier than I expected. He'll move against me, but he's going to do it in a way that can't be tracked back to him. If I can't prove it...

No, there are a thousand reasons to honor my agreement with Persephone and pave the way for her to gain her freedom. There's only one to ask her to stay—I love her. Not enough. It will never be enough with the odds stacked against us.

I'm so deep in my head, it takes a few moments to register the sound of a phone ringing. I lift my head, but it's not my ringtone. "Persephone."

She stirs and blinks those big hazel eyes at me. "Hades?"

"Someone's calling you." When she keeps trying to shake off sleep, I slip out of bed and snag her phone from the dresser. A quick glance at the screen shows Eurydice's name scrolling across. "It's your youngest sister."

That gets her moving. She sits up and shoves her hair back with one hand while reaching for the phone with the other. I expect her to take the call into the bathroom or the sitting room for some privacy, but she puts it on speaker. "Eurydice?"

"Persephone? Oh thank the gods. No one else is answering." The panic in the woman's voice makes the small hairs on the back of my neck rise.

"What's going on?"

"There's someone following me. I was supposed to meet Orpheus at this bar, but he never showed and this guy got really pushy, so I left but..." Her breath sobs out. "He's following me.

There are no cabs. I don't know what to do. There were people around, but we're too close to the river now and all the streets are empty. I tried to call Orpheus, but he's not answering. What do I do, Persephone?"

The more scared her sister sounds, the more Persephone shuts down her own emotions, her voice going brisk. "Where are you? Your exact location."

"Uh…" The sound of the wind in the speaker. "Juniper and Fifty-Sixth."

I meet Persephone's gaze. Her sister is close to the River Styx but not close enough. If she tries to cross over, Zeus's people will attempt to take her. If I do, I'm violating the treaty. "She has to get to the river," I murmur.

Persephone nods. "You need to cross the River Styx, Eurydice. Do you understand me? If you go down Juniper, you'll see the bridge. I will meet you there."

It's a token of Eurydice's fear that she doesn't even question it. "I'm scared, Persephone."

"We're coming."

I'm already moving, hurrying into the closet and pulling on the first items I get my hands on and then shoving a gun into the back of my waistband. I hope we won't need it tonight, but I want to be prepared. I grab jeans and a top for Persephone. She's hanging up as I walk into the room. I text Charon to meet us at the door with a team. We have to play this carefully, but one look at the tightness in Persephone's expression and I know I'm going to throw caution to the wind and do whatever it takes to ensure her little sister is safe.

"This is my fault."

I'm already shaking my head before she finishes. "No, don't take this on."

"How can you say that? Doesn't this sound familiar? A strange man herding a scared woman to the river? It has Zeus written all over it."

She's right, but that changes nothing. We have to get to the bridge. "We'll know more once we get her safe. Focus on that right now."

I half expect her to argue, but she squares her shoulders and takes a slow breath. "Okay."

"Let's go."

We rush downstairs to find Charon and the others waiting. The Juniper Bridge is too far to get to on foot with any degree of urgency, so we all pile into two cars. I keep ahold of Persephone's hand the entire drive. There's no point in trying to dispel her tension, not when someone she cares about is on the line. The only thing I can do is offer what little comfort I have available. She keeps calling numbers and finally curses. "That motherfucker is sending me straight to voicemail. His phone wasn't shut off before, and now it is."

It's not a jump to know who she's talking about. "Orpheus isn't the most reliable." A neutral statement, since I'm not sure what she needs right now.

"I will *never* forgive him for this." Her eyes go cold. "I'll kill him myself if something happens to Eurydice."

There's nothing to say to that that's remotely helpful. *I'll kill him for you* is hardly the kind of romantic statement a person wants to hear, no matter how worried and furious she is right now. I'm saved from having to come up with a better response by our arrival at the bridge.

We screech to a halt and pile out of the car. It feels like a night for people to do bad things, the air cold and close, a low fog drifting up from the river and over the ground. It gives the atmosphere an eerie edge and obscures our vision.

It reminds me of the night Persephone crossed the River Styx.

I follow Persephone to the large columns that the Juniper Bridge has on either side, a clear indication of the boundary on our side of the river. It's one of the better lit bridges, and I know she's searching the other side for signs of her sister, just like I am. We were quick, but even on foot, she should be here by now.

"Hades." The fear in Persephone's voice is a call I can't help but answer. She should never, ever be afraid. Not while she's with me.

"She'll be here." I have no business offering this assurance. I don't know the circumstances, other than Eurydice being pursued.

As if my words summon her, the fog on the other side of the bridge shifts and a woman's form emerges. She's not running. She's stumbling. I can't make out the details at this distance, but she's holding her arm close to her body as if it's injured.

Fuck.

Persephone grabs my arm and utters a wordless cry. She makes it a single step before I catch her around the waist. "We can't cross the bridge."

"We—" She doesn't get a chance to get the rest out. A man moves out of the fog behind Eurydice, a hunting hawk to her injured dove. Persephone goes still, and when she speaks, her voice is freakishly calm. "Let me go."

If I let her go, she will run to her sister, likely playing into Zeus's hands. Whether that means snatching her up off the street tonight or a longer game is irrelevant. It will happen.

If I hold her back while something happens to her sister, I'll lose her long before the end of the winter. More, I won't be able to live with myself if I stand idly by while this woman is harmed. "Persephone—"

The man hunting Eurydice reaches her and grabs her shoulder, spinning her around. She screams, the sound sharp and terrified. I'm moving before I register that I've made a decision. I turn and thrust Persephone into Charon's arms. "Do *not* let her cross the bridge." I'll be the only one to pay the price for tonight's transgressions. I won't allow her to.

She curses and fights him, but Charon wraps her up in a tight hug, pinning her arms to her sides and keeping her immobile without hurting her. It's enough. I sprint across the bridge toward her sister, running faster than I have in a very long time. Not fast enough. I know that as I reach the halfway point.

Eurydice's attacker throws her to the ground. She hits with a thump that makes me sick to my stomach, but she doesn't lie still. She doesn't even look back at him. She just sets her eyes on her sister and starts crawling toward the bridge.

"Eurydice!"

Persephone's agonized cry gives me wings. That and the man

looming over her little sister. His face is twisted into a fierce scowl. He doesn't yell, but his words carry over the distance despite it. "Call for your sister, Eurydice. Scream for her."

I suspected that Zeus is behind this; the man's words confirm it. I don't remember pulling my gun, but its cold weight is in my hands as I reach the pillars on the upper city side of the bridge. "Get away from her!"

He finally, finally looks at me. "Or what?" A flash of metal in his hand as he leans down and grabs Eurydice by the hair. "You're on the wrong side of the river, Hades. Touch me and there will be consequences."

"I know." I pull the trigger. The bullet hits him in the wrist of the hand holding the knife, sending him spinning away from her.

One look at Persephone's sister, and it's clear Eurydice won't be able to cross the distance between us. There's a scarily vacant look in her eyes that I recognize too well. I used to see it in the mirror when I was a child. She's gone somewhere internal, driven there by fear and violence.

The street seems deserted, but I know better. Zeus has his people watching his side of the river, same as I have my people watching mine. If I step off this bridge, it's all over. War will come to Olympus.

The man sits up, clutching his wrist to his chest, his expression ugly. Eurydice gives a broken kind of sob. Just like before, I don't remember making a decision to do this. One blink and I'm shoving him to the ground and hitting him in the face. Fuck, I'm not think-ing at all. The only thing that matters is removing the threat. Each punch feeds something dark in me, as if I can hit this asshole hard enough that the monster in Dodona Tower will feel it. Another, and another, and another.

"*Hades*. Hades, *stop.*" Persephone's scream stops me cold. My hands ache. There's blood everywhere. He's long since stopped moving, though his chest rises and falls. Alive. I twist to look across the bridge. Charon still has Persephone pinned to his chest, but they both look shocked.

They both look horrified.

What the fuck am I doing?

I leverage myself off the man and crouch next to the sobbing woman. "Eurydice."

She flinches away from me. "Don't touch me."

"Eurydice, your sister is waiting for you." I don't have time to be subtle. I grab her chin and move out of the way so she can see Persephone on the other side of the bridge. My bloody knuckles hardly give a reassuring image, but it's too late to take it back now. "Can you walk?"

She blinks big dark eyes, her fear so large, it threatens to swallow us both whole. "I don't know."

"I'm going to carry you. Don't fight me." I don't give her a chance to brace for it, simply hauling her into my arms and hurrying back across the bridge. I was on Zeus's territory a grand total of two minutes, but I'm not naive enough to think it won't count. Even if he didn't orchestrate this—and all evidence suggests he *did*—he *will* take advantage of the opening I just gave him.

I brace for Persephone's fear. She just saw me lose my shit and violently beat a man. She stares up at my face, looking at me as if she's never seen me before. "Hades…"

"We'll talk when we get back home." I maintain my hold on Eurydice and start for the car. "Get in. Now."

For once, Persephone doesn't argue. She slips into the back seat ahead of me and takes her sister's hand as I set Eurydice carefully beside her. Her hazel eyes are shining. "Thank you, Hades," she says quietly. "I know the cost."

"Take care of your sister. I'll meet you back at the house." I shut the door before she can argue and motion to Minthe. "Take them back. Lock the whole house down. No one in. No one out. And so fucking help you if Hermes slips past our perimeter tonight."

Minthe nods and hurries to the driver's side. I keep an eye on the car until it's out of sight and then turn to Charon. "Trouble's coming."

Charon's skin has taken on a waxen tone. "You crossed the river."

"I didn't have a choice."

He opens his mouth like he wants to argue but finally shakes his head. "Doesn't matter, I guess. It's done. What do we do now?"

I try to stop reacting and *think*. Will Zeus go for a frontal strike, or will he try to twist my arm to get something he wants to avoid an all-out war? I don't know. I can't fucking think. All I can hear are the echoes of Persephone's cry. All I can see is the helpless look in her sister's eyes. And all I can feel is the pain across my knuckles from beating a man half to death.

I press my fingers to my temples. What would Andreas say? I snort as soon as the thought crosses my mind. Andreas is going to kick my ass for being so impulsive. "We can't assume they'll come in across the bridges. Pull as many people back from the edges of the territory as we can. If they don't want to go, don't force them, but get word out. War is coming."

Charon hesitates and then nods. "Do you want me to pull in all our people to the main house?"

The temptation almost overwhelms me. I want Persephone safe, and I already know she'll be a target. The urge to bolster our defenses until nothing can get past is a strong one.

But Persephone is not the only person in the lower city who needs protection from what's coming.

I force myself to shake my head. "No, keep the doubled patrols on the river. Dredge up anyone you need to help those who want to get out of the potential conflict zone."

"Hades." Charon has to stop and wrestle the fear out of his tone. "The entire lower city will be a conflict zone if they come for us."

"I know." I clasp his shoulder. "I'll get us through, Charon. Have no doubt about that."

I just don't know how yet. I can't act until Zeus does. I'm torn between the hope that he won't strike immediately and the fear that he'll draw this out until we're all going out of our minds.

The entire ride back to the house, I can't quite shake the fear that I'll arrive and Persephone will be gone. That Zeus will have somehow slipped past all my defenses and taken her back. That she'll have realized I can't truly protect her like I promised and decided to take her chances on her own. That she'll recognize me for the monster the rest of Olympus thinks I am and flee. A thousand scenarios, each fed by the knowledge of how ugly things are going to get. I had planned on multiple scenarios when we started this, but nowhere in those were what happened tonight.

Some things you can't take back.

When I find her and her sister sitting in the living room with the three pups playing around them, it feels like being sucker punched. They're here. They're safe. For now.

I sink onto one of the chairs and catch Persephone's gaze. She piles two of the puppies into her sister's lap and sits back. I approve. Pushing Eurydice right now is the wrong call. She's just experienced... Well, we won't know exactly what she's experienced until she rouses enough to tell us. Which takes time.

So I sit there and watch silently as Eurydice slowly comes back to herself. It starts with her petting the puppies and ends with a shuddering sigh that comes out more like a sob. "I was so scared, Persephone."

"I know, honey." Persephone lets Eurydice lay her head in her lap and carefully strokes her black hair, a soothing touch.

There's nothing soothing in her hazel eyes. She looks at me, and I've never seen her so fearsome. A true dark goddess, bent on retribution. She banks the expression almost as soon as it crosses her face, and I hate that she hides this part of herself from me. A trembling smile pulls at her lips and she mouths, *Thank you.*

In that moment, I'd do it again a hundred times. No matter the cost. It's all worth it for her.

Fucking anything for her.

PERSEPHONE

MY SISTER'S STORY COMES OUT IN FITS AND STARTS. ABOUT how she and Orpheus were supposed to meet in a part of the upper city that she's not overly familiar with. About how he never showed. About how he ignored her texts and sent her calls straight to voicemail, even as her fear grew and a strange man refused to leave her alone.

I keep stroking her temple and hair, soothing her in the only way I can. Her palms are skinned from where she fell, so terrified that she barely noticed the scrapes until now. Her arm is bruised from where he slammed her into the side of a building before she escaped him the first time. There are bruises on her knees from where he threw her to the ground on the other side of the bridge.

I note and file away every single injury. As much as I want to blame Orpheus for this, there's only one person responsible. Zeus. Even thinking his name has rage flickering higher inside me. I want blood for blood.

When Eurydice drifts into silence and her eyes slide closed, I finally look at Hades again. He's already on his feet, draping her in a throw blanket that had been on the couch from the last time I was reading in this room. It feels like a thousand years ago.

He passes me my phone. "Update your other sisters."

Right. Of course. I should have thought of that myself. I accept the phone but don't unlock it. "You made a huge sacrifice saving her." He'd *shot* a man. He'd beaten him. I think if I hadn't yelled his name, he wouldn't have stopped beating him. I don't know how I feel about that. I wanted that man to suffer, but seeing such unrestrained violence was shocking.

"It's nothing."

"Don't do that." It's difficult not to raise my voice, but I'm painfully aware of my sister's head on my thigh. "We'll pay the consequences for this, and I'm not sorry you saved her, but I also am not going to let you brush it off. Thank you, Hades. I mean it."

His big hand cups my face. His dark eyes hold a legion of thoughts that I'm not privy to. "I'm sorry you had to see me lose control like that."

I don't want to ask the question, but I make myself put the words to voice. "Did you kill him?"

"No." He drops his hands. "And you won't pay any price for my decision. I'll ensure it." Before I can argue, he brushes his thumb across my bottom lip and then stalks out of the room.

I have to clench my jaw shut to keep from calling after him. From telling him that he doesn't have to shoulder this alone. *I'm* the reason he broke the treaty. I can't let him bear the cost by himself.

First, though, he's right. I need to update my other sisters. I type out a quick update and send it to a group text with only Callisto and Psyche. They don't make me wait long for responses.

> **Psyche:** I'm so glad she's okay!
> **Callisto:** That fucking asshole.

A picture appears, a screenshot of one of Orpheus's social media accounts. It's a shot of him surrounded by a trio of beautiful women with a giant smile on his face. The time stamp on the posting is right around when he started sending my calls straight to voicemail.

> **Psyche:** He's dead to us.
> **Callisto:** When I get my hands on him, he WILL be dead.
> **Me:** He's not the one ultimately responsible.
> **Me:** It's Zeus.
> **Callisto:** Fuck him. I'll kill him, too.
> **Psyche:** Stop it. You can't talk like that.
> **Me:** We'll figure it out. Right now, Eurydice is safe, and that's all that matters.
> **Psyche:** Please keep us updated.
> **Me:** I will.

Eurydice shifts and opens her eyes. She hadn't fallen asleep after all. "I'm sorry."

I put my phone aside and focus on my youngest sister. "You have nothing to be sorry for."

She rolls onto her back so she can see my face better. The sweet innocence I'm so used to seeing when I look at her is gone. There's a jaded world-weariness that I wish more than anything I could wipe away. She takes a deep breath. "Hades isn't supposed to cross the river."

"Very few outside the Thirteen believe Hades exists." Or at least that was the truth before we started our campaign to rub Zeus's nose in the fact that I'm with Hades now.

"Don't do that. I know I'm the youngest, but I'm not nearly as naive as you all act. It doesn't matter what the rest of Olympus thinks. It only matters what Zeus thinks." She grabs my hand in both of hers. "He's going to use this to get to you, isn't he?"

He's going to try.

"Don't worry about that."

She shakes her head. "Don't shut me out, Persephone. Please. I can't stand it. I thought I could ignore the Thirteen stuff and just be happy but..." Her voice goes watery. "Do you think Orpheus set me up?"

I might be nurturing an intense new loathing for her boyfriend, but I truly, truly want to be able to answer that question with a negative. Orpheus was never good enough for her, but his only real sin was being a musician more in love with himself than with my sister. That makes him a fuckboy. It doesn't make him a monster.

If he sold her out to Zeus?

Monstrous doesn't begin to cover it.

Apparently Eurydice doesn't need me to answer. "I can't help wondering if he did. He was acting weird today, more distant and distracted than usual. I thought maybe he was having an affair. I think I would have preferred that. It's over between us. It has to be."

"I'm sorry." I wanted my sister to leave Orpheus in the rearview, but not like *this*. He was bound to break her heart at one point or another, but this level of betrayal goes so deep, I don't know how she's going to navigate her way through. We've sheltered Eurydice as much as we could, and look how that turned out. I sigh. "Let's see about making you some tea and finding you a sleeping pill."

"Okay," she whispers. "I don't think I can sleep without one."

"I know, honey." I climb to my feet and pull her up with me. She's safe. We're all safe tonight. There will be consequences for our actions, but there's nothing else to do tonight except settle my sister into a room and be there for her.

I thought I could target all Zeus's anger at me. I thought leaving Olympus wouldn't bring down negative consequences on anyone else. I feel so fucking naive.

Even if I left tonight, disappeared never to be seen again, my sisters would bear the consequences of my actions. *Hades* would bear the consequences of my actions. The entire lower city will. I have been so incredibly selfish and I've put so many people in harm's way.

I get a shower going for Eurydice. "I'll be right back, okay?"

"Okay," she whispers.

I'm not sure if leaving her alone right now is a good call, but she really isn't going to sleep without some tea and a sleeping pill. I'm sure Georgie has at least the former down in the kitchen. Someone will know where to find the latter.

I open the door and I'm not even remotely surprised to find Hades there. Somehow, I'm even less surprised to see the steaming mug of tea in his hand and the bottle of sleeping pills. For some reason, his anticipating my needs makes me want to cry. I swallow past my suddenly prickling throat. "Eavesdropping?"

"Only a little." He doesn't smile, holding himself so tense, it's almost like he expects me to turn away. "Can I come in?"

"Of course." I step back so he can enter the room. The feeling in my throat only gets worse as Hades sets down the mug and pill bottle and steps back. I press my lips together. "Can you hold me? Just for a few minutes?"

Just like that, the cold in his expression thaws. Hades holds out his arms. "As long as you need."

I step into his embrace and cling to him. I'm shaking and I'm not sure when I started. This night began with the highest of highs and then plummeted into the lowest of lows. If Hades hadn't broken the treaty, I don't know if that man would have stopped. I might have lost my sister. I bury my face in his chest and hug him tighter. "I can never thank you enough for what you did tonight. Just...thank you, Hades."

No matter what else happens, I won't let him bear the cost of his actions alone.

I'm done running.

27

HADES

I EXPECTED PERSEPHONE TO TURN AWAY FROM ME. SHE'S seen what I'm capable of now. There are no illusions that I'm really a good man playing pretend. I've spent the last thirty minutes bracing for it while I let her get her sister settled upstairs.

I never expected her to turn to *me* for comfort.

"I'm sorry." Persephone releases a long breath, her hands fisting the back of my shirt as if she thinks I'll move away one second before she tells me to. "It seems like I've brought you nothing but problems since I got to the lower city."

"Come here." I press a kiss to her temple. "Never apologize for bursting into my life, little siren. I don't regret a moment of my time with you. I don't want you to regret it, either."

"Okay," she whispers. She clings to me in silence as we listen to Eurydice begin to sob in the bathroom, loud enough to be heard over the shower. Finally, Persephone sighs. "I can't leave her tonight."

"I know." I don't want to let her go, to walk out of this

room. Given enough time and distance, she might reconsider how she feels about what happened tonight. I clear my throat. "Thank you for calling my name. I...I don't know if I would have stopped." I tense, waiting for the inevitable rejection that confession will bring.

She nods slowly. "That's why I did it." She starts to say something else, but the shower shuts off. We both look at the bathroom. Eurydice needs her more than I do tonight.

I give her one last squeeze and force myself to release her. "You'll be safe here. No matter what else has changed, *that* hasn't."

"Hades…" Her bottom lip wobbles a little before she seems to make an effort to firm it. "He's going to use this to force me back and bring you to your knees."

I can't lie to her, even if a comforting lie might sound nice right now. "He's going to try." I turn toward the door. "I won't let him take you, Persephone. Even if I have to kill him myself."

She flinches. "I know." The words aren't happy ones. If anything, they sound sad. Almost like she's saying goodbye.

It's harder than I anticipate to leave her. I can't shake the feeling that she won't be there when I get back. But no matter what else is true, Zeus won't risk throwing away his advantage by striking tonight. He needs the rest of the Thirteen behind him when he comes for me, and that will take time.

I hope.

I find Charon standing outside my study. He's glaring at the door, but I know him well enough to know he's still pissed about how things went down tonight. He gives himself a shake when he sees me. "Andreas is waiting."

"Let's not keep him waiting any longer, then."

The old man is already shaking his head as we enter the room and I shut the door. "I knew it would come to this. He'll crush you just like he crushed your father." His words slur slightly, and the tumbler of amber liquid in his hand is the obvious culprit.

I give Charon a look, but he shrugs. There's nothing to say. Even at his advanced age, Andreas does whatever he wants to. I need my people focused, but I have to deal with this first. I owe it to him, after all. I owe him fucking everything.

"I'm not my father." There was a time when that truth felt like an itch I could never quite scratch. Andreas loved my father, was loyal right down to his bones. The picture he paints of the man is larger than life, a strange sort of expectation that weighed heavily on me as I was growing up. How could I compare with *that*?

That's the trick, though. I don't have to compete with the specter of the man who fathered me. He's gone. He's *been* gone for over thirty years at this point. I'm my own person, and it's long past time for Andreas to acknowledge that.

I sink into the chair across from him. "I'm not my father," I repeat slowly. "He trusted the rules and laws and it got him killed. He never saw Zeus coming." A single truth that I'll never reconcile. If he was as good as Andreas says, why didn't he see the snake that Zeus is? Why didn't he protect us?

I shove the thoughts away. No doubt they'll be back to plague me in the lonely nights ahead, but right now, they detract from my focus. I can't afford to miss a step. "I've spent my entire life studying Zeus. You think I won't be able to anticipate him?"

"What can you do?" Andreas sounds like a ghost of himself,

his once-booming voice faint and cracking. "What can you do against the king of the gods?"

I push slowly to my feet. "He's not the only king in Olympus." I jerk my chin at Charon. "Get him to his room and have someone stay with him. Then we need to talk."

We get Andreas on his feet and I clasp his shoulders. "Get some rest, old man. We have a war to win."

Andreas searches my face. "Hades?" A grin splits his craggy face. "Hades, my old friend. I've missed you."

Not me. My father. My chest sinks, but I give his shoulders one last squeeze and let Charon herd his uncle out of the room. I stalk to my desk and pick up the bottle of whiskey Andreas left behind but put it down without opening it. No matter how attractive the thought of smoothing my rougher edges is, I need to be sharp tonight. Longer than tonight—until the end of this.

The door open behinds me with a faint creak, raising the small hairs on the back of my neck. Every instinct I have screams danger, but instead of spinning around and throwing the bottle of whiskey, I turn slowly, already suspecting who I'll find. Only one person is capable of slipping past my security. Frankly, I'm surprised she actually used the door this time instead of appearing in my office chair as if by magic. "Someday, you're going to have to tell me how you get past my security even when it's at its highest."

"Someday, maybe I'll consider it." Hermes isn't wearing her characteristic grin. She's dressed in a pair of black fitted pants and a long purple shirt that looks like a cross between menswear and a dress. The better to fit in with the shadows, apparently.

I walk around to lean against my desk. "Official business, I take it."

"Yes." Something like regret flickers over her features. "You misstepped, Hades. You shouldn't have given him an opening. It's tied all our hands, even those of us who consider you a friend."

For some reason, that's what gets me. *Friends*. I've barely been able to acknowledge the fact that she and Dionysus might be friends, and now they're gone. Despite my determination to maintain control, hurt flickers to life. "Not that good of friends if we end up on the opposite side of a war."

She narrows her eyes. "You don't know what it's like in the upper city. It's a different world than it is down here. You might be the benevolent king of the lower city, but Zeus is another animal entirely. Crossing him requires paying a higher price than most of us are capable of."

I wonder at that. I've known Hermes for years, but we've never talked about either of our pasts through mutual silent agreement. I don't know where she came from, don't know anything about her family or if she has one. I don't know how high a cost she'd pay to try to stand against Zeus.

A sigh slips out. I don't mean to sound so fucking tired, but the enormity of what's coming will overwhelm me if I think about it too hard. I've planned for this possibility since I was old enough to understand what had happened to my parents and who was responsible.

I never planned on Persephone, though. The thought of *her* bearing any part of the cost? No. I won't allow it. I don't give a fuck what's required of me.

"Let's get on with it, then." I motion for her to deliver whatever message she's obviously brought. "What does the old bastard have to say?"

Hermes nods and clears her throat. Her voice, when it emerges, is a startling approximation of Zeus's booming tones. "You have thirteen hours to return both Dimitriou girls to the proper side of the river. Failure to do so will result in the annihilation of you and everyone within your command. I can't be held responsible for the civilian losses. Make the right choice, Hades." Hermes exhales and gives herself a shake. "End transmission." The joke falls flat between us.

I study her. "Thirteen hours?"

"Never let it be said that Zeus lacks a sense of theatrics. One hour for each of the Thirteen."

"He's not going to back off even if I return them." He's waited too long for an opportunity exactly like this. I don't know what happens if I die and there's no one of my bloodline to continue the name. Does the title die out with me and he splits the lower city with Poseidon? Or does Zeus step in and assign someone of *his* choosing? Neither option would benefit my people.

"No, I don't suppose he is." The conflict on her face says everything I need to know. Hermes doesn't like where this is going, but she won't put her neck on the line to stop it. I'm not sure she could stop it even if she wanted to.

While I'm still contemplating responses, Hermes ducks forward and drags me into a hug. "Please, please be careful."

I return the hug awkwardly, half expecting a knife in the ribs. "I make no promises."

"That's what I'm afraid of." She gives me one last squeeze and steps back. Her dark eyes shine a little before she blinks the tears away. "Do you have a response?"

"He'll have my response in thirteen hours."

She opens her mouth like she wants to argue but finally nods. "Good luck, Hades."

"Use the front door when you leave."

"Now where would be the fun in that?" She flashes me a smile and then she's gone, slipping out the door and leaving me wondering what the fuck I'm going to do.

No matter how intensely I've prepared for this, it doesn't change the fact that the cost will be high. Zeus will strike hard and fast once I've missed this deadline, and he'll bring the war to my territory to ensure my people pay the highest price. It serves a dual purpose of hurting me and potentially damaging their steadfast loyalty, paving the way for them to accept a new leader when he finally succeeds in taking me out.

I have a plan. I have to stick to it.

PERSEPHONE

ONE MINUTE I'M ALONE, TRYING TO DECIDE HOW LONG TO give my sister in the bathroom, and the next I hear a rustle behind me and spin to find Hermes perched on the bed. I press a hand to my chest, trying to soothe my racing heart, but I don't allow myself any strong reaction, not when she's watching me so closely. "Hermes."

"Persephone." Her expression is carefully neutral. "I have a message for you. Will you hear it?"

Nothing good can come of this, because there are only two people who would use Hermes to send a message. The temptation rises to tell her to leave the room, to hide from what's coming next. I'm stronger than that. I won't allow myself to stick my head in the sand and ignore the consequences of my actions. "Yes."

She nods and jumps to her feet. When she speaks, it's with a distinctly male voice. It takes me two words to place it as Zeus. "There is war on the horizon, Persephone. I will crush the lower city and everyone who lives there. You know Hades can't stand against the might the rest of the Thirteen can bring to the fore. Come back now and bring your sister, and I'll reconsider my attack."

I wait, but she falls into silence. "That's his offer? He'll *reconsider*?"

"Yes." Hermes shrugs a single shoulder. "He apparently thinks it's fair."

"He apparently thinks I'm a fool." Zeus won't reconsider anything. He might want me and Eurydice back, either to appease my mother or to prove his might, but he's not going to pass up this opportunity to strike at Hades.

Not unless I give him reason to hesitate.

My stomach twists and my head goes light and staticky. I promised myself I wouldn't hide from the consequences of my actions, but some consequences are too high a price to pay. Hades is more than capable, but against such larger numbers and better-equipped enemies? And even with his precautions, what of his people? All those people I've met over the last few weeks as Hades has shown me around the lower city. Juliette, Matthew, Damien, Gayle. Everyone who frequents the winter market, who has stalls and shops and businesses that go back generations.

They might become casualties. There are *always* casualties in war, and it's always the people who least deserve to bear the cost.

What if I can stop this?

Hermes is halfway to the door when I find my voice, though I hardly sound like myself. "Hermes." I wait for her to face me to continue. If I do this, there's no going back. The price might be too high to pay, but I can't let everyone else fight my battles for me.

The time for hiding behind Hades's reputation is past. It's time for action. "I would like to send a message to my mother."

I second-guess myself a thousand times after Hermes leaves, watching the minutes tick into hours as I wait for a response from my mother. Taking care of Eurydice requires some concentration, but eventually she passes out on the bed and I'm once again left to wait with my own thoughts.

I don't know if I'm making the right call. I wish with everything I have that I could run this plan past Hades, that we could come up with a solution together. A nice rational solution that steers us through these treacherous waters and to a safe harbor.

That's the problem, though. I don't feel rational. My panic doesn't abate as time passes. If anything, it gets stronger. Zeus wants Hades's head on a platter. He's wanted it for years, and I've finally given him a way to make it happen.

I can't let Hades die.

The thought of this world without him in it? The very idea makes me flinch as if my body can repel the thought. He won't be thinking of himself, only of protecting his people. Of protecting *me*. He promised, after all, and I know Hades well enough to know that he'll keep his word even if it means he goes under to keep me above water.

I *have* to protect him. He's got no one else who...

My breath catches in my chest, and I stare blindly at the tasteful blue walls of the room. In a daze, I finish the sentence, if only in my head. *He's got no one else who loves him like I do.*

I love Hades.

I close my eyes and focus on breathing past the tightness invading my body. Love was never part of the plan, but *none* of this was part of the plan. I can't tell him. If I tell him, it might rattle him past the point of reason. He won't see my actions as anything less than a betrayal. He might even do something to put his people at risk, and *that* I can't allow.

No, I can't tell him. I have to bottle this up, shove it down deep. If I succeed, maybe there will be something left of us to salvage on the other side. If I fail... Well, we'll have bigger problems at that point.

I'm still wrestling with my emotions when the window slides open and Hermes climbs through. I stare. "Did you just scale the walls? On the second story?"

"What, like it's hard?" Her grin is a shadow of itself. The night's events have worn on her, just like they have on the rest of us. She straightens and my mother's voice emerges from her lips. "You have a deal."

All the strength goes out of my body for one terrifying moment. I didn't honestly expect her to agree. Now I truly have no choice. I close my eyes and take a slow breath. Things are now in motion. There's no going back now.

I smooth a hand over my sister's hair. "Wake up, Eurydice."

Things happen quickly after that. I take the time to change into another black gown that Juliette made for me. It's long-sleeved with a generous scooped neck and a full skirt, but the real highlight of it is the underbust corset that goes over the top of it. It's black threaded with silver, and it makes me think of stylized armor. In this dress, I feel like a dark queen.

Like a dark *goddess*.

Hermes gives me a long look. "That's quite the statement piece."

"Appearances always matter in the upper city." I'll only have one opportunity to get this right. "It's important to strike the right tone."

She laughs a little under her breath. "When you walk through the door, they won't know what hit them."

"Good." I smooth my hands over the dress. There's no more time to waste. "Let's go."

Eurydice stops me before I can open the bedroom door. "I'm staying."

I stop short. "What?"

"I need time." She wraps her arms around herself. "I'll figure out what I'm doing in the morning, but I'm not going back to the upper city tonight. I can't."

I start to argue, but Hermes cuts in, "Look, if this all goes down the way you want it to, her staying won't make a difference. If things go tits up, her staying here *also* won't make a difference."

She's right. I hate that she's right. Not to mention that the safest place for Eurydice right now is in Hades's home. No matter what happens next, he won't let any harm come to her. I swallow hard. "Okay." I pull my sister into a tight hug. "Be safe."

"You, too." She squeezes me back just as tightly. "Love you."

"Love you, too." I force myself to release her and turn to Hermes. "I'm ready."

I half expect Hermes to direct me to the window despite my wardrobe change, but she leads me out the door and down the hallway to the back staircase that comes out near the kitchen. Then we're down in the tunnels that I haven't visited since the night I met Hades. I silence my questions at her seeming magical ability to navigate Hades's home. It's uncanny in the extreme, but it works. We make it to the exit without being caught.

The night air has gained teeth since we were last outside. I shiver, part of me wishing I'd grabbed a coat, but the one Hades provided me doesn't work with this outfit and I'll only have one chance to make the impression I want to. Besides, it feels fitting that I fled to the lower city without a coat and return the same way.

Hermes glances at me. "Not far now."

Two blocks away, we find a nondescript black sedan tucked between two buildings, an uncharacteristically serious Dionysus behind the wheel. Hermes takes the front seat, and I slide into the back. He looks at me in the rearview mirror and shakes his head. "Damn, looks like Hermes was right after all."

"I'll take my payment in cash." She sounds like she's just going through the motions of their banter, her mind on something a thousand miles away. "Let's go."

Panic gathers in my throat as we wind through the lower city and ease over Cypress Bridge. The pressure is lighter than before, barely noticeable. *Because Hades invited me into the lower city.* I shiver but resist the urge to wrap my arms around myself. My heart sinks as we leave the lower city behind. There's no going back now. Maybe there never was.

I expect them to head west toward my mother's penthouse, but they turn north instead. This is wrong. I lean forward between the front seats. "Where are we going?"

"I'm delivering you to your mother. She's with the others in Dodona Tower."

I'm on Hermes before she can move, my hand wrapped around her throat. "You tricked me."

Dionysus doesn't even slow down. He barely glances at us. "Don't fight, children. I'd hate to have to turn this car around."

Hermes rolls her eyes. "You're the idiot who didn't ask for more details. You offered a deal. Your mother took it. I just deliver the messages—and now the package. Sit back before you hurt yourself."

Instead, I tighten my grip. "If this is a double cross…"

"What will you do, Persephone? Kill me?" Hermes gives a mirthless little laugh. "You can try."

It mirrors something Hades said earlier. That Zeus will try to take me and crush the lower city. The first part of that is a nonissue because of my actions. It's the latter I'm trying to avoid. Damn it, Hermes is right. I asked for this. I don't get to threaten and posture because it's not playing out exactly like I expected.

Even knowing that, it takes more control than I anticipate to unpeel my fingers from her skin and sit back. "I need him to survive this." I don't mean to say it. They might care about Hades, but they're no friends to me. I can't trust them.

Hermes finally looks at me. "You seem to have things well in hand."

I can't tell if she's being sarcastic or not. I choose to take the words at face value and let them boost me when I desperately need it.

Around us, the streets quickly take on a glitzier look. Everything's been renovated in the last few years, more evidence of the way the upper city cares so intensely about how things *look* and less about the content beneath. The businesses stay the same, the people working them the same, at least until they've been priced out. How many of them end up in the lower city? I'm so ashamed of myself for keeping my gaze on the horizon when there were things I should be noticing all around me.

Dionysus pulls up in front of Dodona Tower and stops. When I look at Hermes, she shrugs. "I was only joking about delivering packages. You made this deal, so you should walk in there under your own power. You were right before—perception matters."

"I know," I say faintly. I don't apologize for attacking her, though. She's not on anyone's side but her own, and while I understand, I can't help but hold it against her. Hades could use allies right now, and when he's in his hour of need, she and Dionysus have abandoned him. From the outside, it might look like I've done the same, but everything I did from the moment I sent Hermes with a message to my mother is for him.

I get out of the car and gaze up at the skyscraper in front of me, taller than any of the buildings around it, as if Zeus needs this physical demonstration of his might to remind everyone in the city of what he can do. I find my upper lip curling. Pathetic. He's a child, ready to throw a tantrum and cause untold destruction if he doesn't get his way.

The very last thing I want to do is face him and his shining crowd of flunkies after everything that's happened, but this is what I asked for. This is the price I'm willing to pay to avert war. I can't afford to balk before I even step onto the battlefield.

The elevator ride to the top feels like it takes a thousand

lifetimes. It's been a little over a month since I was here last, since I ran from Zeus and the future he and my mother had mapped out for me without my consent.

It takes more effort than ever to school my expression. I've fallen out of the habit with Hades; I feel safe with him, not like I have to lie with my face and words to ensure a smoother path. Yet another reason I love him.

Gods, I love him, and if this goes poorly, I'll never get a chance to say it aloud. It's not as if he's told me he feels the same. We've been so very careful to dance around any talk of deeper emotions, but I can't help thinking about the conversation we had while naming the puppies. He wouldn't have laid out an alternate future in which we were different people if he wasn't feeling the same. He wouldn't call me *love*. It's too late to worry about it now. I have to set it aside.

One does not swim with sharks unless they're able to focus fully on not losing a limb in the process.

I take one last breath as the elevator door opens and square my shoulders. It's game time.

The room is packed, people dressed in all colors of the rainbow, glittering gowns and elegant tuxedos. Another party in process. It's almost as if they've all been in this room the entire time I was gone, trapped in some warped reality where the party never ends. The clothing is slightly different, the dresses brighter colors tonight than they were last time, but the people are the same. The poisonous atmosphere in the room is the same. *Everything* is the fucking same.

How can they be partying when there is so much death on the horizon?

Fury snaps in my veins, searing away the last of my nerves and any lingering hesitation. These people might not care about the cost their decisions will have on those who don't move in their circles, but *I* do. I stride out of the elevator, my gown slithering around my legs with each step. Every other time I was in this room, I wasn't able to escape the clear power imbalance. They had it. I didn't. End of story.

That's no longer the case.

I am not merely one of Demeter's daughters. I am Persephone, and I love the king of their dreaded lower city. To them, he might as well be king of the Underworld itself, lord of the dead.

I catch sight of my mother deep in conversation with Aphrodite, their heads bowed as they speak in low voices, and turn in her direction. I make it two steps before a voice booms across the room.

"My bride returns."

Ice cascades down my spine, but I allow none of it into my expression as I look at Zeus. He's beaming at me as if he didn't deliver threat upon threat to drive me back to the upper city. As if I haven't spent the last five weeks and change sleeping with his enemy.

As if everyone in this room is ignorant of both those truths.

People step aside as I move forward. No, they don't step aside. They actually trip over themselves to put distance between us and clear my path. I don't look at them. They're beneath my notice at this point. Only two people in this room matter now, and I have to deal with Zeus before I can move into my endgame.

I stop just out of reach and sweep a hand over myself. "As you can see, I've returned safely."

"Safe, but not untouched." He says it low enough only to carry to me, but he grins as if I've promised him the world and lifts his voice. "This is a good day indeed. It's time to celebrate." He moves quicker than I give him credit for and slings an arm around my waist, holding me too tightly. It's everything I can do not to flinch. Zeus waves an imperious hand and tightens his hold on me. "Smile for the camera, Persephone."

I smile easily as a camera flashes, my chest sinking with the knowledge that Hades will see this photo plastered everywhere by morning. I'll have no opportunity to explain, no chance to tell him that I'm doing this for him, for his people.

Zeus skates his hand over my side, though the corset creates a barrier that gives the impression of keeping him at bay. "You've been a bad girl, Persephone."

I loathe the way he talks to me. As if I'm a child to be corrected, except the lust in his eyes gives lie to that perception. I'll kill Zeus myself before I let him take me to bed, but saying so now will undermine my goals. So I smile up at him, sunny and sickly sweet. "I think I can be forgiven for a number of things with the proper penance. Don't you agree?"

The lust in his eyes flares hotter, and my stomach gives a sick twist. He squeezes my hip, his fingers digging in as if he wants to rip away my dress. But he finally releases me and steps back. "Go to your mother's home and wait. My people will collect you when this is finished."

I fight to keep my smile in place, to lower my eyes like a good little obedient wife-in-waiting. I suspect he'll have someone tail me to my mother's home, and this time, there will be no terrified race to the River Styx. It's just as well. My mother's home is the destination I desire.

My mother sees me coming, and the relief on her face is real enough. She cares. I've never doubted that she cares. It's the pride and ambition that get in the way. She pulls me into a tight hug. "I'm so glad you're safe."

"*I* was never in any danger," I murmur.

She moves back but keeps a hold on my shoulders. "Where is your sister?"

I match her low tone. "She chose to stay behind."

Mother narrows her eyes. "It's time to go home." Where we can speak freely.

It's the fastest exit we've ever made from a party. I barely look at the attendees. They only matter in which way they'll fall in the coming confrontation. Without my interference, every single one of them will back Zeus over Hades. I can't allow it. Hades is stronger than anyone I know, but even he can't win a war against the other Thirteen on his own. I'll ensure he doesn't have to.

Mother doesn't speak again until we've safely made the drive to our building and taken the long elevator up to the top floor. She spins on me the second the door is shut. "What do you mean, she chose to stay behind?"

"Eurydice is safe in the lower city. Or she will be as long as we succeed."

She looks at me as if she's never seen me before. "And you? Are you okay? Did he hurt you?"

I step back when it looks like she might try to hug me again. "I'm fine. *Hades* isn't the one who wants to hurt me, and you know it." I stare her down. "He's also not the one who cut off supplies to half the city in a fit of rage."

She draws herself up. My mother always seems larger than life, but we're the same height. "Forgive me for wanting to protect my daughters."

"No." I shake my head. "You don't get to talk about protecting your daughters when you sold me to Zeus without even asking if that's what I wanted, when you *know* his reputation. He's a modern-day Bluebeard, and don't pretend everyone isn't aware of it."

"He's the most powerful man in Olympus."

"As if that makes it okay." I cross my arms over my chest. "I suppose it's also okay that he sent one of his men to chase Eurydice through the street like a doe before a hunter's arrow? It wasn't a bluff, Mother. He had a knife, and he fully intended to use it before Hades saved her. Your precious Zeus ordered that done."

"You don't know that."

I study her. "It's what he did to me. It seems he likes to let his prey get within reach of the lower city before striking, but we both know it was intentional with Eurydice. He set a trap, and if Hades hadn't walked into it, Zeus's man would have stabbed her. Look me in the eye and tell me that you have the utmost faith that Zeus will never, ever do anything to hurt one of your daughters to bring me in line. Do it truthfully."

She opens her mouth, obviously determined to power through this, but stops short. "Gods, you are so damned stubborn, Persephone."

"Excuse me?"

She shakes her head, suddenly looking tired. "You were never in any danger. You simply had to marry the bastard and play the good wife long enough for him to let his guard down. I would have taken care of the rest."

The suspicion I've been harboring since the beginning rises to the fore again. "You had a plan."

"Of course I had a plan! He's a monster, but he's a powerful one. You could have been *Hera*."

"I never wanted to be Hera."

"Yes, I'm aware." She waves that away just like she seems to do with anything that doesn't fit conveniently into her plans. "It's a moot point now. Zeus is a liability."

I stare. "You decided that before I made my offer."

"Of course I did." Her hazel eyes, so similar to mine, narrow. "He threatened two of my daughters. He's outlived his usefulness. I'd rather deal with his son and heir in the future."

I realize what she's implying, and it leaves me breathless. I knew my mother could be ruthless in her ambition, but this is another level entirely. My legs feel a little shaky, but I've come too far to buckle now. "What was the plan? The one I ruined by running away?"

"Nothing too complicated." She shrugs a single shoulder. "A subtle poison to put him out of commission without killing him." Because if he dies, Perseus takes over as Zeus, which means I'm no longer Hera.

"Fuck, Mother." I shake my head. "You're terrifying."

"And you've learned from the best." She motions at herself. "It's quite the deal you're offering."

"Yes. It is." I clear my suddenly dry throat. "I'll stay in

Olympus and encourage Hades to make several appearances annually with our family." The latter I have no business offering, but I'll do anything to prevent this war. *Anything.*

Mother frowns. "You've been planning to leave Olympus since I took this position."

Of course she knows my plans. I don't have the energy to be surprised by it any longer. "That didn't stop you from handing me over to Zeus."

She flinches the tiniest bit. "I'm sorry you were hurt by that." Which is not the same thing as being sorry she did it.

I lift my chin. "Then make amends and take the deal I'm offering. If you really want me to stay, this is the way to do it." I can see her wavering, so I have to press her on all fronts. "*Think,* Mother. The only people a war benefits are the generals. Not the supply lines. Not the ones working in the background. If you let Zeus pursue this personal vendetta and drag our entire city into a conflict, it will undermine the power you've been building since you became Demeter." Nothing that I'm saying is new information. She wouldn't have agreed to my bargain if she wasn't already thinking the same things.

She finally looks away, her jaw tight. "It's a huge risk."

"Only if you really believe Zeus is more powerful than the rest of the Thirteen. You said it yourself; he's become a liability. He's not the only legacy position. He's not even in charge of the most vital resources. Food, information, import-export, even the soldiers who will fight in a war they didn't choose. All of it is handled by others within the Thirteen. If they—if *you*—withdraw your support, what recourse does he have?"

"I can't speak for the others."

I give a mirthless little laugh. "Mother, now you're just being difficult. You know as well as I do that half the Thirteen owes you favors. You've worked too hard to ignore your influence when you finally have the chance to use it for something *good*."

She finally looks back at me. "It will create enemies."

"It will bring enemies you already have out into the open," I correct.

Mother gives a strange little smile. "You've been paying closer attention that I thought."

"As you said, I learned from the best." I don't agree with the choices she's made, but I can't lie and pretend that the persona I've worn for so long is one I came up with on my own. I watched her move among the power players in this city and molded myself accordingly to travel those eddies and flows without making waves. "You have to do this."

She takes a slow breath, and it's as if all her hesitation leaves her on the exhale. "Six events."

"Excuse me?"

"You will ensure that Hades will attend at least six events throughout the calendar year, preferably of my choosing." She holds my gaze. "In addition to that, he will allow himself to be seen with me enough to suggest that we're allied."

I narrow my eyes. "You don't get to control him."

"Of course not. But perception is everything. If the rest of Olympus thinks that Hades is in my back pocket, it will boost my power exponentially."

It's a huge risk. The Thirteen might know Hades exists, but

until recently, the rest of the upper city didn't. If they think he and my mother are allies, it will influence any number of deals she makes. No one wants to open their door and find Olympus's boogeyman waiting because they pissed off Demeter.

But that's the deciding factor. She's asking for the *perception* of an alliance. Hades will not be trapped into supporting her unless he actually wants to. He just has to be seen with her. "Okay."

"Then we have a deal." She holds out her hand.

I stare at it for a long moment. Once I agree, there's no going back. No escaping Olympus. No avoiding the power plays and politics and backstabbing that come with living here. If I do this, I'm immersing myself right up to my neck and doing it willingly. I can't pretend that I had no choice. I can't change my mind later and cry foul. I'm walking in with eyes wide open, and I have to be okay with that.

If I don't seal this bargain, there will be war in Olympus. Hundreds of people could die—likely more. *Hades* could die. And even if he makes it through to the other side, what will the cost be? He's already survived so much, fought his way back from so much loss. If I can save him from more, I want to.

If I don't seal this bargain, I'll never see him again.

I take my mother's hand and we exchange a firm shake. "Deal."

HADES

SHE'S GONE.

I sit in my bedroom as dawn first begins to steal across the sky and stare at the empty bed. The room never felt this large before, this deserted. I feel her absence in my home like a missing limb. It hurts, but there's no source. There's no fix.

I lean forward and press the heels of my hands to my eyes. I watched the security feeds. I saw her leave with Hermes. If it was only that, I might chalk it up to Persephone changing her mind, to her wanting nothing to do with this war and me after what happened tonight.

But she left her sister here.

And she was wearing a black dress.

I'm not a man to look for signs when there are none, but she wore a black dress earlier, too. Tonight represented a turning point for us, one of the latest in a long line of many. She stood at my side in black and we all but admitted our feelings for each other. If Persephone didn't care about me, she wouldn't be dressed as my dark queen when she left. She wouldn't have left Eurydice here, sending a silent message that she trusts me to ensure her sister's safety.

She's making a statement.

I push to my feet and cross to the bed. There will be no time for sleeping, but I need to take a shower and try to clear my head. Things are moving too quickly. I can't afford to let something slip.

I see the paper the moment I walk into the bathroom. It's torn on one side and as I pick it up, I recognize the title of the book Persephone was reading when I saw her last. Her scrawl is almost illegible, which makes me smile despite everything. It's one part of her that isn't perfectly poised. The note is short, but it steals my breath all the same.

> *Hades,*
> *I'm sorry. This will look bad, but I promise that*
> *I'm doing it for you. It's unforgivable to say it*
> *this way, but I don't know if I'll get another*
> *chance. I love you. I made this mess, and now I'll*
> *fix it.*
>
> *Yours,*
> *P*

I read it again. And then a third time. "Gods*damn* it." If she'd left me to save herself or her sisters, that would be easier to swallow. I'd suspected, but suspecting and knowing the truth are two very different things.

Something inside me goes cold and barbed as I pull out my

phone and check the gossip sites. Persephone's only been gone a few hours, but her photos are already all over them. Her in that black dress at Zeus's party. Zeus with his arm possessively around her waist. Her giving him that sunny smile that is fake and sweet enough to make my teeth ache.

She walked back into his waiting arms to save *me*. I can't wrap my mind around it. She's seen my preparations. She knows what I'm capable of. My people and I can weather anything Zeus throws at us. It won't be pretty, but we can do it.

Persephone just stepped in front of a bullet meant for me.

The thought makes the cold feeling inside me go positively frigid. Zeus will make her pay for leaving, for letting me have my hands all over her in front of his peers. For *soiling* her, in his mind. He'll take his rage out on her, and not even Persephone can survive that indefinitely. Maybe her body will, but he'll fracture her soul, the strength that makes her *her*. Zeus isn't the type of man to tolerate any resistance.

I promised I'd protect her.

I fucking *love* her.

I tuck the note exactly back where I found it and walk out of the bathroom. I've ghosted through these hallways often enough that it's child's play to avoid my people and the cameras. Charon will lose his shit when he realizes what I've done. Andreas will never forgive me. None of it matters. Nothing but doing whatever it takes to ensure Persephone is safe.

Even if it means she runs as far and fast from Olympus as she can. As far and fast from *me* as she can. Even knowing that her freedom means I lose her forever. Better that she be lost to me in favor of the world and her freedom than submitting to Zeus to pay the price for sins real and imagined.

I'm going to kill him.

I make it a single block from my house when a dark sedan cruises around the corner and slows next to me. The passenger-side window rolls down, and Hermes gives me a shadow of her normal grin. "You're about to do something stupid."

Dionysus is in the driver's seat, and he looks as exhausted as if he's gone on a weeklong bender. "Hades always did have a noble streak."

"I wouldn't want you to get in the middle. I know how you both hate that." It comes out far harsher than I intend, but I can't help it. Against my better judgment, I started considering her and Dionysus friends and look where that got me. Betrayal. Endless fucking betrayal.

Her smile drops. "We're all playing the roles set out for us. I knew the script when I accepted the title." She glances at Dionysus. "We both did."

"Not all of us had that kind of choice." I can't keep the bitterness, the anger, from my voice. I never asked to be Hades. The decision was taken out of my hands the first moment I drew breath. A heavy mantle to lay on a newborn's head, but no one cared what I wanted. Not my parents. Certainly not Zeus when he made me an orphan and the youngest Hades in the history of Olympus.

She sighs. "Get in the car. It'll be faster than walking, and you don't want to show up to Zeus's all rumpled and messy. Presentation is eighty percent of negotiations."

I stop. The car stops next to me. "Who said I was going to Zeus?"

"Give us a little credit." Dionysus chuckles. "The love of your life just made a deal to save your skin, so naturally you're going to pull a very romantic, very impulsive move to save her right back."

My internal debate only lasts a moment. At the end of the day, they're right. They both have a role to play, just like the rest of us. Holding that against them is like being angry at the wind for unexpectedly changing direction. I walk around the car and slide into the passenger seat. "You helped her leave, Hermes."

"She contracted my services." Hermes twists to look at me as Dionysus pulls back onto the right side of the street and heads north. "Even if she hadn't, I still would have helped." She taps her fingers on the armrest of her seat, not able to be still even for a moment. "I like her. I like you when you're with her."

"I'm not with her right now."

Dionysus shrugs, his eyes on the road. "Relationships are complicated. You love her. She obviously loves you, or she wouldn't be riding off to save you from Zeus and the rest of the Thirteen. You'll figure it out."

"I don't know what I'll do if something happens to her because of this." I'll never forgive myself for not protecting her like I promised.

"Something was already happening to her before you met her, Hades. She was fleeing Zeus when she stumbled into your comforting arms. That has nothing to do with you." Hermes laughs a little. "Well, it didn't used to have anything to do with you, but if there's anyone Zeus hates more than you, it's your father. He'll do whatever he can to annihilate the Hades position. Just grind it to dust with the force of his fury and damaged pride."

There was a time when the vendetta Zeus nurtures made me tired. I want revenge for the deaths of my parents, yes, but hating him for making me an orphan makes sense. His hatred for me does not. Fuck, his hatred for my parents doesn't, either. "He should have let it go."

"Yes." *Tap*, *tap*, *tap* go her fingers. "But he's got it all wrapped up in his head that a son for a son for a son makes sense, so here we are."

I frown. "What are you talking about?"

"What am I ever talking about?" Hermes waves that away. "He won't stop, you know. Even if you manage to negotiate your way out of this mess, he'll be there with a knife aimed at your back for as long as that evil old heart of his keeps ticking."

I want to press her on the son-for-a-son bit. Zeus has four children, two sons and two daughters—that are officially acknowledged, at least—that range from my age to their early twenties. Perseus will take the Zeus title when his father dies. He's just as bad as his father, driven by power and ambition and ready to crush anyone who gets in his way. By all accounts, Zeus's other son was a better kind of man. He fought his father and lost, and he fought his way out of Olympus and never looked back. "Is Hercules dead?"

"What? No. Of course not. By all accounts, he's very happy right now." Hermes doesn't look at me. "Don't worry about riddles, Hades. Worry about what today will bring."

That's the problem. I don't know *what* today will bring. I stare out the window, watching the Cypress Bridge appear. Crossing it feels like entering another world, at least in my head. I can count how many times I've entered the upper city on one hand and still have four fingers left over. Before last night, the last time was when I officially took the title Hades. I stood in that cold room, Andreas at my back while I faced down the rest of the Thirteen. They were whole then, Zeus's first wife still alive.

I was only a child and they handed me a role I had no choice but to grow into.

Now they have to reckon with the monster they created.

I don't speak again until Dionysus pulls up to the curb on a block full of skyscrapers. Even with all the wealth pouring out of the buildings around us, there's no mistaking which one belongs to Zeus. It's taller than the rest by a significant amount, and while beautiful, it's cold and soulless. Fitting.

I pause with my hand on the door. "This feels like walking onto a battlefield I won't survive."

"Mmm." Hermes clears her throat. "Funny story, that. I have a message for you."

"*Now?* Why didn't you give it to me the second you saw me?"

Hermes rolls her eyes. "Because, Hades, you needed a ride. Priorities, my friend." Before I can work up an answer to that, she gives herself a shake and Demeter's voice emerges. "You have the support of myself, Hermes, Dionysus, Athena...and Poseidon." She leans over and presses a gun into my hand. "Do what you have to do."

Shock freezes me in place. I can barely draw a breath. "She just named half the Thirteen." There is a power structure within the

Thirteen and most of the major players have thrown their might in with Zeus—Ares, Aphrodite, Apollo. But *Poseidon* is siding with Demeter? That levels the field considerably. I do a quick count. "We have the majority."

"Yes, we do. Make sure you don't waste this chance." She jerks her chin at the building. "The back door's unlocked. Your window of opportunity won't last long."

I can't trust her. Not completely. Hermes has vowed to deliver messages as they're given to her, but that doesn't mean the originator is required to tell the truth. This could be a trap. I look at the building one last time. If it's a trap, then it's a trap. Persephone is in danger, and I can't turn back now.

If it's *not* a trap, then Demeter just all but gave me the green light to go forward with my plan to kill Zeus. She's clearly signaled her support of it, and she has half the Thirteen behind her.

If I do this, there's a chance Persephone will never forgive me. I saw her face after I beat Zeus's man. She was shocked by the violence of it. Committing murder puts me firmly in the monster category with Zeus, no matter how much he deserves a bullet between his eyes.

I take a slow breath. Yes, I might lose her, but at least she'll be safe.

I'll happily pay any price to make that happen.

It feels like my life has been moving toward this moment for a very long time. Since the night of the fire. Maybe even before then. For better or worse, this chapter ends today.

I check to make sure the gun is loaded and slip it into the back of my pants. The back door of the building opens easily. I step inside and wait, but no one appears to attack or force me out. If anything, the looming hallways feel deserted. Abandoned. I'm not sure if this is Zeus's people being sloppy or Demeter clearing the way, but I can't take this opportunity for granted. I slip down the hallway to the door to the stairs. When I was twenty-one, I researched and planned a full-scale attack on this building—on Zeus. I had blueprints, security cards, and every bit of information I needed to get to Zeus and put a bullet in his brain.

I almost went through with it.

It didn't matter that it was a suicide mission at the time, that even if I survived, the might of the Thirteen would come down on my head. All I could think of was revenge.

Until Andreas gave me a verbal beating to end all beatings. He forced me to see who would really pay the cost for my reckless-ness. He forced me to learn patience, no matter how much it killed me to wait.

I thought all that effort and planning wasted. I was wrong.

There's a service elevator that goes up from the third floor. It doesn't have the same amount of security as the normal eleva-tors, since the only people who use it are employees who are vetted. I don't come across anyone as I move silently through Zeus's territory. Again, I have the feeling that someone cleared the way for me, even if there's no sign of violence. My tension grows higher and higher with every empty hallway, with every vacant room.

Is the entire building devoid of security?

The top floor is dominated by a modern ballroom of sorts that showcases wall-to-wall windows overlooking a balcony set above Olympus and larger-than-life portraits of the Thirteen on the two walls opposite. The River Styx cuts a dark swath through the city, and I don't miss the fact that the lights almost seem dimmer on my side of the river. They would to this fucking crowd, wouldn't they?

They don't bother to see the value in the history written over every surface in the lower city. Why would they when they've systematically purged it from the area around Dodona Tower?

Fools, every single one of them.

I leave the ballroom and walk down the hall. It's double the width it needs to be, the entire space practically flashing a neon sign announcing Zeus's net worth. I poke my head in the next door and find a room full of statues. Like the paintings in the ballroom, they're larger than life, each depicting the sculptor's version of human perfection. These must be the same ones Persephone mentioned right after she arrived in the lower city. The temptation to walk to mine and pull the sheet from it is almost too much to resist, but it doesn't matter what this Hades looks like. He sure as hell won't have my scars, won't have any of the traits that make me the man I am.

Persephone's voice echoes through my mind, soft and sure. *You're beautiful to me, Hades. The scars are part of that, part of* you. *They're a mark of everything you've survived, of how strong you are.*

I release a pent-up breath and close the door softly. There's nothing for me here.

The final door at the end of the hall is a massive thing, designed to intimidate. It stretches nearly floor to ceiling and appears to be coated with actual gold. Holy fuck, Zeus really is unbearable on every level, isn't he?

Like everything else in this place, it speaks to the ego of this man that he keeps his private office on the same floor where the upper tiers of Olympus come and go with regularity. Yeah, he has security, but anyone with a little skill can bypass it. For someone like Hermes? Laughably simple.

After how easy this has been, I half expect to walk through the doors and find the room full of security, ready to shoot me full of bullets. Surely Zeus wouldn't leave himself this open?

I slip through the door and pause to get my bearings. The office is about what I expect—heavy in glass and steel and dark wood, with gold accents everywhere. It's undoubtedly expensive, but it feels just as soulless as the rest of the building.

A grunt comes from the partially open door in the back corner, and I draw the gun Hermes gave me. It takes a few seconds for me to recognize the source of the sound when paired with the rhythmic slapping of flesh against flesh.

My heart stops in my chest. He's fucking someone in that bathroom. I can't tell if the sounds are sex sounds or pained sounds, and the thought that it might be *Persephone* in there...

Thoughts cease. All strategy goes out the window. A numb fury steals over me as I move to the door and edge it open. I'm so busy preparing to save the woman I love that it takes several long moments to understand that it's not Persephone bent over the sink. I don't recognize the woman, but she at least seems to be enjoying herself. Neither of them notice me as I step back into shadows.

I can't quite get my racing heart under control as I take up a position in the corner near the door, tucked back into the shadows where neither will see me when they exit the bathroom.

It wasn't Persephone.

But if I play this wrong, next time it might be.

If she chose him, it would stick in my throat like broken glass, but I'd respect her choice. But she won't choose him. Not willingly. He'll take pleasure in breaking her, and that I cannot allow.

It takes them only a few minutes to finish. I don't know why I'm shocked when they barely exchange a word before leaving the bathroom. The woman comes out first and scurries across the office to the door. Zeus takes longer. I'm bristling with impatience by the time he walks out and drops into the chair behind his desk.

That's when I step out of my hiding spot and level the gun at him. "Good morning, Zeus."

HADES

ZEUS TURNS SLOWLY TO FACE ME. I'VE SEEN HIS PICTURE plastered all over the newspaper and gossip sites more times than I can count, but in person, he seems faded. There is no carefully placed light to maximize his masculine features. His suit is rumpled and he missed a button when he redid his shirt. He's...human. Fit and attractive enough, but not a god or a king or even a monster. Just an old man.

He stares at me, shock sliding over his features. "You look even more like your father in person."

That snaps me out of my shock. "You don't get to speak about my father." I move away from the corner, gun held carefully in front of me. "Get up."

"I can't believe you'd be so damned stupid to show up here." He rises slowly, stretching to his full height. He's got a few inches on me, but it won't matter. I never intended for this to be a fair fight.

He doesn't look particularly concerned about this confrontation. "I have to admit, your plan was clever. I never would have thought the little bitch would run to you and be willing to play *those* kinds of games."

I tighten my grip on the gun. "You don't get to speak about *her*, either."

Pull the trigger. Just fucking pull the trigger and end this.

Zeus smirks at me. "Strike a nerve? Or is it the fact that she scurried back to me fast enough when she realized where true power lies?"

"You're awfully confident for someone being threatened by a man with a gun."

"If you were going to shoot me, you would have done it the second I sat down." He shakes his head. "Turns out you're like your old man in more than looks. *He* always hesitated to pull the trigger, too."

Again, I tell myself to do it, to shoot him now and be done with it. Zeus has committed acts of untold evil. If ever there was a man who deserved to be executed, it's him. As long as he's alive, Persephone won't be safe. My people won't be safe. Fuck, as long as he's around, *Olympus* won't be safe. I'd be doing every single person in this goddamn city a favor by putting this monster out of his misery.

Demeter and a full half of the Thirteen are only too happy for me to be their weapon. There isn't a single fucking person that will hold it against me if I kill him...

Except Persephone.

Except *me*.

"If I pull this trigger, I'm no better than you." I shake my head slowly. "I'm no better than every other member of the Thirteen

who is willing to commit unforgiveable acts to get more power."
I don't want more power, but no one looking in from the outside
would believe it.

Zeus smirks. "You *aren't* better than us, boy. You might play
king down in the lower city, but when push comes to shove, you're
beating a man nearly to death and showing up here to threaten me
with a gun. It's exactly what I would have done in your position."

"I'm nothing like you." I practically spit the words.

He laughs. "Aren't you? Because you don't look like the good
guy from where I'm standing."

I hate that he's right.

I can't kill him.

Not like this.

Slowly, I lower the gun. "I'm nothing like you," I repeat.

He snorts. "That's twice in as many days that you've violated
our treaty. Even if I was willing to look the other way on the
first, the Thirteen won't ignore this attack. They'll howl for your
blood."

"Will they?" I allow myself a fierce grin. Finally, fucking *finally*,
I know something this bastard doesn't. If I can't kill him, at least I
can accomplish this. "You really believe your own fantasy, do you?"

"What the fuck are you talking about?"

"You shouldn't have sent your men after Demeter's daughters." I tsk. "If she was willing to cut off food to half the city to
get Persephone back, what do you think she's willing to do to you
for ordering your man to stab Eurydice?"

"Cut off half the food…" Zeus goes still, surprise widening his
eyes. "That wasn't part of the plan."

I have to fight back a laugh. I'll never forgive Demeter for trying to hand Persephone over to this man, but I can't help my dark amusement at how thoroughly she's undermined him in such a short time. "Maybe not *your* plan. She's been playing at her own game from the beginning. You're just the only dumb fuck who didn't realize it."

"She might have been willing to go through such lengths against *you*, but she knows who feeds her."

"Yes." I wait for him to relax the tiniest bit before cutting his legs out from beneath him. "Olympus feeds her. Olympus feeds all of the Thirteen. Even you—especially you. They've looked the other way time and time again and ignored your sins. Now it's time to pay the piper."

"You're not here for justice." He sneers. "You're here for petty revenge."

My hand tightens on the gun before I regain control. Petty revenge. That's what he calls wanting justice for the death of my parents. I take a slow breath. "Call the whole thing off and I'll consider us even."

Zeus raises his brows. "Call what off? The war? Or my marriage to that pretty little daughter of Demeter? Persephone."

"Keep her name out of your mouth." I stalk toward him.

"That deal is signed, sealed, and only needs to be delivered. She's my reward for crushing the remaining resistance you represent." He grins. "I intend to take a whole lot of pleasure now that you've broken her in."

I know he's baiting me, but now that I'm standing here, nothing seems cut and dried. "She's not yours. She belongs to no one but herself."

"That's your mistake." He laughs. "You put yourself in a position to take it all—my life, that woman, your revenge—and you lose your nerve at the last moment." A mean glint in his pale blue eyes. "Just like your old man."

"Fuck you."

Zeus lunges for me, faster than he has any right to be, and grabs at the gun. He's stronger than I expect, too. Even though I try to wrench away, he maintains his grip on my arm. I pull the trigger reflexively, but the shot goes wide. Zeus jerks me closer, still trying to get my hand off the gun. The look in his eyes spells my death. I might have hesitated to kill him. He won't return the favor.

I distantly register the sound of glass shattering, but I'm too busy fighting for possession of the gun to worry about it. I twist my arm in his direction and pull the trigger again, but he's ready for me and the bullet bites the floor at our feet.

Zeus finally gets a good grip on my wrist and brings my arm down on his knee. Fuck, that hurt. Despite my best efforts, I lose my grip on the gun. I glance down, trying to figure out where it went. Zeus takes advantage of my distraction and punches me in the face.

The room wavers around me. That fucker has one hell of a force behind his hits. Another punch and he might actually knock me out. I shake my head, but it does nothing to quell the ringing in my ears.

Thoughts and plans and strategy fly out the window. Instinct alone rules. I manage to get my arm up to block his next punch, and the impact of the blow sends me sliding back several inches. I slam my fist into his stomach, and he wheezes. He's fast and hits like a freight train, and I'm hampered because even though I hate the fucker, I can still hear Persephone's panicked voice in the back of my head.

Hades, stop.

I can't kill him. I won't. I just need to get enough space between us so I can move, so I can *think*. I shove him back. "Why did you kill my father?"

The bastard laughs. He fucking *laughs*. "He deserved to suffer." He swings again, but this time, I'm ready. I duck under the punch and hammer a left hook into his side. Zeus bends over with a curse, but it's not enough to do more than slow him down. "Shame about your mother, though."

"Fuck. You." There are no answers for me here this morning. I don't know why I thought there might be. Zeus is a goddamn bully determined to mow down any threat that rises up. My parents were a threat, fresh to the roles and naive because they thought they could pave the way to a new and better Olympus. Zeus wouldn't allow anything to affect his power, so he removed them. End of story.

I keep trying to create space between us, but it's no use. Zeus doesn't give me room to breathe. It takes everything I have to keep his fists away from my face. As it is, my eye is swelling shut and it's only a matter of time before I lose the ability to see through it. If the fight is still going by that point, I'm in trouble.

I dodge a right hook and catch his arm, using his momentum to send him spinning away from me. "Stop. It doesn't have to be like this."

"I'm not stopping until you're dead, you little fuck." He shakes his head like a bull and charges me.

I don't register where we are in the room until the cold wind slaps me in the face. *Fuck.* "Wait."

But Zeus doesn't listen. He winds up for a punch that will hurt like a motherfucker if it lands, but he's misjudged his proximity to the broken window, just like I have. He teeters on the edge, arms windmilling as he tries to find his balance.

Time slows down.

He's not to the point of no return yet. I can pull him back. I just need to get there. I dart forward, intent on grabbing his arm, his shirt, *something.* No matter what kind of monster he is, no one deserves to go out like this.

He makes contact with my hands, but his fingers slip through mine despite my best efforts. Between one blink and the next, he's gone, the whoosh of air and a fading yell of surprise the only evidence that he was here to begin with. I stare at the broken window, at the empty dark blue air, at the lights twinkling in the distance.

Did I realize how close we were? Was I intentionally driving him back to a fall to his death?

I don't think so, but no one would believe me if I claimed this was an accident. Not when I showed up to his office with a gun in the early hours of the morning when no one else would be around.

The icy wind slaps me again, knocking me back into myself. I can't stay here. If anyone realizes that I broke the treaty, that I effectively killed Zeus, then my people will pay the price. Right now, I'm relying too heavily on Demeter keeping her word, and our short history has already proven I can't trust her.

I step into the hallway and stop short when I realize I'm not alone. I blink into the darkness, recognition rolling over me. *Speak of the devil.* "I didn't expect to see *you* here."

Demeter pulls on a pair of pristine black gloves. "Someone has to clean this mess up."

Does she mean the scene I left in the room behind me... Or *me*? I exhale slowly. "Was this all a trap, then?"

She arches a brow, and for a moment, she looks so much like Persephone that my heart gives a painful thud. Demeter laughs. "Hardly. I've done you several favors this morning, and it's the least I can do to see that you're still around in the future when I mean to collect payment." She takes a step toward me and stops. "But if you hurt my daughter, I will happily rip out your throat."

"I'll keep that in mind."

"See that you do. They'll never find the body." She examines her gloved hand. "Pigs are very efficient creatures, you know. They're practically nature's garbage disposal."

Fuck, this woman is just as terrifying as her daughter. I move to the side as she heads for the door to Zeus's office. "What will you do?"

"Like I said, clean it up." She opens the door and glances at me. "My daughter must love you very much if she was willing to ask for my help to keep you safe. I expect you to honor the bargain she made."

"I will." I don't have to know the details to agree to them. Whatever price is required, I'm only too happy to pay it. It's the very least I can do after everything that's happened.

"See that you do. Now, get out of here before Ares's people come investigating."

Investigating Zeus's death.

Zeus's death that I caused.

Persephone will never look at me the same after today.

That knowledge weighs on me as much as Zeus's death as I make my way to the ground floor. I step out the doorway to find a small crowd already gathering and people peering up into the sky as if the answers lie there. A few of them look in my direction but don't pay me much attention. Anonymity is a benefit of being a myth.

I turn and walk away. In my darkest heart of hearts, I thought I'd feel victorious once Zeus died. It's a balancing of the scales, a way of paying back all the horrible shit he's done over the years. To me, yes, to my parents, definitely, but also to more people than I care to count. The swath of his destruction is wide and stretches back through the decades.

Instead, I feel nothing at all.

I don't remember much of my trip back to the lower city. It feels like one moment I've tucked my hands in my pockets and am bowing my head against the wind in the midst of upper city shops, and the next I blink and I'm standing in front of my home. Only my aching legs and feet give testament to the fact that I walked this whole way.

I turn and look toward Zeus's tower, barely visible against the skyline from my position. Behind it, the sun is already fully in the sky. A new day. Everything's changed, and yet nothing's changed.

I am still Hades. I still rule my portion of Olympus. The remainder of the Thirteen will have some shit to sort out, but ultimately Perseus will step up as the new Zeus, marry a new partner, and create a new Hera. I'll honor whatever bargain was made with Demeter. Now safe, Persephone will be able to leave the city and chase her dreams. I'll never see her again. Things will continue, more or less as they always have.

The thought depresses the hell out of me.

I walk through the same door I left and make my way to the converted living room. It's all puppy playpen now, filled with toys and several beds. I sink down next to the center bed where all three pups are sleeping. Even though I'm quiet, it doesn't take them long to realize they have a guest. Cerberus comes first, toddling to me on unsteady legs and climbing into my lap as if staking his territory. His siblings follow after his lack of warmth wakes them, pressing their furry wriggling bodies against me.

Petting them releases something in my chest, and I let my head rest against the wall and close my eyes. What kind of monster am I that I feel more loss at the thought of never seeing Persephone again than at Zeus's horrific death? I don't know, but I'm not monster enough to reach out. If I try to cage her, I'm no better than he was. I close my eyes.

She's free.

I have to let her fly.

PERSEPHONE

I WAKE UP TO NEWS OF ZEUS'S DEMISE. IT'S ALL OVER THE COM-
puter where my sisters huddle, watching with varying degrees of satisfaction. I lean over Callisto's shoulder and frown down at the headline
streaming along the bottom of the screen. "He fell to his death?"

"Blew out the window and jumped is what they're saying."
Psyche sounds carefully neutral. "There's no evidence that anyone
else was involved."

"But why would—"

My mother chooses that moment to sweep into the room.
Despite the strangeness of the morning, she's fully made up and
wearing a smart pantsuit that displays her figure. "Get ready, ladies.
There's a press conference this evening with the Thirteen. They'll be
announcing an update on Zeus's death as well as officially naming
Perseus as the next Zeus."

Callisto snorts. "Not wasting any time, are you?"

"There must always be a Zeus. You know that as well as anyone."
She claps her hands. "So, no, I'm not wasting valuable time."

My sisters leave the room slowly, obeying her order but silently disapproving while doing so. I don't. She's too cheery, especially after calling in favors to convince half the Thirteen to betray Zeus last night and then leaving to "run an errand, nothing to worry about." It's too big a coincidence that he died the very next morning. "He didn't commit suicide."

"Of course he didn't. He was the type of man who'd have to be dragged to the Underworld kicking and screaming." She tips my chin up and frowns. "We'll have to do something about the bags under your eyes."

I knock her hand away. "You're not the least bit concerned about the murder?"

"Are you?"

I open my mouth to shoot back that of course I am but finally shake my head. "I'm glad he's gone."

"You and the majority of Olympus." She's already turning away and scrolling through her phone. "Get ready. The car will be downstairs waiting to deliver you to the bridge to the lower city. You'll have to make your way to Hades from there."

We're moving too fast. I stare at her, trying to see through the facade of perfection she presents. "Mother…"

"Mmm?"

How does one ask their mother if they committed murder? She's capable of it. I know she is. But the question still sticks in my throat, jagged and coarse. "Did you…"

"Did I murder the bastard?" She finally looks up from her phone. "No, of course not. If I had, I would have chosen a less public way than throwing him through a window."

I'm not sure if that's supposed to be reassuring, but I believe her. "Okay."

"Now that we got that out of the way." She picks up her phone again. "I'm calling the first portion of your bargain due. Ensure that Hades attends the press conference this evening."

Anticipation curls with anxiety. "You haven't given me much time to deliver my pitch."

"Give yourself some credit, Persephone." She doesn't look up from whoever she's texting. "He's in love with you. He'll agree to anything that keeps you by his side voluntarily. You'd be a fool to ignore that opportunity."

"Fine. I'll see it done."

"And bring Eurydice home." Her tone softens. "It's safe for her here now, and she needs her family while she's dealing with her heartbreak over that idiot ex-boyfriend of hers."

In this, we're in agreement at least. "I will."

There's no point in arguing about my ability to convince Hades. My mother has seen every single one of her marriages as a stepping-stone to something better, her husbands as pawns to be manipulated rather than partners. It would never occur to her that I view Hades as my equal.

I walk into my room without another word. It doesn't take long to get ready, though I do curse softly and add a little extra concealer under my eyes. After some consideration, I dress in a pair of wide-legged black slacks and a red blouse that's so dark, it might as well be black. I pull my hair back into a sleek ponytail and add lipstick almost the same red as my shirt.

I start at myself in the mirror for a long moment. The image

I've very carefully curated over the years is sunny and bright and filled with light colors and pink lips. I look like an entirely different person right now. I *feel* like a different person.

Good. The girl I was a month ago never would have had the audacity to make the bargain I struck last night. Such a small amount of time. So much changed. And we're not done yet.

The ride from my mother's home to the bridge takes less time than I expect. It feels like different worlds, but in reality it's less than thirty minutes, even with traffic. I climb out of the back seat and brace myself. Ideally, I would have liked at least twenty-four hours to bring Hades around to seeing things my way, but I'm working with a few hours.

I still have to apologize for sneaking out like a thief in the night.

Crossing the bridge in daylight feels strange. I brace myself for the same pain I experienced that first time, but it's just a light pressure against my skin. I have the strange thought that it feels like its welcoming me home. I stride quickly across and step through the columns to the lower city. It…does feel like coming home. I lift my chin and start walking, my stride eating up the distance between the bridge and Hades's house. It's still early enough that there are only a scattering of people out and about, and their presence is just another reassurance that I've done the right thing.

None of these people will bear the consequences of my actions.

It's over.

Almost.

I hold my breath as I walk up the steps to Hades's house and knock on the door, my heart in my throat. It opens a moment later and I'm pulled into a hug against a soft body. It takes several seconds to register that it's Eurydice.

"What are you doing opening the door?"

"Psyche texted that you were on your way." She yanks me into the house and shuts the door behind us. "Zeus is really dead?"

"Yes." She looks exhausted, dark circles beneath her eyes and her hair messy as if she's been running her fingers through it. I catch her hands. "Mother would like you to come home. We all would."

She opens her mouth, hesitates, and finally nods. "I will." She gives me a sad smile. "But something tells me you're not here for me. Hades is in with the puppies."

"I won't be long—"

"It's okay." Another of those sad smiles. "Charon offered to give me a ride home whenever I decided that was what I wanted. Don't worry about me."

Easier said than done, but she's right. Eurydice has her own path to walk going forward. I give her another hug. "I'm here whenever you need me."

"I know. Now, go get your man." She gives me a gentle nudge in the direction of the living room currently designated for the puppies.

I find Hades sitting against the wall with his eyes closed, the puppies sprawled over and around his legs. He opens his eyes as I walk into the room and blinks slowly. "You came back."

"Of course I came back." I take a step forward and stop, suddenly feeling awkward and unsure. I clasp my hands in front of me. "I'm sorry I left without saying goodbye. I saw a way through this, and I took it."

He absently runs his hand over the back of the puppy in his lap. "You could have talked to me before you left. I said you aren't a prisoner here, and I meant it."

"I couldn't risk it," I whisper. "You'll go to such lengths for the people you care about, but you're positively ruthless when it comes to your own safety."

"I'm expendable." He shrugs. "It goes with the territory."

"No, Hades. No, you are absolutely *not* expendable." I stride to him and sink carefully to my knees in front of him. It's only now that I get a good look at his face. I can't stop my gasp any more than I can stop from reaching out to ghost my finger along the bruise darkening his cheekbone and blackening his eye. "What happened?"

He still won't look at me. "You made a deal with your mother last night to ensure I could act against Zeus without repercussions. What were the terms?"

"How did you—" I stop when I catch up to what he's saying. "Zeus. That was you?" It must have been, unless Hades wandered into a bar fight in the time between when I left and returned. The most logical answer is also the simplest. He went after Zeus and they fought. Now Zeus is dead and Hades is home and looking like he's come out of a car wreck.

I reach out and tentatively take his hand. He grips me tightly before seeming to realize what he's doing and tries to disentangle our fingers. I tighten my hold on him. "You went after him."

"I thought you bargained yourself to him in order to spare

me. I knew he'd break you, and I couldn't stand back and let that happen." He sounds almost empty. "I wish I could tell you that I didn't mean for him to fall, but…I don't know. I just don't know. If this changes things—"

"Hades, stop."

"Yeah, you said that to me before."

It takes me a moment to understand what he's referring to. "On the bridge."

"I almost killed him, too." His voice is just *wrong*. He hardly sounds like himself. "I might have if you didn't stop me."

I clear my throat and try again. "Zeus was a monster. I'm not going to pretend that murder is the right way to solve a problem, but do you honestly think he wouldn't have killed you if he had a chance? There are so many deaths to lay at his feet. I'm sorry that you have to bear the burden of his, but I'm not sorry he's dead." I reach out with my free hand and cup his face, careful of his bruise. "And that man you beat hurt my sister. I didn't yell because I wanted to save him. I did it because I knew that you'd feel guilty if you lost control."

He releases a shuddering sigh. "I guess this is goodbye, then."

I might laugh if I didn't feel like I'm in the middle of running a marathon. Now is the time for the full truth, but my heart is beating so quickly, I'm suddenly afraid I might pass out. It was so much easier to write the words and slip away before he found them. "I'm not leaving, Hades. I love you. I'm staying and I'll do whatever it takes to protect you—and to help you protect your people."

"But with Zeus gone, you're free."

"I know I'm free." I take a ragged breath. "And because I'm

free, I choose this. I choose *us*." He's not brushing me off, so I scrape up the courage to continue. "A month ago, all I wanted was to get out. I didn't know you existed, let alone that I'd fall in love with you. I didn't know there was a part of Olympus that could feel like home." When he just stares at me in seeming confusion, I give his hand a tug. "Here, Hades. It feels like *home* here with you. In this house, in the lower city. I want to be with you, if you'll have me."

He gives a slow smile. "You mean it."

"With my whole heart and soul."

"I love you, too." He raises our clasped hands and presses a kiss to my knuckles. "I didn't want to trap you into staying by telling you, but...I love you, too."

He loves me. He *loves* me. I suspected, but hearing those three words on his lips makes me dizzy with joy. I wish I could sink into it fully, but my mother's request still needs to be dealt with. "Hades, there's one last thing."

"The terms of your bargain."

"Yes." I clench his hand tightly. "I promised my mother six appearances of her choosing in the upper city. Six appearances with both of us."

Hades stares at me for a long moment. "That's it?"

"What do you mean that's it? Having the man behind the myth of Hades at her beck and call a few times a year is going to increase her perceived power exponentially. Even if you're not her ally, people will *think* you are. It's a big deal."

He carefully moves the puppies and pushes to his feet, tugging me up with him. "It's a small price to pay."

"Are you sure? Because if you have any doubts at all—"

"Persephone." Hades cups my face. "Little siren. Do you think there's a price I wouldn't willingly pay for your happiness and safety? For your freedom? Demeter could have asked for a lot more than she did."

My throat goes tight. "Don't tell her that."

"I won't." He smiles down at me. "Tell me again."

There's no mistaking his meaning. I run my hands up his chest and loop my arms around his neck. "I love you."

His lips brush my ear. "Again."

"I love you."

I feel his lips curve against my skin. "I love you, too, little siren."

"This is probably an inopportune time to make a joke, huh?"

His hands fall to my waist and he pulls me closer, wrapping me up in his steady warmth. "Since when have you let that stop you?"

I laugh. It starts out a little ragged and then evolves into a sound of pure joy. "You're right." I wiggle a little against him. I can barely believe that it's over. Or not over, but just beginning. It feels like it's too good to be true, and I can't stop touching him, reassuring myself that he's here, that this is happening. "In that case, I have a question."

"Uh-huh." He pulls back enough that I can see him grinning. "Ask."

"Do you love me more than you love your precious floors?"

He laughs. A full-bodied sound that seems to fill the room around us. Hades lowers his head until his lips brush mine. "I most definitely love you more than my precious floors. But I'm going to insist you refrain from bleeding on them in the future."

"I make no promises."

"No, I don't expect you do." He kisses me. It's been less than a day since I last had his mouth on mine, but it feels like so much longer. I cling to him and eagerly open to take the kiss deeper, losing myself in the feel of him, the perfection of this moment.

At least until he lifts his head a few seconds later. "If we don't stop, we're going to be late for the press conference."

"They can fuck off."

He gives that delicious laugh again. "Persephone, I heartily do not want to be on your mother's shit list again, especially over something preventable."

He's right. I know he's right. I tangle my fingers in his hair and give a little tug. "Promise me that tonight we'll lock the doors, turn off our phones, and spray Hermes repellent. I want you all to myself."

"You have yourself a bargain."

At that, we reluctantly separate. I still have most of my things here, so I do my best to cover up Hades's bruises, and dark sunglasses do the rest. He wears a black-on-black suit and looks like a villain venturing out during the twilight hours. We hold hands the entire drive to the press conference.

The rest of the Thirteen and their families are gathered in one of the courtyards surrounding Dodona Tower, all dressed to perfection. Zeus's three children who remain in Olympus are all dressed in black, their expressions carefully blank. My sisters stand behind my mother. I give Hades's hand one last squeeze before I start to head in their direction. He tightens his grip on my hand. "Stay."

"What?" I look around. "But—"

"Be mine, Persephone. Let me be yours. In public and in private."

I stare up at him, and really, there's only one answer and it flutters in my chest like a trapped bird. "Yes."

I don't know what I expect. A confrontation. Accusations maybe. Instead, Hades slips seamlessly into their ranks as the reporters appear and Poseidon steps forward to give an official statement to declare Perseus as the new Zeus. People care less about answers than they do about perception, and that works in our favor right now. It doesn't hurt that the reporters are so intensely focused on Hades, either.

Through it all, Hades's expression is as relaxed as if he attends press conferences regularly. The only sign that he's anything less than comfortable is the intense grip he keeps on my hand, down where no one can see. As we begin to disperse, I lean against his arm and whisper in his ear, "You did great. We're almost finished."

"There are more people than I expected." He speaks out of the corner of his mouth, lips barely moving.

"I'll keep you safe. Promise."

We start to head for the cars, and the reporters stream after us, peppering him with so many questions, I can barely keep up.

"Have you been in the lower city this entire time?"

"Why come forward now? Is it because Zeus is dead?"

"Are you the mysterious man Persephone Dimitriou ran off with?"

"Are you two official?"

I lift my hand, bringing their attention off him and onto me. "Friends, we're more than happy to deliver an official statement... tomorrow. Today, we're here to mourn the loss of Zeus." I've had enough practice with public speaking that I don't even trip over the lie. I simply wait in calm silence, and they finally subside and refocus on the matter at hand.

Hades turns to face me when we're finally able to break free, and he's doing that thing he does where he looks at me like he's never seen me before. "My knight in sunshine armor, riding in to save me from the press."

"Yes, well, you're not the only one who likes to play hero." I give his hand another squeeze. "Handling this whole circus takes some getting used to."

"I expect I'll manage just fine as long as you're by my side." He doesn't wait for a response. He just sweeps me into his arms and claims my mouth. I eagerly go up onto my tiptoes and wrap my arms around his neck. I'm aware of the snapping of cameras and the rise of whispers, but I don't care.

When he finally lifts his head, I'm clinging to him to avoid my legs giving out. "Come home with me."

"Yes."

"I don't just mean today. I mean for good. Move in."

"I know that's what you mean." I smile and press a quick kiss to his lips. "And my answer is still the same. *Yes* to everything."

EPILOGUE

HADES

"ARE YOU READY?"

Persephone grins up at me, but it's her happy smile—her *real* smile. "You've asked me that a dozen times in the last hour." She bumps her shoulder into mine. "Are *you* nervous?"

Nervous is too mundane a word. In the last two weeks since stepping out of the shadows and into the glittering vipers' nest that is the upper city, I've had a lot of adjustments. Persephone has been at my side every step of the way, expertly guiding me through each media interaction. I don't know what I'd do without her.

I hope to the gods I never have to find out.

But tonight? Tonight is just for us.

"I'm not nervous," I finally say. "If you're not ready—"

"Hades, I'm ready. I'm *more* than ready." She looks at the door leading into the playroom. It's too soundproofed to be able to hear the people gathered behind it, but we both know they're present. Waiting.

Persephone takes a breath. "How do I look?"

It's another question she's asked half a dozen times since I walked into our room and found her getting dressed. "You look like perfection." It's the truth. She's left her long, blond hair loose and done something to give it waves, and she's wearing Juliette's newest creation. It's another black dress that hugs her body, dripping down her neck in a halter top and skimming over breasts and stomach and hips to flutter about the tops of her thighs. It's also backless, and every time she turns around, I have to fight the urge to go to my knees and kiss the dip at the bottom of her spine. "Little siren—"

"I'm ready." She bounces up and presses a quick kiss to my lips. "I'm really ready. I promise."

I take her at her word. "Then let's go."

We've already talked about how this will go. I've played it out for her step by step. There are times when surprise is part of the game, but I don't want anything to ruin Persephone's night. Our night. Not when this feels like a particularly meaningful step in the midst of a pair of lives that have been turned upside down.

I lead the way into the room. Once again, it's set up to my specifications. The furniture surrounding the dais has been moved back a bit, a clear indication that this is meant to be a show and not an invitation to participate. The lights are down low and every spot is filled.

Persephone's grip on my hand is loose and trusting, and she happily follows me as I weave through the chairs and couches to the dais. Before I can give her one last chance to change her mind, she steps easily up and into the light. She gives me a look over her shoulder as if she knew exactly what I'd been about to do. I bite back a grin and follow her up.

The lights give a different sort of privacy than the shadows do. I can see every inch of Persephone, but the rest of the room is a blurred glare. Another adjustment that can be made later on if this becomes a repeat thing; tonight, everything is orchestrated to ensure she has the best time possible.

I point to the center of the dais. "Stand there."

"Yes, Sir." She says it primly, as if there isn't a wicked smile already curving her lips.

I circle her slowly, building her anticipation. Gods, she's so fucking perfect, I can barely believe that she's mine. That she's made me hers as surely as if she'd tattooed her name on my very soul. I would do anything for this woman. Conquer the upper city. Knock the other Thirteen from their ivory towers. Give another endless interview with a gossip columnist.

I flick the hem of her dress, making it flutter around her thighs. "If I flip up this dress, am I going to find that you have no panties on?"

Her smile widens. "Only one way to find out."

"In a moment." I manage not to grin at her blatant disappointment and step closer to slide my hands up her arms, over her shoulders, to cup her face. I lower my voice, speaking just to her. "You have your safe word, but if you want this to stop at any point, just tell me. It stops."

She lightly grips my wrists. "I know."

"Good."

"Hades?" Persephone smiles at me. "Would you like to see the best thing about this dress?" She doesn't wait for an answer, the little brat, before reaching to the back of her neck and unclasping it. The fabric flutters down her body and floats to the ground, as delicate as a flower petal.

She's not wearing a single thing beneath it.

I take her hand and lift it over her head, urging her into a slow spin. "You want to put on a show, little siren? Let them see." I enjoy the way a blush steals across her golden skin in response.

I drop her hand long enough to walk to the edge of the dais and grab a chair I had placed there earlier this afternoon. It's made of black metal with a wide seat and a back just high enough to bend over comfortably.

I motion for her to sit in the chair. "Spread your legs, Persephone."

Her breath is coming in little gasps now, and when I place my hand on the back of her neck, she leans hard into my touch. Because what my little siren needs isn't only to be on display; it's to have me grounding her while she is.

I lean over the back of the chair and stroke my hands up her thighs, wrenching them wider. A light stroke of her pussy finds her wet and needy. I press my lips to her temple as I stroke her. "They look up here, and do you know what they see?"

"No," she gasps, lifting her hips to try to guide my touch. "Tell me."

"They see their golden princess fallen." I push two fingers into her. "Their dark goddess rising in her place."

She whimpers and I can't help myself. I catch her mouth. With Persephone's taste on my tongue, I temporarily forget myself.

Forget the audience. Forget everything but doing whatever it takes to cause her to make that sound again. I press the heel of my hand to her clit as I slowly fuck her with my fingers, driving her desire higher. Her movements get more frantic as she chases her pleasure, riding my hand even as I give her exactly what she needs to send her soaring.

I break the kiss to say, "Come for me, little siren."

And she does. Gods, she does.

I send her wave cresting again twice more before I finally gentle my touch and ease my fingers out of her. "I'm going to bend you over this chair and fuck you now."

Persephone gives a dazed smile, her hazel eyes full of love. "Yes, Sir."

She's a little wobbly as I help her up and guide her into the position I want, bent over the chair back. I nudge her feet wider and step back to get a good look at her.

Fuck.

The trust this woman places in me. It makes me want to be a better man, to ensure I never fail her. She shivers, and I close the distance between us, smoothing my hands over her ass and down her back. "Ready?"

"Oh my gods, just *fuck* me already."

A chuckle moves through the room in a wave, multiple voices joining mine in response to her. I give her ass a light smack. "Impatient."

"Yes. Very." She wiggles a little. "Please, Hades. Don't make me wait any longer. I need you."

In the end, I don't want to tease her any more than she wants to be teased. Another time, perhaps. The need is riding too high tonight. I free my cock and grip her hip as I guide my length into her. Persephone lets out a low moan that almost masks my sharp exhale.

I'll never get tired of this, either. The way she clamps around me as if she never wants to let me go. How she pushes back against me, needing me as deep as possible. Her little whimpers and moans.

The rest of the room might think they're getting access to this, too, but their only role here tonight is to amplify *her* pleasure.

I reach down and wrap her hair around my fist, tugging until she looks up into the darkness surrounding the dais. "They're watching. Greedy for whatever bits of you we'll allow. Tonight, they'll be chasing their pleasure to the memory of me fucking you."

"Good," she moans. "Harder."

I give a rough laugh and obey. Fucking her in harsh strokes even as I hold her in place. There's no hiding from the fact that we're on display, and from the way she clenches around me, she's loving every moment of it.

And then she's orgasming, her cries sharp and needy. It takes everything I have not to follow her over the edge, but tonight is about *her*. Not about me. I take a slow breath and ease out of her so I can tuck my cock back into my pants. Then I pull her up and toss her over my shoulder. Persephone's squeal has me biting back a grin. I turn in a slow circle. "I hope you enjoyed the show. It's over now."

"We did!" Someone from the audience shouts. It sounds a bit like Hermes.

I shake my head and climb off the dais, Persephone's laughter trailing behind us. She sounds so fucking *happy*, the sound a perfect match to the warmth in my chest. I stride to the throne and sink onto it.

This is our kingdom, our throne, *ours*.

Persephone's still laughing a little as she arranges herself on my lap. "'I hope you enjoyed the show. It's over now.' *Really?*"

"Succinct and to the point."

"Mm-hmm." She shifts to straddle me. "I was going to suggest a second throne down here."

I grip her hips lightly, letting her guide this. "The person who created this one still lives in the lower city. I can commission a second if you'd like."

"No." She palms me through my pants. "I like sharing. It gives me access to you." Persephone leans down until her lips brush my ear. "Did you hold off coming so I could fuck you on this throne, Hades?"

"Yes."

She laughs again. Gods, I love her laugh. "Insatiable."

"Only for you." I smooth my hands up her sides. "I love you, little siren."

"I love you, too." She kisses me, a slow, decadent kiss that makes the room spin away for several long moments. Persephone digs her hands into my hair and grins against my lips. "And it's a good thing you're just as insatiable as I am, because I'm nowhere near done with you yet."

COMING SOON:
ELECTRIC IDOL

"BRING ME HER HEART."

"Yes, you said that already." I don't look up from my phone as my mother paces from one side of the room to the other, her skirt swishing about her legs. Knowing her, she chose her clothing today in order to maximize her dramatic flouncing.

She's nothing if not a showwoman.

"And yet you're still sitting here." She spins on her tall heel and glares down at me. She's fifty, and though she'd skin me alive for saying as much in public, no wrinkle or gray hair betrays her. She spends a fortune to keep her skin smooth and her hair a perfect icy blond. Not to mention the countless hours with her personal trainer to accomplish a body twenty-year-olds would kill for. All in the name of her title, Aphrodite. When one has the role of the goddess of love, one must meet certain expectations.

It's unfortunate for everyone that my mother takes replicating the original Aphrodite's reputation to heart. The goddess wasn't exactly known for her even temperament, after all, and my mother is even worse than her namesake.

"Eros, put down that goddamned phone and listen to me."

"I'm listening." My bored tone betrays my waning patience, but I'd like to fast forward past all the dramatics to where she tells me what she wants done and I take care of it so she can keep her hands lily white. "You're going to have to be more specific, Mother. Do you literally want her heart?"

She makes a sound suspiciously like a hiss. "You are such a little shit. Call me by my title or nothing at all." This is the Aphrodite she doesn't show anyone else in Olympus. Only I get the dubious privilege of witnessing what a monster my mother truly is.

But then, I'm not one to throw stones.

I make a show of turning off my phone and giving her my full attention. "You're about to send me out on another one of you little errands, so why don't you dial it back and give me a pretty smile before you ask me again—this time with more details."

Another person would flinch in the face of my mild tone with the threat of violence beneath it. Aphrodite just laughs. "Eros, darling, you really are too much. You know very well that I want her literal heart. After what Demeter pulled last fall, nothing else will do. With Hades in her corner and the new Zeus untried, she's throwing her weight around as if she's anything other than a glorified farmer."

Considering Demeter is responsible for ensuring that all of Olympus gets fed, and Aphrodite mostly handles arranging for vapid Olympians to marry other vapid Olympians, one could argue that Demeter *should* be in charge.

That's not how Olympus works, though. No matter what my mother thinks, there will never be one ruler of this city. Instead, we get the Thirteen. Zeus, Poseidon, Hades, Aphrodite, Demeter, Artemis, Hephaestus, Ares, Athena, Hermes, Dionysus, and Apollo. And, of course, Hera, though that title will be unoccupied until the newest Zeus marries someone and fills the position.

That's what my mother should be focusing on. She arranged all three marriages for the last Zeus—the fucker kept killing off his wives, which suited my mother quite nicely, as she loves a wedding and hates everything that follows. She should be frothing at the mouth to parade Olympus's eligible people in front of the new Zeus.

Instead, she's hyper-focusing on her revenge. It's annoying as hell. "How's Zeus doing these days?" Up until a few months ago, he was Perseus, but names are the first thing sacrificed at the altar of the Thirteen. Part of me wonders if that bothers him. I let the thought drift away. Perseus isn't my problem. He's been Zeus's heir for his entire life. He knew he'd take the title when his father died. If it happened a bit earlier than anyone expected... Well, that's also not my problem. *I* didn't kill the asshole.

"Don't change the subject," she snaps. "Ever since Persephone ran off and shacked up with Hades, the power balance in Olympus is off. Someone needs to check Demeter, and if no one else will step up, then we'll have to."

"You mean *I'll* have to. You might be demanding a heart, but we both know that I'm the one doing all the work." It's not even that I mind it, exactly, though I try to keep murder to a minimum. It's messy and I have no desire for someone to start calling for my head. It's so much easier to remove an opponent with a well-placed rumor or simply observe them until their own actions provide the ammunition for their downfall. Olympus is filled to the brim with sin, if one believes in that sort of thing, and no one in the Thirteen's shining circle is without their fair share of vices.

Except, apparently, Demeter's daughters.

I've been keeping an eye on them for months, ever since the old Zeus decided he wanted Persephone for his own. I snort. For all that good that did him. He drove her right into Hades's arms, which in turn, brought Hades out of the shadows of the lower city. No one saw *that* coming.

But the bottom line is that the remaining three of Demeter's daughters are careful to color inside the lines. They don't drink too much, they don't do drugs, they don't date or sleep with anyone they shouldn't. The most scandalous thing any of them have done in the last two months is when Callisto, the oldest, attacked a guy who grabbed her youngest sister's ass in a bar. It was a gorgeous takedown. One second he was leering at Eurydice, and the next she'd punched him in the throat, knocking him on his ass, and said something in his ear that made him turn a sickly shade of green.

If I have my choice, I wouldn't cross Callisto. I'm better than she is, but she's got a rage that makes her unpredictable. Being unpredictable makes her dangerous.

"Eros." Mother snaps her fingers in front of my face. "Stop daydreaming and do this task for me."

I sigh. "Which daughter?"

"The daughter no one but her mother will miss." She smiles slowly, her blue eyes going icy. "Psyche."

Years of training keep my response to a minimum. I should have known Psyche would be her choice. Callisto is a wild card and as likely to harm Demeter's reputation as help it. Persephone is untouchable as Hades's dark queen of the lower city. That leaves Psyche and Eurydice. Eurydice is sweet and as close to innocent as someone can be in Olympus, even with her recent heartbreak. Beyond that, she flits back and forth across the River Styx and spends too much time in Hades's domain to risk messing with.

Psyche?

She's something else entirely. She plays the game and plays it well, all without seeming to. She's got this unassuming thing going on, but I've been watching her long enough to notice that she never makes a move by accident. I can't prove it, of course, but I think she's got just as savvy a brain in her head as her mother does. "The daughter no one will miss?" I raise my brows. "Or an excuse to punish the Dimitriou daughter who gets more press than you do?"

She sneers. "She's a fat girl with little style and no substance. The only reason MuseWatch and the other sites follow her around is because she's a novelty. She's not even close to my league."

I don't argue with her because there's no point, but the truth is that Psyche is gorgeous and has a style that sets trends in a way Aphrodite can only dream of. Which is exactly the problem. My mother's decided to take down two birds with one stone.

"The reason is irrelevant." She props her hands on her hips. "I want this taken care of, Eros. You have to do this for me."

Something in my chest twinges, but I ignore it. If I believed in souls, I would have sacrificed mine long ago. There is a price for power in Olympus, and with a mother in the Thirteen, I never had a chance at innocence. I don't mourn the loss, not when I enjoy the benefits so immensely. If it means that sometimes I'm required to do these little *tasks* for my mother? It's a small enough price to pay. "I'll see it done."

"Before the end of the month."

That doesn't give me much time at all. I stomp down on the flicker of resentment and nod. "I'll see it done."

"Good." She twirls away, her skirt once again flaring dramatically around her feet, and strides out of the room.

That's my mother, all right. Here for the proclamations of revenge and heavy with the demands, but when it comes time to actually do the work, she's suddenly got somewhere to be.

It's just as well. I'm good at what I do because I know when to be flashy and when to fly below the radar. Aphrodite wouldn't know how to be subtle if her life depended on it. I wait a full thirty seconds before I push to my feet and walk to my front door. If she changes her mind and comes back to spout off some more bullshit, she'll be pissed to find my door locked, but I don't like being interrupted once I get to planning.

And, frankly, it's good for my mother to be foiled from time to time.

I head down to the ground floor and flip the lock there and then lock the actual door to my apartment for good measure. Then I head through the rooms to the safe room. Oh, it's not technically a safe room even if I like to refer to it as such. I use it to store things I don't want nosy guests—or Hermes—to get their hands on. She's tried at least a dozen times to break into it, and so far my security has held, but I'm all too aware that eventually she might prevail. Still, it's the best option available to me.

Once I lock *that* door, I sit down behind my computer and consider my options. This would be so much simpler if Aphrodite just wanted to make a non-lethal example of Psyche. She might be crafting a reputation as an influencer in that quiet way of hers, but reputations are easy to burn to ash. I've done it dozens of times over the years, and no doubt I'll do it many more. All it takes is some patience and the ability to play the long game.

But no, my mother wants her literal heart. How very Evil Queen of her. I shake my head and bring up my files on the Dimitriou sisters. I have files on all the Thirteen and their immediate family, as well as close friends, but Demeter is a relatively new addition. She's been around over a decade, and since then her daughters have become something of favorites among the Olympian paparazzi. There's not a week goes by without some kind of info about them being dropped on the online gossip site MuseWatch.

I click through the most recent articles, if one can call them that. Persephone visited her family last weekend briefly and caused quite the stir because she brought her new husband with her. The Hades-Demeter alliance is one nobody saw coming, and it's feeding into my mother's paranoia. She had the last Zeus on a leash, but his son hasn't taken the bait she keeps dangling in front of him. It's got her worried.

I stop on a picture of Psyche and Persephone together shopping.

They always seem to be shopping. It's enough that someone who isn't paying close attention would assume they're just as focused on appearance and power and money as the rest of those who surround the Thirteen. Everyone with a little bit wants more than what they have, and they're all willing to drag others down to claw their way higher, closer to the Thirteen.

But then, if that were true, Persephone Dimitriou wouldn't have braved crossing into the lower city to try to get away from a marriage with Zeus.

Psyche wouldn't have helped her.

Even I'm not sure exactly what happened that night, but I know Psyche was involved—and it wasn't to play the part of the rational party convincing her sister that this marriage would help their family's position. If they were any other family, Psyche would have taken advantage of her sister's absence and placed herself in front of Zeus as a candidate for the new Hera.

I study the image of her. She's got long dark hair and pouty full lips that she never seems to wear bright color on. There's a reason that she's become something of a trend setter in Olympus. She's never overt about it, but one week she'll be wearing high-waisted pants and a flouncy crop top and within two weeks, I'm seeing the look everywhere. The fact that she's plus-sized only makes people watch her more closely. She seems comfortable in her body, and that kind of thing is sexy as hell.

Or it would be if I was interested in someone like Psyche Dimitriou.

I curse and close the window. It doesn't matter if she's hot as hell, or that I respect the way she's so effectively dodged the power games since her family arrived on the scene. My mother has a task, and I know the consequences of failing.

Exile.

I might not love Olympus most days, but it's my home. Normally the threat of exile would be bullshit—it's not easy to leave this city, and that's for people who actually want to get out—but when your mother is one of the Thirteen, anything is possible.

Best not to think about that too closely. I'll take care of the task and then I'll find a few partners and lose myself in a week of fucking and drinking and anything it takes to numb me out completely. Just like I always have.

I already know how to lure Psyche in. She might not play the power games, but she's got a weak spot a mile wide. With another curse, I pick up my phone.

A chirpy female voice answers. "Eros, my favorite little sex god. It's my lucky day."

"Hermes."

She gives a sigh. "So it's business, then?"

"If it was personal, you'd be breaking into my house and eating my food. But I suppose you're too busy doing that to Hades's house these days." She and I have hooked up a few times over the years, but ultimately settled into something resembling friendship. I don't necessarily trust her—her title is practically spymaster, after all—but I like her.

"Don't be mad just because Hades banned you from his sex dungeon. You would have done the same thing in his position."

She's right, but that doesn't mean I'm about to admit it. When

Hades cut me off, he cut off my main outlet to blow off steam. "I have a message I'd like you to deliver, but it's delicate in nature."

A pause. "Okay, you have my attention. Stop toying with my emotions and tell me what you're up to."

I allow myself a grin as I sketch out what I need from her. Hermes's role in the Thirteen is a little bit messenger, a little bit spy, a little bit agent of chaos for her own amusement. Her only real allegiance is to Dionysus and even then, I'm not sure that friendship would hold if things got really intense. He's not my aim, so I have no doubt she'll do exactly as I request.

When I finish, she gives a merry laugh. "Eros, you sly rake, you. I'll have the message delivered by morning." She hangs up before I can respond.

I sit back with a sigh and rub my chest. No matter my personal thoughts on this, things are in motion.

Psyche Dimitriou will be dead before the end of the week.

ACKNOWLEDGMENTS

Huge thanks to all my readers for loving Hades enough that you're willing to read two different versions of him. Will there be more? Only time will tell! I appreciate you more than words can say. I hope you enjoyed this story!

Big thanks to my editor, Mary Altman, for hearing me ramble about my idea for a supersexy Hades and Persephone retelling and immediately demanding I send you a proposal. I am so, so happy that *Neon Gods* found its home with you and Sourcebooks. This book is approximately a thousand times better than it was when we started because of your input.

Thank you to my agent, Laura Bradford, for working with me on this book. Yet another weird little story that's found a home because of you and your belief in me and the stories I tell. Thank you!

Writing a book is a solo endeavor, but I wouldn't have pulled it off without the support of my amazing friends. Big thanks to Jenny Nordbak for chatting mythology with me, brainstorming different pairings, and being in total agreement about the various fuckboys of Greek myths. All my love and appreciation to Piper J. Drake and Asa Maria Bradley for always being ready to knock me out of a tailspin or help me navigate a tricky plot point.

All my love and gratitude to my family. This book was written during 2020 and, suffice it to say, it's been a particularly hellish year for everyone. Thank you to my children for rolling with the punches and adapting to this new version of life while we balance online school and my working with no office door and all the new challenges that arise. Thank you to Tim for never once doubting that I can accomplish my lofty goals, for always being willing to jump in when I need something, and for loving me even when I'm being kind of an asshole. Love you!

ABOUT THE AUTHOR

Katee Robert is a *New York Times* and *USA Today* bestselling author of contemporary romance and romantic suspense. *Entertainment Weekly* calls her writing "unspeakably hot." Her books have sold over a million copies. She lives in the Pacific Northwest with her husband, children, a cat who thinks he's a dog, and two Great Danes who think they're lap dogs. You can visit her at kateerobert.com or on Twitter @katee_robert.